GHOSTED

MARK McCRUM

BLOODHOUND
— BOOKS —

First published in 2023 by Bloodhound Books.

www.bloodhoundbooks.com

Print ISBN: 978-1-5040-8881-7

CHAPTER ONE

'**B**e *thou our guard while troubles last,*
And our ete-e-rnal ho-ome.'
As the congregation thundered their drawn-out conclusion to Isaac Watts's famous hymn and lapsed back into a rustling semi-silence, Lucille the vicar climbed the wooden steps up into the pulpit. She stumbled halfway and there was a loud creak as she steadied herself. But once ensconced she was back in control. She grasped the ornately carved rostrum and gazed out lovingly over her tortoiseshell half-moons onto the expectant faces below. As if on cue, a shaft of April sunshine beamed down through the stained-glass window at the far end of the nave, casting, for all of fifteen seconds, ethereal coloured patterns on the shoulders of her white cassock.

'I didn't know Adam that well,' she began, 'but he's always been a great believer in the church...'

Right on the first point and most definitely wrong on the second, Adam thought. I have always been polite to you, Lucille. I attend your services occasionally, yes. To please Julie, generally. Or for some sentimental throwback to my childhood, some probably misplaced desire to feel the holiness that you, of all people, so signally fail to impart. I even put my hand in my pocket for the restoration. Of course I didn't want to see the place falling down; the church is the architectural centre of the village and whatever nonsense you practice here, it's still important to keep it going. But please don't try and make out that I believe in your mumbo jumbo: the Afterlife, Heaven and Hell, the Resurrection, all that patent absurdity. Especially not the happy-clappy version you put about, with poor long-dead Jesus in attendance on our every waking movement.

'Adam was many things,' Lucille continued. 'As well as being an extremely successful architect, he also had his poetic side. He wrote lovely verses and in the village we all looked forward to his annual Christmas offering...'

Give us a break! If I strive to be one thing with my occasional bardic efforts, which certainly aren't verses, thank you very much, it ain't to be lovely. Mid-thought, Adam found himself double-taking. His gaze roamed away from Lucille's ever-sincere, nodding-dog features and out over the packed rows of chairs. Almost everyone, he realised suddenly, was wearing black – or close to it. All his relatives were here, in the front rows. On the left of the aisle, his second wife Julie, splendidly got up in figure-hugging velvet, with a tiny black hat and veil perched on her bobbed blonde locks. On the right, more elegant and understated, let's face it, his first wife Serena, in a discreet dark blue satin number. Next to her, on one side, his children, Leo and Matilda, with Leo's surprisingly good-looking fiancée Abby beside him; and on the other, Walter, Serena's frankly uninspiring new man. In the row behind, his sister Claire, her irritating husband Dan, and their ten-year-old daughter Maya. Just next to Claire, clutching her indeed, was his mother Patricia, as frail as a waif under her neat coif of bone-white hair; on her other side, the staunch but smiley Polish woman who was the latest in her roster of carers.

As Adam got closer, and saw the crimson tear stains, like

watermarks, on his daughter's pale cheeks, it finally dawned on him what this was.

'And in tragic circumstances such as these,' Lucille was saying, 'it may be hard for us to believe that Adam, after a life that had clearly troubled him much more than any of us had realised, has found peace at last. But I can assure you' – she paused, significantly – 'that he has.'

The penny had dropped. This was no ordinary service. It was – Adam could hardly bear to articulate the thought – his funeral. How had that happened? The last time he'd looked he had been robustly alive. Having dinner with Julie, no less, on a Friday evening, after a windy and rain-swept drive back up the motorway from his offices in Covent Garden. God, perhaps that was it – he'd been in a car crash. Had he even imagined the dinner? Or perhaps they had gone out to the pub afterwards? Drunk too much and driven the Disco (as they called their beloved Land Rover Discovery Sport) into a wall. But no, he could remember the candles that his wife had put out; the sirloin steak she had cooked – medium rare as he liked it; the yummy chocolate pudding she had prepared; the awful feeling that now was not quite the right time for the confession he needed to make, sooner or later. As the special food had come out, he'd been quietly dreading that she might be about to come on to him, which would have put him in a difficult, not to say confusing position. But no, they had kissed chastely and he had woken in his own bed, breakfasted with her, civilly enough, then waved her off for her usual Saturday morning of shopping and gossip in Tempelsham.

And there she was now, looking as if butter wouldn't melt, with Roland Herrington next to her. Adam saw that his old friend was holding her hand. For support? Out of grief? With her other hand she removed a dainty embroidered hanky from her bosom and dabbed at her lovely blue eyes.

'The idea that those,' Lucille continued, 'who, for one reason or another, feel compelled to take their own life, do not find a place in the Kingdom of Heaven, is not one that Christians like myself believe in any more...'

Adam was treble-taking. Was this what accounted for all these drawn, shocked faces; more so, he realised now, than at your average funeral? Was Lucille really suggesting... suicide?

It seemed that she was.

And where was *he*? he wondered suddenly. Not with them all in a corporeal sense, that was for sure. So was his body in that shiny teak coffin that stood central on its stand in the aisle, decorated with his favourite spring flowers: yellow narcissi, white tulips, blue and white hyacinths, pink ranunculi, blue and purple irises.

He watched on in disbelief. The service took the form of hymns and readings, interspersed with four-minute addresses by close friends and colleagues, up at a microphone below the pulpit, giving their take on his life: Adam the architect, Adam the poet, Adam the man. Adam knew it was four minutes because Roland had taken at least thirty seconds of his precious quota to tell them all so. As was only to be expected, the rest of his supposed tribute was all about him. Roland, that is. You would have thought that in death the old tosser would finally have let the rivalry go. But no. He still had to get the digs in about the poor corpse in the box. 'And now, let us pay tribute to Adam's poetry,' he said, pausing weightily, as was his wont. He stroked his ridiculous beard, a hipsterish attempt to look younger that unfortunately, with the long streaks of white amid the piratical black, failed entirely. He smirked, and there were a few knowing chuckles from the more irreverent lightweights in the audience. 'It wasn't Keats, or even Armitage,' he went on – or even Roland, was the clear and tedious implication – 'but it wasn't *bad*. In fact, for a man who had spent his main energies on becoming such an accomplished architect, it was surprisingly good. I even found myself, on one occasion, wanting to steal from it.'

On one occasion! Roland, for God's sake, was the one who sometimes got his compositions into *The Times Literary Supplement* and the *Spectator* and the *London Review of Books*, not to mention all those strange specialist publications with which Adam had never bothered. Yes, Roland had spent his professional life working in the City (like T.S. Eliot, as he would happily tell you) but he had published three collections, albeit with obscure presses. So why the continuing beef?

The strangest address was by Gideon Bloomberg, who went over his slot by three long minutes and argued, against the noise of rain now drumming down noisily on the roof, that Adam had had every right to take his own life. With that long, lugubrious face more animated than Adam had seen it for some while, Gideon spoke movingly of Adam's 'courage' in taking up his 'moral right' to end his own life. 'His *own* life,' he repeated, gazing challengingly around the disbelieving faces. 'We who are left behind may be tempted to succumb to anger at this terrible act, but we would be wrong. It was Adam's pain and, hard though it may be for us to accept it...'

'What pain!' Adam wanted to scream out. I was fine, thank you very much. There were a couple of recent hiccoughs, granted. Julie and I haven't been getting on that brilliantly. Jeff's been trying to push me out of my own firm, the one with my name on it. But there's nothing I would put my head in the oven for, even if that were something I would consider anyway, however bad things got. So don't cast your weird philosophy onto me, mate. I didn't do it.

Whatever state Adam was now in, he found that he could see, all too clearly. Every face in the church, in close-up if he wanted. He could hear, every word that the speakers were saying, and the audience reactions too. Every sob, every gasp, every muttered aside. But if his spirit – if that's what he now was – had eyes and ears, it had no mouth. He couldn't articulate. He couldn't intervene.

He could still smell, however. How odd was that? Sailing close up to the spring flowers on the coffin, he caught their delicate scents in his non-existent nostrils. Hovering elsewhere, he got all kinds of audience whiffs: body odour from Gideon, the familiar costly pong of Diorella from Julie.

There was another of his favourite hymns – 'Abide with Me' – and then his sister Claire was on her feet, with a poem she knew well that he was fond of and admired: Christina Rossetti's 'Let Me Go'.

> When you are lonely and sick at heart
> Go to the friends we know.
> Laugh at all the things we used to do
> Miss me, but let me go.

As she came to the end of that powerful fourth stanza, Claire's bright voice cracked and she let out a sob. Then she brushed her long, grey-flecked dark hair away from her face and looked up, determinedly. Bless her, she wasn't going to allow Gideon to get away with his deranged and depressing thesis. With all due respect to the previous speaker, she said, and very much expressing her own point of view, she didn't understand it. She had known Adam, obviously, since she could remember. There had been ups and downs, of course. He could be difficult; we all knew that. (Did we? Adam thought.) But the idea that her brother would take his own life. No, she couldn't see it. 'Sorry, everyone,' she gulped, tears now pouring down her pudgy pink cheeks. 'I'm sorry…'

As she broke off and strode away from the mic stand, a mobile went off. It was Adam's ringtone, 'By the Seaside'. Involuntarily, he reached for his phone, before realising that he had no phone. No hands either. Ten rows back he spotted his devoted office manager, Lynsey Turner, shuffling furiously in her handbag. She had the same ringtone; he had never realised. Eventually she located the offending device and clicked it off. Lynsey of all people, anal about her filing, spickety-span about coffee cups, would be more embarrassed than most about such a public gaffe.

Claire, meanwhile, had made her way back to her pew and the strong arms of hubbie Dan. He was a bully, as Adam knew, but he did a good job of looking like a decent enough guy in public, with his thick blond hair and CGI cartoon hero good looks. He hugged her close, looking round and nodding sympathetically at the surrounding folk as he did so. It was an ongoing mystery to Adam why Claire was still with him, even if they did have little Maya, their 'late addition', as a reason to stick together.

Now Matilda was up by the mic. What an absolute beauty his daughter was, with her silent-movie-star face and those tight dark curls. Was she going to sing, bless her? She was. 'Pie Jesu.' God help him, this was what he had asked for, now he remembered, in that plan of his own funeral he had once drawn up, almost as a joke, though Julie had insisted on keeping it on file, 'just in case, sweetheart'.

She might be trouble, darling Matilda, but she could pull it off when she wanted to, couldn't she? As the final note faded away, there was loud applause. Lucille nodded approvingly. It was okay to clap in God's house these days, even at a funeral. Not that Adam minded. He was in tears. Not literally, obviously. But his spirit, or whatever it was that he had become, was moved in exactly the same way as if he had been alive.

From the sublime to the ridiculous. The final four-minute offering was by his business partner, Jeff: 'a short encomium' on his 'remarkable career'. The remarkable career, Adam thought, that you were actively trying to scupper, you fat hypocrite. Adam's architectural philosophy had been 'truly admirable', Jeff went on. He had always stressed the need to think of designed space in terms of people. 'The people who would be living there, the people who would be working there, the individuals, if you will, who would inhabit Adam's lovingly devised and always carefully thought-through spaces and places...'

As the congregation nodded along to this sententious bullshit, Adam caught sight of Eva, his colleague, protégé and dark secret, ten rows back, with, well well, Reuben and Simone from the firm too. Eva's face was an absolute picture. She knew exactly what a virtue-signalling slimeball Jeff was; and exactly what Adam would be thinking, were he here among them. Which, oddly, he was.

Afterwards, Adam stayed with them all as they trooped out behind the coffin and up through the churchyard. The charcoal-grey clouds had passed over and the place was dazzled with spring sunshine, casting dark shadows from the gravestones onto the wet grass. Bright droplets gleamed on the still-naked branches and furled buds; pale curlicues of steam swirled up from the paved path that ran down to the lychgate.

Beynton St Marys was, it had to be said, the perfect place for an old-fashioned English funeral. Even though it was only an hour and a half from London, it was still not overpopulated. Its position in an Area of Outstanding Natural Beauty had saved it from the tacky new-build add-on crescents and closes that had spoilt so many of the little villages outside that designation.

Adam's grave was not in the main churchyard, with its tilting and rackety old headstones and sumptuous green-black yews, which grew so well, his father Philip had always joked, because they were fertilised by corpses; it was up in the new section in the repurposed field beyond. Julie had insisted he buy the plot, three years ago, alongside one that was intended for her. 'You're always telling me you want to be buried, not cremated, so we might as well get organised,' she'd said, bossy as ever. Now that very organisation seemed almost sinister. Adam was hungry to find out exactly how he was supposed to have died. Taken pills, hung himself, jumped under a Tube train? Whatever, it was a monstrous lie. Unless he'd been so severely traumatised that he'd forgotten how he'd done it. No, don't gaslight yourself, Adam. Even if you had done it, you'd have remembered the preparations, the planning. Wouldn't you?

As they followed the coffin, borne by four blank-faced undertakers' operatives, up the gravel path out of the old churchyard, people were quietly acknowledging each other, falling into loose groups. Given the solemn context, there were no loud whoopish greetings. But there was plenty of warmth, Adam noticed, among the silent nods and muttered and mouthed 'How are you?'s. Something as desperate as the suicide of a friend brought people more intensely together. The shock of it. How could he? Adam, of all people! And yet, we're still here. Let's love each other all the more, despite and indeed because of this horror.

All sorts had turned out. Besides family, office colleagues and old friends he hadn't seen in years, there was a sprinkling of fellow architects, structural and services engineers ditto, along with a good crowd of sub-contractors ('subbies' in the trade), some of them looking as if they'd put on a suit for the first time in their lives.

As they reached the annexe field, with its neat rows of newish headstones, its clearer cut, more recent dates, its fresh or artificial floral arrangements, the perambulating congregation quietened down again. They were silent as they approached the stark oblong of the open grave, with the wheelbarrow of earth and spade to one side. Reverend Lucille was waiting, her white robes billowing in the chilly breeze.

What a marvellous rite it was, the old English *Order for the*

Burial of the Dead. How had Julie persuaded Lucille to use it? She must have promised her good money for the restoration fund to have got her not to employ an alternative liturgy, something altogether more upbeat and 'relatable'.

'Man that is born of a woman, hath but a short time to live, and is full of misery. He cometh up, and is cut down, like a flower; he fleeth as it were a shadow, and never continueth in one stay…'

It was almost worth dying to hear Lucille mouthing these wonderful ancient words. 'Full of misery' was certainly not her style. Her church services were so convivial that Adam had found them closer to a kindergarten lesson than anything sacred. There was chitchat, there were toys, there was tea and coffee and biscuits, there was a sing-song around the electric piano. Where was the ritual, the long slow build up, through Collect and Epistle and Gospel and Sermon, to the solemn celebration of Communion? Gone with the lovely Victorian pews that Lucille had got rid of last year, citing health and safety and improved disabled access among other absurd reasons. Toe-numbingly boring those services might have been, on the sunny Sundays of his childhood, but at least they had felt holy. Mysterious. 'Other', as his father used to say, when justifying his wavering faith.

Eventually Lucille stepped forward, bent down and scooped up a handful of earth from the waiting barrow.

'Forasmuch as it hath pleased Almighty God of his great mercy to take unto himself the soul of our dear brother here departed: we therefore commit his body to the ground; earth to earth, ashes to ashes, dust to dust…'

Adam wondered if he would feel something as the first fistful of damp soil clattered down onto the shiny varnished lid of his coffin. Or if not feel something, hear something. No. Whatever was in that long, slim box, it wasn't him. He was up here, flying free, with the fat wood pigeons that perched on these leafless white-trunked birches. He felt as he had always felt, albeit without a body. So this was it. You got older, you got used to seeing a wearier face in the mirror, teeth that were greyer or yellower or made of zirconia, lines around the eyes, hair that was thinner or gone completely, a body that couldn't do what it used to, a brain that could no longer recall words that had once sprung immediately to mind, the titles of books and films, the names of celebrities and even old friends. And then you passed on. Literally. But you still felt the same. It was a revelation.

As Adam watched his relatives and friends step forward, one by one, to claim their handful of earth, to chuck it down with a kiss or a sob or a goodbye ('Farewell, old friend,' Roland muttered theatrically), he had another revelation. It was an obvious one. If his death had not been suicide – and it hadn't – it had been murder.

CHAPTER TWO

There was, of course, a wake. Back at the house, which was a convenient five-minute walk through the preserved-in-aspic village. Adam had designed and built the place himself, and the development, which had involved taking down a rotten old barn in a field raddled with nettles, brambles, burdocks and hogweed, had caused minor ructions at the time. Protests to the council, that sort of thing. But Adam had charmed the objectors, and used his long experience of dealing with metropolitan planning officers to outwit the local low-rent apparatchiks, pointing out that he wasn't doing anything that radical with 'Fallowfields'. Though it was, yes, a raw white concrete oblong, it sat on a plinth of knapped flint, referencing the local vernacular. With its floor-to-ceiling windows and concealed external water pipes, it was, above all else, a beautiful, clean shape. The low-angled grass roof was a nod to a Scandinavian tradition and, of course, the famous Australian Parliament House in Canberra, but it was hardly outrageous. It fitted in light-heartedly with the village green just down the road, not to mention the neat lawns of other, more traditional properties round about.

Inside, Adam had allowed himself more freedom – and fun:

2.7 metre doors linked rooms with high, 3.3 metre ceilings. At the centre of the property, industrial scale etched-glass doors opened to reveal a huge double-height sky-lit galleried space; polished white concrete with oversized art works and an arching chandelier (more Antony Caro than Vienna crystal). The glass and steel staircase that led up to the bedrooms was tucked to the side until it emerged as a bridge spanning the view to the terrace, garden and hills beyond.

It was great to see these beloved spaces of his full for a change. It seemed ridiculous that it had taken his death to have a repeat, indeed an improvement on their original, rather damp housewarming party, fifteen years before.

For now the sun had come out properly. Coats and jackets were flung off, ties loosened or discarded as people gathered on the terrace, in and out of the long sequence of casement windows that led into the mighty oblong of the living room. The fire blazing behind the pristine glass of the Nestor Martin rotating stove at the far end was starting to look a bit superfluous.

With flutes of champagne in their hands, the mourners were letting rip. Their voices were raised, their emotions flying free. Though Adam could see and hear everything in front of him, there was, quite apart from his muteness, one key limitation to his spectral capabilities; he couldn't be in more than one place at a time. More's the pity, as everywhere he looked there were old friends he hadn't seen for ages. What a turnout! He was, despite himself, quite impressed. And they were all talking about *him*. In largely flattering terms. 'His buildings were always about people, that's what I admired...' 'Such a talented man...' 'He *was* kind, wasn't he?' How quickly, though, they had relegated him to the past, like a shocking news event becoming history.

One or two were even starting to get frank little digs in. 'I did love Adam, but he could be rather too...' Adam overheard Lynsey Turner opining, before she was drowned out by a roar of laughter from bald, jowly structural engineer Keith Henderson, looking almost stuffed in his shiny grey suit. 'He was! He was!' he cried, clapping his beefy red hands; though what exactly he was supposed to have been, Adam had missed.

A gang of subbies were gathered around Paddy O'Neill, that bearded goliath of a builder, who liked to boast, in his un-Irish South London accent, that he had over two hundred painter-decorators on his books. Adam had missed his comment, but its noisy reception suggested a level of political incorrectness that was presumably off the scale. The wit tended to match the job with this crowd: plumbers, scaffolders, demolition crew, ground men – the dirtier the work, the dirtier the humour.

Against this racket, some of Adam's older friends were talking about the service, how lovely it had been. 'Had Adam actually planned it?' asked Louise Burbage, an architect he'd done Part Ones with at Bristol, but who had subsequently dropped out and become an interior designer. 'It's the sort of thing he might have done.'

'No, Julie did, I think,' their friend Nicola Newman replied. Nicola had been a conceptual artist back then, when such a thing was a novelty. Having pulled off a number of powerful stunts, including putting a live horse in an empty office space, a work she had called 'Galloping Inflation', she had changed tack, and was now a key figure in the Green Party.

'Julie, did she? She did well.' Louise had never liked Julie; had indeed told Adam, over a plate of fajitas in Notting Hill in 2006, that he was making a huge mistake leaving Serena for her. 'I liked the mini-addresses,' Louise went on. 'It all added up to a very rounded portrait, I thought.'

'What about that chap that spoke in favour of suicide...' asked skinny, thoughtful Mike Boyston, another Bristolian, who had spent long years at the BBC in some IT capacity and now had his own outfit.

'Gideon Bloomberg,' said Nicola.

'The egg-headed guy with the scraggly beard?'

'That's him. He's a philosophy professor at King's.'

'Is he? What – in London?'

'Yes.'

'It was a brave thing to do.'

'Actually,' said Louise, 'I thought it was completely inappropriate.'

'Isn't that what philosophers do?' Mike countered. 'Ask the difficult questions. And he had a point. It was Adam's life. I mean it's very sad for us, obviously, but if that's actually what he wanted...'

'"Very sad for us",' Louise repeated scornfully. 'Suicide.'

Adam hovered. He was touched that Louise was so defensively emotional about the manner of his death, though not surprised that Mike wasn't. But why wouldn't, didn't, any of them just say exactly what that manner had been? All these oblique mentions of 'a horrid death' were no use to him at all.

Somewhere in this noisy throng someone was having that conversation, surely? The question was where? He didn't think that those who were commiserating with Julie would exactly be quizzing her for details. That story had been and gone, by phone and WhatsApp, days, even weeks ago. Now it was in the category of the unmentionable; or perhaps, the not-necessary-to-mention.

How long had he been dead, anyway? In one group Adam passed he overheard the word 'inquest'; and although that hadn't been followed up, it seemed that such a thing had taken place. Adam could glean no details. What had it involved? A coroner, presumably, and a verdict. What had that been? More to the point, why could he remember nothing about any of it?

A small group around his business partner were discussing Adam's obituaries. *The Times* one had been better than the *Telegraph*'s, apparently. 'I'm not sure they quite got how significant his work was,' Jeff was saying. 'In terms of placemaking, thought-through living spaces...'

'I'm glad you think it was significant,' Eva chipped in, looking mischievously over at her work colleagues, Reuben and Simone.

'I did, Eva.' Jeff gave her a covert glare. How Adam wanted to swoop down and join in, offering perhaps a quick supportive wink for his girlfriend and her mates before he floated off.

'Did you hear the *Last Word* piece on Radio Four?' asked Joanna Peterken, an architect from a rival firm who had nonetheless been a friend.

'I was in it,' said Jeff, proudly.

'Of course you were! You were good, I thought. You got his humour, his mischievous side.'

'Thank you.'

Revolted though Adam was that Jeff had clearly been swanning around capitalising on his death, he was quietly chuffed. An obituary in *The Times*, no less. And *Last Word*, that was a great honour. Julie, little snob that she was, must have been thrilled.

His second wife was, it had to be said, looking radiant. She was standing beyond the living room near the island in the kitchen and dining area, holding court, as mourners and old friends trooped up in singles and pairs to offer condolences.

'Julie,' said Pete Frobisher, who had trained with Adam for his Part Two at the Architectural Association in London – AA in the biz – but had traded in his considerable talents for a less stressful career designing house extensions in the West Country. 'What can I say?'

Julie smiled nervously. 'You don't need to say anything, Pete.'

'No, don't say anything,' echoed Pete's wife, Daphne, a twitchy sparrow of a woman, tugging at his arm.

'What I will say,' Pete said, ignoring her, 'is hugs. Big hugs.' Actions followed the words. Julie was almost suffocated by his bearlike embrace. 'You know we all love you, Julie,' he murmured into her ear. He stepped back and shook his head, slowly. 'I'm so sorry. None of us can understand what happened. Adam. Of all people.'

Adam wanted to thump his old friend. What did happen, Pete? Spit it out. And why don't one of you sympathetic old chums put two and two together and draw a conclusion from the fact that you can't – understand – what – happened.

That conclusion being: it didn't.

Serena, Adam's first wife, was keeping well away from this area of public sympathy for the official widow; though in truth she had every right to feel as sad about his death as Julie did. She had been married to Adam for longer than Julie, and the pair of them had met when they were younger, when days and years were surely longer, in imagination if not in fact. There were times, indeed, especially recently, when Adam had found himself regretting that he'd ever left his original partner; but there you are, that was then, this was now. She had her new fella, Walter, who seemed to make her happy, even if he was a bit of a useless idiot, in Adam's humble and obviously only slightly biased opinion.

'Very, very upsetting,' Walter was saying now, to Belinda Briarstone, another of Adam and Serena's original Bristol circle. Of all the couples he knew who had got together in those far-off days, she and her husband Eric were the only ones who had stayed the course. Sad, really, when you considered what a jolly gang they'd all once been. Belinda was being nice to Walter for Serena's sake, but you could see from her over-polite expression that she didn't rate him. 'It's such a shame,' Walter was going on, 'because surely, if he could have seen all this,' he gestured round, 'his friends, all the love there is for him out there, he would never have done it.'

Guess what, Walter, you twat. I didn't do it. Whatever it was.

If only he could ask directly. Of, say, his mother, who was now sitting proprietorially on the old carved padded chair she had given him when his father had died and she had decided, on a whim, to declutter her house. Patricia was looking surprisingly perky, chatting away to dear kind Damian McIntyre, who was on his knees before her and didn't look as if he knew, now he was down there, how to get off them and away. Or of his daughter Matilda, who didn't look so great, despite her triumph with 'Pie Jesu'. 'Matilda, darling, you seem so very sad under that bright smile. The one thing I would love to do is give you a hug, a Daddy-hug, as of old, but I can't. I have no arms. But please, please tell me how I was supposed to have died.'

Then an odd thing happened. Adam's black-and-white cocker spaniel, Tonto, was suddenly in the room. Julie must have shut him away, but being Tonto, he wasn't having any of that. He was barrelling through the crowd towards Adam. He wasn't usually a big barker, Tonto, but he was yapping away now. He came up to where Adam was, or where Adam thought he was anyway, and stopped abruptly, wagging his tail, looking up with his pleading let's-go-for-a-walk face.

Adam didn't know where to put himself.

'I'm not here, Tonto,' he whispered loudly; and even though Adam could hear these words himself, it was clear that the gathered mourners could not. They were looking instead at a whining, excited dog, with a focus none of them could see.

'What's wrong with Tonto?' asked Matilda. She leant down and tickled his neck. 'Tonto, Tonto, what are you worrying about, you silly dog?'

'Oh, Tonto,' Julie sighed, marching over, 'what are you up to, you naughty animal?' She always called him 'animal', much to Adam's annoyance. 'Come on, darling, you're supposed to be nice and cosy in the boot room.'

Tonto turned and snarled at her and Adam laughed. Good for you, Tonts, you were always my dog.

'Now, Tonto, that's not nice. You come along with me and we'll find a lovely bone for you.'

'We can let him stay out here, can't we, Julie?' Matilda said. 'I don't think anybody minds. Poor old Tonto. He hates being cooped up.'

'Adam's dog,' said someone.

'Yes, let him stay,' came a chorus of voices.

Julie always knew when to concede. She turned to the crowd, smiling, as if this compromise were entirely her idea. 'Let's let him stay, then. Come on, Tonto. Matilda will look after you.'

But Tonto continued to whine. Was Adam more corporeal than he realised? Was he visible or audible on some higher frequency that mere humans couldn't access? He still, it seemed, had his sense of smell; perhaps that worked in reverse as well?

CHAPTER THREE

M uch later, when the sensible guests had departed, and the less sensible (in every sense!) had stuck around for far too long, hugging each other, swapping old Adam stories, laughing, crying, in one case both simultaneously, there came a moment when enough was clearly enough and it was time for the remaining hard core to hit the pub. Luckily, Beynton St Mary still had a pub, and a nice one too, The Cat and Whistle, right on the little triangular village green, run by a long-established couple who liked to keep pace with their punters in the drinking stakes. Famously grumpy at opening time, they were usually in an excellent mood mid-evening, before becoming a bit leery and impatient at last orders. Adam followed the inebriated gaggle up the road and hung around for a while as they told more tales of his life, often with zero relation to the historical truth; then, in ones and twos and threes, sloped off; in taxis to the train station, or to cars driven by the soberer partner. Finally, there were just four left, none of them coherent. It was time to leave.

Back down the lane at Fallowfields, only Adam's wife and business partner remained.

'I should go,' said Jeff, stretching out his arms, yawning. 'Get back on the yellow brick road.'

Well, if you should go, why don't you, Adam thought; he knew his partner's devious tactics of old; what on earth was he up to now?

'Haven't you drunk too much to drive?' Julie asked.

'I'm sure I'll be fine. I've been pacing myself.' Jeff grinned, slyly. 'Up to a point.'

'Stay and have a bit of supper if you want. There's loads of leftover canapés, I ordered far too many. And I've got some cold meats in the fridge. I could make you a coffee.'

'Now there's a tempting thought.' Jeff gave Julie the benefit of his chemically-whitened smile. 'Maybe I will.' His nickname in the firm was 'the Weasel' and, quite apart from his behaviour, he really did look like one with his bright, dark, button eyes, the substantial snout, the receding mouth and chin – albeit that weasels didn't generally have goatee beards.

'You'd be welcome to stay the night. I've got more than one empty guest room.'

'I didn't bring pyjamas.'

'I could lend you some of Adam's.'

'Bit spooky. Or a toothbrush.'

'We have spares.'

Jeff gave Julie a measured look. 'I'd have to phone Susan,' he replied.

Julie shrugged. 'It's up to you. But the offer's there.'

Watching this exchange, Adam was sincerely hoping that he wasn't about to observe anything inappropriate. But it seemed, as the pair of them sat down a little later at the glass table in the kitchen area, that any moves Julie wanted to make on Jeff were not physical. Nor – thank God – vice-versa.

'Thanks for staying, Jeff,' she said. She yawned, and stretched, and did one of her neck-circling yoga moves. 'It's been a hell of a day, one way and another. I couldn't quite face being alone.'

'I imagine,' he replied. He was shaking his head, slowly and with great meaning. 'Such a terrible, terrible thing to have happened. I don't know how you've coped.'

Julie held up her hands. 'Please, Jeff, no sympathy. Not now. Otherwise, I really will crack up.'

'I understand,' Jeff replied. He plunged his fork greedily into the smoked salmon mousse that Julie had magicked up from somewhere, as a preamble to the promised cold meats. He was back on the leftover bubbly, Adam saw, so he presumably really was sticking around. Well, he loved a random adventure, did Jeff. That was one of the things Adam had liked about him, in the days when they'd first got together, when Adam's original partner Stanley had pulled him into the firm, enthusiastic about his computer modelling skills. Jeff had always been one for the second cappuccino, the extra glass of wine at lunch, the unnecessary nightcap at the conference.

When Jeff had scoffed the mousse, he gazed across at Julie, weightily.

'Now may not be the time, Julie,' he said, 'but at some point you and I are going to have to sit down and decide what you want to do with Adam's share of the business.'

Straight to the point, as always. Not that Julie seemed to mind, the heartless bitch. On the very evening of my funeral, Adam thought, mournfully.

'I know there's all that stuff to do,' she replied. 'I guess when it comes to the business side, I'll be guided by you.'

'Obviously, you'll need to have total scrutiny of everything,' Jeff went on. And this was how he did it, the duplicitous shit. The last thing he wanted was total scrutiny. But by proposing it he was playing Julie just right. She was always one to do or want the exact opposite of what you suggested to her. Back in the early, loved-up days of their relationship, when Julie was helping Adam design and decorate Fallowfields, for them both, and who knew, their possible future babies, Adam had laughed about this wayward stubbornness of hers. 'I've worked out that if I want Dutch Orange I should recommend Hague Blue,' he'd joked to his friends. Later in their relationship he'd learned the hard way never to even signal his intentions.

Julie fetched the cold meat platter and found a half bottle of leftover red wine. Tonto had been let out of the boot room and allowed to pad around the living room, though Julie was as strict as ever about giving him treats from the table.

His dog had identified his business partner as a soft touch, and was standing a yard off, wagging his tail and looking up expectantly.

'No, Tonto,' Julie said. 'Jeff is not giving you anything, are you, Jeff?'

'Not if you say not.'

'Adam was always so naughty. Used to feed him titbits. With the result that, look, he still begs.'

'Must be nice to have him around, though, now you're on your own.'

'We'll see how we get on,' Julie replied; and watching, Adam didn't hold out that much hope for poor Tonto's long-term chances at Fallowfields.

Suddenly Tonto gave up on Jeff and rushed across the room, barking. Now he was looking up towards Adam, his big brown eyes full of their usual plaintive appeal.

'Tonto, come here, stop that!' Julie was calling after him, getting to her feet. 'There's no one there. That's the second time today he's done that.'

Adam backed away, high up towards the far end of the room. With one more yap, Tonto turned and slunk over towards the table.

'*Shall* I give him something?' Jeff asked, holding out a scrap of salami.

'Really, Jeff, it's not a good idea.'

With the dog finally settled, Julie listened patiently as Jeff explained that after Stanley's sudden death from a stroke two years before, he had ended up with half of Stan's equity in the firm, leaving him with forty per cent and Adam with sixty per cent, a controlling share. Now Jeff was recommending that he took most if not all of that sixty per cent, which would be very good for Julie financially, what with the current high value of the company, not to mention that of the premises in Covent Garden, which they owned outright. The London commercial property market was currently buoyant, but who knew for how long? Julie nodded along, sweetly enough. But just when Jeff thought he had his deal in the bag, she suddenly met his eye.

'But you were trying to force him out anyway, weren't you, Jeff?'

Stranded in his ethereal dimension, Adam couldn't help but chuckle as Jeff all but choked on his mouthful of prosciutto and caramelised endive.

'Whatever makes you think that?'

'Adam used to rant and rave about it.'

'Did he? When?'

'Whenever he was home. How Stanley and he had basically discovered you, and made you, and now, like the young cockerel in the run, you were trying to get rid of him.'

Jeff laughed, that genial fake laugh that Adam knew all too well, having sat in at client meetings with him over the years. It was the laugh that bought him time, allowed him, even as he gurgled away, to think out his next move.

'Nonsense,' he said, after a few moments. 'We hugely valued Adam. I think we all thought that maybe it was time he moved to a less hands-on position, but we wouldn't have wanted to lose him.'

'Really?' Julie cocked a plucked eyebrow.

'Believe me.' Thousands wouldn't, Adam thought. 'But I have to say,' Jeff went on, 'with the best will in the world, that Adam created most of his own problems.'

'Such as?'

'Being a bit of a dinosaur, dissing our branding and social media strategy on a regular basis. It was just silly. And counterproductive.'

'Was it? Does a successful firm, known in the business by and for its actual work, need to rebrand endlessly, or waste time boasting about itself in largely meaningless terms to a wider public? I don't think so.'

Adam wasn't sure whether he had spoken these words or not. In his current state, his thoughts and his words seemed to be much the same thing. It didn't matter anyway, because neither of the others could hear him.

'He hated Twitter,' Julie agreed. 'Thought it was a waste of time.'

So not the case, Adam thought (or was he actually speaking?) I was an early adopter. I was there when Stephen Fry was sharing his amusing thoughts on breakfast meetings, Grace Dent was updating us on toenail varnish and Alain de Botton pumping out gnomic utterances on an almost hourly basis. I just didn't like what it's become: a sewer for the pointless outrage of ill-informed nobodies and has-beens, its rebranding as X (-rated crap) amusingly appropriate. Which hardly made me original. You knew that, Jeff. We talked about it: 'I don't need to share my half-formed thoughts,' I explained, 'about every last thing that happens, do I? There is a merit in keeping your counsel. Especially with the freaks out there now, the weaponised green ink brigade.' Jeff had grinned and agreed, repeating the last phrase with his characteristically phoney, 'I like that.'

'Adam wasn't exactly woke, was he?' Jeff was saying to Julie now. 'There was a big argument at our last Christmas lunch about transgender rights, for example, and he didn't make himself popular with some of the younger staff, telling them that he'd always wanted, deep down, to be a seagull, but had learned to live with the disappointment.'

Classic Jeff! Repeating what had been no more than a tipsy party riff in a way that indicated he understood the joke, yet disapproved of it in the same breath; thus having his right-on cake and eating it.

Not that Julie noticed. She was making her sympathetic I-understand-though-millions-wouldn't face, the humourless cow. These two, really, were made for each other.

'It just wasn't appropriate,' Jeff went on. 'Especially as one of our most talented designers was seriously considering transitioning at the time. He left shortly afterwards.'

Which was, as you well know, you fraud, nothing to do with me. If anything, it was to do with you, Jeff, and the way you were threatened by Gary's spectacular computer modelling skills, which put your own late-forty-something efforts to shame. Not to mention, ahem, the sneaky jokes behind his back that Eva alerted me to on several occasions. Garyella. Wasn't that your nickname for him?

'To be fair,' Julie was saying. 'I don't think you could accuse Adam of prejudice… in that sort of area. On a personal level–'

Up went the bogus palms. 'Please! Julie! Don't get me wrong! I really wasn't doing that; I was just saying…'

Just saying, Adam thought. You were always just saying, weren't you, Jeff? Just saying to A, about B, and to B, when the time was right, about C. What a massive stirrer you were, and undoubtedly still are. Well, you've got your way now, haven't you? Woke or not, dinosaur or not, I'm off the scene. What I'm wondering now is whether it was you that helped me off that scene.

Adam smiled to himself as he watched his widow put up objections to Jeff's carefully-prepared plans. It was something she was very good at doing, and for once it wasn't him in the firing line. Jeff visibly didn't like seeing this new side of his partner's partner, the stylish yoga teacher who had previously treated him only to vapid charm and flattery. In particular, he didn't like her suggestion that her friend Roland Herrington, 'a bit of a financial whizz', might get involved in the negotiations on Julie's behalf.

Eventually they agreed to call it a night. Julie showed Jeff up to the largest and nicest of the three spare rooms, the east-facing White Room, designed, as it had been, to maximise on the early morning light. With the blinds up on the floor-to-ceiling windows you woke, on a good day, bathed in sunshine. In the early days of their marriage Adam and Julie had often spent rogue summer nights at that end of the house, just for that delicious experience.

'Goodnight, Jeff. I do hope you sleep okay. Guests always tell us it's a very comfortable bed.'

Adam's worst fears were not to be realised. There was a quick hug, instigated by Jeff, and that was it. Julie hurried off downstairs to lock up the house and put Tonto in his crate.

Feeling relieved and slightly furtive, Adam followed his business partner along to his room. What was he hoping to witness? An incriminating phone call, even just a celebratory high-five in the mirror? He watched as Jeff stripped off his lightly creased Armani suit and padded, skinny-legged but fat-bellied, into the marble tiled en suite wet room, where he stood under the domed chrome Grohe power shower and – good God! – masturbated. This was a side of his partner Adam really didn't need to see, but intriguing nonetheless. What kind of a man pleasures himself after a funeral, indeed after dining *a deux* with the attractive widow of his allegedly suicided partner? Perhaps he'd been turned on by Julie's hardball negotiating tactics.

Smartly clad finally, in a pair of Adam's best tartan PJs, Jeff opened his briefcase and took out a crime novel, *Murder Comes To Wincanton*, by P K Tresimmons, doubtless some hot new name in the genre; apart from architectural stuff, crime was all Jeff ever read; the paradox being, Adam thought, that if anyone could help him with his search for his murderer, it was probably Jeff. Unless of course Jeff was his murderer. Ha! He didn't really think that, did he?

Bedtime reading matter laid respectfully on the bed, Jeff now reached into a side pocket and found a little octagonal silver box. He opened it carefully and took out three white pills, which he threw back with a glass of water from the en suite. Poor man, he was a mere forty-seven, but already he had ongoing issues with his heart; perhaps that's why he was in such a hurry to get his hands on the equity and his name on the door. Albury Atkinson Trelawney it would presumably be now; the two deceased partners offering continuity and reassurance to the established clients, even as they rolled in their graves as the new chief trampled on their legacy.

Along the corridor, Julie was sitting in a cream silk nightie at her dressing table, applying moisturiser with her forefinger while talking on the phone.

'...okay, darling, will do. You sleep well. Night night. Love you too.'

Damn. Adam had completely missed the conversation. Who was this darling that she loved too? Husky Jane? Daffy Diana? Mean Merielle? Of course it would be one of her close girlfriends, even though they'd all been at the funeral and the wake. Why did she need to talk to them again the very same day? Well, that was Julie for you. Her mobile was like an extension of her brain. She liked to be connected, even as she sank into sleep.

He followed his widow as she climbed into their king-sized double bed. He floated down next to her and turned to look at her. If she really was nervous about being alone in the house, perhaps now was the moment to make her fears real.

'Hi, Julie,' he said.

She didn't flinch.

'Julie,' he repeated. 'It's me. Adam. Your dead husband who didn't kill himself. I'm here. In your bedroom. Right beside you.'

Nothing.

I'M HERE!' he yelled in her face. 'RIGHT BESIDE YOU. CAN'T YOU HEAR ME? DID YOU ACTUALLY KILL ME, YOU MAD BITCH?'

He had made less impression on her than a midge.

He backed off across the room and watched as she sighed, held her hand to her lips, closed her eyes and kissed her fingers, then slowly opened them again and put the light out.

CHAPTER FOUR

J ulie soon nodded off. Adam could hear that familiar breathing, peppered with the light snores that his second wife always denied making. He was the one that snored. Not her. But ha! Now that he was no longer around, her creaky wheezes were all too clear.

Did he need rest himself? As whatever he was now: a spirit, a ghoul, a spectre, a spook, a phantasm? What did ghosts do? Did they sleep standing up, like horses? But he wasn't standing up, because there was nothing of him. And yet what had Tonto seen? It must have been something, otherwise, surely, his dog wouldn't have reacted like that.

It was all the more confusing because Adam didn't even believe in ghosts. As a small boy, granted, he had been frightened of a long uncarpeted staircase that ran up from the corridor outside his bedroom at Larks Rise, the old family home where his mother Patricia still lived, into a dark loft. He had several times imagined that he had heard noises from there. Nothing would have induced him to venture up those stairs alone in the middle of the night, and even during the day he had kept away. But once he'd reached teenage years, he had determined to leave such silly superstitions behind (even though he'd continued to dream about that staircase all his adult life). In drunken late-night discussions in friends' rooms at Bristol, where he'd done his RIBA Part One, then later in flats in London, where he'd done his Part Two, qualified, and stayed, Adam had been the firm voice of sanity on the subject of the supernatural, while loopier friends and acquaintances had talked about poltergeists and past lives and murdered kitchen maids and farmers dressed in old-fashioned clothes.

If and when Adam had ever believed, his main fear had been that ghosts could do stuff. Move things. Write in a spectral hand. Talk. There was one story, that Jeff, of all people, had told him when they had been staying together in an old hotel in Dorset after a site meeting. This quaint half-timbered hostelry, dating back to Elizabethan times, had made a bit of a thing about its supposedly haunted status. It had suits of armour on the main staircase and an empty back dining room with oil paintings on the dark, wood-panelled walls, some, apparently, of the alleged ghouls. Jeff had refused to go into it, though Adam had and found nothing to freak him out. Eva, who had come along to assist, had made a point of going in there on her own and turning the lights off for ten minutes to 'experience the vibe', a vibe which she maintained had 'zero real spookiness' in it. But over dinner that night, Jeff, wide-eyed, had told the pair of them about this dead Italian monk who had haunted a chapel in the Vatican; whose slowly-moving facial expression, accompanied by a husky and 'infinitely evil' whisper, was so terrifying that it had driven at least one seminarian insane. Obviously that tale was for the birds; or maybe just for lapsed Catholics like Jeff; but then again, as Adam had joked, he wouldn't have volunteered to spend the night in that chapel.

Though Adam had been an adult sceptic, he hadn't ruled out the idea that it might be possible for some kind of imprint of a person to be left on the ether. The intensity of some particular experience, a murder, a rape, an abandonment, some other human cruelty, had been such that the poor victim's spirit had no choice but to leave something of their anguish behind. Stone tape theory, some called it; the idea that certain types of stone – quartz and limestone were cited in particular – could store the memory of unusually horrific events for playback to sensitive souls in due course. His first wife, Serena, had seen a ghost as a teenager, in a holiday cottage her family had rented in the Cotswolds. But this particular spirit hadn't looked at her, or said anything, it had just been there. An old woman, floating past, in a long black Victorian dress. Perversely, Adam found that story comforting, in that it ruled out the idea of conscious, active ghosts.

But here he was: conscious, for sure, and active too. But invisible and worse, powerless. Unable to interact with the world he had left behind.

He had two big things on his mind, if 'mind' was the word for the thinking facility that he still apparently possessed. Well, three actually. First, obviously, how had he died? Even in the drunken aftermath of the wake, up at the pub, he had managed to overhear no conversation that had explained what his method had been. The nearest he'd got to it was, 'Nobody expected him to go *like that*.' This from the lips of his favourite quantity surveyor, Duncan McFarlane, a rubicund Scot who never knowingly turned down a pint of ale, or a glass of free bubbly for that matter. 'Like *what*, man!' Adam had yelled, but none of the gang of well-oiled subbies around Duncan had done anything more than nod solemnly.

Second: what was he now? He had no hands, no body, no lips, no ears, no eyes; and yet he could hear and see. He had no nose and yet he could still smell. How did that work?

Third, moving on from that: how long did this state, if state it was, last? Would these lingering privileges of the living world be soon denied him? Would he slowly fade away? Or vanish as if in a puff of smoke, extinct? That was the thought that terrified him the most. He didn't, in theory, mind oblivion. Indeed, in life, he had always argued for it. What could be more comforting than sleep, rest in peace, etc.? Who could bear an eternity of the same self? But now he was halfway there, he found that he desperately wanted to cling on. More than anything, he wanted to find out who had done this to him, snatched away his life twenty or thirty years before his allotted time. Adam had never been a vengeful type; far from it. But he wanted at least to know.

Suicide was an absurd idea for him. When he'd been alive, he'd sometimes joked that now he was coming to the end of his sixth decade he could do with *another* life. To do all the things he'd failed to do in this one. Backpacking, for example. How had he managed to miss out on full moon parties on the beaches of Goa or sex with a raven-haired stranger on the terraces of Machu Picchu? Because, obviously, architecture was a seven-year course, and then he'd gone straight from Part Two at the AA into Bywater Shaw Melrose, the firm where he'd done his practical training. Once he'd passed his professional practice exams and was allowed at last to use that coveted protected title 'Architect', the idea of heading off to India or Thailand or South America with a knapsack hadn't been on the agenda, so keen was he to crack on, get ahead, gain the experience that would allow him to leave BSM, supportive and encouraging though they were, and put his own name above the door. Albury & Atkinson. He had done it. By the age of thirty-one. With Stanley's help. They had made a success of it. First in the UK, then latterly, in the Middle and Far East too. From Camden to Chengqing, as Stan liked to say, referencing one of Adam's more successful 'regenerations'. *The Architectural Review* had described Adam's refurbishment of the old town of that uber-modern metropolis as 'an even better example of people-friendly placemaking in a modern Chinese city than Ben Wood's famous Xintiandi in Shanghai.'

Three years before, his friend Lionel Leesome, whom he'd

known since his Bristol days, had killed himself; a shock that had resonated through his extended friendship group like a sonic boom. None of them had ever thought that Lionel, of all people, would have taken his own life. Happily married, an organiser of excellent parties, with a house in Islington and a cottage in North Norfolk, he had made enough money as a partner in a City law firm to retire in his late fifties. He had years of good times ahead of him. And then suddenly – bang. His poor wife Amanda had found him, after two days of silence, in the cottage in Cley, a place Lionel had always loved to be. He had walked out along the shingle and through the long stretch of dunes to Blakeney Point, to see the seals basking in the sun on that beautiful empty strand for one last time; then he'd returned and hung himself from a light fitting in the upstairs bedroom.

Sorry, but no, Adam could never have done something like that. Wasn't life precarious enough anyway? Quite apart from Lionel, his older friends and acquaintances seemed to be dropping dead of this and that all the time. He would open Facebook, and there it would be: someone he'd known for years, hadn't seen for a while, suddenly succumbed to cancer or a heart attack or an aneurysm or one of the numerous other booby traps that awaited men and women from this age upwards; the sad announcement by a closer friend or relative; the shocked stream of condolences below.

Adam loved life. If not raindrops on roses and whiskers on kittens he would, if asked, have come up with a long list of favourite sensations of animate existence that included, off the top of his head... what?... a pint of decent bitter and a packet of cracked sea salt crisps after a hard day's work in the office; sharp and tangy home-made marmalade on hot buttered toast on a sunny Saturday morning at home; the smell and taste of – God help him, how he missed it! – freshly ground coffee anytime; a decent Cab Sav cutting across, say, a well-crisped duck confit; warm apple crumble with, yes, please, cool, thick double cream;

the heavy scent of jasmine on a Mediterranean summer's night; the rattling hum of crickets ditto (a sound the ever-pretentious Roland called 'stridulation'); swimming languidly in a warm turquoise sea; a freshly powdered ski run under a brilliant blue sky; tartiflette washed down with génépi in a warm and fuggy chalet bar... where, really, did you stop? Quite apart from the pleasure he got from his design work, a seemingly endless uphill climb that would continue to challenge and reward him till the day he died.

Oh shit. The realisation had hit him again, an all too real punch in his non-existent stomach. He *had* died. And there were no more sunlit afternoons of drawing at his stand-up A0 desk for him now – let alone tartiflette after a spirited morning's skiing.

Or were there? Was it impossible for him ever to pick up one of his favourite Faber-Castell Wasserlack pencils again? Would he never tear open another roll of detail paper? Mightn't he in due course learn how to do stuff again physically, move things around, stop being so damned impotent?

Or might it be that now he was on the other side, wherever that was, he would be able to encounter old mates who had passed on. Lionel, even. Or Stanley, his partner of many years, friend from his first week at the AA. Fresh from Liverpool, Stan (as he was then) had been rather lost in London, and it had been Adam's youthful delight to show the freckled, ginger-haired newbie round, to take him out from those raffish old buildings in the corner of Bedford Square to the haunts he had got to know in his practice year. Kettner's, in Romilly St, Soho, where you could eat a cheap pizza in swanky surroundings, piano music drifting in from the adjacent cocktail bar. Jimmy's in Frith St, down steep steps to huge plates of Greek food and rough retsina, the 'instant hangover' as they had jokingly called it then. The Stock Pot, over in Chelsea, where the nosh was even more basic, but Serena was to be found, waitressing, getting big tips from the punters with her helpful manner and wide smile.

Stan had been the better designer; Adam had always known that. But he had needed Adam. To be the front man, the one who could bring in the business and keep it. And also, to be fair, the one who wouldn't laugh at him as he gradually morphed from Liverpudlian Stan into London Stanley, with his tasteful but funky flat in Camden Square...

Adam must have finally fallen asleep, if that described what ghosts do. Put it this way, his active mind faded out, and the next thing he knew it was morning. Julie was still in bed, eyes closed, breathing rhythmically and grunting from time to time, but the birds were awake in the garden, marking their territory with noisy song. As he floated silently along the familiar gravel paths, Adam could make out the chirrup of a robin, the classic trill of a blackbird, the harsh caw-caw-caw of a crow, the rat-tat-tat door creak of a woodpecker, the distant coo of wood pigeons. It was almost unbearable, now that he was no longer part of it, to hear these customary cries; to see but not to be able to touch the sculpture at the end of the lavender walk, an idea he had stolen from a favourite secret corner of Regent's Park.

Further down, beyond the long sloping lawn, were the plants around his natural swimming pool, waiting for their big moment in high summer: galingale, flag iris, purple loosestrife, bulrushes, marsh marigold. Adam had been an early installer of such a thing in the UK; certainly one of the first to have had it written up, in *Homes and Gardens*, with Julie posing in her white one-piece by the driftwood diving board (his idea). Up on the long bank by the woodland beyond, the yellow daffs were already over, dying back to tawdry brown, while the primroses kept going and the bluebells struggled up next to the white stars of wild garlic, the tangy smell of which filled the air, even this early in the season.

Indoors, his widow stirred. He watched her roll over and reach out across the bed, as if for another body. Ah, she did miss him then, now that he was gone! He watched her slowly realise that he wasn't there. Then she sat up. Even though he knew her so well, it was hard to make out what her expression meant. Resignation? Longing? Relief?

Out of bed, she put on her turquoise silk dressing gown and went downstairs to let Tonto out of his crate and make herbal tea: jasmine and green mix, her morning tipple. She was against caffeine at any time and had given Adam repeated gyp for his coffee and tea habit, his beans, his grinder, his Assam, Darjeeling and Lapsang, all marking different times of the day. As she put the pretty little box back, alongside the jars and tins that contained her other teas – chamomile, rosehip, Wahama seaweed sencha, mint (dried from the garden), fennel, nettle and lemon verbena (ditto), echinacea, Valerian Plus – Adam noticed how neat and bare the cupboard looked. She had cleared him and his noxious stimulants out already.

Jeff was down before she could even start on her yoga. They greeted each other, a little over-cheerily, like a couple who had almost made a pass at each other in an empty house but hadn't.

Jeff wanted coffee. This was amusing. Luckily Julie hadn't, as it turned out, got rid of all Adam's supply. She had just moved it to a lower cupboard.

'Adam was very particular about his coffee,' she said, as she pulled out a leftover bag of beans and the little grinder. 'Here. I never use it.'

'He was,' Jeff agreed. He plugged in the machine and whirred the beans around noisily. Ah, that smell! How Adam, hovering enviously, longed for a taste as well.

CHAPTER FIVE

Once Jeff had had his breakfast and left, with a kiss on both cheeks for the new widow he planned to do business with, Julie did her yoga as usual. There had barely been another word about what she wanted to do with Adam's equity. As she had suggested last night, Jeff was going to put his proposals in writing for her lawyer – and maybe Roland too – to scrutinise. This morning seemed to be all about setting a cheery tone for future negotiations, which Jeff was keen to wrap up as quickly as possible. Jeff was, by turns, apologetic (about wanting coffee), grateful (about being put up for the night, then having an egg and toast cooked for him), bogus (about offering to help clear up) and enthusiastic (about seeing Julie very soon, in London, or even back here, 'to take things forward').

On her neat blue mat, with her blue block beside her, Julie breathed in through her lovely little upturned nose and out through the soft, and you would think forgiving, lips of her full mouth. She let the love in, and then she let it out again. She shifted effortlessly between Vrikshasana ('tree pose') and the torture (but not for her) of Adho Mukha Shvanasana ('downward facing dog'). Then her supple body slid from Trikonasana to Kursiasana to Naukasana to Bhujangasana, ending in Adam's old favourite, from the days when he had slavishly done these stretching exercises alongside her: Shavasana ('corpse position'). Allegedly the hardest one, though he had always found it the easiest, lying still on your back with your arms outstretched. 'Coffee position,' he had joked in the early days and Julie had laughed, as he trotted off to get her jasmine tea and his three-star Columbian roast before they had retired to bed for a rather different sort of exercise.

After her routine, she showered, and dressed in blue jeans and an alarmingly practical top. She headed downstairs and ate a slice of rye bread topped with home-made blackcurrant jam. Then, with a deep sigh, she got going on the clean-up of the wake, assisted by Becky from the village, who had arrived to her usual enthusiastic greeting from Tonto, who loved their warm, young, wide-hipped cleaner more than his official mistress, Adam often thought.

After an hour or so, Julie put down her J-cloth. 'Right, Becky,' she announced, 'I hope you don't mind me leaving you to finish off here, I'm going to get started on Adam's shed. It's about time.'

Adam followed Julie down through the garden to his beloved work space. She was clutching a roll of heavy-duty black bin bags and her expression looked ominous. Tonto followed her, wagging his tail, his shifty lugubrious eyes ever hopeful.

'No, Tonto, Mummy is not taking you for a walk. Mummy has more important things to do. Clearing out the shit of ages,' she muttered, more to herself than the dog.

She opened the door and paused on the worn wooden step, as well she might. One of the hard-fought agreements she and Adam had had to keep their marriage going was that this was Adam's space, his 'man cave', and Julie didn't enter without permission, whether he was there or not. Julie had initially protested, but Adam fought his corner. Becky was allowed in to tidy and clean, but not Julie. If Julie went in, he knew his peace of mind would be disturbed. She would be unable to resist sorting out his stuff, closing the drawers of the plan chest, stacking up his drawings in neat piles, when sometimes what an artistic soul like him required was a carefully modulated chaos.

Now she was in. He could see what she was staring at, a slightly demented smile on her lips. The corkboard over his beloved A0 drawing desk. Why couldn't he put his ideas in a portfolio, like anyone else, she had asked him, many times. Why did they need to be laid out in this mad jumble of sketches and notes to self and lists, on the wall, where anyone could see them? 'Because,' he had replied, patiently, 'a) no one can see them because this is my private space and b) that's how I like to work. You remove that corkboard over my dead body.'

Ha! There was no obstacle now, was there? Julie marched towards it, grasped with delicate but strong hands its wooden frame and tugged. It came off with two wrenches. As she half lowered it, half dropped it onto the floor, she was laughing.

'That was easy,' she said as she looked at it, shaking her head at the yellow and pink Post-it notes that had already fallen to the worn varnished boards like autumn leaves.

With that she got going in earnest. There was nothing Adam could do except watch as she flew into his stuff like a vengeful harpie, bulking out the heavy-duty black bin bags with his life's work. After ten minutes she ran back to the house and got the portable Bluetooth speaker, then set up a hi-energy Spotify playlist ('You Can Do It').

Now she was actively having fun.

It was not only Adam's current projects that were being chucked out to the sound of 'Told You Once' and 'We Can Come Together', but all his past ones, stretching way back to a time before Julie. One of her frequent complaints to her friends, often made jokily over a meal, but always with a rasping undertone of barely-concealed frustration, was that Adam was a hoarder. 'Like all men,' her grim chum Merielle had replied, sexist to a fault. And it was, perhaps, true. Maybe a man who kept all his journals and notebooks and sketchbooks stretching back to teenaged years was a bit of a hoarder. But it wasn't just hoarding for the sake of it. It was all part, as he had often tried to explain to her, of his ongoing thought process. Sometimes you needed to look at the details of your early projects, to see their very naïveté and lack of experience, to get the confidence to move forward.

It was all toast now. In due course, doubtless, Julie would move on to the London flat, and then presumably tell Jeff there was no need to hang on to anything in the office and that would be that. He would have been cancelled. The background to his long life's work, his legacy, in fact, gone. He watched as his second wife paused for a moment, wondering whether to hold on to his beloved notebooks, the black-bound A5 plain paper Moleskines, stacked up in a row on their dedicated shelf. Here were his ideas in writing, elaborated and developed with pen and ink line drawings, often enhanced with watercolour. They went back years, to the day, pretty much, when Moleskines had first appeared, some time in the late nineties. Serena, bless her, had given him his first one, for his birthday. Before that he had used a random collection of more ordinary notebooks, which were also here.

'Aren't you going to consult my children about them?' he shouted, as she held one thoughtfully between thumb and finger. 'Matilda might like them. As a keepsake.'

But there was no reply. Nor did Julie pause for long. She did a mad little jig to Jübel's 'Dancing in the Moonlight' and then she was off, chucking them merrily into her growing line of black sacks.

You would have thought that a wife who had loved you, who had told you when you first met that you were such a huge talent, that it was a privilege to meet you, yadda yadda, would have wanted to hang on to your effing notebooks. Had Serena been in this position, keeper of the holy flame, she would have done for sure. Adam was tempted to race over to her house now. 'Serena, please, it's urgent, come down to Fallowfields and rescue my notebooks before they reach the dump.'

But how would he even get there? Serena was in north London, thirty-five miles away. He could hardly drive there in this state. What did ghosts do to get around over long distances? Take public transport? Fly?

The only thing that interrupted Julie's frenzy was the trill of her ringtone, the mindful 'Swan'.

'Julie Albury.' It was one of the oddest quirks of his second wife that she always answered her mobile as if it were an old-fashioned landline.

'Merielle darling... hang on... no, not shagging, naughty,' she giggled, 'just breathless... tidying... yes, it was, wasn't it... well, I'm glad... I think we did him proud, one way and another... I agree... to try and *justify* it... he's always been one of Adam's weirder friends...'

Adam, watching from the corner, could only follow Julie's side of the conversation. He got up, floated over, tried to get in close enough to hear Merielle, but he couldn't. They gossiped on, not just, it seemed, about Gideon Bloomberg's odd speech, but all the other events of yesterday afternoon. 'I do hope he would have been happy with it,' Julie said at one point; and Adam was surprised, touched even, by her concern.

When she eventually clicked off the phone, Julie took a long, slow, deep breath. Then she closed her eyes tight, pushed her lips together and visibly shuddered. For a moment, Adam thought she was about to cry. Now, after all his anger about what she was doing with his stuff, he felt for her. He wanted to put his arms around her and say, 'It's all right, Julie. I know things haven't been so great recently between us. I'm sorry you've been left alone.'

But he had no arms.

At another level, he had to admit that he found this sudden display of emotion comforting. He had hardly admitted it to himself, but Julie was one of his key suspects in this murder that was masquerading as something else. Julie had, as the crime buffs would have put it, both the proximity and the means to do away with him; it was just her motive that raised a doubt. He knew she loved Fallowfields: the house itself, the garden, her friends in the neighbourhood, her yoga class, the fast train from Tempelsham to London for those things she liked doing there: shopping, going to exhibitions, attending kooky workshops and courses. But she hadn't needed to *kill* him to keep (most of) those things.

Had she?

Just after noon there was the crunch of tyres on the gravel and a van arrived. It was Rod Richardson, known to the locals as 'the posh plumber'. Not that he was actually that posh, but he was ex-Army, or rather ex-Marine, and had been some sort of officer. It was rumoured that Richardson had been in the Special Boat Section, but that may well have been a story put about by himself, because Rod did like to talk the talk. He had come, originally, from South Africa, and still retained a good twang of the accent. The plumber thing was a bit of a misnomer too, as though he could do plumbing, if pushed, Rod was really more of a handyman-cum-painter-decorator. He had repainted most of their upstairs, Farrow and Ball all the way.

He was a bit of a flirt too, as well he might be with his physique. As Clive James had said of the young Arnold Schwarzenegger, he looked like a brown condom full of walnuts. Particularly perhaps with that shaved and shiny head of his, where the all too obvious male pattern baldness had been repurposed as a sexy asset. He always got Julie simpering and making unnecessary cups of tea (it was okay for *him* to have caffeine, for some reason). But nonetheless Adam had always liked him. There was something about his chirpy, can-do energy that was appealing. Rod was not a man to tell you a particular replacement tap couldn't be found, or a soakaway not dug. Rod would sort it, one way or the other; and he didn't do that typical builder thing of rushing off on another job when he was supposed to be finishing something for you.

To Adam, who saw himself as a genial, middle-of-the-road liberal, albeit perhaps of a somewhat old-school variety, Rod's politics had always been on the suspect side, with his crazed enthusiasm for Brexit, his desire for 'ex-colonials' to be put back on the favoured immigrants list, his belief that everyone should stand on their own two feet, come what may. 'Let's put it this way, *Eddam*,' he would say, 'there were never many Poles or Romanians after your job as a top-notch architect, were there? So why would you give a toss? But I was undercut every *stip* of the way. It's a no-brainer, mate.' Rod liked his shooting, too, both in the range at the Tempelsham Gun Club and out in the winter fields. If he couldn't get behind a gun, he would happily beat, walking ahead of the guns on the local shoot, shouting and banging sticks to raise the game from the undergrowth, a poor man's day out, in Adam's opinion.

Why had Julie called him now? Was there a skip coming just behind him, for the final disposal of Adam's treasured sketches and notes? Was she planning to have her way immediately with the paint shade in the hall, return it from Skimmed Milk White, the wrestled-over compromise, to her favoured Dayroom Yellow?

The van door slammed and the human condom got out. He was wearing tight blue jeans and – yes, for real – an orange and black lumberjack shirt, opened to reveal a seventies-style hairy chest. He was walking up the gravel path to the front door when Julie appeared, almost coquettishly, at the door of the shed.

Tonto shot out between her legs and barrelled across the gravel, barking.

'Rod!' she called. 'Over here.'

She turned on the doorstep and he followed her in, the fickle hound now slinking along next to him, tail wagging. Inside, they stood for three seconds looking at each other, as if, Adam thought, in congratulation. Then: 'Sweetheart,' she said softly, her snaky arms reaching up to his neck as her lips met his.

Tonto yapped enthusiastically.

CHAPTER SIX

They were up in the bedroom in the main house before Becky had even left. Had their cleaner known all along? Adam wondered. Did this explain the sheepish, pitying looks she had been giving him for the last few months when he'd been at home?

Adam followed them. He couldn't help himself. At first, he wanted to make sure that this lingering, passionate kiss wasn't something else; that he was indeed witnessing, first hand, that corniest of clichés, an affair with the help. But then, as the door closed behind them, and Rod was out of his lumberjack shirt before you could say Bhujangasana, he realised he was. Rod hadn't even made it to his funeral and now he was fucking his widow.

It was hard to watch, but strangely fascinating too. Adam didn't want to stay, he really didn't, to see his wife's face contorted into those expressions he'd not witnessed himself for a while. Rod was quite the lover. He took his time. He toyed with her. Then came on strong when she wanted it. And boy did she seem to want it. The funeral had made her needy.

Watching them, her specifically, Adam was swept back to the

early 2000s, when Julie had been like this with him. He had almost forgotten recently why he had thought it a good idea to leave Serena and the children. Now he remembered.

It had been an exciting and dreadful time. Julie in her shared flat in Notting Hill, twenty-something PA to an important client, deferential, flirtatious, *fun* for God's sake! Serena and the children back at the family house in Tufnell Park. Twelve and fourteen was not a good age to put your kids through a marriage break up, was it? Older Leo, bless him, had been remarkably stoic, though he'd had his flare-ups. Younger Matilda had not behaved so well. Sometimes, in his guiltiest moments, Adam wondered whether she had ever recovered from the effects of his selfish abandon.

Was he aroused, watching his wife in this mode? No. There was nothing to arouse. He felt strangely detached, like someone with vertigo looking out of an aeroplane window and feeling no fear about the ground far below. Yet his jealousy was intact. There was a part of him that wanted to fly in and pull Rod off, throw him to the floor, punch him hard in the face. But what with? There was nothing he could do.

Or was there? Surely a decent ghoul would have chucked a shoe onto the bed or picked up Rod's lumberjack shirt and floated it spookily out of the window. But Adam hadn't even the beginning of an idea how he could do that. He had no hands, no feet, no voice, no purchase. On anything.

How long had this been going on? Now that he thought about it, Julie had been much less tense than usual in recent weeks. How had he not spotted it? He knew the answer. He'd been so worried about Julie finding out about Eva that he hadn't seen what was going on right under his nose. Now he laughed, bitterly. The trouble he had gone to, to keep *his* dark secret: the dedicated Outlook account, the second phone, 'the burner' as Eva laughingly called it, like something out of a TV box set thriller.

He had even felt bad about how well they had been getting on recently, he and Julie. Was this what I needed to improve things, he'd thought guiltily, as he drove home on Fridays after another discreet week with his young lover, an affair? And all along that new glow on his wife's face had not just come from her yoga.

No, he couldn't watch them a moment longer. He took himself out into the garden, down the long sloping green lawn to the natural pool. He settled for a while on the island in the middle, another of his ideas. As a boy, he had always liked islands, particularly little ones in the middle of rivers and streams that you could make your own.

This one was full of promise at this time of year, with the mix of rushes and lilies he had planted and encouraged, dotted among them the weeping sedge. Nor was there any need for the tiny rowing boat, *The Coracle*, as he and Julie called it, that normally brought him here. He just floated over – and there he was, in among the reeds, looking out over the tight green buds of the *Nymphaea*, the burgeoning white waterlilies that gave a Monet-style vibe to this part of his creation.

What he should do, he thought, was to wait until Julie and Rod had exhausted their mutual energies and then go back and eavesdrop on them, find out exactly what was going on. From being temporarily out of the frame, Julie had shot straight back to number one suspect. With ex-military, go-getting Rod as her assistant, doing away with Adam would have been easy. Now the motive was there, writ large: the house, the lion's share of his money and his equity in Albury & Atkinson. Why, the negotiations had already started, with him barely cold in the ground. How long would they have to wait before Julie announced her new romance; before Rod's canal boat outside Tempelsham became just a fun place to visit on a warm summer's day, and horny Rod had the full run of Fallowfields?

Despite, or perhaps because of his anger, Adam suddenly felt a powerful longing for Eva. Obviously he couldn't hold her, or touch her, or even make himself known to her, but just to see her would be a relief, a salve to his jealous spirit. Yesterday, at the funeral, and in the noisy crush of the wake, he had only glimpsed her, and always in company. He had longed to talk to her, to find out what she made of this suicide nonsense, but there had been no chance of that. On the two or three occasions when he'd got close to her, the conversation he had found himself listening in to had been inconsequential. Even though Eva was not one to show her true feelings in public, hiding them always behind her carefully cultivated ironic mask, she had looked troubled. 'Even if you're not making an issue of it, you don't believe it, do you, my darling?' he had wanted to ask. 'That I would do that. Top myself. Especially now that I have you.'

Where would she be now? he wondered. Twelve thirty. At the office, unless she was out with a client or nipping down to Pret to get an early lunch. How good it would be just to see her! At her desk, eating as she worked. Sneaky bites of sushi or her favourite 'soggy BLT' accompanied by sips of her traditional skinny soy latte. From his glass cube of an office, Adam had often watched her; long before they had got together, too.

It had all been innocent enough at first. She was, God help him, over twenty years younger than him. Not that it had ever occurred to him, as he had helped her through her year's practical training, the functional filling in the sandwich that was RIBA Parts One and Two, that they might be anything other than boss and student. Of course, as he had taken her under his wing and out to the site visits and planning meetings that would look good in her logbook, he had noted her particular charm and beauty. But never in the context of any intimacy with him. She was 'the mixed-race girl', later 'the woman of Thai-Mauritian heritage', whom Jeff was thrilled to have on board because it upped their diversity quotient, and Adam because she was keen, and good, and thoughtful, and provocative and a delight. With the extra bonus that she generally saw things his way. That London, for all its dirt and ugliness, was still a treasure trove of fine and historic buildings, and it was more than just a shame to tear them down and put up yet another identikit glass and steel tower. They could do that in America, where their idea of a historic building was a colonial timber-framed house from the 18th century, something that probably wouldn't even be listed in the UK.

On Adam's advice, Eva had done her Part Two at the AA, where he could keep an avuncular eye on her; before welcoming her back to Albury & Atkinson for her Part Three, her professional practice year. Even then, anything other than a business relationship and warm friendship had never crossed his mind, though he had often sat so close to her they might as well have been in bed. He knew that soft sigh of hers when she was frustrated, the way she bit her lower lip when she was concentrating, all that stuff.

It was Butcher's Yard that had brought them together. Her passion to hold on to the essence of that picturesque and, to use the word properly for a change, unique bit of old Clerkenwell had chimed with his. Together with her team leader Reuben they had come up with a scheme whereby the existing buildings would be incorporated into something new, yes, but not overwhelmingly so. The historic yard would remain intact, complete with the existing facades. Behind that, the ramshackle old houses, where the offices of two legal firms and an august Royal Society were jammed together higgledy-piggledy, would be completely stripped out and redesigned, to create the big airy sunlit spaces that were Adam's trademark. It would be a fusion, as Adam liked to say, of the best of the old with the best of the new.

They had been on the same side as the tenants, against the designs of the client, who had always known how much more they could make out of the site with a brand-new £100 million pound tower, not a mere £4–5-million-pound regeneration scheme. Jeff had brought the job in and Adam, with his conservation expertise, had initially carried it forwards. But then decent Stewart, the senior planning officer on the case, had fallen foul of council restructuring and been replaced by Dodgy Dave, and suddenly the story had changed and Jeff was gung-ho with the 'iconic tower' idea. Had this been his plan all along? Had backstage influence and brown envelopes been involved? Adam could never prove it, though he distrusted the clients, (Steve) Sugar and (Tim) Savidge, a dubious pair if ever there were one. It was galling that he was suddenly fighting his own business partner on this project, that Stan was no longer there to back him up, that Jeff now had more heft because he had an extra twenty per cent of the equity from Stan, that Adam was losing control, not just of what was happening to Butcher's Yard, but of Albury & Atkinson itself.

One night in the dark little garden area behind his favourite local, The Prosperous Parson, fired up and furious after a passionate defence of his scheme, staying for an extra tipple after Reuben had left, he and Eva had kissed. Just like that. After all those long years. He was ashamed to admit that at that moment Julie hadn't even come into the equation. Whatever remnants of love they had wasn't enough for him to resist Eva's entwining fingers.

So what could he do now? Glide out of the garden, down the lane, onto the main B4021 into Tempelsham. How long would that take him? Could he somehow hitch a ride on a car to speed things up? What would happen at the station? Would he sail down onto the platform, slide in through the doors and find an empty seat on the train? Is that what ghosts did, when they wanted to transport themselves?

Even as he was worrying about this, he realised that the garden was fading out. The chirruping birdsong had been replaced by the hum of traffic and the distant whine of sirens. The quiet tappety-tap of laptops. Adam was in the Sheridan Street offices of Albury & Atkinson, Architects.

Now he was floating, amazingly, right through the long glass wall that he himself had installed when they had first taken over these premises, almost thirty years before; when for all the burgeoning swank of the colonnaded shopping arcade, Covent Garden still had its run-down corners, and it was possible for a thrusting young firm to buy, freehold, a couple of semi-derelict warehouses on the tattier edge of the area.

Adam was in the conference room. The weekly management meeting was just coming to an end. Eva and the others were on their feet. The Weasel, at the end of the long glass table, was still seated.

'Eva,' he was saying. 'Could we just have a quick word?'

'Jeff.'

'Shove the door to, could you. Have a seat. Great ideas today on the Peabody project.'

'Thanks.'

'On another matter, if I may, how did you get on yesterday?'

'At Adam's funeral?'

'I hardly saw you.'

'It was super-busy, wasn't it?'

'How did you think it went?'

'The funeral of a suicide, Jeff. It was never going to be a jolly occasion, was it?'

'No. Having said that, I found the service intensely moving.' Jeff paused, then repeated the last two words, as if to convince himself of his own sincerity.

'What did you make of the friend who tried to justify it?' Eva asked.

'That long-faced professor guy?'

'Him, yes.'

'It's a point of view, I suppose.'

'Did you agree with him, Jeff?'

'Certainly not. Why would I? No. Suicide's a terrible thing. Weird to try and justify it, actually.'

'Agreed. D'you think it's cowardly? Selfish?'

Jeff sighed. He hated to be put on the spot about anything that challenged his comfort zone of right-on, generally acceptable ideas. He looked down for a moment, as if his crotch might offer him some answers. 'I suppose,' he said, 'deep down, I do think it's a bit cowardly. At one level. But also brave.'

'One or the other, Jeff.'

'I get that. But it must take quite something to try and gas yourself in a car.'

'And succeed.'

'To sit there, waiting, inhaling the noxious fumes...'

'How long does it take before you lose consciousness?' Eva asked. 'Do you have any idea?'

'No.'

So that was it. Jesus. He had gassed himself in a car. In a garage? In *his* garage? Had he done the full trope? Exhaust, hosepipe, windows closed. How did you even fix a domestic hosepipe to something as wide as a car exhaust? Did you have to tape up the window the hosepipe went through? These operational questions confirmed to Adam what he already knew. That he hadn't somehow managed to blank out the whole thing in some kind of post-traumatic amnesia. He had never done it. Okay, so he'd had some quasi-suicidal moments in his life, on vertiginous sheer cliffs or on bridges above raging rivers, where a powerful desire for extinction had momentarily overtaken him. There had, more to the point, been dark days of despair, when the idea of living and working had seemed both pointless and absurd. But forget about raindrops on roses or tartiflette and génépi, the idea of ending it all just wasn't in his mindset.

Like Celine Dion, he had wanted to go on and on; looking, engaging, creating, *living*, till the bitter end. He had even joked that if things ever got that bad with his existing life he'd get on a plane and find another one; and not in the Maldives or Seychelles, where life might seem even emptier over a cocktail by a glinting blue pool, but somewhere gritty, uncomfortable, even dangerous: the Gaza Strip, the Yemen, the Congo, Ukraine. Somewhere to make him wake up to his own remarkable fortune in being alive at all, let alone the privileged white stale old male, yadda yadda, that he was. He remembered an argument he'd once had about this with Julie.

'Do you really think,' she had countered scornfully, 'that if you were seriously suicidal, you'd have the *energy* to relocate to a war zone? It doesn't work like that.'

'It would with me,' Adam had replied stubbornly. Bottom line, even if a volcanic depression had swept in and overcome him, so that he couldn't wrench himself from some benighted solipsistic hell, a hosepipe in a car was never the method he would have chosen.

'Three hours,' Eva told Jeff. 'With carbon monoxide.'

'Christ on a bike!' his business partner replied.

'Christ on a bike indeed. It shows determination, doesn't it?'

'Certainly does.'

'Did you see it coming, Jeff?'

The Weasel seemed taken aback. 'No, I didn't. Though Adam hasn't exactly been at the top of his game recently.'

'You were trying to get rid of him, though, weren't you?'

Just as he'd done with Julie, Jeff feigned surprise. 'What do you mean?' he replied.

'Come on! We all know what's been going on.'

Jeff was leaning forward. 'Sit down a minute, Eva.'

'Why?'

'Please. You obviously want to have this conversation. I think it might be healthier for us to level about things in an honest fashion.'

She sat, a little reluctantly, two or three chairs away from him. It was more of a perch than a full sit. *I can run away from his bullshit at any time*, her body was saying.

'I do understand,' Jeff went on, 'that this has all been very hard for you.' He gave her a meaningful look.

'Why particularly "for me"?' She made the quotes with her fingers, disdainfully.

'Come off it, Eva. You say you all know that I was trying to force Adam out, which is absolutely not the case. But by the same token, I'm sorry, it's hardly as if your little liaison has been a well-kept secret.'

The cast-iron shit. But he was hardly acting out of character.

'Okay,' Eva replied, slowly. She didn't seem shocked that he knew; nor was she going to bother to deny it. 'So what?' she replied.

Jeff shrugged. 'As I said, Adam's tragic death must have been difficult for you. Especially as you've not wanted to talk about your private loss with anyone here.'

'How the fuck do you know who I've talked to?' Eva looked down at the table, then up again. 'What did you want to say, anyway?'

'Partly this, really. I totally get that you were, are, a great believer in Adam's vision, in his way of doing things, but we have to accept that he's gone now. We need to move forward.'

'To your vision? The Clerkenwell Tower?'

'Not specifically just to my vision. But I don't want us to be hung up on a lot of things that Adam was, to put it mildly, a bit of a dog in the manger about.'

It was all coming out now. Adam's vision, Jeff elaborated, was admirable. Obviously, buildings needed to be built, primarily, for the people who were going to live and work in them. Jeff too was a believer in 'sensitive placemaking'. That went without saying. But it was also possible to go too far in that direction.

Was it? Eva asked, and they were suddenly deep into a tense theoretical discussion about the purpose of architecture. It was one that Adam was screaming to join, if only to remind Eva what a profit-seeking wretch Jeff was. How for all this fashionable talk about placemaking, he was forever trying to increase density, reduce public space and turn projects into the most expensive versions of themselves possible. Which was, frankly, why his more unscrupulous clients liked him so much.

'Look, Eva,' Jeff said eventually. 'What I wanted to say is this. I really don't want you to think that now that Adam's gone, I'm gunning for you. I'm not. I like your style. You've got a great deal of talent and once the Peabody thing is up and running, and we've resolved Butcher's Yard, I'd be keen to make you a team leader on a new project.'

'Okay,' she replied. She didn't refuse his offer or tell him to sling his hook because she was going elsewhere. Was it that easy to win her round? 'For what it's worth, Jeff,' she added, 'I don't think Adam killed himself.'

Jeff made his best taken-aback face. 'No? So what did happen?'

'I don't know. But he had no reason to. He was enjoying life.'

'With you?'

'Partly with me, yes. He was frustrated by what was going on here, between you two, but that wouldn't have defeated him, to the point of taking his own life, even if you had succeeded in driving him out.'

'I'm not sure we're getting anywhere here, Eva.' Now Jeff's bad cop was peeping through. The charm had gone, and his tone was more matter-of-fact. 'Poor Adam was found in his wife's garage, dead in his car, overcome by carbon monoxide fumes. There was a note, too, by all accounts. I do understand, Eva, why you might be tempted to deny what happened, but...'

A note! Good God! So someone had made a thorough job of this.

Eva was on her feet. 'You're not going to change what I think,' she said.

Did she also know about the note? If not, why wasn't she asking Jeff about it?

'Okay,' he replied, suddenly reasonable again. He held up his hands in fake surrender.

By the door Eva paused. 'Thanks for your faith in me, by the way.'

Jeff grinned, Teflon tyrant that he was. 'It's what we do, Eva,' he said, the master of smarm, as always.

But what on earth was *she* playing at?

CHAPTER SEVEN

I should go back to Fallowfields, Adam thought. Now that he knew about the mechanics of his so-called suicide, he needed to see what his wife and her handyman were up to; what they were saying. Were they rubbing their hands with glee, even as they loaded up a skip with the rest of his lifetime's work? And what about this note that Jeff had talked about? Did it exist? And if so, who had written it? Because it certainly hadn't been him. One of Julie's numerous passing interests had been graphology, and she had developed a party trick whereby she could give people an amusing summary of their character based on a line or two of their handwriting and their signature. But she wasn't an expert forger (as far as he knew).

But he found that he couldn't go, couldn't indeed quite bear the idea. Something deeper in him wanted to stay with Eva, to watch her as she went on with her day; to see her smile open up for the colleagues she liked; that studied blank face of hers freeze out those she didn't.

At the close of play, he followed her home. It was easy enough, floating along quiet Sheridan Street and crowded Long Acre, down into the Tube and its warm and acrid underground passages, crowded with tired office workers, some already tipsy and over-loud after an early Friday night drink. Nobody saw him, nobody heard him, nobody bumped into him – there was nothing to bump into.

Eva strap hung and flicked through an *Evening Standard* she'd picked up from an empty seat. And then she was out, up the neat red-brick steps into her neighbourhood, along the wide street to her studio, in the top floor of the old white stucco house. How often had he let himself into this nondescript London hallway, a shared space littered with old letters and junk mail, a herringbone seagrass carpet that had presumably once been smart, but was now worn down and ingrained with dirt? How often had he sprung eagerly up these flights of stairs, guilt in his heart, lust in his brain? How often had he lied to Julie that he was in their little flat in Bayswater, four miles away? How often had he thought: she's bound to find me out, sooner or later? I'll do something idiotic like leaving the burner phone in a coat pocket; or she'll dig down into my computer files one evening when I'm not home and find the secret Outlook account. And what an appallingly incriminating sequence of interchanges that was, right from that very first tentative email wondering if, after what had happened last night at The Prosperous Parson, Eva would like to meet again.

I'm free this evening, as it happens. How about a cocktail at that swanky-looking new place on Long Acre? Redemption, is it called? Appropriate?! Exx

He remembered her first teasing reply verbatim. Redemption was dangerous, too close to the office, but he had gone, and things had moved on from there. Despite her rather cool public manner, her formal work emails, Eva enjoyed letting rip on

Outlook. Particularly on the weekends, when Adam was at home with Julie. He would sometimes sneak a risky look on a Saturday evening and find himself reduced to a quivering wreck by what she'd written. She was playing with him, he knew; but she was in London, single, young, she could do what she liked. That she did was a deliberate reminder of her status.

He'd been astonished really that Eva was interested in him. At thirty-seven, still lithe and smooth-skinned, why would she be? Yes, he was her boss, and yes, he was successful. If not quite the kind of 'starchitect' that the Great British public knew as a household name, still highly respected within his profession, his firm in the top fifty of the key list published by the *Architects' Journal*; a name to conjure with in that always cut-throat world.

But it was more than that, wasn't it? They had something, the two of them, despite the age difference. In leaving Serena for Julie, Adam had made a huge mistake, he had realised that a long time ago, even if it had been hard to admit. Sex and novelty had led him foolishly down that primrose path to hell. But now, with Eva, he had not just requited lust but an intimacy – a 'connection' in her lingo – of the kind he'd always craved. He was back up there with Serena when he'd first known her; when they had been carefree students at Bristol, lying in his narrow single bed at Goldney Hall gazing dreamily at the parallelograms of sunlight on the wall. *My face in thine eye, thine in mine appears, And true plain hearts do in the faces rest.* Not that he read Donne to Eva, as he had, once upon a time, so innocently, to Serena. But he could have done.

Now he followed his paramour through the low door into her living space. No danger of banging his head now! It was basically just an attic room with a kitchenette strung along one wall, a flat window with a Velux blind let into the roof, and a tiny bathroom shoe-horned in on one side. Eva was lucky to have it, even though at some years younger than her age, he and Serena had already bought their first house together, the three-bedroomed terrace with a twenty-foot garden, in the then unfashionable and rather grotty suburb of Tufnell Park. Now the once-bleak Fortress Road was a string of artisan bakeries and cafés and home-made ice-cream shops where owning a house made you a de facto millionaire.

It was odd, and rather spooky, to watch Eva, as she reached down into the fridge for the half-empty bottle of Sauvignon Blanc, glistening with condensation; how she sighed, heavily, as she took a glass from her washing-up machine and slowly filled it; how she walked over to the purple IKEA couch, the famous Flottebo, and sank down onto it; how she gazed out blankly at the wall and her black-and-white poster of Greta Garbo. What was she thinking about? With such a sad face. Him? Surely she was.

'Eva,' he said, in his gentlest voice, 'I'm here. Right beside you. I love you. Did you know that, my darling?'

But there was, again, no reaction. Even with Eva, he was clearly on a different plane. He sat and watched her as she tapped her phone and switched on music. Beethoven's Concerto for Violin and Orchestra, something else they had bonded on, back in their earliest days. She closed her eyes as that delicious opening poured over them both. Her dark lashes quivered as her lips pushed tightly together. Then, with the dancing intricacies of the first violin solo, tears slipped down her cheeks. She was shaking with sobs. Adam yearned to hold her, comfort her, but there was nothing he could do.

Later, after she'd made herself a light supper – smoked salmon, smashed avocado, toast, an Eva special – finished the wine and opened a new bottle, he followed her into the tiny bathroom. She ran herself a deep Ortigia Fico d'India bubble bath, then lay in it, white foam prickling round her ears.

Around nine, naked but for the navy and gold silk kimono Adam had brought back for her from his last Tokyo trip, Eva picked up her now fully charged iPhone 12 Mini and made a call.

Her first friend was clearly out, or not picking up. She didn't leave a message. She tried another, ditto. On her third attempt, she got through to someone.

'Katya!' Adam heard her sigh with relief. 'I'm sorry, I just had to talk to someone and that someone turned out to be you... it's strange, I kind of feel him around me... it *is* silly, I know that he's dead and gone... I guess yesterday brought it all back, it was such a beautiful service...'

Adam had slid in so close to her that he could now hear Katya's side of the conversation too, as Eva gave her a detailed report of the funeral, the wake and her journey home by train with Reuben and Simone. 'And when we got back to London we just went off to Redemption, you know, that cocktail place on Long Acre, and got rat-arsed on negronis. Which was bizarre, because I was barely drinking at the actual wake itself.'

Then Eva was telling her friend that she still didn't believe that Adam had killed himself. Why would he, how could he? Especially with important projects ongoing.

'I thought you said George, or whatever he's called, the slimy partner, was trying to push him out?'

'Jeff. He is, was, completely, though now he's done a total reverse ferret and Adam's like the world's most brilliant talent ever and Jeff's thinking of having a permanent exhibition of his work in the lobby. He's such a toad really, because there's simultaneously a massive rethink going on with one of Adam's key designs...'

They talked for almost half an hour, during which Katya posited the idea that if Jeff had wanted rid of Adam that badly he might have been responsible for faking his suicide for him. Eva didn't believe that 'for one minute', but agreed that it was certainly convenient for Jeff that Adam was gone.

Alone again, Eva picked up her violin and started to play. It was comforting to hear the familiar repertoire. 'This one's for you, Adam,' she said eventually. It was the famous Cuban song

'Quizás, Quizás, Quizás' ('Perhaps, perhaps, perhaps'), which had started as a jokey criticism of his supposed attitude to their affair, but had segued into something of a theme tune. 'I can't believe I'm in this position,' she had told him barely a month ago, 'over twenty years younger than you and begging you to leave your wife.'

'You know I will,' Adam had replied. Though at one level he had meant it, he had hardly believed he was saying it, promising such a huge upheaval, which would leave him, for sure, without the house he had built, in his lovely protected AONB valley, in his favourite county, not far from his elderly mother and his sister to boot. To start all over again with Eva, who knew where? For the second time in his life.

'Thank you,' he said, when she'd finished. 'That meant a lot. THAT REALLY MEANT A LOT, MY DARLING!' he shouted.

She didn't turn a hair. She put away her violin, carefully, as always, made a cup of chamomile tea and went to bed.

'Eva,' he repeated, as she undressed and slipped into those familiar dark blue cotton pyjamas. 'Eva, Eva, EVA, EVA-A-A-A...'

Nothing.

She read her book.

After a while the light clicked off and he watched her sink into sleep. He could see her chest rising and falling in the neon-yellow streetlight from outside.

How could he get to her? If not speak to her, at least communicate with her? Old King Hamlet had spoken to his son, hadn't he? The ghosts of Christmas Past, Present and Future hadn't had a problem. Even the Alan Rickman character in the film *Truly Madly Deeply* had got through. That cello-playing ghoul had not only spoken (repeatedly) to his widow, played by the lovely Juliet Stephenson, but brought other ghosts back to her flat. Black-clad north London types. They had filled the place, chatting away noisily.

But here, now, Adam was entirely alone. The shock of his new situation was wearing off and he was realising, viscerally, that he was dead. 'Dead and gone.' That was the phrase, used so idly by the living. There was more in it than he'd ever realised when he'd had the careless privilege of life. Dead *and* gone. Gone from the world. No going back. His body, a corpse rotting in a box. His spirit, floating invisibly. No way of communicating. At the very best, a vicarious observer: of the fallout from this vicious and repellent lie that he had taken his own life.

What was he going to do now? Spend the whole night watching his girlfriend sleep, like some overzealous attendee at a conceptual art event? Shouldn't he make more productive use of his time? Try, somehow, to transport himself back home and see what his fickle wife was up to? How would he even do that? It would be absurd for him to attempt to make the journey conventionally: down the stairs, along the familiar paving stones to the red brick steps of Pimlico Tube, then strap hanging invisibly up to Paddington. Would there even be a train at this time?

Could he somehow repeat what he'd done with Eva? How had that even worked? *Please*, he articulated silently, *take me there. To my second wife, for God's sake.*

Nothing happened.

He visualised Fallowfields. It would be beautiful out in the garden on this clear spring evening: cowslips, cuckoo flowers and bluebells in the moonlit long grass.

Nada.

He put his hands together in the namaste gesture of formal prayer. He had given up on God in his teenaged years, around the same time, in fact, as he'd stopped believing in ghosts. But now he was a ghost, and there was clearly some sort of afterlife, so who was to say that God didn't exist, after all.

'Take me home,' he begged.

And all of a sudden, he was home.

In his study, just like that. It took him a moment to realise that it was his study, because the place had been stripped bare. Only the old conference table and the surrounding stackable black chairs remained to indicate that this had once been his idiosyncratically cluttered man cave; more than that, the repository of his life's work.

'There's nothing left,' he muttered into the empty silence. 'How could she?'

CHAPTER EIGHT

The sun emerged slowly through the woodland, a crimson glow behind silhouetted top branches. It climbed free of the trees and became a brilliant yellow, backlighting the bushes in the garden with golden outlines, casting long shadows on the glistening dewy grass. Birds sang.

Finally, Adam was ready. He floated in through the bedroom window. In their king-sized bed, Julie was fast asleep. Alone, thankfully.

He hovered by her antique dressing table, which he had canvassed repeatedly to get rid of, but failed. It had been Julie's mother's and she had loved it since she was a child. Random bits of make-up littered the embroidered cloth that covered and protected the polished mahogany.

He twiddled his spectral fingers like a yogi. His fingers! What was happening? Until now he had just been a presence, nebulous, insubstantial. Now, looking down, he saw legs, his legs – and wearing the dark blue Boss jeans he habitually wore at home. Very slowly and carefully, he got to his feet, which were, he realised, clad in his favourite brown Camper Pelotas. He tiptoed over to the long mirror behind the door. There he was. Almost as solid as when he'd been alive. Exactly the same shape, unfortunately. His face still had the same telltale lines, crinkling his forehead, spreading from his eyes to his upper cheeks. Those almost-sixty jowls were still all too grimly prominent. His bald patch unchanged. Even the belly he had fought so hard to keep trim over recent years had survived the shift into the supernatural. You might have thought that a ghost would be allowed to shape their own image; but no, it seemed that, even on the ether, he was stuck with himself; styled by God knows whom.

Adam approached the wall by the bathroom. He paused for a moment and shook himself like a dog. Then, experimenting, he walked straight at it. Amazing! The solid mass failed to stop him. He was through, without feeling a thing. Looking round at the familiar taps and units and mirrors, he felt exhilarated, but also disconcerted. He turned slowly and sailed back through. On the other side again, he found that he was laughing. This was like scuba diving or something: completely unreal.

Julie was still sleeping. Adam sat down on her favourite little yellow chair and watched her. You would think that if you were able to float through walls, sitting on a chair would be impossible. You would sink to the floor, maybe even drop through that too. But no. Adam found he was easily able to perch. The chair held him. How, he didn't know.

She was still beautiful. Twenty years on from their first encounter at L'Arbre Bleu in Chelsea, at a client lunch. 'I've been sent to flirt with you,' she had told him, and he, silly man, had found her honesty refreshing. Or so he had told himself.

After a while, he coughed.

Julie stirred, grunted and rolled over. Surely she hadn't heard him? Tentatively, he coughed again, a little louder, like some Jeeves-style butler.

Julie sat up abruptly. She scanned the room like a nervous cat. So she had heard him, even if she couldn't see him.

He coughed again.

'What in God's name...' she muttered. She shook her head and got to her feet. She walked over towards the door, then pushed it back and looked out into the long upstairs corridor. She stood stock-still, listening. Then she turned, walked slowly back across the room and sat down on the bed.

Adam gave her a minute of peace. She was nodding to herself, even starting to smile. Then: 'It's me,' he said in a loud whisper.

She jumped, visibly.

'What... the... fuck?' she squealed.

Adam hated to admit it, but he was enjoying himself. He let her stew in the silence for another minute. Then: 'How are you?' he asked.

She was frozen like the proverbial rabbit in the headlights. 'What?' she repeated. 'Who? Where?'

'It's Adam. I'm over here.'

She turned to look in his direction, then, 'No!' she cried. She leapt off the bed and ran back towards the door.

'Julie!' he called after her. 'It's okay. I'm not going to do anything to you. I *can't* do anything.'

She paused, as if realising that she had nowhere, really, to go. Then, very slowly, she turned round. She was breathing heavily, he saw; in and out, in and out, that calming mindfulness technique that she routinely recommended to her more anxious clients.

Now she was staring at him.

'What... what... what *are* you?' she asked, eventually.

'It is I, Adam – your former husband – whom you and your painter-decorator boyfriend did away with for your own gain. Admit it all, you scurvy varlet!' A gothic fantasy span through his head. Maybe he should run at her, waving his arms madly to freak her out. But no, he didn't need to.

'It's me, Adam,' he said quietly.

'Adam,' she repeated, as if in a trance. 'But you're... you're–'

'Dead, I know. Nonetheless, here I am.' He heard his own voice, measured, unthreatening.

'Is that... is that... really you?'

'You can see me all right?'

'What are you?' Julie had sat back on the bed now. She was visibly shaking. 'Where are you?'

'I'm not sure. In some netherworld, I think.'

She was nodding, taking him at face value. This was the thing about Julie. She was never one to panic. 'But you're speaking to me,' she went on, 'so you're not like some sort of ghostly image. You're conscious.'

'So it seems.'

It was extraordinary. They were talking, man and wife, as if he were still alive. How long would that last? Would he suddenly vanish or fade away? Would his voice become inaudible to her again? He had no idea, other than thinking he had better get on with it, grill her before anything changed.

'How did I die, Julie?' he asked.

'What?'

'You heard.'

'I... I... you,' she muttered, oddly. Then: 'You must know. Adam, don't you even know?'

'Tell me.'

'You... you killed yourself,' she said softly.

'How did I do that?'

'Can't you remember?'

'No,' he replied, honestly enough. 'I can't. Perhaps because it's not the sort of thing I would have done.'

'But... you did... do it. It was horrible.' She was suddenly in tears. 'It was me that found you. In the garage. In the car.'

'The Alfa Romeo?'

'No. The Disco. For fuck's sake, why does that matter?'

She was angry now, though why he deserved that wasn't clear.

Because he'd had the gall to ask about his own death? If anyone deserved to lose their cool it was him.

'You had the hose fixed up through the window. From the exhaust. You were in there, head on one side, mouth open, drooling, the skin on your face and neck blotched with bright pink, vomit on your chest. It was horrible,' she repeated.

'Which hose did I use?' Adam asked.

'What d'you mean?'

'Which hose? I'm just interested, because I don't imagine the garden hose would fit the exhaust, would it?'

'It wasn't the garden hose. It was a black one. A wider one. That you must have got from somewhere. You tell me. There was a special adapter thing on one end.'

'To connect to the exhaust?'

'Yes.'

'I see. And when was this, exactly? That you found me.'

'In the afternoon. It was a Saturday. I'd been in Tempelsham, shopping, and having lunch with Claire.'

'When was this?'

'Weeks ago. There's been an inquest, Adam. We couldn't bury you before that was all concluded.'

'I thought as much. So why were you lunching with Claire? It's hardly something you do regularly. And on that day of all days.'

'We didn't know then that it was "of all days", did we?'

'Not unless you were meeting her to set yourself up with a nice little alibi.'

'Don't be silly. It was Claire's idea to meet.'

'Guess what, Julie. I have no recollection of any of this. Certainly not of going out and buying a special hose. Or an adapter. Odd that, isn't it?'

'Maybe you blanked it out?'

'D'you know what my last memories are? Of my life on earth? Having dinner with you. On the Friday night. After I'd driven back down a wet and windy motorway from London. At first, when I realised I was dead, I thought I might have been in a crash. But then I remembered crossing the gravel, crunch, crunch. Letting myself in. You cooking me steak. Almost as if you wanted to soften me up for something.

'Then, in the morning, after breakfast, Serena came by to talk about Leo's wedding arrangements. You shot off into town, so you missed a pleasant chat over coffee, during which I agreed, as expected, that I would pay for pretty much everything, Abby's parents having no money to speak of, and the alternative being one of those ghastly occasions where you get a single welcome glass of Prosecco and then there's curly sandwiches and a pay bar.'

'You snob. I'm glad I wasn't there.'

'My only son. Having punched seriously above his weight in his choice of bride, the least I could do was fund a decent meal and some champagne. You also missed an excruciating conversation about a ridiculous idea Serena had that Walter might want to publish a collection of my poems with his silly Bullfrog Press. As if!'

'So Walter was there too?'

'Walter is always there too. He hangs around. Like a bad smell.'

'Then what happened?'

'They finally buggered off after a second coffee, and I fixed myself some lunch.'

'Did you?'

'Yes. I was looking over this file of poetry that I'd lent to Walter. To see if there was any way, going forward, that I might actually do a collection. Obviously not with Walter, though.'

'What did you eat?'

'Does it matter?'

'It does if you can't remember.'

'Actually, yes, I can. A sliced baguette and some cheese and salami and salad you'd left out for me. A bottle of Doom Bar. Beethoven's *Violin Concerto* on the Sonos. I was enjoying myself.'

Eva had called him too, just as his first wife was vanishing up the drive, and they had ended up having phone sex, though he didn't mention that.

'Are you sure they left?' Julie asked.

'What are you suggesting?'

'Just that when I came back late afternoon, there you were, dead in the garage. By this account, Serena and Walter were the last people to see you alive.'

'I waved them off. They were going to look at antiques in Fowlton Bennett. Hideously lovey-dovey. Surely the inquest would have covered all that?'

'It did. They were as shocked as anyone else, they said. You'd been in good spirits about the wedding, apparently.'

'I'd been in good spirits, exactly. And then, guess what, as soon as they'd gone, I topped myself. It makes no sense, Julie. What was the coroner thinking?'

'So you have no memories after that: your boozy little poetic lunch?'

'It wasn't boozy. I had one beer. But no. The next thing I knew I was at my own funeral. Some weeks later, it seems.'

'You were at the *funeral*?'

'Very much so. I can't say I enjoyed it, but I was impressed. Extremely well organised, I have to say.'

'Thank you. But... I mean... God... so you heard... all those addresses?'

'And the rest! Roland crapping on, about himself as usual. Gideon Bloomberg was a bit over the top, didn't you think? My moral choice and all that. So what did you do when you found me?'

'Found you?'

'In the garage, Julie. Drooling, blotchy-faced...'

'I phoned an ambulance.'

'And they came, quick enough?'

'Super quick. They were here in twenty minutes. They tried to resuscitate you. But it was too late. Then I had to call the police.'

'And who else?'

'It was just the police.'

'No friends? Rod, for example.'

'Rod?' she spluttered. 'Why would I call him?'

'Why indeed, Julie?'

He sat there on her chair, watching her closely. She had swung her legs around now, and was sitting forward.

'Or perhaps he was already on site,' he added.

'What the heck are you talking about?' Her tone was brisk, but she looked rattled.

'The interesting thing about being in this state that I'm in,' Adam went on, 'is that you're not always visible. Most of the time you're not.'

He continued to smile at her. Her eyes, big and blue, the colour of cornflowers, he'd once told her in a loved-up moment, were trying hard to appear innocent. But guilt shone out of them.

'And you can control that, can you?' she asked.

'Not at all. I've got no idea why I've suddenly appeared to you now. But I was invisible yesterday. When you were in the studio, binning all my stuff. And afterwards...'

'What are you trying to say?'

'You and Rod. I saw you. Yesterday. Here. In our bedroom.'

'What! You mean...?'

'Not really a spectator sport, sex, is it? Still, I managed to hang around for a bit. I gave up when he started spanking you. You never told me you liked that, in twenty years.'

'You're a fine one to talk,' she replied, defensive as ever.

'Meaning?'

'Don't think I don't know about your little friend in London. Eva or whatever she's called. Don't think I didn't guess months ago, Adam. When I phoned you at the flat and you were never there. When you stopped telling me about the lonely calamari in Côte or the boring queue for takeaway at the Taj Mahal.'

'It's over,' Adam replied.

'Of course it's over. You're dead.'

Painful though it was, Adam had to laugh at that. And this was the odd thing about his second marriage. The passion had long gone, the mutual frustration and scorn was there, almost inevitably it seemed, on a daily basis, but he and Julie could still, sometimes, make each other laugh. Had they both wanted it, there might even have been a way back; to some kind of loving relationship. But they hadn't wanted it, had they? Even before Eva.

'Why didn't you say anything then?' he asked. 'About that – Eva?'

'It might have been a bit hypocritical, mightn't it? To be frank, I didn't give a shit. I was hoping it *would* go somewhere. Then I could have this place and Rod too.'

'At least you're honest. But here's the thing, Julie. I didn't kill myself. You know me well enough. Am I the suicidal type? No. As I've often joked, to you and others, if anything I'd like another life. To do all the things I haven't had time to do in this one.'

'Like shag a few more women.'

'Very funny. So it seems clear to me that someone did me in. The only question is who. As my wife, my widow, wouldn't you like me to find out?'

'Adam, do stop being so self-righteous and ridiculous. You left a note.'

'Did I?' So Jeff had been telling the truth.

'I have it here.' Julie walked over to her dressing table, reached behind the oval mirror that formed that piece of furniture's elegant focus, found her little tarnished brass key, and unlocked the top drawer, the one in which she kept all her most precious stuff, her passport, her jewellery box. 'Here,' she said, unfolding a white piece of A4 covered with typescript. 'Can you see it?'

'Yes.'

'Can you hold it?'

He reached out for the paper, but his fingers slipped through, gaining no purchase.

'Put it down on the dressing table, please,' he said.

He hovered above it. Good God! This was no suicide note. It was the typed-up version of a poem he had written after poor Lionel had hung himself in Norfolk, three years before. 'Suicide Note' was the all too appropriate title. It was full of angst and emotion about that horrid tragedy. Awful to admit it, but he had, at the time, been rather pleased with it.

'This isn't a suicide note, Julie.'

'What is it then?'

'It's a poem I wrote. About Lionel. Leesome. My lawyer friend, who killed himself. Remember?'

He read out the title.

'Why's it in the first person?' she asked.

'Because… it is. That's how it's structured.'

'I wasn't to know,' she replied, giving him a pouty and unconvincing look.

'I showed it to you, after… all that.'

'Did you?'

'Yes. You claimed to like it. You thought I should show it to Roland.'

'Did I? Did you?'

'Yes. Amazingly, he quite liked it.'

'So why's it signed then? By you?'

'Is that supposed to be my signature?' Adam looked closely at the scrawl at the bottom of the page. He wasn't in the habit of signing poems, as if they were paintings or something. Had he ever put his name to a poem, even in a manuscript? No. And though this wasn't a bad copy of his signature, there was something about the trailing-away 'bury' in Albury that wasn't right. Too laboured, too flowery.

'It *is* your signature,' Julie insisted. Then: 'The inquest was perfectly satisfied.'

'I bet they were. If you told them this was a suicide note. Where did you tell them it was left?'

'Where was it left?' she replied, her musing question almost an echo, and one, moreover, that was playing for time. 'Next to you, on the car seat.'

'Hm,' Adam grunted, studying it some more. On the left-hand side of the page were two tiny telltale half-moons, duplicated hole punches. 'This isn't even a typescript,' he said, 'it's a photocopy. A bogusly signed photocopy, Julie. All I can say is that whoever did me in had the whole operation very well planned. And knew me well.'

'Unless it was you, Adam, and you've somehow just blanked it. Horrific near-death shocks do sometimes cause amnesia.'

'But this wasn't a near-death shock,' he pointed out.

She didn't laugh.

He sat there, staring at her. With his non-existent but seeing and visible eyes. 'Was it you?' he asked bluntly. 'Who murdered me.'

'Oh come on! Why would I want...?' She looked down, then slowly up again, almost unable to meet his gaze. 'That's a horrible accusation, Adam. D'you really think I've got it in me to do that?'

'I don't know, Julie. You've certainly started cleaning me out of the house fast enough.'

'You know I hate mess. I'm sorry, Adam, but you've been dead for eight weeks and it's time to move on. That studio's been a tip for years.'

'Going to move Rod in, are you? Hunky Rod. With his little business?'

'Rod and I are very casual, as it happens.'

'Handyman with benefits, is that it?'

She didn't answer.

'It didn't look that casual to me,' he went on. 'I haven't seen that look on your face since, God, 2007.'

'Ha *ha*. Perhaps that's why it is casual. Perhaps I like having a bit of no-strings action without all the crap that came with it with you.'

'What crap? I always enjoyed sex with you. In the days when we used to have it.'

'*You* enjoyed it, yes. That was part of the problem.'

'Oh right, so handyman Rod is a more considerate lover than me, is that it? Spankety spank.'

'Fuck's sake, Adam! It's a little pathetic for a ghost – or whatever you are – to start feeling jealous about sex. I'm a widow now. I'm allowed a lover.'

'Within a few weeks! Some widows keep their dead husband's stuff around for years. They cherish it. Sniff their old shirts.'

'Yuk. You won't catch me doing that.'

'Mum still has all Dad's old suits in a cupboard.'

'Tragic.'

'I find it touching.'

'You never said that when you were alive. You were always going on about what a sentimental pain in the arse she was about Philip. Why couldn't she let him go? Et cetera, et cetera, ad nauseam.'

The house phone was ringing. Which, ironically, could only mean one thing. 'The only person who ever calls on the landline is Patricia,' Adam had often complained. 'Why do we bother with it?' It was either his mother or a scam caller.

CHAPTER NINE

'Speak of the devil,' Julie said, striding across the room to pick up the phone. 'Julie Albury...' She raised her eyebrows meaningfully at Adam. 'Patricia,' she said warmly, 'I thought it might be you... I SAID, I THOUGHT... IT MIGHT... BE... YOU. Deaf as a post,' she muttered. 'DON'T BE SILLY,' she went on. 'YOU TOLD ME THAT YESTERDAY...YES...'

Adam could hear his mother's clear, old-fashioned tones ringing out from the receiver between Julie's loud replies, though he couldn't quite make out her words. He decided he would see if he could transport himself to her side. He pressed his hands together, as before, in the prayer-namaste gesture and concentrated hard; and before he knew it, Julie's voice was fading out and the sunny bedroom at Fallowfields was replaced by his mother's conservatory, that lovely, glass-walled, plant-filled space he had known since childhood. A huge, thick-stemmed plumbago grew up the orange brick back wall, its pale blue flowers spreading prettily across the roof panes in summer, strewing the tiled floor with blossom in early autumn.

What would his mother say when she saw him? Her beloved only son, reconstituted? Would she freak out like Julie? But as he

78

hovered round the conservatory he realised he had become invisible again, even to himself. No hands, no arms, no legs, no belly, nothing. He floated in front of the tarnished old mirror that stood at the far end. But no, he didn't even have a reflection. His mother chatted on, unaware.

Her hair was still coiffed from the funeral, not the bedraggled mop it could become after a week or so without a visit to 'lovely Keith' in Tempelsham. Her chestnut brown eyes, set in that criss-cross palimpsest of wrinkles, were bright and expressive as ever, her thin-rimmed gold specs haphazardly perched on that familiar arched nose. She was *chez elle*, alone with her carer, but she still had pale pink lipstick shining on her thin lips. There was nothing much she could do to improve those jagged yellow-brown teeth, but at least they were her own. A trio of white hairs curled from her chin, but they would be whipped off before she had a visitor. As a young woman she had been something of a beauty, and taking care of herself was still important to her. Her mind was intact and she wasn't going to let her body go either; though her now substantial girth revealed her weakness for cream cakes and cheese straws, not to mention the nightly glass or two of Fino sherry and the Sunday lunchtime gin and tonic, a habit and a treat she would never let go, whatever the instructions said about 'no alcohol' on her pack of daily tranquillisers.

She was sitting up, a little hunched, in the big, cream, frankly hideous leatherette recliner that Philip had, bizarrely for a man of his good taste, grown so fond of in his final years. It had several levers which meant you could adjust it in interesting ways, not that Patricia ever used them. *The Times* was open on her lap, her coffee cup on the wobbly cast-iron white table beside her. From here she had a clear view down over the terrace to the sloping garden. Even when Philip had barely been able to walk out onto the lawn, let alone down to the woodland, he had never wanted to downsize or move out of the house that Patricia had inherited and he had taken on to share when he'd married her. Nor was she going to leave Larks Hill either. It was the house she had been born in; and she was going to die there too.

'I expect you *will* feel like that, Julie,' she was saying. 'I hate to go on about Philip,' (not true) 'but you'll find that it'll all take much, *much* longer than you think, just let the emotions come, anger is a perfectly acceptable, no, more than acceptable, necessity... You know the five stages of grief, don't you...?'

Of course Julie knew the five stages of freaking grief, albeit they had probably been updated since Kübler-Ross. Adam had a feeling that 'mindfulness' might be in there these days, perhaps just after the final 'acceptance' stage.

It was funny, Adam thought, watching his mother chat away with Julie, just how quickly Patricia had switched allegiance from his first wife to his second. One of his big worries, fifteen years ago, before he'd finally actioned the awful upheaval of leaving Serena, was that his mother would remain loyal to his first wife and never accept flashy young Julie. Far from it. Julie, it soon transpired, was 'making Adam happy', in a way that Serena had somehow failed to do. Perhaps it had something to do with the ironing, which Julie enjoyed doing, or at least said she did, while for Serena, ironing, at least for her husband, had always been a step too far. For Patricia, who had never quite bought into feminism, in any of its waves, and still, years later, would articulate the tired old mantra that 'behind every successful man stands – or was it lies? – a strong woman', ironing was something a woman did for her man, alongside other necessary domestic services. If you didn't do it, you were somehow failing, in your loyalty, perhaps even your love.

Now Julie was in the widows' club, which made her even more popular. Her bereavement gave Patricia the right, if not the duty, to phone her up whenever she wanted. Would his mother have minded if she knew Julie had murdered him? Probably not. '*Well, it's understandable, Julie. Even though he was my son I know he could be difficult. The main thing now is that you learn how to deal with your grief...'*

Eventually, Patricia rang off and addressed the first of her two helpers, Alexa. Once there had been nothing but a cracked old Bakelite bell, which had run on a greasy twisted white wire cord up from the conservatory into the main part of the house to summon whoever might be there: cleaner, cook, carer. Now, by the wonders of modern technology, she had a series of Alexa Echo 3rd generation speakers, ordered for her and installed by her kind, hands-on, techie grandson Leo.

'Alexa!' Patricia commanded. 'Could you ask Jadwiga to come here, please.'

It always amused Adam that his mother treated Alexa as she would any other helper or servant; with the studied if superior tact of one who had grown up with such people around her.

After a minute the carer appeared on the concrete step that led up into the house. This latest one was in her forties, dark-haired, pink-cheeked, Polish, and quite the success, in that she'd been there, as part of Patricia's month-on, month-off system of rotation, for almost a year. Patricia's normal carer sequence usually began with guarded enthusiasm on day one but rapidly soured into a list of 'issues' as the days went by: the carer didn't 'lift a finger'; was always on her mobile; sat watching TV on her laptop upstairs; cooked the wrong things or 'couldn't cook'. Alternatively, she did too much; wouldn't leave Patricia alone; insisted on watching TV with her; wanted to read to her to improve her English (the carer's, not Patricia's); in one case, 'prayed all over' her. The best ones were the Eastern Europeans, who seemed inured to boredom and servility; the worst, the South Africans, who often had 'problems of their own'. One was 'rather an unhappy woman', another was 'with a man who, well, I'm not sure it's for me to judge, but he doesn't seem to treat her at all well'. With one exception, who hadn't worked out, and not because he was gay, which was perfectly all right ('I'm more than comfortable with that, as long as he doesn't bring anyone back'), they had all been women.

'So sorry, Jadwiga,' his mother asked. 'Would you mind terribly if I had another pot of coffee?'

'That'll be your second and last for the day,' the carer replied.

Patricia grunted and Jadwiga hurried off, to return five minutes later with the favourite oval tray. Coffee in the silver pot, one of the old blue and white willow pattern Wedgwood cups, and a plate of garibaldi biscuits too, even though it was barely half nine. Jadwiga could be tough, but she knew what his mother liked all right.

'You okay in here?' she asked. 'Warm enough? You don't need that little heater?'

'*Ryvita?*' Patricia glared at the garibaldi in a puzzled fashion. 'Not at the moment, thank you, Jadwiga. Maybe later.'

'I said, Do... you... NEED... that LITTLE HEATER, madam?'

'Oh yes, I think I will have the little heater, thank you. It is a bit chilly.'

Julie was right. His mother was getting deafer by the day, though she refused to consider a hearing aid, regarding such a device as a 'horrid old people's thing'. No one apart from Adam thought she needed one, she had repeatedly told him, though of course they all did.

Adam watched as the carer returned and set Patricia up. She didn't really need the heater, but what she did need was someone to boss around. Jadwiga had not only worked that out, but, amazingly, seemed happy with it. Perhaps she was just very professional, and this is what the best carers did.

'Are you okay, Jadwiga?' his mother asked. 'Got enough to be getting on with?'

'I'm just tidying up those files for you. In the little study.'

Patricia stared at her blankly.

'FILES,' Jadwiga repeated. 'In your STUDY.'

'Oh yes, good. We might look over those later.' Patricia

returned to her *Times*. 'Just going to see what this useless government's been playing at now.'

'Whenever you're ready, madam.'

She was the only carer who called his mother 'madam'. Patricia seemed to like it, even though there had been the usual kerfuffle when Jadwiga had first arrived and insisted on this old-fashioned deference. 'I just don't know whether I should let her,' she had said. 'All the others call me Patricia. But she insists. Says it helps her with her boundaries.'

'If she's happier calling you madam,' Adam had advised, 'I don't see it as a huge problem. Unless you really don't like it.'

'I don't dislike it.'

'Well then.'

So after further consultation with his sister Claire, and the usual phone posse of other friends and confidantes (those that weren't already dead) it had been settled. To Jadwiga, she was 'madam'.

As Adam watched the carer retreat, and his mother return to the important business of news, he wondered what Jadwiga was up to. What files was Patricia letting her tidy up? It was odd, because Patricia was normally very protective of her private material.

After a bit Adam realised that his mother's urgent interest in current affairs had abated. She had asked Alexa to switch to *Essential Classics* on Radio Three, a favourite of both hers and Philip's, loyally stuck to, of course, after his death. But even as the lovely Georgia Mann was outlining today's 'playlister challenge', Patricia's head was nodding forward, and then, as Renaud and Gautier Capuçon and the Radio France Philharmonic took it away with Camille Saint-Saëns's Op 132, 'La Muse et le Poète', *The Times* slid out from under her bony fingers and tumbled to the floor.

Patricia slept on, her chin sinking down lower with each rasping snore.

Adam watched her with alarm, even as the violin and cello raced to a fiery climax. He might very well not have been here, but now that he was, he didn't want his mother falling off her chair. Shouldn't Jadwiga be keeping an eye on her, rather than 'tidying files'? A crash down onto these hard tiles might hurt her, even, at her age, kill her. Carer indeed!

'Mother!' he shouted. 'Mother, wake up!'

Nada. Whatever luck he'd had with Julie wasn't being repeated here. Not that he minded, at one level. Did he want his mother knowing he was still around? No. The news that he had appeared to her in ghostly form would get out on the family and friends phone network sooner than you could say 'spook'. Maybe they would all just assume she had gone mad with grief. Then again, Patricia was persistent and convincing. He didn't want to jeopardise his chances of learning anything significant about his death.

She was leaning right over, on the point of toppling off. He had to do *something* – and fast.

'Alexa!' he shouted. 'Play Queen's "Another One Bites the Dust".' That should wake her up all right. But the virtual assistant didn't respond. Either she was programmed only for command by Patricia or Adam's ghost voice was not getting through. As his mother's chin juddered dangerously downwards again, he reached out to an empty flowerpot that was resting near the edge of the long, wide, gravel-covered shelf that ran down the garden side of the glasshouse. With his imagined hand he gave it a hefty push.

It fell to the floor and smashed noisily. Adam jumped back. How on earth had he managed that? Patricia jerked awake. She stared around her, blank-eyed for a moment, fearful.

Then: 'Adam,' she muttered.

Help! Was he visible? Had he, by using his 'hand' like that, somehow materialised and blown his chances of listening in?

But she wasn't looking *at* him. She was looking slowly around. Albeit in the wrong direction.

'Adam, is that you?'

He sat tight, like a small boy playing hide and seek; the small boy he'd once, long ago, been with her. The only sound was Georgia's next tune, the soupy slow movement of Mozart's 23rd piano concerto.

'Very strange,' Patricia went on. 'I could almost imagine you were in the room with me, you naughty boy. Alexa,' she went on, 'stop playing that music. And get Jadwiga for me, please, could you.'

Adam watched his mother as she waited in the sudden silence. She scanned the room, eyes bright, head up, senses tuned. For some people, old age meant degeneration, a slow slide into fading faculties, dementia. Not for Patricia. If anything, she had become beadier in her dotage.

'Yes, madam?'

'Ah, Jadwiga, there you are. A flowerpot just came crashing down. I have no idea how.'

'Don't worry, I can sweep it up. Did you knock it over by accident perhaps?'

'No, Jadwiga, I didn't touch it.' Patricia was cross now. 'I was nowhere near it. I was having a little nap.'

'Of course you were. Now are you okay staying here or do you want to move? Up to bed? Or we could have a little game of Piquet if you like?'

Another thing the saintly Jadwiga was happy to do; play this boring card game that Patricia liked to inflict on her carers.

'Actually, it was the oddest thing, Jadwiga. I thought Adam was here for a moment. My son.'

'Ah, that's nice.'

'It wasn't nice, it was alarming. I felt his presence quite strongly.'

Jadwiga nodded. 'Yes, madam.'

'You don't believe me, do you?'

'If you felt that he was here, I do believe you. Now shall we move you through into the sitting room for a bit?'

'I'm fine here, with Georgia. Alexa, play *Essential Classics*, please.'

Even as the music started up again, Patricia's phone was ringing. She flashed a brisk smile at her carer as she looked down at the screen. 'My daughter, Claire,' she said, although Jadwiga hardly needed to be informed that Patricia's daughter was called Claire. Jadwiga and Claire spoke most days, between themselves, though not always within Patricia's earshot.

'Hello, Claire, my darling, how are you?... Hang on a moment, I just need to mute Georgia. Alexa, mute *Essential Classics*, please, thank you. That's better. Sorry, darling, I was just listening to *Essential Classics*... Yes, Jadwiga and I are doing a little tidying up... Although a strange thing happened just now, a flowerpot flew off the side and smashed onto the floor... In the conservatory, yes... No, it wasn't on the table... How many times do I have to tell you, that table isn't wobbly, your father had his coffee on it for years... It absolutely wasn't near the edge... Jadwiga and I are always very careful about that... No, Claire, I didn't knock it over... If you'd like to come round and have a look for yourself you'd be more than welcome... It would actually be quite nice to see you in the flesh for a change...'

This was often the way with those two. A phone call started equably, enthusiastically even, but within a couple of minutes they would be trading passive-aggressive barbs. It was a mother–daughter thing, Adam told himself, because even though he could and did find Patricia infuriating, he generally managed not to rile her in quite the expert way that Claire did.

Adam had seen enough of his mother for the time being. He decided he would try and take advantage of this call to see if he couldn't transport himself to his sister. Might he even be able to appear to her too? Find out what her take was on his 'suicide', over and above what she had expressed, publicly, at his funeral.

He put his hands together and focused in on Claire's voice on the other end of the phone. And yes, wonderfully, it grew louder, his mother's grew fainter, and the sedate, tatty surroundings of the old conservatory were replaced by Claire's state-of-the-art kitchen with its real granite worktops, maple cupboards and limestone floor tiles. Claire was standing by her picture window, looking down over her short, paved drive at a rather smart car that was speeding in through her neat stone gates.

It was his car. The crimson Alfa Romeo Giulia. He was shocked to see his widow at the wheel. Julie didn't drive the Alfa; she drove the Disco. What on earth was she thinking? Then it hit him again. He was dead. Dead, dead, dead. He would never feel the beautiful thrust of that vehicle under his right foot ever again.

'Sorry, Mum,' Claire was saying, 'I've got to go, Julie's just showed up.'

Even from where he was, across the room, Adam could hear Patricia's loud squawk. 'Julie? I was just talking to her, darling–'

But Claire wasn't going to let her mother join in with this encounter, was she?

CHAPTER TEN

Now Julie was marching up the steps towards the kitchen side door. Claire was kissing her on the cheek and welcoming her in with her best shit-eating grin, offering her coffee or sorry, no, herbal tea, because Julie didn't do caffeine, as well she knew. Even though they were forever going on about how hard-up they were, Claire and Dan were usually well-stocked with the finest brands, in this case teapigs, individual net pyramids containing whole dried chamomile flower heads, none of your off-the-factory-floor crushed-dust rubbish.

Matching Emma Bridgewater mugs in front of them, they had soon cut through the awkward preliminaries and were onto the subject in hand: Adam. The funeral was discussed. Julie was congratulated on the arrangements and the wake. Claire had been impressed by the number of work colleagues who'd turned up to pay their respects. And not just the posh ones, the builders and carpenters and painters and all.

'The subbies loved Adam,' Julie said.

'Subbies?'

'Sub-contractors. Adam always felt very at home with those rough and ready types.'

'He wasn't a snob, certainly,' Claire replied. They chatted on, slightly at odds with each other, as always.

'D'you know what, Claire?' Julie said eventually.

There was a pause. Claire looked at her sister-in-law with anticipation. 'Yes?' she said.

Julie's fingers tapped nervously on the smooth surface of the reclaimed timber table. 'It's really difficult for me to express this, but...'

'Go on.'

'I almost... sometimes... feel as if... Adam's still around.'

'How d'you mean?'

'As if his spirit's still... here.'

'Oh... kay...'

'Have you sensed anything like that, Claire? At all?'

'No.'

'I know how close you were.'

'We were. Although, as you know, we were pretty good at winding each other up too.' Claire laughed, dismissively, but Julie wasn't listening. 'This might sound ridiculous,' she went on. 'But he appeared to me.'

'He *appeared* to you? Who did?'

'Adam... of course.'

'But... how?'

'It's hard to say. Almost like a ghost, I suppose. In fact, exactly like a ghost.'

'What are you saying, Julie? I don't quite understand.'

'You'll probably think I'm crazy, but Ad-Ad-Adam' – she was stuttering nervously, which wasn't like her at all – 'visited me this morning. At home. He was in our bed- bed-bedroom.'

'In your bedroom?'

'Yes. Maybe not one hundred per cent, but ninety per cent. Like a sort of hologram.'

Claire was looking at Julie as if she were insane. Fair enough,

Adam thought. 'So what was this ninety per cent Adam wearing?' she asked.

Julie shrugged. 'I can't remember. Usual sort of Adam clothes. Jeans. Campers. V-necked jersey over a T-shirt. You know Adam. Scruffy at home. Smart in the office.'

'Not his blue burial shroud?'

'No, he was fully dressed, right there in front of me. Sitting by my dressing table when I woke up. Asking me questions.'

'He talked to you?'

'Yes. We had a long conversation.'

'About?'

'Stuff.'

'Such as?'

Adam could almost see the cogs in Julie's brain whirring. She wasn't going to confess to the Rod liaison, that was for sure.

'We talked about his – his... suicide,' she said eventually.

'Did he tell you why...?'

'No, this was the thing. He insisted he hadn't done it. That he wasn't the type.'

'Did he?' said Claire. She looked down at her hands and shook her head slowly from side to side. 'I must say, Julie, I have found that very hard to accept. Suicide. Adam isn't – wasn't – that kind of person, was he? He was always so energetic and upbeat. About everything. Things didn't get to him in the same way as they do to lesser mortals.'

'He concealed his anxieties well, that's true.'

Claire was studying her sister-in-law with narrowed eyes. 'So what did he think? This ghost of Adam? How did he reckon he'd come to be in your garage with a hosepipe in his mouth?'

'He thought someone... had done him in.'

'*Murdered* him?'

'Yes. I told him he must have been so shocked by what he'd done that he'd blanked it all out.'

'And what did he say to that?'

'He wasn't having it. He wanted to know who had discovered him... and all that.'

'But that was you, Julie, wasn't it?'

If Claire had been hoping to wrong-foot her sister-in-law, it hadn't worked. Julie looked unfazed. 'Yes,' she replied. 'In the garage, right after that lunch we had in Tempelsham. You and I. To talk about Patricia.'

'And Eva, more to the point, as I recall. Serena was determined you should know.'

'Of course she was, the old witch. Why couldn't she tell me herself? She just can't deal with me at all, can she? Even though I've been with Adam for nearly eighteen years.'

Claire shrugged, as if to say, *'Can you blame her?'*

'Not that it mattered,' Julie went on. 'I knew anyway.'

'Did you?'

'I'd guessed. Though I wasn't going to tell you that. Then. Was I?'

'So what did you conclude?' Claire went on, after a moment. 'You and... this ghost... Adam?'

'He accused me of meeting up with you to create an alibi.'

'For what? You being involved in his death?'

'Pretty much.'

'So how would that work if you weren't even there?'

'He was kind of implying... that someone else might have done it. Staged the suicide.'

'While you were lunching with me? Who?'

Adam got the feeling, from the expectant expression on her face, that his sister knew all about Rod.

'We didn't get onto the details.'

'He must have had some idea.'

'There was no one in particular,' Julie said briskly. 'Then your mother rang. And he'd suddenly vanished.'

'Adam had?'

'I looked up and he wasn't there anymore.'

'Aha. So he came,' – Claire waved her hand floppily – 'and went.'

'Don't mock me, Claire. This happened.'

Adam's sister and his second wife had never much liked each other, had they? Julie had always thought Claire was a bit absurdly right-on, with her comfortable lifestyle and 'self-righteously leftie' views; while for Claire, Julie had always been the gold-digging interloper, albeit of the kooky, yogatastic variety. When Adam had left Serena, his sister had stayed quite openly loyal to his first wife, regularly winding both Adam and Julie up with stories about how Serena had been with Adam, funny things she'd once said, et cetera. Claire had also always 'been there' for his children, and had loved it when Matilda, as a teenage provocation, had given Julie a book called *Second Wife, Second Best?* for Christmas.

'Are you sure you didn't just imagine all this, Julie?' Claire asked. 'Like when you're still awake, but dreaming. A hypnagogic state, it's called. I heard a programme about it on Radio Four. You can have totally realistic-seeming encounters, but they're actually hallucinations. You've been upset about Adam. Your mind is trying to rationalise it. Maybe you feel guilty.'

'About what?'

'You tell me.'

There was silence. Julie stared straight back at Claire. 'No,' she said. 'I didn't imagine it.'

Claire sighed. 'I think I'd be more convinced if I saw him myself.'

'Another of the things Adam told me,' Julie went on, 'was that he could be invisible, watch people without them realising he was there.'

'So he could be here right now?'

'I guess he could.'

Claire looked over towards the window and did a theatrical

wave. It was in completely the wrong direction. 'Hi, Adam!' she called.

Adam laughed. Out of frustration as much as anything. Part of him urgently wanted to do something. What? Try and slide a mug along the worktop? Push it off, like he'd done with Patricia's flowerpot? That would show them. But did he really want to confirm what Julie had just said? Where would that leave his efforts to find out the truth about his death? Silly idiot. Why had he even told her he could watch people?

Now Julie smiled back at her sister-in-law, a sympathetic but businesslike smile. 'I suppose it simplifies the whole Patricia inheritance issue,' she said.

'How d'you mean?'

'With Adam gone, you get everything.'

Claire looked flabbergasted; and a bit caught out, too.

'Do I? I've actually no idea what's in Mum's will.'

Adam didn't like that 'actually'; was his sister protesting too much?

'Not me, I don't think,' Julie returned, with a mocking smile. 'Remind me how far you are through that seven-year tax evasion thing?'

This was naughty of Julie. When Adam had mentioned their family tax plan to her, he'd made it clear that it wasn't for general discussion. In a nutshell, and, frankly, on Claire's insistence, they had persuaded their mother to hand over Larks Hill to them six years ago, under the government scheme that meant that after seven years it would become theirs and they would therefore be spared inheritance tax. As this came in at a hefty forty per cent above the basic threshold, the saving would prevent the house from having to be sold on Patricia's death, and make for quite a chunk of money, if they decided, further down the line, that they wanted to sell it. Larks Hill, with its surrounding fifteen acres, was prime building land, in an area between Tempelsham and Fowlton Bennett that had been allocated for development in the local government plan. Sad though it would be to see the back of the rambling old garden, the lily-covered pond, the huge chestnut tree that the two of them had climbed up in their childhood, with its favourite, now rotting, old treehouse, there was always the option, once Patricia had gone, to flog it – and the empty fields around it – off for Barratt boxes. Though Claire loved her old home, Adam had always known that, with her and Dan's endless and much-vaunted money problems, she might eventually feel enabled to kiss goodbye to the happy memories.

'How do you know about that?' Claire asked.

'Adam told me.'

'Not… as a ghost?'

'No, ages ago.'

Claire nodded thoughtfully. 'It's not tax evasion, Julie,' she replied. 'That's a crime. It's tax avoidance.'

'Same difference.'

'Well, it's not the same difference is it, because otherwise Adam and I would have gone to jail. And guess who would have grassed us up? My husband. Whose job, in case you've forgotten, is chasing tax evaders. If you're genuinely interested, I'm happy to tell you that we're six years into it.'

'So one more year and you're squids in?' Julie was grinning.

Claire gave her the basilisk stare, familiar to Adam since childhood. He knew his sister well enough to know that she was now so angry she could barely speak. 'Obviously, I don't think of it like that, Julie. But there's really no point in handing over a huge chunk of our inheritance, such as it is, to the Exchequer.'

'Except that, I guess, you know, we all have to do our bit to pay for hospitals and nurses and social care and such like.'

Given what she knew of Claire and Dan's politics and general philosophy of life, this was a provocative and frankly hypocritical dig. Julie, Adam knew, did everything she could to set her expenses against her meagre earnings. She had even tried to claim for haircuts, on the grounds that she had to look good in her online yoga videos.

'It would also have meant,' Claire went on, 'that Larks Hill would have to be sold just to pay the tax. Which would have been a bit sad. This way we can keep it if we want to.'

'The beloved family home. Passed down the generations. But do you want to? Keep it? You and Dan?'

'I think that's for us to decide.'

Tense smile matched tense smile. Julie sipped at her – now surely cold – chamomile infusion. 'How is he?' she asked.

Claire wasn't going to tell Julie how her husband really was, that was clear. He was 'ground down by work,' she replied. Dan was always ground down by work, even though he'd been made redundant from his job as a Grade 6 tax inspector over two years before. That had had nothing to do, obviously, with his tetchy, bullying manner. It had been a 'restructuring' matter, plus the fact that Head Office had moved from Kingsway in central London to Croydon, which was a heck of a commute from Tempelsham. So Dan had taken the payoff and set up as a freelance 'fraud investigation specialist', which could, in Adam's albeit cynical view, mean anything. As he'd joked to Julie at the time, perhaps the first thing Dan should investigate was himself.

'Well, once your mum pops off,' Julie replied, 'he can pack it all in and the pair of you can swan off around the world on a perpetual Saga tour.'

'I don't see Dan taking early retirement. He's very committed to his job.'

Watching these two sparring, Adam realised that he had no idea who had done him in. His initial instinct had been that it had to be Julie. She had the opportunity, the motive and, yes, with a bit of help from handyman Rod, the capability. If it had been anyone else, why would they have done it in her garage? Because it was Adam's garage, so the obvious place? To frame her? All that was troubling.

But now he was starting to wonder about his sister too. He and Claire had been 'joint tenants' of Larks Hill, which meant that now he was gone, she did indeed get everything. 'Survivor takes all,' in lawyer's jargon. They had laughed about the phrase at the lunch after the decisive meeting at Kumar, Rogers and McPherson, the family solicitors in Tempelsham. Laughter which seemed rather hollow now. It was an arrangement Dan had advised, pointing out that the legal alternative, 'tenants in common', could prove 'problematic' if one of them were to predecease the other.

And what about the rest of Patricia's estate? The carers were running through her funds on a daily basis, but there was still plenty there. Did Claire 'actually' know who that was all left to? Was it conceivable that under all her tears, her protestations that Adam hadn't killed himself, she knew he hadn't killed himself because it was a double-bluff... and she and Dan had done it?

Who had suggested that Saturday lunch in Tempelsham? If it had been Claire, perhaps it had been her alibi and not Julie's. Get Julie out of the way, so Dan could sweep in, sedate their victim, bump him off, then set up the theatrical suicide scene?

No. Don't be ridiculous, Adam told himself. Your mind is running away with itself. If Dan had turned up that day, you would have remembered it, wouldn't you? He could hardly have sedated you if he wasn't there.

Now he followed his sister and his widow down the drive to Julie's car. They were chitchatting inconsequentially again and hugging goodbye, as if the serious financial issues had never been raised, as if the pair of them were not reluctant sisters-in-law but old friends. Embracing in mutual, guiltless grief.

CHAPTER ELEVEN

A dam was left alone with Claire. Was now the time to try and talk to her, get her version of things, the Tempelsham lunch included? On balance, he thought he wouldn't even attempt it. At the moment his sister was clearly sceptical about Julie's account of his visitation (if that was the term for his probably far too low-key haunting of his second wife). Even if he were able to appear to Claire, that would be it: a) she would believe Julie unequivocally and b) there'd be no catching her out in possibly compromising chitchat with Dan. Adam's advantage, as invisible eavesdropper, would be gone.

So he watched patiently as she tidied up the kitchen, listening to some political podcast, as was her wont. Earbuds in, she hoovered through the house, fixed herself lunch, then at three thirty drove into Tempelsham to pick up little Maya from school. Adam slipped into the back of the car and went with her, enjoying the view, then following her out to hang with the mums and dads at the school gates, to see his niece's happy face as she came running across the playground towards her mother's outstretched arms.

Back home, Claire fed her daughter macaroni cheese, played

with her and put her to bed, and was back in her kitchen preparing a grown-up supper when Dan returned. Since redundancy, he'd rented an office above the music shop in Tempelsham, though what he did there other than read the papers and drink takeaway Costa lattes was anyone's guess.

'Hiya,' he said as he strode in.

'Good day?' Claire asked.

'So-so,' Dan replied as he headed to the larder and fetched himself a green net bag of carrots. 'Where's my juicer?'

'Where it always is. Next to the grinder in the tea and coffee cupboard.'

'I wish you'd leave it on the side.'

Dan grunted as he fetched it down, plugged it in, then started feeding carrots into its noisy maw. He paced over to the big wooden fruit bowl on the granite topped island and helped himself to two apples, which he cut into quarters before slicing out their pip-filled cores and dividing them again. These segments followed the carrots. A trip to the fridge added a fistful of spinach leaves.

Finally, his healthy drink was ready. He headed off upstairs to enjoy it while reading to his daughter and kissing her goodnight.

As they sat down together to eat, half an hour later, Claire smiled hopefully at her husband. After his long, fruitless day, Adam was agog.

'Julie came by,' Claire said, after a bit.

'What did *she* want?' Dan replied, his mouth full of pasta, like a washing machine in mid-cycle.

'I didn't know why she'd come. Maybe to tell me Adam had left us an unexpected chunk of money.'

'Fat chance of that.'

'Quite. No, she was really jittery. Couldn't quite bring herself to spit it out.'

'Spit what out? Has he?'

'No.' Claire told him about Julie's visit from Adam.

Dan barked with laughter. A pasta shell shot across the room and landed on a distant tile. 'A *ghost!*' he cried. 'It's hardly surprising, Claire. Julie's a Grade A Froot Loop. We've always known that.'

'I know, I know. But this was a whole step further. She really thinks she's talked to… him. He was wearing Adam's jeans and favourite shoes and everything.'

Dan was rolling his eyes. 'As opposed to his burial shroud.'

'Exactly what I said!'

'So what did this well-dressed spook have to say? That it wanted a post-mortem divorce.'

'No, apparently that it, he, Adam, hadn't committed suicide.'

'What did Julie say to that? Did she admit to first degree murder? On the grounds of wanting a fat uncomplicated income and a nice house for her and her not very secret lover to live in?'

Claire laughed. 'She didn't mention that. I don't think she realises we know.'

'More fool her. Everyone knows. Didn't you raise it?'

'It didn't seem the right time.'

Dan chuckled scornfully. 'What else did this ghost have to say?'

'That it could be invisible, apparently, watching her, us, anyone, at any time.'

'We'd better be careful what we say. "Hello, Adam!"' Now it was Dan's turn to wave in the wrong direction.

'It also accused her of having lunch with me, in Tempelsham, on the day of the–'

'Death,' Dan cut in, finishing her sentence for her. Did he not want to hear the word 'suicide', or even the word 'murder'? It was odd.

'In order to create an alibi,' Claire went on; she was looking round nervously, almost as if she thought that the ghost they had been laughing about might really be with them.

'Okay,' Dan said slowly. 'So once Julie had her alibi then

what?'

'"Someone" murdered him.'

'According to ghostie?'

'Yes.'

'He didn't know who?'

'If he did, she wasn't going to say. Then Patricia rang and the ghost vanished. Apparently.'

Dan laughed out loud. 'Your bloody mother would be enough to drive off any spook. Even down the phone. What did you say to that?'

Claire explained about her scepticism, then how Julie had suddenly switched to quizzing her about their arrangements for inheritance tax avoidance.

Dan leant forward, knife and fork poised. 'For fuck's sake! How does she know about that?'

'Adam told her.'

'What – as a ghost?'

'No, no. Some time ago, apparently.

'So much for "total confidence".'

'She wanted to know how far through we are.'

'With the seven years? Did you tell her?'

'I couldn't not, Dan.'

'Claire, it's none of her business. Not now anyway. I do wish you'd keep this stuff to yourself.'

'She raised it!'

And they were off, suddenly, into one of the spats that Claire always tried to pretend didn't happen with her grumpy shit of a husband. Now Adam could watch the escalation objectively; feel sorry for his sister, even as she tried to point out that Julie had been married to Adam, so did in fact have a legitimate interest. 'I guess Julie knew more than we'd realised,' she said eventually, still trying to play the peacemaker.

'Lucky we managed to keep her out of it,' Dan replied testily. 'She's pretty fucking beady. Don't forget, she's still a potential beneficiary of the rest of Patricia's estate. And Patricia likes her, Julie makes well sure of that.'

'So Mummy can still leave her what she likes?'

'Of course. We can hardly influence that.'

'But I thought the whole *point*–' Claire began, before she was cut off by the upbeat trill of her mobile. It was Serena. Great timing from his first wife, Adam thought. At the very moment that Claire was finally about to reveal something significant, he was suddenly listening to her affectedly upbeat chitchat with the mother of his children. Perhaps to annoy Dan, perhaps to put a stop to the argument, Claire had clicked her mobile to speakerphone.

Serena was just touching base, she told Claire. After the funeral. How was she? And Maya? And Dan? (She had never liked Dan, but then who had?) Had she seen Julie?

She had. Claire had something to tell her about that, she said, backing out into the garden away from her husband's scowl. No, not over the phone. It would be better face to face. How about lunch soon? Tomorrow? Why not? Should she come up to London or would Serena come to her? Actually, Serena quite fancied a day out in the country, now the blossom was out.

'Could you pick me up at the station?'

'Of course. We'll go to the White Duck in Tempelsham.'

'Perfect.'

By the time Claire had finished the call, Dan had stropped off upstairs. Adam stuck around, hoping that Claire would follow him, that they might return to their conversation, to: 'We'd better be careful what we say' and 'But I thought the whole *point*–'

But no. Adam watched while his sister did a half-hearted clean-up of the kitchen, then slumped back on the L-shaped sofa, sighed deeply, and clicked on the TV. Upstairs, Maya had gone to sleep and Dan was now hunched in front of his home computer. Playing some game and sulking, it looked like. He might be there all night.

CHAPTER TWELVE

Adam was on tenterhooks as he sat watching his sister and his first wife, clinking glasses, sipping their naughty lunchtime Sauvignon Blanc, nibbling fat green olives, dunking fresh bread in the White Duck's specially sourced Cotswolds extra-virgin oil, enjoying each other's company again, one to one, on this sunny end-of-April day.

As a regular customer, Claire had managed to secure a table by the window, with a view down the grassy slope to the River Mead, which wound its way through lush green meadows at the back of Tempelsham proper, a copse of trees to the right conveniently hiding the sewage works. How nice it was to be out here, Serena said, away from the terrible fumes of London, all the worse at this time of year. The particulates combined with the pollen from the ornamental cherries and plane trees gave her terrible hay fever.

'How are you?' Claire asked, reaching out a sympathetic hand.

'I'm fine. Really. Still shocked, obviously, but I'm slowly coming to terms with it all. You?'

'I suppose I have. Starting to, anyway.'

But the funeral had been perfect, Serena went on, brightly.

Insofar as such a dreadful occasion could be perfect. Presumably Claire had had input?

'What do you think, Serena?'

'Endless overruling by the blessed Julie, I suppose?'

'Maybe just a little.' But Claire had, as Serena knew, been allowed to organise the music.

'Which was wonderful, I meant to say. Obviously, I loved the "Pie Jesu".'

'What a star Matilda is.'

'This is the absolutely infuriating thing about her. When she wants to do it, she can. And then...' Serena shrugged, encompassing the numerous occasions their daughter hadn't wanted to do this, that, or the desired other, the frustrations that caused even the most reasonable and doughty of mothers.

'How is she?' Claire asked. 'Now?'

'All over the place again at the moment. Basically, she's heartbroken. She argues with me, she argues with Walter. She refuses to believe that Adam could have killed himself.'

'She's not alone in that.'

'But, Claire, do you really think he didn't?'

'I'm afraid I do.'

'It's hard to believe, isn't it? Particularly with Adam. I know you're not supposed to say this, but suicide is a dreadfully selfish act. Especially if you have children.'

As she finished off chewing a corner of bread, Claire was nodding, encouragingly.

'I know Adam could be selfish,' Serena went on.

'And how.'

'But was he *that* selfish? And I'm speaking as the abandoned wife.'

'You're always so forgiving, Serena.'

Adam's first wife shrugged, accepting the compliment, but in a humorous rather than a smug way. What an easy, relaxed, natural woman she was! Why had he ever thought it a good idea to leave her? He had taken her for granted. He had got together with her too young, then let himself forget what a prize she was.

'But if it wasn't,' she replied, leaning forward and dropping her voice, *'suicide...* what are you saying? The implications, as Walter keeps reminding me, are shocking.'

'I know,' Claire agreed.

As an invisible spirit, seated at the adjacent empty table, reserved for who knew what important customer, Adam could smell everything: Serena's fish soup, Claire's meaty duck pâté, the slightly overdone toast (which he would have sent back), even the freesias in the slim glass vase at the centre of the table. But he had no menu envy. These powerful aromas didn't arouse an appetite in him, as they would have done in his human frame. Once again, his strange state was brought home to him; he was in the world, but no longer of it.

More to the point, he could see and hear, even if he couldn't, at the moment, be heard himself. How he wanted to chip in, though. As the pair of them chivvied over the now familiar ground of his death. 'It was a *poem!*' he shouted when Serena brought up the suicide note. 'And not even in manuscript. Photocopied!' Neither of them turned a hair. He reached out with his right hand and tried to grab a piece of Claire's toast. That would make them sit up. Flying toast! But his fingers had no purchase. The toast could have been a small, low-lying wall that he'd glided through. Why was this, when with his mother he'd been able to push over a flowerpot? Because there were two of them? Because that had been a dangerous situation and this wasn't? He had no idea.

'So you had something to tell me,' Serena said eventually. 'About Julie coming to see you.'

'Yes!'

Claire recapped their conversation, excitedly. When she explained about Julie's visit from the ghostly Adam, she raised her finger and waggled it sideways by her right ear in an old 'doolally' gesture that she would never have dared use with her Gen Z niece Matilda.

'But perhaps he *did* appear to her,' Serena said.

She didn't really imagine that was true, did she? Claire replied. Adam's ghost had been wearing jeans and Campers. Why not a burial shroud? And then he had insisted that he wasn't a suicide, that someone else had 'done him in'.

'And what d'you think about that?'

'A ghost! Suggesting that. For real.' Claire was laughing. 'No. Dan agreed with me. She must have dreamt it.' She explained about hypnagogic states.

Serena was nodding. 'You're probably right. Julie's always been away with the fairies, hasn't she? I suppose it's nice to know that she's missing him. The bitch,' she added with a laugh.

To Adam's disappointment, they left the fascinating subject of him. They didn't even speculate, as he had thought they might, about who might have been his murderer, had his ghost been real and telling the truth about his 'suicide'. Instead, they danced off into a long and clearly mutually enjoyable reminiscence of their friendship, from when Serena had first met Claire, coming up to Larks Hill with Adam from Bristol in the holidays. A spiky teenager.

'Was I spiky?' Claire asked, making a face.

'You were a bit. But sweet with it. You were always quick to give Adam grief.'

This was true.

'Were you jealous of him?' Serena asked. 'He was such a golden boy, wasn't he?'

Claire paused to think. As well she might.

Come on, admit it, Adam thought. Envy runs through your character like the letters in a stick of rock, even if you do a great job of concealing it (most of the time).

'No,' said Claire. 'Not exactly jealous. I suppose it was a bit annoying that he always knew what he wanted to do. And was so good at it.'

'Perhaps he was good at it *because* he always knew what he wanted to do. Whereas you…'

'Still don't know what I want to do.' Claire laughed.

Serena, it had to be said, always brought out the nice side of his sister.

'I personally think there's merit in that,' Serena said. 'It's like I keep saying to Matilda, "You've got so many talents, darling, it's just a question of which one you want to use." Whereas dear old Leo…'

'Is much more predictable.'

'Solid, I like to think. But yes, he's a very different character. Funny isn't it, how the same gene pool can deliver two such contrasting personalities.'

They were like a pair of conversational dragonflies these two, dancing over their long-shared experience with no coherent thread. One subject led off into another, then back again. As their main courses arrived, they were remembering Claire's long string of disastrous love affairs, before she had finally met Dan.

'Mr Right at last,' Claire said.

'Although,' said Serena, 'I was always rather jealous of some of your more glamorous Mr Wrongs.'

'Were you?'

'That Polish conceptual artist. What was his name?'

'Olek.'

'Olek, yes. What a very handsome fellow he was.'

'He was a bit, wasn't he?' Claire grinned. 'Crap artist, though. All those things he found in skips.'

'And the tenor.'

'Lend me a tenor Charles. The meanest man on the planet.'

'I'd be up to my knees in nappies with Leo and Matilda and in you'd waltz, with one of these men, or off on your travels; it all seemed so glam.'

'It wasn't that glam. Otherwise I'd have stayed with one of them. And some of that travel was pretty lonely. I was jealous of your happy family life.'

'The grass is always greener. Anyway, that didn't last, did it?'

'No.'

Was it because Adam had died that they were allowing themselves to get into these deep waters, or was this how it usually was? Adam had no idea. But now his sister was onto her third glass of Sauvignon and telling his first wife that she had never understood why Adam had left her. For Julie of all people, who was so obviously such a flashy little tart.

Serena shrugged. It had probably been her fault as much as his, she said. 'The children were still young; I was so wrapped up with them. Adam was in town all the time, working hard, he always told me, which he was, but also getting up to who knows what. I was in north London, driving them to playdates and sleepovers and birthday parties and all the rest. I'd rather gone off sex. And there was Julie, all pert and willing. She saw her opportunity and took it.'

'Don't you hate her?'

Serena looked down, and there was, for just a moment, Adam thought, a proper flash of loathing in her eyes. But then that melted away and her wide, forgiving smile took over. 'It's all such a long time ago,' she said. 'She is what she is. And what she must be going through now I have no idea.'

'Unless she did it.'

'Claire! You don't really think that, I'm sure.'

'The whole ghost thing could be a massive bluff.'

CHAPTER THIRTEEN

A dam was back in his sister's house. Was he now ready to try and manifest himself to her? After Claire's scornful remarks to Serena about his visit to Julie, he couldn't wait to see her face if he did manage to appear to her in the non-flesh. How exactly would he do it, though? What was it that had meant he had suddenly appeared to Julie, but couldn't even get through to Eva, whom he cared about so much more?

Claire was upstairs in Maya's colourfully decorated bedroom. After her chequered romantic career, and then Dan's problems with committing, she had come so close to not having children that Adam found it sweet to see her there, cuddled up with her miracle *in vitro* child, reading her a bedtime story.

'So what happened about the maths test?' she asked Maya when she'd finished the chapter, had a little fight about reading another one, then closed the book carefully on its cloth bookmark (a worn green and gold one that Claire had herself had as a child).

Maya laughed. 'Everyone failed.'

'*Everyone* failed?'

'Apart from Grace. And she only just passed. Rebecca was really cross with us. Said she was *disappointed* with us.'

'I'll bet she did,' Claire muttered.

Downstairs, half an hour later, she was arguing with Dan about the school. 'Everyone failed the maths test. What does that tell you about the teaching?'

'Sounds like the teacher set too hard a test.'

'But how, why, would you set a test you clearly hadn't taught to?'

Dan shrugged. 'Perhaps she's trying to raise standards.'

'That school is rubbish.'

'It's the best in the area.'

'What does that mean? You never go there, so how would you know.'

This jibe prompted a furious response from Dan. He did go there, he said, he went there a lot. In fact, he went there so much that one of the mums had suggested he join the PTA.

'Which mum was that?'

'Sasha.'

'Typical!' Claire snorted. 'What does Sasha know about anything? She's never there either. She waltzes in for the quizzes and brings her lovely dish for International Day, but that's it. So are you joining?'

'What?'

'The PTA. They could do with another man besides drippy Gareth.'

'Who's Gareth?'

Claire sighed. 'A hopeless weed of a stay-at-home dad. So keen to please he's virtually vanished up his own arse. Okay, so what are the names of Maya's teachers?'

'Amanda,' Dan replied, after a pause worthy of *Mastermind*.

Claire gave him a flat smile. 'Form teacher, very good. And?'

Dan was unable to name another.

'I rest my case. Do you even know the name of the head?'

'Martin.'

'Brilliant. Surname?'

'I have no idea.'

'Fiddledick.'

Another bark of laughter from Dan. 'He's called Martin Fiddledick? Seriously?'

'What's wrong with that?'

'Not the greatest of surnames for a primary head.'

'Dan! You're being silly. And gross. It's a perfectly good English name. What's his favourite topic?'

'His favourite topic?' Dan repeated.

'If you ever went to one of the assemblies, you'd know the answer, because it's all Martin ever talks about.'

'I don't know… climate change?'

'Close, but no filthy polluting cigar, I'm afraid. His favourite topic is growth mindset. Do you even know what that is?'

'Yes.'

'What is it then?'

And so they went on, baiting each other about their commitment to their daughter's education. Despite her principled defence of his unusual name, Claire couldn't bear Martin, couldn't bear the fact he insisted that all the teachers be called by their given names, yet refused to act over the obvious bullying by the boys in Maya's class; that he'd banned all nut products, and yet had been found, by Lana Tillotson, one of the feistier mums in the PTA, scoffing pistachios out of a jar in his office; that he'd decided to treat the fox that had made a den on the edge of the school's celebrated 'rewilded playground' as a pet not a pest, right up until the moment when it had eaten the Reception class's pet rabbit, Dolores, and he'd finally allowed the Polish builders to take it away and 'liberate' it on Tempelsham Common; that he'd equivocated disastrously with the Muslim parents who'd objected to LGBTQ + History Month, leading to an exodus of the same and consequent reduction of important diversity. Eventually, she reached the point Adam knew she was building up to. Why couldn't they just pull Maya out, send her to Heathcote House, the independent school up the road?

'You know the answer to that,' Dan replied coldly. They couldn't afford it and, more to the point, it was against his principles. As well she knew. So why did she even bring it up? No, he was sorry, he was not prepared to buy his child an unfair advantage. Anyway, there was zero diversity at Heathcote.

What was he talking about? Half the sixth form was Chinese. There were Africans.

'Posh ones.'

'So what?'

They ranted on. Claire brought up Dan's beloved convertible Audi A3, a much more expensive car than your average Joe Bloggs would ever be able to afford.

'It's a car, Claire. Not an education.'

'What's more important? Our child or your fucking middle-aged fantasies of being James Bond? If there's one thing we can't afford, it's that car.'

At this Dan strode over and grabbed her by the collar. 'Don't aggravate me, Claire.'

'Dan, back off.'

His face was crimson and the tendons in his neck were quivering. Was he about to hit her?

'You know what happens if you don't,' Claire said, slowly and with practised purpose.

Adam watched, appalled. Could he intervene? Not in this state.

But then, just as another surge of powerlessness swept over him, his brother-in-law dropped his wife like a dog might drop a ball and stepped back. God. Adam knew there had been issues about Dan's temper, but Claire had always said they had been resolved in couples' therapy. This was ugly.

'Dan, I'm sorry,' Claire said, after they had stood staring at each other, breathing as heavily as if they'd just had sex. 'I'm not trying to provoke you. But this is our daughter we're talking about here. I know you think we can't afford it, but being blunt, now that Adam's gone, we have Larks Rise, which is potentially worth a fortune, and in any case we stand to get a whole lot more from Mum anyway. When she goes.'

'She might hang on for years, Claire.'

'She's ninety-two.'

'With all her marbles. Maya might be in college before she pops her clogs.'

'I doubt it.'

'In any case, Robin's Lane is a perfectly good school.'

They were back to it; and it looked like a battle Claire wasn't going to win. Dan didn't want a 'lady of the manor' for a daughter. He wasn't impressed by the huge sports fields at Heathcote House. He certainly didn't want Maya playing lacrosse, even if it was a game invented by American Indians (and where had Claire got that delightful titbit from?) Eventually Dan stormed off upstairs and Claire collapsed into an armchair, sobbing. Adam's non-existent heart went out to her. She was always so loyal to Dan in public; and here, now, was the private reality he had glimpsed so often, but never been privy to. Should he, could he reach out and offer her sympathy? His earlier desire to scare her had melted away completely.

'Now, now,' he said, tentatively. Just for luck, and as an experiment, he put his hands together in the prayerful namaste.

His sister's head turned. Her pink, lightly-veined cheeks were gleaming with tears.

'What?' she muttered. 'What's that?'

'It's okay,' he said gently.

'What? Who's... this?'

'It's your brother. Adam.'

'Adam! How? Where?'

'I'm here. Just across the room.'

'I'm imagining it. Stay calm, Claire,' she was telling herself, out loud in her typically practical way. 'It must be an aural hypnagogic state. You're not going mad. Or having a panic attack. You're fine.'

'I'm not sure you can have an aural hypnagogic state,' Adam replied, and as he did so, he realised he had materialised. Just like that. No slow fade in. There he was – in best hologram mode.

'Oh my God!' Claire cried. 'Julie was right. Adam, is that really you? What... how... what are you doing here?'

'Just keeping an eye,' he replied. 'Seeing that you're all right.'

'But... how long... have you... been here? Did you just see that... our little row?'

'Afraid so.'

'How much of it?'

'All of it. I was here when you were reading Maya a story.'

His sister walked across the room and sat down in the armchair, as if exhausted by her own fright. 'Dan's being such an arsehole,' she said. 'It's not as if we can't afford it now. I mean...' She broke off.

'You mean what?' he asked.

She was staring at him. 'How do I even know it's you?'

'Look at me. What do you see?'

'A 3D image of my dead brother. But, but... why should I assume it's you? Perhaps I've got so stressed I've started seeing things.' She slumped back in the chair and began to sob again.

'Claire, please stop it. I'm real.'

'I'm clearly going mad.'

Adam floated towards her, then back, not wanting to freak her out. He planted his spectral feet carefully in line on the floor to one side of her.

'Ask me something about our childhood,' he said gently.

His sister's tears slowed. She pulled out a handkerchief from her jeans pocket and blew her nose. Then: 'Okay,' she said finally. 'What was the name of my first pet?'

'Very funny. You didn't have a pet. Daddy hated animals.'

'I was allowed a goldfish for a bit, though.'

'Were you? I'd forgotten about that. What was its name?'

'Goldie.'

'Original.'

'Don't you remember, Adam? Goldie. I won him as a prize at a fair, and he had a little glass bowl and everything. The cat got him and you very sweetly helped me bury him in a shallow grave. Okay, another question. What was the name of the club you had, with your friend Roland, that you wouldn't let me join because I was too little; that met in the summer house at Larks Hill, whose mascot was a stuffed animal you found in a junk shop?'

'Did we find it in a junk shop? I don't remember that bit.'

'Come on, no bluffing,' Claire insisted. 'What was the name of the club?'

'The Ferret Club.'

'It is you.'

'D'you remember his sharp teeth? You scratched my leg with them, you horror.'

'Did I?'

'Yes, Claire.'

There was silence – bar the sound of the old clock on the mantelpiece. It was an heirloom that his sister had been given 'on permanent loan' by his mother. This meant that whenever Patricia came to her house she said, 'Are you looking after my lovely mantel clock? I might have to take it back one day.' Tick tock, tick tock. It was one of the sounds of their mutual childhood. There was no getting away from that; even if there had always been the five-year age gap and they had latterly grown rather apart, they had grown up together.

'Where are you?' Claire asked. 'What are you?'

'I don't know. It's just, I'm still here, somehow.'

'So you are.' She was shaking her head in continuing disbelief. 'So are you in some kind of… what… purgatory?'

'I don't know. I don't feel much different, to be honest. Only that I don't have a body.'

'I can still see you.'

'That's an illusion, obviously.'

'I almost feel like I could hug you.'

'You can't do that, sadly. My physical body is somewhere else.'

'In the ground, yes. Unless that coffin was empty. Which it wasn't. Adam, did you really kill yourself?'

'No.'

'I knew you didn't. Dan doesn't agree with me. His point was that you were in that garage with the hosepipe. You left a note on the car seat. They went through it all at the inquest.'

'You went to the inquest? What was that like?'

'Very thorough. Impressively efficient female coroner. Asked a lot of questions. Julie broke down.'

'Of course she did.'

'The note was the decisive thing. It was so final. If you didn't kill yourself, why did you leave a note?'

Adam explained about 'Suicide Note'; also the troubling fact that he had shown the poem to Julie three years before.

'So if she knew it was a poem, then...'

'She claimed not to remember.'

'But it was signed,' Claire said.

'Not by me. I never write my name by my poems.'

'So someone must have forged your signature.'

His sister was looking at him pityingly now. Did he know, she went on, that Julie had been seeing someone. Adam laughed bitterly. He did now, he said. He'd caught them at it. No! his sister exclaimed. What had that been like? Interesting, Adam replied. Actually horrible.

'I'll bet,' Claire said. 'Did they say anything revealing?'

'They didn't realise I was there. I was invisible at the time.'

'So how does that work?' Claire asked. 'Can you just choose to be visible or invisible? At any time?'

'It's not that simple. I'm learning as I go. It's almost as if I can only appear if my feelings for the person I'm with are strong enough. Like you, just now. I just felt... you know... you were sobbing...'

'And then there you were...'

'There I was,' he agreed. 'But how, or why, I have yet to understand.'

So what did he want her to do, she asked, suddenly. Should she contact the coroner? Tell her about this conversation.

'I'm not sure a coroner's going to believe you, Claire.'

'But you can't be the victim of a miscarriage of justice. If you didn't kill yourself, Adam, you were murdered.' His sister dropped her voice to a whisper, even though there was no one else in the room. 'We need to find out who did it. Whoever it was, they can't be allowed to get away with it. Can they?'

CHAPTER FOURTEEN

I n the conference room at Albury & Atkinson, Jeff Trelawney was in a meeting with... Jesus... the Butcher's Yard clients, Sugar and Savidge. Quieter Steve was the numbers man, 'the bean counter' in Stan's cheery parlance, while smooth Old Harrovian Tim was the front man, what Stan used to call 'the rain maker'. They were still young, mid-thirties probably, but well on their way to achieving their stated aim of being 'the next Candy brothers'. Reuben Green, Adam's old team leader on this project, and Eva were also present, so there was at least a faint hope that things might be staying on track, that S & S weren't after all taking the change of direction that Jeff had been quietly (or not so quietly) pushing for, ever since he'd first brought the job in. Adam didn't like it that the council's new development control officer, 'dodgy' Dave Purbeck, was also in the room, but not the nice – and sound – conservation officer, Tom Ireton. And what on earth was smarmy Trevor Wealdstone doing there, Jeff's favourite team leader for new-build projects?

Listening in, Adam soon realised that they had all just returned from walking Dave around the site, informally and off the record. Now, with the plans for the scheme laid out on tables around them, they were into a discussion about the pre-app, the formal meeting with planning and conservation officers at the council offices, in which problems around a planning application were discussed, with the idea of ironing out any wrinkles and objections before that document was formally presented to the council committee. But this wasn't going to be a pre-app for Adam's conservation project, that was all too clear. With Jeff in charge, the gathered gang were talking about daylight and sunlight infringements on surrounding properties and how they would need to be dealt with in the inevitable, and now compulsory, consultation process. But there were no daylight infringements in Adam's scheme. He had planned to preserve the charming higgledy-piggledy façade intact; the roof, invisible from the yard itself, was going to be heightened by a mere two feet. A quick glance at the drawings only confirmed the horror: this was the Clerkenwell Tower they were on about. He had thought he'd stopped it, but he hadn't.

'It's going to be a headache,' Jeff was saying, 'but I'm sure we can get through it. There's some group calling themselves Save Butcher's Yard that's sprung up, but most of them don't even live there, they're just people that work there, and other conservationist busybodies, calling themselves concerned residents...'

'Concerned residents.' Savidge laughed. 'Professional pains in the arse, more like.'

Reuben's face was a picture, though weirdly he was saying nothing, just shooting charged looks in Eva's direction as Jeff moved on to discuss which demolition contractor would be right for the job, and how that always tricky process would need to be covered in the construction management plan.

'Sadly,' said Dodgy Dave, 'Tom Ireton is going to be away on holiday next week, but you can be sure he's going to have plenty of questions about all this.' He made a knowing face. 'Particularly when it comes to the kinds of materials that may be used at the base of the building to make sure it sits in its context better.'

Wealdstone was smirking, as if at a private joke. How long had this coup been in the planning?

'May I just ask?' Reuben piped up. 'Why we're even having the pre-app without Tom? The application can't be submitted without his approval anyway.'

Dave was laughing. 'No fault of mine, Reuben. Tom has worked for the council for so long that he's built up over three months of annual leave. He can't wait to get down to his cottage in St Ives, especially at this time of year.'

'Fortunate timing for you, though, Dave.'

'If Tom wants to pottle round the beaches in his Birkenstock sandals there's not much I can do about it, is there?'

After the meeting was over, Jeff took Savidge, Sugar, Purbeck and Wealdstone off for a drink at his favourite bar round the corner, the ever-pricey New Deal, while Reuben and Eva slipped down the back stairs and along the familiar little alleyway to the Prosperous Parson. Adam was burning to know what the pair of them were thinking, why they had kept so quiet, what exactly was going on.

'What the fuck happened there?' Reuben said when they were settled with their drinks.

'Classic Jeff is what happened. He's been working on Dave for months.'

'Tom is going to be "conveniently" on holiday.'

'Dave deliberately picked his week.'

'Tom'll be furious when he finds out.'

'Furious and powerless. Unless he cancels his holiday. Which he really won't want to. Sugar and Savidge can't wait for the demolition ball to start swinging...'

'Tim Savidge,' Eva scoffed, 'the man who told me he bought Butcher's Yard because he'd always loved it, had discovered it one

June morning coming out of a club after an all-nighter. What a bullshitter!'

'So is that the end of it?' Reuben asked. 'Adam's plan. All that work we did wasted?'

'That's how Jeff works. You know that. Fait accompli. We're just grist to his mill. Once he's persuaded the client, we have to go along with it.'

'I hardly think the client needed much persuasion. Their eyes were glinting. They're suddenly looking at a hundred-million-pound new build rather than a boring five-million-pound conservation project. Now I see why Jeff's had us flat out on Peabody for these last few weeks. Weren't you tempted to say something?'

'What could I say? Jeff's in charge now, isn't he? I'd just be risking my own position by going up against him in an open meeting.'

'So is that it, Eva? Your job security is more important than voicing an objection to a plan that is completely against everything that Adam stood for?'

'I didn't notice you speaking out.'

'I wanted to talk to you first.' Reuben looked down sulkily. 'So party's over for Butcher's Yard? Bang goes four centuries of history. Up goes another identikit glass-and-steel box.'

'There's still the consultation process.'

'Ha fucking ha. Have Your Say, you furious plebs, in what we've already decided. It'll be the usual joke; watch this space.'

'Of course it will.' There was silence between them. 'Then again,' Eva said, 'life moves on, Reuben.'

'That's not what you used to say, Eva, when Adam was here.'

'Adam's gone.'

Reuben eyed her thoughtfully. 'Did you know what Jeff was going to say, Eva? What's going on? Have you gone over to the dark side?'

'Reuben, there is no dark side. The bottom line is we're

powerless without Adam. Either we move on elsewhere – or we learn to work with Jeff.'

Later, Adam followed Eva home. Yes, he was dead. Yes, he had no influence anymore on how the firm operated. But Reuben was right. Jeff should not have overturned what had already been agreed. In any case, the destruction of an historic site like Butcher's Yard was more significant than any one human life. Than his life, even. He had lasted fifty-eight years, hadn't even made it to sixty. The charming little cobbled triangle of Butcher's Yard had been around, in some form or other, since the early seventeenth century. The Great Fire had, remarkably, swept past it. Wren's plans for rebuilding the area had also failed; though approved by both king and parliament, they had been 'unhappily defeated by Faction'. Jeff was no Wren, but was he really going to achieve what that great architect had failed to do? Take a demolition ball to this quaint corner, albeit that it was a rabbit warren inside, that extensive (and appalling) alterations had prevented it from ever being listed, that wartime bomb damage and subsequent crass rebuilding right next to it meant that it had also just missed out on being included in the local conservation area.

Adam waited until Eva was safely upstairs and into her studio. He watched her make and eat a lonely bowl of noodles. When she was finished, she slumped down on the Flottebo with a glass of Sauvignon Blanc and started to cry.

Powerless, he watched her. Were these tears for Butcher's Yard? For letting Jeff compromise what had once been her values? Even, for him? Overwhelmed suddenly, he decided that now was the time. His feelings for her were surely strong enough for him to appear to her. He put his hands together, as before.

'Eva,' he called gently, from where he stood, invisible, by the little window.

She didn't look up.

'Eva,' he repeated, louder.

Nothing.

He got up and walked over to her violin, which sat face up in its open case. He tried to pluck the strings, but his fingers found no purchase.

He turned back towards her. 'EVA-A-A-A!' he shouted.

Not an eyelid flickered.

CHAPTER FIFTEEN

Matilda was, as Adam had hoped she might be, in her old bedroom at Serena's house in Tufnell Park. His house, as it had once been: a bog-standard London terrace with two rooms at the front (knocked into one), a kitchen at the back (now with side return), three bedrooms on the first floor, and a converted attic. He had left his first wife there early one fine June morning and never gone back. With the new-found wealth from Albury & Atkinson, he'd taken Julie off out of town and built Fallowfields – to his eternal shame because that had always been something he'd talked about doing with Serena.

His son, Leo, had long ago moved out for good, but Matilda still had the room she'd always had, with its view out over the roof of the side return to the little back garden beyond. Though she was now twenty-nine, and came and went to flat shares and boyfriends, it was still, really, a teenager's den. There were old posters of Beyoncé, Shakira, Taylor Swift, Hermione Granger, W.H. Auden. There were scented candles, a bookshelf made of bricks and planks of golden pine, flowery drapes covering the double bed.

Serena and Walter were downstairs, watching TV, but Adam

wasn't bothered about them. He floated upstairs, through Matilda's closed door and slumped down on the leather beanbag he had brought back for her from a business trip to Rio, many years ago. He had seen it in a market and known her nine-year-old self would love it. Back home, they had unfolded it and stuffed it with little polystyrene balls together. Then Leo had wanted one too. The painted wooden toucan suddenly wasn't enough.

He sat watching her, silently, as she tapped away busily at her laptop. He longed to talk to her. Surely it was worth a try? He did the namaste again, but without expectations.

'Hiya,' he said, eventually.

His daughter looked up. Her dark eyes were wide with surprise, but she didn't scream or freak out in any way. 'Daddy,' she replied, as if his presence were the most natural thing in the world. Then, double-taking, looking hard at him, grinning with delight: 'Is that really you?'

'Matty,' he murmured. He could hardly believe he'd got through to her; and so effortlessly too. He had materialised even more quickly than he had with Claire. He had no idea how or why; he was just grateful that his burning desire to talk to his daughter had been recognised. By who or what, he didn't even have the beginning of a concept; even if there was a who or what.

He grinned back at her, happily. He was biased, obviously, but what a lovely young woman she was: his own dark, penetrating eyes coupled with her mother's wide smile, the one he'd first fallen for at the Freshers' Fair, where he had been a third year running the Architects' Society stall and she had been one of the new first year intake, fresher indeed! He remembered it as if it were yesterday. Sexy Serena in her pale blue jeans. Signing up for his club. He had asked her out the next day.

'Where are you, Daddy?' Matilda asked. 'What are you doing?'

He explained, taking her through everything that had

happened to him since he'd regained consciousness at the funeral: 'Quizás, Quizás, Quizás', 'Suicide Note', everything.

'So you saw me singing?'

'Of course I did. You were wonderful.'

'I thought I wasn't going to be able to go through with it, that I'd get up there and break down at the thought of you in that horrid box. You know, centre stage.'

Adam smiled. He disliked coffins too.

'But then I felt,' she went on, 'like, buoyed up. Almost like you were watching me.'

'And I was.'

She clapped happily. 'That's so cool.'

Her face reset itself to serious. 'So you really think... that someone murdered you, Daddy?'

'I don't think. I know. There's no way I would have killed myself.'

'That's what I said to Mummy. Walter thought you could have done it, but Mummy wasn't so sure. Walter has this idea that you're basically, like, this secret depressive...'

'Great.'

'That under your upbeat exterior there's this guilty person who's done so many bad things in his life...'

'I'm sure he knows best.'

'He's a dick, don't worry.'

'Should I agree with that?'

'You don't have to, Daddy. Trust me, he is. A total, prizewinning plonker.'

So, she went on, after a moment, if Adam was able to do this haunting, visiting, whatever he called it, why hadn't he been to see her – or any of them – before the inquest, when they could have done something? Maybe even reversed the verdict.

'I wasn't around, Matty. I don't know where I was before the funeral, but I wasn't in any conscious state.'

'You really don't remember anything between your death and the funeral?'

'I don't remember my death.'

'You've blanked it out. You're probably suffering from whatsitsname syndrome. Post-traumatic stress thingy.'

'Disorder. No. This is more like post-traumatic amnesia. The last thing I remember, and it's crystal clear in my head, is sitting at home in Fallowfields eating lunch on my own and reading through some of my poems.'

'Where was Julie?'

'Having lunch with your aunt Claire in Tempelsham. Then she drove back and found me in the garage, apparently...'

He spared her the graphic details; she was his daughter, after all.

'So what are you saying?' she asked. 'You suspect Julie of killing you? Maybe with Rod's help?'

Adam groaned inwardly; even Matty knew about his wife's lover. 'It seems kind of likely, though, doesn't it?' he replied. 'Given that I was found in our garage. And we only have Julie's word for it that she discovered me at the time she did.'

'But wouldn't you remember her coming back? Before... she... or they... did... whatever...'

'Not if she'd sedated me in some way. Or even finished me off with some powerful drug. She left this special little lunch out for me.'

'Doesn't she often do that?' Matty was giggling now, in that familiar, nervous, endearing way of hers. 'You being a completely useless cook.'

'All I'm saying, Matty, is that it was odd that eating Julie's food was the last thing I remember. Julie could have drugged the food, then she and Rod set up the suicide scenario, which would have been easy enough to do.'

'Would it, though, Daddy? How would they have got you to breathe in the carbon monoxide?'

'Perhaps they didn't. Perhaps I was already dead.'

'But they wouldn't have wanted to leave evidence of some killer drug in your system, would they? And anyway, they would have had to get you breathing the gas, for quite a while, because that's what the post-mortem found. Carbon monoxide poisoning. You had the bright crimson skin, what's it called, lividity, and everything.'

'You think?'

'For sure. It takes ages to die from carbon monoxide. The doctor at the inquest went into it in detail.'

'So if not them,' Adam asked, 'who? My sister?'

'Claire?' Matilda rolled her eyes. 'I know you have problems with her sometimes, Daddy, but she's hardly a murderer. She's been one of the ones consistently saying you wouldn't ever have killed yourself. You should have seen her at the funeral...'

'I did see her at the funeral.'

'Tears streaming down her face. What's her motive supposed to be, anyway?'

Adam explained. But though they did have a sound financial reason for getting rid of him, Adam didn't really think his sister and her grim partner were in the frame. Watching her alone with Dan had been uncomfortable, but the chat had never been that suspicious, had it? 'We'd better be careful what we say' was surely just Dan's joke. 'But I thought the whole *point*' had led nowhere. Once Adam had spoken to Claire directly, any doubts he'd had about her had melted away.

'What about that dodgy business partner of yours?' Matilda asked.

Jeff had a good motive, Adam agreed, in that he was trying to get him out of the firm and Adam had been resisting. But if he really were the culprit, why would he have staged the suicide in Adam's garage? Surely it would have been easier to set it up at the office after hours. Adam discovered at his desk, comatose with pills, an empty whisky bottle to one side; hanging from one of the old leather ceiling loops they had kept as features of the ex-warehouse; even tumbled down one of the steep stone staircases.

'Who else is there?' Matilda asked. 'Eva?'

Adam laughed. 'Please. Why on earth?' She loves me, doesn't she? 'Whatever she thought of me,' he went on, 'my death gives her zero advantage, in fact removes her greatest supporter from the firm where she loves working.'

Matty nodded. She was playing devil's advocate, he realised that. She liked Eva, even if only because she represented a betrayal of the hated Julie. Matty had rumbled her and Adam in a flash when the three of them had got together for a drink. She had promised to keep her dad's affair a secret; though Adam suspected she had told Leo, and who knows whom he had told, dreadful gossip that he was.

But: 'You're sure she isn't working below the radar with Jeff?' she went on.

No, Adam absolutely didn't think that. On the other hand, he would never have suspected, he said, even for a moment, that Eva would have backed Jeff in the abandonment of their long-nurtured plans for Butcher's Yard.

'What d'you expect, Daddy? It's her job. She can't go out on a limb for you when you're no longer around, can she?'

Adam reluctantly agreed.

'Is it even possible,' Matilda went on, 'that she started your affair so that she could talk you into leaving her a nice little something?' Seeing her father's expression, she smiled. 'Don't tell me that's happened already?'

How intuitive was his bloody daughter? But Eva had never asked for anything from him; had initially resisted when he'd offered to give her the small slice of his assets he had now handed over, enough to put a deposit down on a flat, to free her from her stupidly expensive rental. He'd only done it because he'd felt sorry for her, throwing all that money away every month, and because he was simultaneously cross with Julie. And yes, it had bought him a little bit more time with her in their easy status quo, before he was forced to upend his world all over again.

One thing he was sure about: Eva hadn't faked that passion over all these months. Had she? No.

'It's a ridiculous idea,' he replied. 'Engaging in a full-blown love affair in order to get close enough to me to bump me off. In any case, she'd have been taking a big risk.'

'Of falling in love with gorgeous you?'

'I didn't mean that.'

'The starchitect twenty years her senior.'

'Come on, Matilda. I'm not a starchitect. Or even approaching.'

'Your obituary in *The Times* said that you will be seen, in due course, as one of the five most influential architects in the UK in the post-millennial period.'

'If only that were true,' Adam said. He shrugged, as if he didn't care, but his whole spirit glowed with this filial flattery. Was it possible that posterity would rank him alongside Baron Foster of Thames Bank and Baron Rogers of Riverside? Baron Albury (honoured posthumously) of Embankment?

'So what risk?' his daughter asked.

Adam shrugged. 'Of being caught out, obviously.'

'And that means she wouldn't have done it?'

'Matilda, darling,' Adam replied slowly. 'I know her. I know what we were like together. Really. She might have been frustrated I wasn't moving as fast as she wanted to reorganise my life, but she didn't want to kill me.'

'So who else is there? Some other rival who envies you, hates you? More to the point, needs you out of the way.'

Adam could think of no one. His old friend Roland Herrington, of course, had always been weirdly jealous of him, but a) he was still, despite that, a friend and b) would he murder him to prove he was a better poet? Hardly.

Adam's only frustration about Eva, he went on, was that,

despite his strong feelings for her, he seemed unable, in his present state, to get through to her.

'Get through?'

'Talk to her. Appear to her. Like I'm doing to you. Find out what she thinks. Of my death. And everything.'

'But she played you that tune. On the violin. She must have wanted to communicate...'

'You would have thought so, wouldn't you? It was so easy with you.'

'I am your daughter.'

'Still.'

Matilda was studying his face, reading his distress, as only a daughter could. 'Would you like me to talk to her?' she asked. 'See whether she really has given up on you?'

'D'you think that would be a good idea?' Though Adam had hoped she might say this, he felt as nervous, suddenly, as a brand-new lover.

'Why not? I like Eva. I hardly got to speak to her at the funeral, what with one thing and another. But how am I going to report back?'

'I could just be there, I guess. Watching. If you tell me where you meet. Or if you went and met her right now, I could follow you.'

'At eleven o'clock on a Friday night?'

'There are places open, surely. What about that club I bought you membership of?'

'Tea and Sympathy.'

Matilda picked up her phone from the white cuboid bedside table where it was charging. This is what Adam loved about his daughter. She'd inherited that Serena thing; of never dithering around; just deciding things and getting on with them. Adam had Eva's number off pat.

But his girlfriend wasn't answering.

'Sorry,' Matilda said. She didn't look that sorry. 'I'm kind of tired anyway. I'll try her in the morning. She's probably gone to bed.'

'And how will I know whether it's happening?' Adam asked. 'Or where you're going. You can hardly text me, can you?'

'This is true. You'll have to hang around. Or come back. I tell you what. I can write whatever we agree on a piece of paper and leave it somewhere. How about here?' Matilda pointed to a pink scented candle in a glass jar by her bed. 'Will that work?'

'Okay,' Adam agreed, reluctantly. How weird and frustrating it was when you no longer had a mobile. He was swept back to his distant youth, when arrangements to meet up had to be made on a landline, and that was that, you just waited and hoped. He remembered once hanging around for ages for Serena under the clock at Waterloo, a famous rendezvous. And her arrival, very late, through the hurrying commuters, smile wide, breathless with apology, into his arms in her favourite blue headband and black leggings, that oversized electric green sweater she always used to wear, tumbling off one bare shoulder.

Happy days.

CHAPTER SIXTEEN

Tea and Sympathy was a private members club in Soho that wasn't actually terribly private, in that non-members could use it when it wasn't busy. It had started out life as a women's only teetotal club, then segued to being a teetotal club for both sexes, before becoming a place where alcoholic drinks were allowed and eventually what it was now; a bar famous for its cocktails. But it had a nice enough vibe, Adam had always thought, with its roomy leather chairs and plumped velvet cushions, low round tables and soft lighting. Eva had taken him there, as a change from the Chelsea Arts and Groucho clubs, his usual hangouts. He had liked it enough to get Matilda a membership; had hoped it might help her have an independent base, away from her mother and Walter, from scuzzy flat shares out in God-knows-where-land, from the noisy and often intimidating chaos of London pubs.

Eva was already there, scrolling through her phone as she sipped at a Singapore sling, her glass topped with a triangle of pineapple decorated with two shiny glacé cherries.

Adam sat opposite her, studying that lovely, familiar face. His girlfriend was wearing an embroidered maroon jacket he had bought her for her birthday, which looked as good on her as he'd hoped when he'd spotted it in the window of the fancy Hampstead boutique. He didn't hold out any hope that he could speak to her; or even pick up one of the Twiglets from the little lacquered bowl on the table in front of her and zoom it around like a toy rocket; or perhaps do something humorous with her pineapple slice. If he couldn't reach her when he was alone, what chance was there now, in this crowded place, with the hum of conversation and laughter over the tinkling dinner jazz?

But here came his daughter, his representative on earth, weaving her way skilfully through the chairs.

'Matty!' Eva cried, rising to her feet, holding her arms out wide.

'Eva,' Matilda replied, giving her a tight little hug. She was looking tentatively around as she spoke, and Adam imagined she was wondering whether he had seen the scribbled note she had left folded in her bedside candle and was here too, with them, observing, but unable to indicate his presence.

'I'm sorry we didn't really get a chance to chat at the funeral,' she said, once they'd got the preliminaries over, hailed a waiter, and Matilda had dithered between a margarita and a whisky sour.

'You were busy with family,' Eva replied. 'I didn't stay long. Bundled back on the train to London with some colleagues.'

'I know Dad meant a lot to you.'

'It's weird, not having him around. I know we weren't exactly public, yet. But we saw a lot of each other. At work, and then, outside, in the flat and places. Here, even.'

'You miss him?'

'Terribly, at first.' She sighed. 'More than I thought I would.'

Oh my darling, Adam thought.

'But then, recently, since the funeral...' Eva looked up at Matilda and smiled. 'Loved your singing by the way...'

'Thank you.'

'…it's really come home to me that it's all over. You know, it's been almost two months now. I need to move on.'

'Of course you do.'

And whose side are you on? Adam thought, as pain stabbed his virtual heart. I thought you were here to argue my case.

'Tell me,' Matilda asked, after they'd chatted a bit more about Eva's feelings. 'Do you ever get… like… a sense of him?'

'How do you mean?'

'Like, he's still around in some way.' Matilda laughed lightly.

'Do you?'

'Maybe. I miss him. Obviously.'

'When you miss someone that much you can almost imagine they're there, can't you?' Eva said. 'The night after the funeral, when I was at home, it was a bit like that.'

'Really? How?'

'I actually spoke to him, called his name. Crazy, eh? Then I played him this song on the violin that he used to like.'

'"Quizás, Quizás, Quizás",' Matilda said.

As she hummed the tune, Eva sat forward. 'How d'you know about that?'

'He told me.'

'What! When?'

'Before… he died. When you were… er… dating.'

'Oh.' Eva looked puzzled. 'Weird sharing. It was, like, a theme tune for our relationship. You know, "What's happening, dude? You going to leave the bitch or what?"'

Matilda grinned. She hated Julie. 'How d'you find work?' his daughter went on. 'Without him? What's happening with the rogue partner?'

Eva laughed. 'Is that how your father described him?'

'And the rest. He was trying to take over, wasn't he? Push Daddy out of his own firm.'

'It's not quite like that. They have – they had,' Eva corrected herself, and Adam was happy to see a sad look flit across her face, 'very different visions. Adam was always a bit old school for Jeff.'

'Old school?'

'Just ways of doing things. You know, a wizard on the drawing board, but he didn't really understand how to design on computers, thought social media was a waste of time–'

'Total bollocks!' Adam interrupted. 'I had a Twitter account for years. You know I was on Instagram, Eva. Stylish pics of buildings in their settings, different views of street widths, nice details and use of materials. Come on, you helped me with my posts. Facebook too, 900 plus so-called friends, most of whom I hadn't seen in the flesh for years, if ever.'

But these were words that fell on deaf ears; or rather, didn't fall on any ears at all. As Eva carried on with her revisionist view of Butcher's Yard, Adam's heart sank. Jeff had got to her. In the space of a few weeks, Adam's perspective had been thrown out of an ultra-modern, triple-glazed, iconic tower window.

'And what about you, Eva?' Matilda was asking.

'What about me?'

'Which vision do you believe in? Adam's or Jeff's?'

'ATTAGIRL!' Adam shouted. But nobody noticed, except for one pale-faced young woman with long, lank blonde hair, sitting on her own drinking jasmine tea, who looked up and stared straight at him, as if trying to make him out. He smiled at her, then waved. If she could see him, he thought, all well and good. If she said something, even better. It would be wonderful for Eva and Matilda to know he was there. But maybe she had been looking at something else, as people in crowded places do, because her gaze went straight through him, oblivious to his increasingly frantic gestures.

'Don't get me wrong,' Eva was saying. 'Adam's philosophy was and is totally cool. The importance of people in built environments, "placemaking", I'm not letting go of that. It's just, you know, realities. Adam's gone. Jeff's running the show now. I have to be on side, otherwise I might as well not be there. You have to be in the room, don't you?'

'So, with Butcher's Yard,' Matilda asked coolly. 'You don't care about all those quaint buildings being knocked down and replaced with yet another glass and steel box? The Clerkenwell Tower.'

Eva looked gobsmacked. 'Who told you about the Clerkenwell Tower?'

'Dad.'

'But this was only finalised yesterday.'

'I know. But you've all been discussing it for some time, haven't you?' Matilda looked down, then very slowly up again. 'You know I was just asking you whether you'd ever sensed him, like, around. This might sound a bit crazy, Eva, but the fact is he *is*… still around.'

'What are you talking about, Matty? Around where?'

Matilda explained about Adam's visit to her at home and Eva laughed in disbelief. No, Matilda insisted. It had all been real. Her dad had been lurking around for a while, following people. Eva even, when she'd gone to The Prosperous Parson with Reuben after the Savidge and Sugar meeting…

'You *what*?' said Eva. 'How d'you even…?'

'He was there. Dad. Watching, listening. That's why he was so upset, why he visited me. Because he's freaked out that you…'

'That I what?'

'Seem to be backing Jeff. That all his plans for restoring Butcher's Yard have been chucked out.'

'So why has he spoken to you about all this stuff, and not to me?'

'He said he'd tried. Twice. But he couldn't get through to you.'

'Why not?'

'He doesn't know. He was worried you'd lost interest and moved on. That's why he sent me to see you. Or rather, why I offered to speak to you.'

'He's dead, Matilda. It's not a question of moving on.' Eva fell silent, her face lost in thought. 'Has he visited anyone else?'

'Yes, my aunt Claire...'

Eva nodded, blankly, in a 'fair enough' way.

'And Julie.'

'He's spoken to Julie but not to me?'

'That's what he said.'

'Fucking hell!'

'Eva!' Adam cried. 'She's getting this arse over tit. I've tried, twice, to get through to you. Please don't blame me for failing. I was shouting at you, for God's sake!'

But there was no point in this tirade. He still wasn't getting through. In any case, Matilda's phone was ringing. She pulled it from her pocket and looked at the screen. 'Eva, sorry, it's my mother. D'you mind?'

Eva waved her on.

'Mum... hi... yes... I *am* sitting down... I'm in a club in Soho... It doesn't matter, what's wrong... what?... oh my *God*... I'm coming now.'

'What?' asked Eva, concerned at Matilda's sudden change of expression. She was white-faced.

'It's Leo. He's been in a car crash.'

'Leo? Your brother?'

'Yes.'

'Is he okay?'

'No.' Matty was shaking her head. 'No, he's not okay. He's dead. I've got to go, Eva. I'm sorry.'

CHAPTER SEVENTEEN

Adam got to Serena's long before Matty. For him, it was just a conjuring up of the image of the little terraced house in Tufnell Park and he was there. Later, he wondered whether he should have stayed at Tea and Sympathy until his daughter and his girlfriend had actually parted. Followed the pair of them out and down onto the busy Soho street. Heard their last revealing words to each other.

But he had gone. As devastated as any father would be at a fatal accident involving his child (even though he was dead himself).

At Serena's he found a scene of shock. His first wife's cheeks were puffy and red from crying. Leo's lovely fiancée Abby sat straight-backed on the sofa, a blank expression on her face. Walter was striding around like a spare part, trying, unsuccessfully, to be helpful. He had opened a bottle of Italian red, which he was quaffing freely.

As he waited for Matilda to return, Adam stood to one side, watching and listening, hoping to pick up more details of what exactly had happened. Leo loved his cars, always had done, since he'd been a small boy who called out the marques of vehicles parked up on the street as he passed them. Recently, he had got rid of his diesel BMW 4 and invested in an all-electric VW e-Golf, much to everyone's surprise, as he'd never been that bothered about climate change.

But that was Leo. He had bought Steve Jobs's game-changing MacBook Air when he was still a teenager; a Dyson bag-free vacuum as a student; ditto Alexa as soon as she had first appeared. Since then, pretty much any fab new device that added a bit of tech fun to his life. If he hadn't been the broad-shouldered, jolly, rugger-playing fellow that he was, you might have accused him of being a geek.

And now he was dead. In a head-on collision with a lorry on the A10, apparently. Adam could hardly cry. He had no eyes, no tear ducts. But he felt gutted to his soul. His lovely boy Leo, with his whole life ahead of him. Leo, who had always been the happy-go-lucky one, whose easy charm meant that he'd so often punched above his weight. He had sailed through school, accumulating friends. He had got into a better uni than his raw intellect perhaps deserved and had had a great time there too, popular and productive. He had got his degree and then treated himself to a gap year, travelling the Far East and Australia, Instagramming as he went. On his return he had walked straight into a good job. And now he was marrying Abby, with her big blue eyes and easy smile. How had he managed to land her? his mates had joked. But they all knew. Leo was always the jammy one, wasn't he?

But his luck had run out. It was heartbreaking, even if you no longer had a heart to break. Leo had been taken from Adam, before he'd even had a chance to get through to him and say goodbye.

Now, it seemed, that would never be.

'Hello, Dad.'

Adam spun round. He could see nothing.

'Dad, it's me, Leo.'

'Where?'

'Here,' came his son's voice again, clear as a bell. 'Where are we? I thought you were—'

'Dead. I am.'

'How come... I mean, what's happened?'

As Leo was speaking, he was materialising. Why so soon? Adam thought. It took me close to eight weeks to 'go through'. But he was relieved, as his son's image thickened into a three-dimensional likeness, that he didn't appear to be damaged in any way. His cheerily-grinning face was much the same as it had been in life.

'I think you've had an accident,' Adam replied.

'An accident,' Leo repeated. 'How d'you mean?'

The poor boy clearly had no recollection of his death.

'A car crash, was what your sister said.'

'Matty. Where is she?'

'She's on her way... here.'

'Here...' He was looking round. 'Where am I?'

'At your mother's house.'

'Mum!' Leo cried. 'Mum,' he repeated, seeing Serena below him. He sailed down towards her.

'Leo, stop!' Adam said. 'She can't hear you,' he explained. 'Or see you. I'm sorry to have to tell you this, but it seems that this accident you were in was fatal. Have you got no memory of anything like that?'

'No.'

'So what's the last thing you do remember?'

'Actually, yes, I was driving.'

'Where?'

'On the A10. I was coming back from this super-boring meeting in Royston.'

'Driving what?'

'The e-Golf. It has amazing acceleration. It can literally do nought to sixty, just like that.'

'But what happened, Leo? Can you remember?'

'That's what people don't realise about these electric cars, Dad. Guys like me aren't buying them because they want to be part of some worthy green revolution, although, sure, we're happy that that's part of the package. But we actually slam down the cash on the table because of the fucking torque. It's like driving a turbocharged milk float.'

'Sure,' Adam agreed. It didn't seem that what had happened to him had fully hit home.

'So where am I now?' Leo asked.

'You're on the other side.'

His son looked baffled. 'The other side? Of what?'

'It's an expression, Leo, for what lies beyond…'

'You mean…?'

'You're dead,' Adam said bluntly. 'Like me.'

'Like you? So… Abby…?'

'Is still alive.'

'Walter?'

'They're all still alive, mate. It's us who are dead.'

'But they're just over there.' Leo gestured at his fiancée, his mother and her partner, across the room.

'They're in another dimension. You can't get to them.'

'Watch me!' Leo cried. 'Abby!'

But his fiancée didn't turn. Leo ran towards her, but when he reached out for her, his hands didn't engage. They were flailing, round and round and through her. Eventually he gave up and looked back at his father.

'So where… are we? In this room? I mean, surely–'

'But we're not in this room. It's like a parallel world.'

'You mean… we're some kind of ghosts?'

'So it seems.'

'Wowsers!'

Leo stood stock-still for ten seconds, digesting this, then he strode purposefully across to where Walter was standing. He stepped back, theatrically, squared up to him and unleashed a punch. It cut straight through him.

'Okay,' Leo said, laughing. 'So he is in a different dimension. Boy, would I like to freak him out, though.'

Leo's genial frivolity had always amused Adam when he was alive. But now, you would have thought that his own death would have wiped the smile off his face. Presumably he was in some weird kind of shock.

'It's not that simple,' Adam said. He had just started to explain to his son about the apparently random way in which he was sometimes invisible, sometimes in visible form; sometimes able to speak to people down in the world, and then sometimes not – when the front doorbell rang. Matilda had arrived, flushed from her journey from Soho. She ran to her mother and enfolded her in a long hug. They wept together, while Walter stood by with a glass of wine he'd poured for her. More hugs with Abby, then she eventually sat down. She drained her glass in a single gulp. Adam and Leo kept schtum, watching.

'What happened?' she asked.

Serena was beyond words, so Walter took charge. 'We don't quite know,' he said. 'Leo was driving that new electric car of his and he somehow smashed into a lorry in the opposite lane. His vehicle was a total write-off. He was killed instantly.'

'It's coming back to me,' Leo said, looking over at his father. 'I was overtaking. On a long bend. But I could see clearly. Then suddenly there was, yes, this big lorry coming from the other direction. I jammed the brakes on but I didn't slow down. Dad, *I didn't slow down*. Something was wrong with the brakes. They'd been a bit soft, but nothing I didn't think a service wouldn't sort out....'

Down in the room, Matty was sobbing. 'But Leo was a sensible driver,' she was saying.

'Was he?' said Walter. 'Not when I was with him.'

'Walter!' Serena warned.

'I'm sorry, but it's the truth. He drove like the proverbial bat out of hell.'

'That's not fair,' Matty said. 'He was fast, but always careful. He totally understood cars.'

'He did,' Leo agreed.

'He even did that advanced driving course,' Matty continued. 'That police drivers do. Somebody sabotaged the car, Mum. Somebody killed Leo, just like they killed Daddy.'

'Now come on,' Walter said. 'Let's not get hysterical here.'

'Hysterical! I've just lost my brother... and my father.'

'*Could* it have been sabotage?' Adam asked his son. 'You can fiddle with brakes, can't you? Cut leads or something.'

'Lines,' Leo replied, correcting him. 'You wouldn't really cut them. Or if you did the driver would know about it pretty much straight away. I guess you could drill small holes in them so the brake fluid slowly drained off. That might have explained why they felt soft. But there's a warning light that should come on to prevent that. Anyway, why would anyone want to kill *me*?'

'A very good question, Leo.'

'The plain, if unfortunate truth,' Walter was saying, 'is that Leo has had an accident and your father killed himself. It's all very shocking and sad, but–'

'Daddy didn't kill himself,' Matilda interrupted.

'Matilda, we've been over this,' Serena said.

'You may have "been over" this, but you don't know, do you?'

'Your mother and I were at the inquest,' Walter said. 'The coroner reached a clear verdict. Suicide.'

'You think what you like.'

'I'm afraid there was no question about it.'

There was silence. Matilda sat stony faced.

'She hates Walter,' Leo said. 'With a vengeance.'

'She did say he was a prize plonker,' Adam agreed.

'She's right about that. First prize in the annual plonker parade.'

Walter was speaking again, attempting to pour oil on troubled waters and failing. 'And now this is even harder to face. Leo, a young man in the prime of life, soon to be married to Abby here. It's heartbreaking, but with the best will in the world, I don't think anybody could countenance foul play.'

'Foul play?' said Matty. 'What's that?'

'It's an expression for… murder, darling,' Serena explained.

'Fowl play,' Matty repeated, then laughed wildly as she made the noise of hens clucking. 'If it was "fowl play", Walter, maybe that was because whoever murdered Daddy realised that Leo had sussed them out.' She ended with a long cock crow, which Walter ignored.

'Matty, darling, please,' Serena said. 'Stop being silly. Nobody murdered Daddy.'

'I don't know who did it, but I know it happened.'

'This is my fault,' Adam said to Leo. 'She knows because I told her.'

'You told her, what, that…?'

'I didn't kill myself, yes.'

'When?'

Adam explained about his visit. 'She actually never thought I had,' he said.

'Nor did I, Dad.'

'Not unless I managed to do it in a trance. Surely I would have remembered if I'd felt so despairing that I'd had to go into my garage and set up a hose, complete with special adapter and everything. Apart from anything else, it's just not my style. I've had a few disappointments recently. But I basically loved my life.'

For a moment Adam paused, doubting himself. Had he in fact done himself in, and all this frantic looking for his murderer was just part of a massive state of denial? Had he fixed up that hose himself? No, no, no – and then again no.

'That's what I said to Abby,' Leo said. 'Dad loves life; he's always on the go. Abby's argument was that energetic people were also the kind who could kill themselves. That despair is the other side of the coin of great activity and passion. Grandma didn't agree with me either. She was adamant, in that way she is sometimes. "The fact is," he mimicked Patricia's cut-glass accent, "the police and the inquest have determined..." I had to face both of them...'

'What, Grandma and Abby...?'

'No, Grandma and her annoying carer, parroting away.'

'The carer thought I'd killed myself? Which one?'

'The interfering Polish one who doesn't believe in climate change.'

'Jadwiga?'

'Her, yes. Granny loves her. God knows why.'

'Because she behaves like a servant,' Adam said dryly. 'While most of the others have delusions of grandeur. Or at least of basic equality.'

They were laughing together now, father and son, in their parallel dimension. But neither the noise, nor the mood, carried across to the room in the real world, where Matilda had now moved on to positing suspects for the murders of her father and brother.

'You can't just start casting wild aspersions against people, Matty,' Serena was saying. 'None of us know this Rod character.'

'It's actually offensive,' Walter added, 'to say that because he was once a marine he would know how to kill Adam.'

'Well, he would,' Matilda riposted. 'That's what they learn in the army, isn't it?'

'The marines aren't the army.'

'They're all professional killers.'

'So what exactly is his motive supposed to be, Matilda?' Walter had topped his glass up to the brim with Rioja and was now standing like the counsel for the prosecution in a courtroom; or more likely, some bogus legal inquisitor on daytime TV. Rod's motive, Matilda replied, was the same as

Julie's. With Adam out of the way, they would get Fallowfields all to themselves, together with whatever Adam had left Julie in his will, which had to be a lot, quite apart from the life insurance.

'I hate to disillusion you, Matilda.' Walter's features were triumphantly smug. 'But life insurance companies don't pay out on suicide.'

'No?' Matilda looked only momentarily deflated. 'Well, he and Julie still get all the other stuff, don't they? So he goes from being a painter-decorator living in a houseboat on the canal by the sewage works in Tempelsham to lord of the manor in one bound.'

'How do you know he lives on a houseboat?' Walter asked. 'Or even where it is.'

'I have my sources.'

'Did you tell her?' Leo asked Adam.

'I didn't know he did.'

'I must have done.' Leo chuckled.

'You knew about Rod as well?'

''Fraid so. Everyone did, Dad. I was actually planning to tell you. I just didn't know how to do it.'

'I really think this is a most unlikely scenario, darling,' Serena was saying, across the room. 'I think Walter's right. You can't go around making accusations about people you barely know. I mean, Julie–'

'Mummy, why do you always persist in seeing the good in people? Julie is an evil scheming bitch.'

Serena was laughing. 'That's a little harsh, darling.'

'How can you say that? When she ruined your life...'

'Don't be silly. Your father and I grew apart, that's all. Our split was as much my fault as his.'

'You didn't used to say that, Mum.'

'I'm not Julie's greatest fan, as you know,' Walter cut in, 'but come on, she isn't a murderer. This whole idea is preposterous. If what she wanted was to be with Rod rather than Adam there is a perfectly civilised way of organising that that doesn't involve killing people, like something off a second-rate Netflix series. You tell your partner you no longer want to be with them, and then you separate. In due course, if you want one, you get a divorce.'

'The point is,' Matilda returned, scornfully, even as she misquoted him, 'if Julie had followed that "civilised procedure" she wouldn't have got the house. Would she, Mummy? Or anything like so much money. There's no way Daddy would have let her stay in Fallowfields with some handyman shag. It's his house. He designed it.'

'So where does Leo fit into this analysis of yours?' Walter asked. 'Were Julie and Rod behind his death too? And if so, why?'

'I told you. Leo found something out. So they had to kill him as well.'

'Don't be ridiculous,' Walter scoffed.

'I'm not being ridiculous.' Matilda was sobbing again.

'Oh, Matty, darling,' said Serena, going to her. She held her tight and stroked her hair, looking angrily over at Walter.

Eventually Matilda looked up, eyes gleaming with tears. 'I don't believe it was an accident. I'm sorry. I just don't think it was.'

CHAPTER EIGHTEEN

'Do *you* think it was an accident?' Adam asked Leo, beckoning him away from the disputatious family group, through the glass doors, and into the front living room, whose bay window looked out on the quiet, gently sloping street outside.

'I don't know,' his son replied. 'It was an accident, obviously, if I smashed into this juggernaut...'

'But the brakes?' Adam said, pushing the doors gently to behind them, more for their benefit than anything else, as the others couldn't see or hear them. 'They felt soft, you said. How does that feel anyway?'

'It's like, spongy. You have to jam your foot right down on the floor to slow down.'

'So you seriously think someone fiddled with them?'

'I don't know. But I don't see how else–'

'D'you think Matty could be right?' Adam interrupted. 'That because you'd sussed it out, realised my death wasn't a suicide, my murderer felt they had to eliminate you?'

'But I hadn't sussed anything out, Dad. For certain. I just

wasn't convinced that you'd killed yourself. It wasn't as if I was going around telling everyone that's what I thought...'

'Who did you tell?'

Leo couldn't exactly remember. Abby, obviously. His mother. Granny Patricia, as he'd said.

'Not Julie?'

'No. But then I suppose Granny is hardly known for keeping stuff to herself, is she? And she talks to Julie pretty regularly.'

'Who else might she have spoken to?'

'Matty, obviously. Claire maybe.'

'Claire,' Adam repeated, thoughtfully.

'You don't seriously think that Claire would have... done anything to you. Dan possibly. Let's face it, he's never liked you. Or me, to be fair.'

'Who does he like?'

'Himself.' Leo was laughing. 'Actually, I'm not sure he even likes himself that much.'

Adam explained about 'Survivor takes all'. 'At the time, it seemed fair enough. Keep the money strictly in the family and all that. But now, even though at one level it seems ridiculous, I can't help wondering...'

'Why don't we go and check them out?' Leo suggested.

'What? Who?'

'Aunt Claire. And Danny boy. In their house. Right now.'

Wasn't this one of the advantages of being a ghost? he went on. That you could descend on anyone, anywhere, and just watch. 'And nobody even knows you're there...'

Adam felt inspired by his son, as go-getting as his sister when he wanted to be. But did he have any idea, he asked him, how a ghost did this? Just turned up somewhere.

'No,' said Leo with a grin. 'But they do, don't they?'

Adam laughed at his certainty. He explained how you put your hands together, visualised your destination and hopefully that would get you there. 'Can you remember what Claire's front room looks like?' he asked.

'I can see it in my mind's eye,' Leo said. 'But I've no idea what's actually in it. Armchairs, couches?'

'Yellow and black, ugly check pattern.'

'Oh yes. Then there's that child's rocking horse in one corner that they got for Maya but she never uses.'

'Brilliant. Focus on that.'

So they were there. Together. Standing right by the rocking horse in the middle of the noisy living room. Claire and Dan were hosting a dinner party. George Ezra was riding shotgun on the Sonos sound system and ten-year-old Maya was handing round crisps, picking up compliments for her star-spangled black leggings. Dan was playing a clumsy *mein host* with the sparkling wine, while Claire was up the kitchen end of their big, open-plan space, putting the final touch to the starters, some fancy smoked eel and seaweed arrangement, helped by one of the female guests.

'They don't yet know, do they?' Leo said. 'About me.'

'Doesn't look like it, does it?'

'Should we tell them? You and me. Right now.'

Adam shook his head. 'It's all too noisy. There's no place for spooks like us. We wouldn't get through to them.'

'Wouldn't we?'

'Trust me, no. You can only really talk to people, humans, down there, when they're alone.'

'Why?'

'I've no idea. But that's what I've found.'

Leo shrugged. 'Really? If we appeared now, think of the impact we'd make.'

'But imagine if we could, did. They would all have witnessed us. Whereas I suppose that if ghosts can only appear when people are alone, in the small hours maybe, a bit scared, doubting what they see, the mystery remains. Perhaps that's why.'

Leo, typically, wasn't taking advice. 'I'm dead!' he cried,

suddenly, zooming around the room, waving his arms like a banshee. 'Dead, dead, dead!'

But nobody turned a hair.

Eventually he calmed down.

'I guess you're right,' he said, returning to his father a bit sheepishly.

Even though Claire had done all the cooking, Dan was very much in charge. Now he was telling his guests where to sit at the long, reclaimed timber table; then, embarrassingly, changing his mind and putting beardy Garry next to tall, blonde Sasha after all.

'Can't have couples sitting together, can we?' he said. 'Otherwise they just talk about the drains.'

'The drains!' shrieked Sasha.

'Or their sex lives,' said Garry. 'Even worse.'

'Garry!' said Gita, a small, round-faced woman who was clearly his partner. Her deep brown skin was set off nicely by a bright pink trouser suit.

But all Dan's careful efforts to create social harmony were in vain, because no sooner had they got stuck in to their smoked eel, with many a compliment to the chef, than a noisy argument had broken out: about schools again. Adam realised that the guests were all parents of kids at Maya's primary and were concerned about where their Year 5 darlings might apply to go next, a decision that appeared to be imminent. There was Robin's Lane, the big mixed-sex comp in Tempelsham, and then a smaller grammar down the road in Partelsfield. Although if Claire had her way, Dan said, looking dangerously at his wife, Maya probably wouldn't be going to either of them; she was seriously looking at the fee-paying Heathcote House, up on the hill, where the yummy mummies in huge SUVs jostled at teatime and it didn't matter what catchment area you were in.

After a short, stunned silence, Claire was defending herself – 'it's only a possibility' – and then all hell had broken loose. Dan had an ally in Sasha, who was as uncompromising about state provision as he; but Claire found an unexpected supporter in Garry, which was funny because he was a builder with a local accent, not the uni-educated tones of the others. If he had the money, he said, or could pull in enough effing work to make the money, he would send Darren private, of course he would. 'No-brainer, mate!'

Just as Garry had moved on to tease Sasha about her regular trips to the White Duck in Tempelsham, not to mention recent holidays to Minorca and Madagascar, the landline rang.

Claire covered the receiver with a hand. 'My mother,' she mouthed, backing away. 'Won't be a moment.'

The others continued, rather less enthusiastically without their hostess as the victimised focus. Only Gita spotted Claire's expression crumple as she received the news that was coming down the line.

'I'm sorry,' Claire announced, walking back to the table, face blank with shock. 'There's been a horrid accident. My nephew, Leo, has been in a car crash.'

'Serious?' asked Dan.

'He's dead.'

'You're fucking joking me!' said Garry.

The party broke up. No, no, please, said the guests, we'll be fine. I'm sure you need to go over there, or be on your own. Nobody knew what to say. Coats were fetched, the front door banged, the hosts were alone with an untouched main course.

'All that food wasted,' said Dan.

'Dan! How can you even think that, let alone say it?'

Dan realised he'd gone too far. He walked over and put his arm round his wife, like a highly-trained robot acting in sympathy mode. 'First your brother,' he said, 'now this.'

'I can't get my head around it,' Claire muttered, looking up at him with shining eyes. 'Poor Leo. And Abby. What about her?' Then: 'I should go over to Mum's.'

'What about Serena? Shouldn't you call her?'

'Maybe tomorrow. She's got Walter. And Matty presumably. She'll have her hands full. Mum sounded distraught.'

'Haven't you had too much to drink to drive? You've been on the wine since five thirty. Plus two hefty gin and tonics and a negroni.'

'If she's not going to Granny's, perhaps we should,' Leo said, after Claire had reluctantly agreed that neither she nor Dan were in a fit state to drive the fifteen miles to Larks Hill.

How sweet Leo was, Adam thought. Looking out for his old grandmother even though he was no longer alive. They had always had a special bond, Patricia and Leo, from the days when he'd been a cheery, fat-faced little baby, and Patricia would take him for long weekends while Adam and Serena swanned off to a nice gastro-pub in North Norfolk or wherever took their fancy. Before Matilda had come along they had been good at that, keeping the romance going: starter, main course, pudding, coffee, digestif, sex. It was only later they had let that happy routine slip.

Patricia was in her sitting room, still on her landline, even though it was late. Her carer hovered in the background.

'Well, Jadwiga,' she was saying, putting the receiver down with a deep, sad sigh. 'I think I've done all I can for one evening. Spoken to everyone who needs to know.'

'Yes, madam. Time for rest now.'

Patricia sat forward, eyes bright. 'My best *what*?'

'TIME... FOR... REST... NOW,' the carer repeated, loudly, slowly, impeccably patient.

'If you say so,' Patricia replied, sinking back. 'Though I hardly think I'm going to sleep tonight.'

'You must try, madam. Shall I mix you your special sleepy drink?'

'Actually, you could tonight, Jadwiga. That would be kind.'

As Jadwiga ushered Patricia out of the room, and along the corridor towards the stairs and bed, Leo raised his eyebrows at his dad. 'I spoke to her about all this sort of thing last week,' he said.

'All what sort of thing?'

'This controlling stuff. On the one hand, the "special sleepy drinks", to knock her out. On the other, visits to town, to shop and have little lunches in Tempelsham. Whatever suits Jadwiga, basically.'

'You spoke to Granny?'

'No, to Jadwiga. Aunt Claire doesn't see the problem. She thinks Jadwiga is being kind. But I thought it was best to tackle her directly. Warn her off before she ends up with power of attorney or something.'

'How on earth is that going to happen?'

'Because Jadwiga is on a mission, Dad. She often has Granny's paperwork out. Helping her tidy her files, is what Granny says. But it's more than that. I've seen her will out on the table in the dining room.'

'Her *will*. Seriously?'

'Yes,' Leo insisted. 'And they went to her solicitor's together, in Tempelsham. Shortly after you died.'

'How do you know that?'

'Granny told me.'

'But surely Jadwiga's just accompanying her, as she always does, while Granny does her stuff.'

'Is she? When I asked Granny about that trip she gave me this big wink. "Redrafting," she said. "Now that Adam's gone." Then: "You two haven't come out of it too badly." I thought she meant me and Matty, but then I realised she was talking about me and Jadwiga.'

'No!'

'Yes. Jadwiga made herself scarce when she said that. So I asked Granny directly whether she really had left Jadwiga anything. D'you know what she said? "A little something." Then she gave me one of her naughty smiles. "Actually, rather a large something," she said.'

'Did you tell Aunt Claire?'

'Yes. She didn't think Granny meant anything much by it. She thinks, "rather a large something" is a grand, tops. For her loyal carer's devoted service. I'm not so sure. The trouble is, Aunt Claire is hoodwinked by Jadwiga too. Because Jadwiga does everything for Granny, so Aunt Claire is, like, freed up, isn't she? So she refuses to think badly of her. Actually, I'd been planning to go down and talk to her about it all face to face this weekend. With Matilda.'

'You told her too?'

'Why wouldn't I? It's her inheritance as well.'

What a bossy meddler his son could be, Adam thought. But he'd always liked things his way. 'Bit late for a visit now,' he said.

'Unless I could talk to her like this. Would that be possible? Or you could. On my behalf.'

'I've already spoken with Claire,' Adam said. 'Why don't you try?' He smiled over at his son. 'You might as well get some practice in while I'm with you.'

CHAPTER NINETEEN

The evening clearly hadn't ended well for Dan and Claire. Downstairs, the debris of the dinner party remained uncleared; upstairs, they had passed out in separate bedrooms. Dan was in the king size in the master; Claire in the queen size in the spare room.

Adam and Leo stood on either side of Claire's bed.

'Now what?' Leo asked.

'Try waking her up.'

'But how do I know she can see me?'

'You don't. But go carefully, because if she can, she's going to be freaked out.'

'Obviously,' said Leo. 'I'll try not to be too spooky,' he added, with that familiar grin.

He did a little dance around the room, waving his ghostly arms madly. Irrepressible lad, he was; even now.

He leant over the bed. 'Aunt Claire,' he called, softly.

There was no reaction.

'Aunt Claire,' he repeated, more loudly.

'Gently does it,' said Adam.

'And she won't be able to see *you*?'

Adam shrugged. 'I don't know. She could before, but then again–'

'Aunt… CLAIRE!' Leo shouted.

'Steady on!'

'She's not reacting.'

Adam thought fast. What was it that had worked for him?

'Try touching her,' he said.

'Really? Aunt Claire?'

'You're a ghost, Leo. It's fine.'

'It feels weird. Okay, here goes.'

Leo went over, sat down on the edge of the bed and reached out for one of Claire's sprawled hands. Then he turned and looked back at Adam.

'Can't get a grip. It's like Abby. My fingers are slipping through.'

Maybe, Adam thought, it was because there were two of them in the room. He would go downstairs for a bit, while Leo tried by himself. But this didn't work either. After five minutes, Leo appeared at the top of the stairs. 'No dice,' he said. 'I'm not getting through to her.'

'Shit,' Adam said. Perhaps he had spoilt things for Leo by talking to his sister already. Maybe if she'd seen her brother, she couldn't see her nephew. Or perhaps it was just simply that she wanted to see *him* more than Leo. Perhaps it was the desire of the particular human, or at least their receptiveness to your visit, that made the contact happen. But in that case why had he had such problems getting through to Eva?

'Can I put the light on?' Leo said. 'I can hardly see where I'm going.'

'Don't do that. It might wake them.'

'Wouldn't that be a good thing? If either of them woke up, maybe we'd have better luck.'

Leo found the switch. Adam wondered if his fingers would have any traction, but it seemed that with this at least they did.

The big open-plan kitchen-dining-living area was flooded with light. Father and son sat there together for a minute, half-expecting a noise from upstairs. None came. The unhappy couple were sleeping soundly.

'Let me have a go,' Adam said. Someone had to warn his sister about Jadwiga. But when he went upstairs and found her, he was unable to rouse her either.

'Maybe we should go to Mummy's,' Leo said. 'You never know, I might have more luck with her. Getting through. Being her son and everything.'

'I suppose it's worth a try,' Adam said, uncertain. But Leo had already put his hands together in the namaste.

In the house in Tufnell Park, Serena was still up. Walter and Matty had taken their differences upstairs, it seemed, and Serena was sorting out her kitchen. This was how she always behaved when she was upset. She would get on with some mindless task. She was never one to sit hopelessly and stare.

She lived up to her name, Serena. Always had done. None of that edgy neurotic energy that Julie had. She exuded calm. Prickly, pompous, incompetent Walter was lucky to have her. Not for the first time Adam found himself wondering why he had ever allowed himself to be tempted away to that crazy, lust-filled drama that Julie had dangled before him. It had been fun, of course it had been fun, but when the madness was over, and he realised what he held in his hands, he had been filled with regret, even if he hadn't allowed himself to admit it for years. And now the crazy bitch, not content with ruining his life, had murdered him. Or so it seemed. What kind of payback was that?

Leo was standing watching his mother with the look of love. Dear Leo. Adam had meted out such shit to him over the years and it had never seemed to affect him. He had abandoned the family when Leo was just fifteen, the worst possible time, and how had Leo repaid him? By flipping out; by taking drugs; by harming himself; by truancy; even by a critical or sarcastic attitude towards his dear papa? Not a bit of it. Leo had just ploughed on, a model if somewhat dogged pupil, the man in the middle, the friend of all, the upbeat, dutiful son. He had risen above his circumstances and maybe for that Adam had Serena to thank, because she too was possessed of that imperturbable niceness. She would go to her grave thinking the best of people, doing her bit, never boasting or striking attitudes about the good things she did, all the time, routinely.

His son turned to him with that smile of his, still somehow preserved into this afterlife, or semi-afterlife, or whatever it was that they were in now.

'Okay,' he asked, 'what do I say?'

'Whatever you like, Leo. I'll just watch.'

'How come she's going to hear what I'm going to say in a minute and she doesn't hear this?'

'We don't know that she is going to hear what you're going to say in a minute, do we? But it's when it's addressed to her, directly, that it seems to work. If it doesn't, I'll back away into the other room.'

'Okay, let's give it a try.' Leo giggled nervously, then tiptoed stagily towards his mother (always the clown). 'Hi, Mum.'

Serena turned. Then she stepped sharply back, her hand over her mouth in silent shock.

'Good... h-heavens!' she stuttered eventually. 'Leo...'

'So you can see me?'

'Are you... alive?' For a moment there was a desperate inflection of hope in her voice, a pleading look in her large, ever-thoughtful brown eyes. But her son was shaking his ghostly hologram of a head.

'I had an accident,' he replied.

'I know, darling. The police have been.'

'I didn't make it, Mum. Sorry.'

Serena was staring at him. 'So where… where… where… are you?' she managed finally.

Leo grinned. 'I'm on "the other side". Apparently.'

'The other…?'

'Side, yes. You know, the afterlife or whatever. Dad's here too. I didn't even have to look for him. It was like I came round and there he was. Right in front of me.'

'Your dad is… there too?'

'Yes.'

'Adam?'

'Yes.'

Serena was shaking her head, very slowly, trying, visibly, to take all this in. 'But where exactly *are* you?' she repeated.

'Some netherworld or something, Dad says. It feels totally normal, to be honest. Like I'm still myself, you know. Just without a body. Actually, it's quite cool. I can float around. Go through walls and stuff.'

'Can I speak to your father, Leo? Just briefly, please.'

In the background, Adam was shaking his head. Leo had got through to Serena just fine. He didn't want to risk messing up that connection by trying to join in. There was too much at stake.

'What's that, Dad?'

Adam waved a single finger, back and forth in a firm 'no' gesture. 'Lay-ter,' he mouthed.

'He says he'll speak to you later.'

'Claire,' Adam added, with meaning.

'Claire,' Leo repeated slowly. 'Oh right, yes, Claire. Mummy, this is the thing. You need to go and talk to Claire for us. Because Dad spoke to her once but neither of us can get through to her again for some reason.'

'Your father's already spoken to Claire?' Serena sounded incredulous.

'Yes.'

'When?'

'I don't know. A day or two ago maybe.'

'He's been dead for eight weeks!'

Leo shrugged.

'How?' Serena asked.

'Like this,' Leo said. 'A visit. Or a visitation, as Dad calls it.' He explained their concerns about Patricia's will and Jadwiga.

'You want me to talk to Claire about all this?' Serena asked, when he'd finished.

Leo was looking over at Adam, who was nodding and making thumbs-up gestures. 'Yes, yes, we do,' he said.

Adam leant forward towards his son. 'Tell her,' he said slowly. 'That... it... might... even... impact... on... why... we're... here.'

Leo repeated his father's words.

'What are you saying?' Serena asked. 'That Patricia's carer has got something to do with... with what's happened to you and your father?'

Leo turned to Adam. 'What are we saying, Dad?'

For a bright young man, Leo could be a bit obtuse sometimes. 'Exactly that, yes,' Adam replied, sotto voce. 'Someone killed us... well, definitely me... and we're keeping all options open. We don't want any more victims, do we?'

'Okay, tell your father I'll go and see Claire,' Serena told her son, after he'd repeated that too. 'If not tomorrow, the next day.'

'Tomorrow,' Adam insisted. 'We need to get on with this.'

'He says you need to go tomorrow,' Leo echoed.

Serena laughed. 'Crusty old git. Still bossing me about. Even from the other side.' She rolled her eyes. 'Okay, I'll go tomorrow. Why can't he just speak to me now?'

'I can't risk it,' Adam said.

'He doesn't want to risk it,' Leo repeated.

'Risk what?' Serena asked.

'It's complicated,' Adam said.

Leo repeated that too, and there was more kerfuffle, as Adam tried, through Leo, to pin his ex-wife down to a time for her visit. He was just getting Leo to explain that he might sit in and watch, when the kitchen door pushed open and Matilda was there, in a nightie, looking a bit like a ghost herself.

'Who are you talking to, Mummy?'

Serena span round. 'Matty! I thought you were asleep. I was just… chatting away… thinking aloud…'

Matilda didn't look convinced.

'Are you okay, Mummy?'

'Who else would I be talking to?'

'Daddy, maybe.'

'Don't be silly, darling. Daddy's dead.'

Adam watched the pair of them agog. Was Matilda about to confess to her mother about his visit to her? She had told Eva easily enough, after all. But no. She looked back at Serena and stayed schtum.

'I know,' she replied. 'And Leo. It's so hard to take in.'

She went to her mother and gave her a long hug.

'And Leo,' Serena repeated, breaking down into sobs. He daughter held her tight and comforted her.

'It's all right, Mum,' she said, stroking her hair.

'It's *not* all right,' Serena half-squealed. 'It's not all right,' she repeated, sobbing some more. For a moment, Adam thought she was going to tell her daughter what had just happened. But no. Recovering herself she looked out over the empty kitchen, eyes like blank pools. Her son had retreated. Back into the netherworld. She seemed to have understood that without even saying goodbye.

When Matilda went up to bed she shook her head sadly, and followed.

'Why didn't you try and show yourself to Matilda?' Adam asked his son.

'She's sensitive. I wasn't sure she could handle it. She's freaked out enough as it is.'

Adam decided not to tell him that of the three people he'd spoken to so far, his sister had been the easiest and most accepting.

'Now what?' asked Leo. 'Do we sleep too?'

Adam explained what he'd done so far, in resting ghost mode.

'So it's just like, we hang?'

'That's quite a good word for it. You hang.'

'Shall we hang in my old room, then? Since we're here. You've really never seen my old room, have you, Dad?'

'Not since you were about fifteen, no.'

Leo laughed. 'It's changed a bit since then. But I'd love you to see it.'

CHAPTER TWENTY

Claire didn't seem at all surprised that Serena had made a special journey out to see her in the sticks, just forty-eight hours after her son had been killed in a road accident.

'Oh darling,' she said, throwing her arms around her. 'I'm so very, very sorry about Leo. But I'm so glad you feel you can come... here.'

'Thank you,' said Serena, hugging her back, planting an affectionate kiss on her lower left cheek.

They stood there, holding each other, for a good twenty seconds.

Dan, in the background, was doing his best to behave like a human being. 'Sorry for your loss,' he said clunkily as they parted, holding out his hand for the required shake.

Claire made fresh coffee in a cafetière and the two women settled at the table in her sunny kitchen. They talked about the terrible shock of Leo's death; then, after some more tears, and another long hug between Claire and her original sister-in-law, about what Serena was planning for the funeral; the inquest that might be needed, it being a fatal road accident; how Abby and Matilda were taking it all...

'I keep thinking Mum's about to say something,' Leo said to Adam. 'About you and me, visiting.'

'She'll get to it,' Adam reassured him. He knew Serena. She never put her cards on the table straight away.

Sure enough: 'Claire,' Serena said eventually. 'There's one thing I did want to ask you.'

'Here we go,' said Leo. 'Finally.'

'It's about Patricia,' Serena went on. 'Possibly a little on the personal side. But it concerns Leo, and Matty, so...'

'Fire away.'

Serena started to relay their concerns about Jadwiga.

'You've got absolutely no worries there,' Claire insisted. 'Jadwiga's a saintly woman. She does everything for Mum. She even insists on calling her "madam", which Mum grumbles about but secretly loves.'

'The thing is,' Serena went on, 'Leo told me...' there was a gulp while she got control of herself, 'this was just before he died... that he'd been round there, and he'd seen that Jadwiga had been looking at the will. The latest one, reflecting Adam's death. Under the guise of helping Patricia with her paperwork...'

'Don't be ridiculous!' Claire replied. 'She was probably just helping Mum tidy up.'

'They went to the solicitor's together. In Tempelsham. Shortly after Adam died, apparently.'

'That's what she does. Takes Mum to her appointments. I very much doubt that she went into Hemal's office with her. She'd have sat outside, or gone to a café.'

'Hemal being the solicitor?'

'Hemal Kumar, yes. She deals with all Mum's bits and pieces.'

'Leo also said that Patricia had said something to him about the will. While Jadwiga was there. She winked, apparently, and said, "You two haven't come out of it too badly".'

'She'd have meant Leo and Matilda, Serena.'

'D'you think?'

'Of course! She's hardly going to tell her carer that she's a beneficiary in front of Leo. I know she loves playing games with us, but even so...'

Serena was looking back at her sister-in-law. Unless she was about to admit to Leo's ghostly visitation, there was no way she could put his deeper suspicions to her, was there?

'Matilda was worried that she might have had something to do with the deaths,' she said, after a few moments. 'Adam's and Leo's.'

'*Jadwiga* might have done?'

'Yes.'

'How, exactly?' Claire looked genuinely gobsmacked. 'I'm sure Matty's very upset about all this,' she went on. 'Her father and brother. I do understand, it's beyond shocking. But no. Even if Jadwiga had got Mummy to leave her a shedload of money, it's preposterous to think... I mean, whatever happened to Adam, why would Jadwiga have been involved? As for Leo, that was just an accident. As Dan says, four people die on the roads every day in this country. Something like seventy are seriously injured. It's not something we like to think about, but it happens. I've always worried about Leo's driving. He just can't help himself, the boy racer...'

'I know,' Serena agreed. She was shaking her head, her eyes blank, as if struggling to contain the memory. 'He always had his reckless side. Even when he was just a child with a push bike, he used to get up to the craziest stunts. Riding "no hands". Wheelies. All that. And then there was the motorcycle phase, before his Dad bribed him out of it–'

'Honestly, Serena,' Claire cut in. 'I think you can put any thoughts about Jadwiga being in any way suspicious to one side. How would she even get access to Adam? Let alone Leo who lives miles away. What are you saying? That she somehow got down to London, an unfamiliar city, made her way out by public transport to Leo's flat in Hendon, and then did something quite detailed and difficult to his electric car while his back was turned. On the street, presumably, with passers-by.'

'I'm glad I was able to raise it,' Serena replied. 'I'm sure Matilda will be reassured.'

'Is that it?' said Leo to Adam. 'She's going to pretend this was Matilda's concern. Not mention us.'

'She doesn't want Claire thinking she's crazy, I expect,' said Adam.

'But she knows you paid Claire a visit.'

'Only if she believed you, Leo. Claire hasn't said anything about that, has she? Doesn't want Serena thinking *she's* crazy.'

'This is so ridiculous,' Leo said. 'Shouldn't we say something?'

'How?'

'Or do something. Get the frigging ball rolling with these two. Why don't I push that cafetière over?'

'That's a bit aggressive.'

'I don't care.'

'It might not even work.'

'Let's see, shall we?'

Leo strode across the sunlit room to the kitchen table. He walked round the far side and stood between his mother and his aunt, casting, for Adam, a shadow over the table and the lovely limestone floor. It didn't seem to be a shadow that either of the two women saw, as Claire held Serena's hand as she sobbed again about Leo.

'I can't believe it. My poor boy. He was just getting going in life. With Abby and everything. Their sweet little flat. It seems so very unfair...'

'Not now, Leo,' Adam said, as his son held up his hand, theatrically, ready to strike. 'Your mother's crying.'

'About me, yes! All the more reason I should assert myself.'

Leo thrust his palm down towards the half-full cafetière. It wasn't going to be pretty, Adam thought. Coffee and grounds everywhere. Maybe it would topple to the floor and the glass would smash.

But Leo's hand passed straight through it.

'Shit cakes!' he cried, as his arm swept back up again. 'Did you see that, Dad? What do I have to do to engage?'

He tried again.

Nothing.

'Top up?' Claire asked Serena, as she reached out for the immobile cafetière.

'Thank you, Claire. Actually, I will. It's been so good to talk about all this. Walter and Leo never quite saw eye to eye, so it's harder with him, although he's obviously been very sympathetic and supportive.'

'Obviously,' said Claire.

'Bloody hell I'm frustrated,' said Leo. 'What's wrong? I could speak to Mummy last night all right.'

'Maybe you can't now because you did then. It seems to be very random, this accessibility. I did warn you.'

'But *you* didn't speak to her. You should be able to get through. Shouldn't you?'

Adam shrugged. 'I don't know.'

'And what about me and Aunt Claire? I've not spoken to *her* yet. Why don't I get a go with her?'

Adam was as flummoxed as his son. What worked and what didn't in relating to the human world seemed to have got less clear rather than more. He stepped out through the sliding glass doors of the kitchen and into Claire's sunny garden. Leo followed.

'We don't actually need her,' he said, after a few moments. 'Why don't we visit Granny ourselves, see what Jadwiga is or isn't up to?'

'D'you seriously think it's possible?' Adam replied. 'That Jadwiga could have something to do with your accident?'

'It seems unlikely, doesn't it. On the other hand, her boyfriend is a car mechanic.'

'Her boyfriend is a car mechanic? You're joking.'

Leo nodded. 'Yep. Omar. Turkish guy. He works in that Volkswagen dealership outside Tempelsham.'

'How on earth d'you know that?'

'I chat to her, you know. When I go up there. Listen and learn, that's me.'

A car mechanic who knew not only how to sabotage brakes, but also how to fake a carbon monoxide poisoning. Was that too improbable? Surely yes, because what did it imply? Jadwiga and Omar setting the scene somehow in Julie's garage? Or maybe even Jadwiga and Omar working with Julie and Rod? The dream team! Adam's thoughts raced ahead with unlikely scenarios.

'It was weird, though,' Leo continued. 'Because I'm certain I jammed those brakes down hard. And the more I think about it, the more I think nothing happened. Otherwise, why wouldn't I have pulled back, behind the lorry I was trying to overtake? I was going fast, but that's the thing, so were they. So normally, in that situation, you brake hard, you slip back behind them. It can be a bit hairy, but...' He closed his eyes, as if the memory of the next frame of the film was too much to bear. 'That was it. Blackout.'

His eyes opened again. 'The next thing I knew I was coming to. And seeing you.'

'So you don't have any recollection of this lorry you supposedly hit?' Adam asked.

Leo was turning his head from side to side, very slowly. 'Nothing. Actually... hang on... no.... there was a cab. It was pale blue, big window, coming at me. The grille.'

'Anything else?' Adam asked, excited by this recall. 'A driver?'

'There were trees. We were on a bend. We were on a long bend and there were trees on both sides. There was nowhere for me to go. Except back.'

'But you were alone?'

'Yes. Why did you think I wasn't?'

'You said "we".'

Leo grinned. 'The royal "we", sorry. No, I was alone. Wanting to get home. I wouldn't have driven like that if Abby had been there.'

'Okay,' his father replied slowly. He was looking down the grassy slope towards Claire's lily pond, which was, amusingly enough, pretty much a direct copy of Patricia's, up at Larks Rise, only half the lilies were plastic. That had been Dan's brilliant idea. Claire had wanted lilies, as she'd had in her childhood. They didn't grow naturally in that deep shade. So Dan had bought fake ones; an ersatz replica of her happy memories.

'Whatever happened to you,' Adam went on, 'my death wasn't an accident. It was orchestrated by person or persons unknown. Which makes it all the more likely that your death wasn't an accident either.'

'Let's go there now,' said Leo. 'To Granny's. What's stopping us having a little nose around? We could have a sneaky look at Jadwiga's phone. See if there are any unlikely calls to family members.'

He raised a quizzical eyebrow. Death hadn't diminished him one bit.

CHAPTER TWENTY-ONE

As Adam and Leo floated down towards the lovely green demesne of Larks Hill, surrounded though it now was by the dreadful, unimaginative boxes of cheap new-build housing, they saw a familiar battered green Fiat Panda bowling up the long, steep, lime-tree-lined drive.

'Matilda!' said Leo. 'What's she doing here?'

'Come to console Granny maybe,' said Adam. 'Or be consoled. About you.'

Halfway up, on the bend, the car paused, and pulled in, to let a sleek silver Volvo V60 go past. Adam glimpsed a man at the wheel, heavy set, with thick dark specs, a woman with a dyed-looking blonde bob beside him.

'Who are they?' Leo asked.

'God knows. Some of Patricia's numerous visitors that she never lets on about. Even as she gives us grief for not visiting enough ourselves.'

Jadwiga stood at the top of the steps up to the beautiful brass-studded oak door. A murderer in a black dress? With that round, pink, smiley face it was hard to credit.

'Matilda, hello, this is a good time. Your grandmother is down from her rest.' Jadwiga moved towards her and put both hands on her lower left arm. 'I'm so sorry... for your loss. For Leo,' she added, as if a clarification were necessary.

'Thank you, Jadwiga.' Matilda looked up at her with her hurried, shy smile. 'That's kind of you. It's all been such a horrid shock.' She followed the carer through into the familiar hall, with its wooden panelling and worn black-and-white tiles.

'I imagine,' Jadwiga went on, 'so soon after your poor father's–'

'Quite,' said Matilda, cutting her off before she articulated the alleged nature of Adam's death. 'Is Granny in the yellow sitting room?' she asked.

'Yes. She's just been talking to some police officers. What they want, I do not know.'

'Despite listening at the keyhole,' Adam said, and Leo laughed.

'They have to report a death like this, don't they?' Matilda said. 'In this country, anyway.'

'Yes.' Jadwiga looked visibly relieved. 'And in Poland, too. That's it, of course.'

'But it isn't,' Adam said to his son. 'Because Patricia's not your immediate next of kin. The police would have gone to Serena.'

'So what do they want with Patricia?' Leo asked.

'Maybe they're suspicious about your death after all.'

'Or yours.'

'I doubt it,' Adam said. 'My case has been and gone. Anyway, you said Patricia was adamant that the inquest was right.'

'So she said. Though you can never entirely trust Granny, can you? She's always up to something.'

'Shall I bring you some tea?' Jadwiga was asking Matilda. 'Or coffee, would you like?'

'Actually, Jadwiga, coffee would hit the spot. I imagine Granny will have tea.'

'Herbal, yes. Madam only has coffee at breakfast time nowadays. It doesn't agree with her gut.'

'Was that your doing, Jadwiga, talking her out of it?'

'Any coffee drunk after two o'clock in the afternoon affects your night-time sleep. So when she keeps complaining to me about her insomnia, not to mention her sore tummy, I tell her that.'

'As well as offering her the famous "sleepy drink",' Leo added. 'Which gets Granny off nice and early so Jadwiga has time to chill out.'

'Look through the will, that sort of thing,' Adam joked (though he wasn't smiling).

Matilda followed Jadwiga down the hall, turning right at the end into Patricia's favourite little den, from which the sound of loud classical music rang out. It had always been called 'the yellow sitting room' though the sofas and chairs were a mixture of peach and pale blue, and the walls were papered with a pink, green and cream pattern of peonies.

Patricia looked up. 'Matilda, what a lovely surprise! Alexa, turn… the music… *orf…* please.' Funny to hear her accent, Adam thought. It struck him more clearly now that he was no longer there, beside her, in the flesh. His mother was from a previous age, really. If anyone should be dead and gone, it was her, not him. Once again, the sheer injustice of what had happened to him hit him hard. And as for Leo, a young man with his whole life ahead of him, that was beyond unfair.

Patricia shifted in her chair, as if to get up, another piece of old-world courtesy, long since abandoned by even the politest and most-refined of folk.

'Don't move, Granny.'

'You don't approve?' she cried, her eyes flashing. 'I've just turned her *orf*, for goodness' sake!'

'I said, "DON'T MOVE, Granny",' Matilda repeated loudly.

'No need to shout.' Patricia took in that she had misheard, but she certainly wasn't going to admit that or apologise. 'I wasn't *going* to move,' she said softly. Now she was shaking her head.

Slowly and with dismay. 'You poor love. Sit down. There, yes, on the chesterfield. You can shift those bits. Sorry, Jadwiga and I have been having a bit of a clear out. What a business, what a business. First your poor father... and now Leo. I've just had the police here, asking me questions, though what I'm supposed to say I have no idea. What's going on?'

'I wish I knew, Granny.'

'Did you see Jadwiga?'

'Yes. She let me in. She's bringing coffee.'

'Not for me!' Patricia cackled. 'I'm not allowed it after breakfast. Herbal tea all the way. But they have some lovely ones now. There's one from Waitrose called Digestif that Jadwiga's found, that I particularly like. It's got a kind of mint flavour. And rooibos, have you tried that?'

'Yes, Granny. You introduced me to it.'

'That was another of the carers that brought that one in. I can't remember her name. *Seth Effrikan.*' Patricia's mouth twisted downwards as she did a strange version of a South African accent that sounded almost Welsh. 'She was rather grand, I remember, fallen on hard times. I don't think she was quite cut out to be a carer. She was always telling me how many servants she'd had, back in *Seth Effrika.* I used to tell her she was talking to the wrong person. I've never had a servant in my life.'

'Since you were a child anyway.'

'That was a very long time ago. As I have no need to remind you. Anyway, I was a child. So they weren't *my* servants, were they?'

'And your carers, of course,' Matilda joked.

'Matilda, please. They're not servants.'

'Jadwiga calls you "madam".'

'She's Polish. They like that sort of thing. All the Eastern Europeans do. No need to make that face, dear, I'm talking from experience. To be honest, I don't mind it. You know where you stand.'

'On top, yes.'

'Do stop being so silly, Matilda. So how's your poor mother coping?'

'She's okay.'

'Is she?' Patricia gave her one of her famous beady looks.

'As okay as she can be,' Matilda said.

'You're all still in shock, I expect,' said Patricia. 'As you would be. Idiot boy. I always said he shouldn't drive those fast cars. There's a reason they have such high insurance premiums.'

'It wasn't fast, Granny. It was an electric Golf, actually quite sensible for Leo.'

'Electric. Well, there you are. They've only just invented them; I expect they're full of faults. I was reading in *The Times* about these huge, high-voltage batteries they have. Not safe, in my opinion. Imagine if you went through a deep puddle. Was he actually electrocuted? In the smash?'

'No, Granny. I don't think so.'

'Are you sure?'

'He ran into a lorry head first. It wouldn't have mattered what car he was driving.'

Patricia was shaking her head. 'Why didn't he see it? He was a good enough driver, wasn't he?'

'He was overtaking on a bend or something and he misjudged it.'

'On a bend!' Patricia scoffed. 'Philip was the same. Such a kind, reasonable man on his own two feet, but get him behind the wheel of a car and he was a terror. "Don't back seat drive, Patricia!" he used to shout. When for a start I was in the front seat, right next to him, and for seconds, it was often a matter of life and death. His terrible driving.'

There was silence, as if they were suddenly struck by the awful reality of what had happened. Neither Adam nor Leo said anything, both agog to hear what either of them would come up with next. Over the noisy birdsong outside the window, they could hear footsteps, clickety click, on the tiles of the corridor floor. The door pushed open and Jadwiga appeared with a tray.

'Coffee and green tea. You did want it black, you said, Matilda?'

'A little milk would be amazing if you had it. Actually, Jadwiga, if you could be bothered, could you hot it up, please?'

'Yes, madam.'

Jadwiga used 'madam' as a put down, Adam realised, watching her closely as she addressed her charge's granddaughter. Away from her mother, and her generation, Matty was more like her granny than perhaps she realised.

Jadwiga gave Patricia her tea and left the cafetière and cup on the tray. When she'd gone, Matty leant forward and pushed the gleaming chrome handle that drove the ring of wire netting down through the swirling dark liquid. She grinned as she filled her white bone china cup.

'Proper coffee,' she said.

Patricia was holding out her empty cup with a perky, questioning expression. 'Might I have a sip?'

'I thought you weren't allowed.'

'Only when *she's* watching. A little sip won't hurt me. The stuff she gives me at breakfast is instant anyway. And decaf. What's the point of that?'

'I'm not sure I should, Granny.'

'Don't be such a meanie. When you were a child, I kept you well supplied with orange juice. Juice, not squash. That was a treat in those days. There was a restaurant in Tempelsham that had it on the menu as a starter. Orange juice. One pound. You wouldn't get that now.'

Matilda laughed. 'Okay, then. Just a little one.'

Patricia took a long greedy gulp and sat back. 'Ah-h!' she sighed, savouring it. 'You can't beat proper coffee, can you?'

'No,' Matilda agreed. But she seemed distracted. 'Don't you think it's a bit strange, Granny, that Leo should have an accident now? Barely two months after Daddy "supposedly" killed himself.'

'One thing you learn when you get to my age, darling, is that accidents happen at the oddest times. Just like that, out of the blue, when you least expect it. I never thought your grandfather would keel over when he did, but there you go, perfectly fit one day, striding around happily, and then, bang, he's flat on his back, dead as a fish on a slab. Myocardial something or other. Didn't even have the decency to have an illness first.'

Jadwiga was back, with a little white jug of foaming hot milk.

'Thank you so much, Jadwiga,' said Patricia, as the carer put it down on the octagonal occasional table that Adam had known and loved since childhood. She smiled up at her, with a grateful, slightly fearful smile. 'Lovely herbal tea, by the way.'

She waited for Jadwiga to exit before she spoke again. 'It's actually horrid. She leaves the bag in too long. But I don't want to upset her. We have to get on. Even though she is terribly bossy.' She made a face and looked back at her granddaughter. 'I don't think it's strange about poor Leo, Matilda. I think it's life. It's hard, but that's what we have to do, as we get older, accept what comes along, however appalling it is. You know, I never really got over your grandfather's death, it was all so sudden, I never got a chance to say goodbye, but I've learned to accept it and you must learn–'

'Of course I accept it!' Matilda cut in, impatiently. 'I'm just saying: what if it wasn't an accident?'

'I'm not sure I understand what you mean.'

'If Leo's car crash wasn't an accident and Daddy's suicide wasn't a suicide...'

Patricia sighed. 'There was an inquest, Matilda. Expert professionals looked over all the evidence and agreed that very sadly, your father killed himself. Why, we shall never know, given that his suicide note was really so very vague about reasons...'

'It wasn't a note, Granny. It was a poem. Someone used it as a note.'

'A poem? What are you talking about?'

Matilda explained.

'Sounds most unlikely to me. Why would Adam write a poem about his own death? Though he did write poems about the oddest things, I have to admit. Don't know why he bothered, to be honest. They were never very good, in my opinion. You'd think he'd have been happy with his architecture. But he was one of those people, wasn't he? Like his father. Couldn't keep his blasted fingers out of every pie going.'

Matilda's face was a picture. 'He wasn't writing about his own death, Granny. That's the whole point. Oh, never mind. I was talking to Mummy about it and–'

'Your poor mother,' Patricia cut in. 'She won't have been so upset about your father, because, frankly, he'd already gone, but Leo...'

'She *was* upset about Dad. Very upset.'

'Not in the same way, darling, believe me. Those precious bonds of trust were broken many years ago. Once broken, never replaced.' Patricia was leaning forward now, wagging a bony finger. 'It's like a glass bowl, marriage. You can't piece it back together again. If and when, Matilda, you finally find the man of your dreams...'

'It might not be a man, Granny...'

'I do hope you're joking. Obviously I'm not one to stand in the way of your happiness, especially these days. I like to think I'm forward-thinking, as you know. But whoever it is, when you do find that special person, I do hope you will value those bonds. It's never bond*age*, even though it may feel like that at times. But actually, in a way, it's the bondage element that makes it all so precious. If you can always remember to look past those tight ropes and see the good intentions of your other half–'

'May I ask a blunt question?' Matilda cut in.

Patricia laughed, that 'very amused', high-pitched, borderline cackle that was one of her more endearing features. 'No blunter than usual, I hope, Matilda.'

'When Daddy died, did you change your will?'

Adam looked over at Leo, who gave him a double thumbs up. 'She's on it, finally,' he whispered; though there was of course no need.

'Is this what this is all about?' Patricia said. 'Serena's sent you over to check that you haven't been disinherited?'

'No,' Matilda replied. 'It's nothing to do with Mummy. I was just–'

'The answer is yes, naturally I had to adjust my will after Adam died, because he was one of the main beneficiaries. But other than that necessary redistribution, nothing substantial has changed. You can tell your mother that you'll still get your share, no need to worry about that. And some of Leo's too, I expect, come to that. As will your aunt Claire. Even if she hardly ever comes to see me, leaves all the hard work to someone from a distant country to whom I'm not even related.'

'Oo-er!' said Leo, raising his eyebrows at Adam.

'Is that fair, Granny?' Matilda was saying. 'Aunt Claire does come to visit you. All the time.'

'Is that what she tells you? Once in a blue moon, darling. And she only lives down the road. Of course that husband of hers has never liked me, but there you are, touché, I've never liked him. A charm-free zone, as I told her several times before she married him.'

'She took you to the garden centre only last week,' said Matilda.

'Last week, yes. Nothing this week, even though my poor grandson has been killed in a car crash. I've had no more than a brief phone call. Anyway, that trip to the garden centre was two hours, tops. She didn't even want to stop for tea and cake. When I go with Jadwiga we always stop for tea and cake. They do a particularly nice lemon drizzle–'

'To be fair, Granny, Jadwiga works for you. She is your carer.'

'She certainly is. What a dreadful word that is. What a dreadful world, really. When I was young, people didn't have carers. Your grandfather and I took in his mother in her last years. Seven years she lived here with us. Buffy, I've told you about her before, I expect.'

'You have, Granny.'

'I'm not saying she didn't drive me up the wall. She did. With all her little demands. You know Buffy always insisted *The Times* had to be ironed. Because the newspaper boy stuffed it into the basket of his bike and it came in creased some days. So poor old Mrs MacNamara, you wouldn't remember her, but she used to help us in those days, used to have to iron the paper every day before it could be taken into Buffy in the conservatory. And then her little peccadillos on food. She couldn't eat soft eggs, because one of her nannies had forced them on her as a child. She couldn't eat coconut, for some reason I never quite fathomed. Not that we had much coconut in those days, except after the village fete, when Philip usually managed to knock down a couple. Anyway, we had Buffy here until she moved into St Luke's right at the end. It wasn't ideal, but she was family. And that's how we did things. We didn't talk about it, or boast about it, or bang on about the caring sector, or our mental health, or any of that claptrap, we just got on with it. All this huff and puff now about whether the government should sort out care or not. It's the families who should sort out care. The families,' she repeated, as if that somehow made her opinion truer. 'I mean,' she went on, 'most of those coloured folk we've let in to this country look after their elderly better than we do. It's a thing with them. You know I'm not the hugest fan of everything they do, forcing their young girls to marry–'

'Granny, stop! You know I don't want to hear this kind of nonsense.'

'Why not? It's the truth.'

'You can't use the term "coloured" anymore, anyway.'

'Why not? How else do I describe them if they're not white. They're not all actually black, are they? I doubt I'm allowed to say "brown" these days…'

'That's actually less offensive. Correctly, you say "people of colour".'

'Do I? "Correctly". People of colour. Coloured. What in heaven's name is the difference? Obviously we're all people.'

'There was a recent Home Secretary who had to resign for using the word "coloured".'

'I thought the Home Secretary *was* coloured. Last time I looked.'

'Granny! It was before her. Anyway, the Home Secretary is Asian. Of Asian heritage.'

'What is she? A clock. Asian heritage, my foot.'

Despite her mock outrage, Patricia was chuckling quietly to herself. She knew more than she let on about this stuff, Adam knew (as she did, really, about everything around her). She read *The Times* from cover to cover daily: the news, the comment, the leaders, the letters, the register. On Sunday she took both *The Sunday Times* and *The Observer*, as she and Philip had done forever. She watched the TV News several times daily, on different channels, including, amazingly, Al-Jazeera.

'Granny, really,' Matilda said. 'None of this is at all funny.'

'It's not supposed to be funny. I was actually just trying to make a point about how much more caring those coloured, sorry, Asian heritage folk are about their old people than we are. You see them in Tempelsham sometimes, piling out of minivans. The parents, the children, *and* Granny. Surely that's a good thing. It's us whiteys who've got spoilt and cruel, forgotten who we are, who nurtured us, brought us into the world, wiped our bottoms–'

'Granny!'

'No, I'm serious now. Your blessed people of colour haven't forgotten that. Even if they soon will, if they stay over here too long.' Patricia's deep sigh was almost a scoff. 'They wouldn't be pestering their poor old relatives about who's leaving what to whom, you can be sure of that.'

CHAPTER TWENTY-TWO

In the corner, under the window of Adam's office stood a rowing machine. Concept 2, it read, in fancy font on its shiny black spine. Had Julie decided to improve her upper-body fitness to better than yoga levels? No. This ergometer belonged to Rod. The handyman, it seemed, was moving in.

Good God, Adam thought, surveying his once beloved space. It's a total takeover. His favourite oval conference table, with its surrounding black moulded stackable chairs, was the one item to escape Julie's cull. So far there was nothing on it except one of those executive toys with swinging shiny metal balls that you presumably clinked together in intervals between work. At the moment it almost looked as if it *was* Rod's work.

'Remember this,' Adam said to his son, as they scoped around together. 'Used to be my man cave.'

'Not anymore, Dad.' Leo laughed.

Though Adam and Leo had not, obviously, arrived by car, someone else had. Jeff, no less. Their luck was in. Adam's (ex) partner's gleaming silver-grey Aston Martin Vantage was parked on the Fallowfields circular drive and he was up in the kitchen, signing off, it seemed, the paperwork that would give him total control of Albury & Atkinson at last.

At last, at last, the bastard! How long had he waited for this? He had made it all happen rapidly enough now that he finally could, that was for sure. What had even happened to the idea of Roland being involved? Any scruples Julie had previously entertained had clearly melted away in the fierce warmth of the Weasel's charm; not to mention the fierce warmth of his bank transfer.

'There we go,' she was saying as she put her big flowery signature at the bottom of the document. One of Julie's graphological theories about autographs was that the size of the initial letters compared to the rest indicated the relationship between fantasy and reality in a person's idea of themself. By which token, Julie's giant J and A indicated an extremely high opinion of herself and maybe her talents too. Well, Adam knew that. It was funny that it had taken him until he was dead to notice it so starkly on the page.

Rod, as someone who had as yet no documented relationship with Julie, was co-opted as the witness of this hugely significant transaction. It was paradoxical, really, that at the probable apex of their intimacy there was no register of it. As the passion dropped away, the formal recognition of their union would creep in, as usual, in an inverse ratio. The human condom's mark was surprisingly banal. Small caps, small lower case, almost straight, descending only slightly; intriguingly, that was supposed to mean he was a) straightforward and b) lacking in confidence, pessimistic. Was that the reason behind the frenzied exercise routine and the colourful Lycra: to give himself a diet of life-affirming endorphins?

He handed the pen to Jeff, then leant down to fondle Tonto, who was watching this betrayal with his usual devotion. Jeff's matchingly huge swirly 'J' told you all you needed about his ego too. Jeff Trelawney, wannabe starchitect. Baron Trelawney of the

London Mudflats. Well, he had a shot at it now. Having bought Adam out, the next thing would be a change of the firm's name. At first linking himself to Adam and Stanley and their success; then, in due course, presumably, dumping the Albury & Atkinson bit so that he was out there on his own, a solo artiste, untrammelled. For the moment, though, he still needed that name, even if not the dead people who came with it; obituarised, recognised by peers, Adam and Stanley came with more heft than when they had been alive.

Effectively, this moment of flowing ink on paper marked the death of Adam's ideas, his take on things, his philosophy. Good God, he thought, looking again at his ex-partner's shifty features, perhaps he *had*, after all, been his murderer?

It was a sunny day. But Jeff wasn't going to stop for lunch on the terrace, no thank you, Julie, very kind, but not this time. He had to be getting back, there was an important meeting, at the council – he grinned – about his big new project, Butcher's Yard, soon to be the Clerkenwell Tower, immensely exciting, though a few of the difficult locals still had to be satisfied, not to mention the usual suspects who would turn up with their placards, protesting about any change whatsoever, even if they didn't know what it was. Had Christopher Wren had this trouble? Jeff didn't think so. He laughed. He would, yes, thank you, just take a very short stroll around the lovely garden, breathe in the country air, and then he'd shoot.

It was a victory walk, really, wasn't it? Jeff was casting his eye over one of Adam's, yes, signature buildings, even – ha! – at the moment of signature. He was looking at it with envy and awe, maybe; but also thinking, *It's my time now.*

'You have to say,' he said to Julie and Rod, whose lean and muscly figure trailed respectfully two paces behind, with Tonto trotting beside him, 'Adam did a wonderful job with this place.'

'He did,' Julie agreed. 'Though you know we really built it together. A lot of the ideas were mine.'

'Is that so?'

'Yes.'

'Sometimes one's best work is in collaboration,' Jeff replied slimily, not even risking pushing back on Julie's preposterous fantasies. For what, really, had she contributed to Fallowfields apart from ideas for some of the interior, a paint colour here and there, a few of the internal fittings? The Grohe chrome taps in the master bathroom, he gave her that.

'Having turf on the roof, that was one of mine,' Julie said.

'Good call!' Jeff said, eyes creasing up with intelligent interest.

'Total bollocks,' Adam said to Leo. 'It was an idea I pinched from the Australian Parliament building in Canberra. Though it's actually a traditional Scandinavian thing, to have turf on a roof. It gives you excellent insulation, at the same time as letting the building blend in to the landscape, if it's done well.' It was a style that had been picked up also by a couple of forward-thinking Scottish architects in recent years. Not that Julie, bless her, would have a clue about any of that; nor about the fact that the smooth green lawn on the Canberra hill had dried up so horribly in recent droughts that there was talk of replacing it with more appropriate native species, something Adam would have done in the first place, had it been his baby.

Adam watched with quiet amazement as Julie gave Jeff a garbled version of what he'd just told Leo, then went on to explain about the playful postmodern use of vernacular elements to offset the central bold statement of the main house: the plinth of local knapped flint; on the side building and outhouses, the dark orange pantiles that echoed those to be found on many of the original village houses round here.

'Perhaps we should consider getting you in to the practice. On an ad hoc advisory basis.'

Was the Weasel teasing? Julie clearly didn't think so.

'That would be good,' she replied, with a nicely judged flirty smile, which made full allowances for her actual – and watching

– lover. 'Perhaps we could schedule in a preliminary meeting in the next fortnight or so.'

'Let's do that,' said Jeff. 'I'll get Asha on to it when I get back.'

Adam knew what that meant. He doubted whether Jeff would even mention it to his bright little button of a PA; though if he did, it would be with instructions to gently fob Julie off. He was a master of fobbing off, as he was of genial prevarication. If he didn't want to do something, he would stall. Endlessly. Meanwhile getting on with whatever it was that was currently rocking his selfish little speedboat. Adam should have got rid of him when he'd had the chance, years ago. It was a bit late now, to put it mildly.

Back in the kitchen Jeff gave Julie a stiff hug and shook Rod's hand, man to man. Did he realise the handyman's true status?

'Thanks, guys.' Perhaps he did. 'Well, I think you've got an excellent deal there.'

'And so have you,' Julie replied.

'Let's bloody well hope so.' Jeff was squeezing the handle of his briefcase nervously. 'Lots of work to be done.' He turned through the long open window and trit-trotted down the steps towards the Vantage.

'All the best!' he shouted up, waving as he reached the gravel.

Tonto chased after him, barking noisily, intelligent animal that he was.

Adam and Leo were still in the kitchen. So they were there to witness the long, triumphant look that passed between Julie and her lover.

'We did it!' Rod said, as the door of the Vantage clunked shut.

He was silenced by his mistress's slim white forefinger, pressed against his thin lips and bristly black 'tache. 'Walls have ears, darling.'

'Sorry,' Rod said quietly, making a caricatured apologetic face and looking round the room, almost as if he expected Adam to appear.

As they walked forward without speaking, Rod put his right arm around Julie's shoulders, in a way that Adam would never have done. Reflexively, she did that yoga neck thing, then smiled sideways at him, her handsome younger man. What did she really think of him? Adam wondered. At that moment, she looked, frankly, a little nervous.

Down below, Jeff's pricy motor sped off down the gravel, sending tiny coloured stones flying. He was already on speakerphone, doubtless relaying his good news. To whom, though? Sue, his wife? Adam doubted that. An ally in the firm? Or out of it? More likely. But who would that be?

Once the car had gone, out through the gateposts, swinging left on the lane that led down to the village green and the main B road beyond, Rod pulled Julie round to face him.

'Do naughty rich ladies like to be fucked before lunch?' he asked.

Julie giggled. If she really thought Adam might be watching her, she didn't mind him seeing this. With a frankly gross leer, Rod reached out and fondled her bottom with his muscular right hand. His fingers moved on her wobbling buttocks like someone playing scales on the piano. There was something almost exhibitionist in the backward roll of Julie's eyes, a roll Adam remembered from long ago, up into her head like a doll as she submitted.

'They do,' she sighed, tipping her lips towards his, snuggling her body closer.

Leo turned to his father and made a face. 'Yuk,' he said. 'D'you want to get out of here?'

'One moment,' said Adam, holding up a finger. In this moment of lust, might their caution slip, might they make another, more revealing remark. But no, they were too busy snogging. It didn't look as if they were even going to make it to the bedroom.

Leo had already gone, out onto the terrace, down the steps towards the office.

'Sorry,' he said, when Adam caught up with him. 'I couldn't quite cope with that. I'm surprised you could, Dad.'

'Needs must,' said Adam. 'But it seems as if they've moved beyond words for the time being.'

'Double yuk. What d'you want to do? Shadow them until they give themselves away.'

'I'm not sure they will.' Adam shrugged. 'I made a basic mistake, right at the start of all this. Which was letting Julie know that I could see her even if she couldn't see me. And then she told Claire, not that I think she took it seriously. But still. It's a handicap.'

'So what was that all about?' Leo asked. '"We did it!"'

'Well, I suppose they did, didn't they? Got out of Albury & Atkinson with the cash in hand. Was that all, though?'

'Quite,' Leo replied. 'I wouldn't have put it past that muscly shit to have tinkered with my brakes.' He was turning into quite a useful partner in crime, Adam thought, or rather (ha!) in the detection of crime; something more than just a Watson to his Holmes.

'So what now, pardner?' Leo asked, picking up on his thoughts, albeit in a dire comedy American accent.

CHAPTER TWENTY-THREE

S o there he was, Adam's one-time business partner, conked out on the bed, after what looked like a good post pre-app lunch. The meeting at the council had presumably gone well. Sugar and Savidge would have piled on the congratulatory brandies and greedy Jeff would have drunk them.

Jeff's eyes were closed and he was snoring fitfully. His mouth was half open, that fat lower lip hanging down, exposing rows of yellow teeth dense with crowns and fillings. Adam floated round, surveying him, wondering how to play it. He wasn't even sure that he needed to do much. Jeff was already terrified of the supernatural, as Adam knew; his mere appearance would probably be enough to solicit a confession, if confession was what he was going to get.

That was, of course, if Adam was able to appear. Part of his instinct about whether or not he would be successful relating to the human world was that solo visits seemed to work better, so he had come alone. In any case, there was no point in Leo being here too. It was better that his son was making himself useful back at base, keeping a close eye on Julie and Rod. Might Leo indeed be proved right? Would 'We did it!' be followed up by something altogether more incriminating?

Okay, time to give this haunting a try. On the long bookshelf, below the serried ranks of crime fiction paperbacks, Adam saw a suitably weighty hardback on its side. *Art Deco Britain* by Elain Harwood. It had a screenprint-style picture of Battersea Power Station on its cover. Amusingly, this was a building he and Jeff had never agreed about. Adam had always thought it ugly, would have torn it down, given half a chance, and replaced it with some beautifully-designed new build. Jeff, on the other hand, thought it iconic, overlooked the fact that its listed status had meant it had stayed empty for over thirty years, that its eventual restoration was in Adam's opinion, a grim travesty.

Hey ho, no time for such arguments now. Tentatively he reached out for the book with his spectral right hand. He could feel it. Solid as a rock. Well, as a book, anyway. Whey-hey! Gently, slowly, he pushed it to the edge of the shelf and watched as it teetered and then crashed down to the floor.

Jeff started, but he didn't wake.

The next to go was an even chunkier tome. *S, M, L, XL* it was titled; heavy black type on an off-white background. *A graphic overture that weaves together architectural projects, photos and sketches, diary excerpts, personal travelogues, fairy tales, and fables, as well as critical essays on contemporary architecture and society.* The kind of pretentious shit Jeff was into, although deep down, of course, he wasn't. Adam tipped it off. There was another resounding thump. Hurrah! Jeff started again and opened his eyes.

Adam immediately shoved another. Make the most of it, man. You have no idea how long this empowered state will last. *A Field Guide to American Houses* this one was called. Actually, it looked quite interesting.

Jeff sat up suddenly, stared from the three books on the

ground up to the bookshelf. 'What... the... fuck?' he muttered, blearily.

Adam was starting to enjoy himself. *Yes is More. An Archicomic on Architectural Evolution* was the next to go. It made a good sound thud on the carpet.

'What's going on?' Jeff said, louder now. He looked at his watch. Saw that it was 1.17 am and he was still in his clothes on the spare bed.

He stumbled to his feet and opened the door.

The house was silent. His wife and children were asleep. He closed the door, gently, then stared for ten long seconds at the fallen books. Eventually, he bent down to pick them up. He replaced them on the shelf, one by one. Then he sat down on the bed and leant forward to remove his shoes. From far away across town came the screech of a siren. He shook his head, groaned and lay back down again.

Adam waited for five minutes until Jeff had closed his eyes, perhaps willing himself to doze off, because, as yet, his breathing was not the regular in and out of a sleeper. Then he moved quietly over to the far end of the bed and picked up one of Jeff's shoes, his beloved brown Timberlands. He held it over Jeff's belly and dropped it. As it bounced and fell sideways, there was a sudden yelp and Jeff sat bolt upright. He was wide-eyed now. Scared.

Adam picked up the second shoe and threw it against the bookcase. It didn't dislodge any of the books, but it made a satisfactory thump, then fell back down to the floor again, bounced a couple of times and lay still.

Jeff was looking from the shoes on the floor to the bookcase and back again, as if trying to convince himself that what he'd just seen hadn't in fact happened.

'Hello, Jeff,' Adam said, quietly; he was confident now, looking at his ex-partner's petrified face, that he was getting through.

Jeff sat there, ramrod stiff, breathing heavily, listening, still appearing to refuse to accept what he'd just heard. Adam gave him a minute or so to savour the silence, or rather the continuing background noise of semi-suburban London at night: the distant banging of a car door, a random shriek of laughter from a nearby street.

'Hello, Jeff,' he repeated.

'What the... fucking... fuck?' Jeff was shaking now; all over, like a man out in a shirt in the winter cold.

'What the fucking fuck indeed,' Adam repeated. It was almost worth having died to be able to tease his disloyal business partner in this way.

'What is this?' Jeff whimpered. 'Who are you?'

'Who d'you think?' Adam replied, measuredly.

'I... I... I don't know,' muttered Jeff.

It was pathetic to see him like this. Of course the poor man was a lapsed Catholic so sudden proof that there was a life beyond, after all, was bound to hit him hard. Jeff had once been an altar boy, unlikely though it seemed, looking at his baggy, debauched features now.

'It's your old business partner. Remember me?'

'Adam.'

'That's the one.'

Adam willed himself to materialise. And there he was, back in hologrammatic form in jeans and Campers. Jeff could have caught flies his mouth was so far open.

'Gone before my time,' Adam continued. 'Sad, eh?'

'What...what... are... you?' Jeff was gasping.

'Adam... Albury. Spirit of. Now on the other side. Limbo, purgatory, the Bardo, call it what you will. I thought you believed in that kind of thing. You did once.'

'Bloody hell,' Jeff muttered. 'Was that you chucking my shoe around?'

'Certainly was.'

'How... how do I know?'

'How do you know what?'

'That it's you, you fucker.'

'Doesn't it look like it?'

'It does. But you could be an imposter. Or some metaverse avatar or something.'

Adam laughed. 'Okay, here's something that even the most sophisticated avatar wouldn't know. What was the name of the major east central London development that you've managed to conjure out of what was supposed to be a straightforward restoration job?'

'Butcher's Yard.'

'Correct. Only from the pre pre-app discussion I attended last Monday morning with those egregious shits Sugar and Savidge, it seems that it isn't Butcher's Yard any more, it's the Clerkenwell Tower.'

'You… were… there?' Jeff stuttered. 'How the fuck…?'

'I returned, in spirit form. But never mind about that. Once you've squared the poor old businesses and locals with your usual mixture of lies and charm and bribery,' Adam continued, regardless, 'Have Your Freaking Say and all that, the demolition ball goes in, destroying centuries of history in favour of some steel-and-glass monstrosity that could be stuck up anywhere in the world…'

Jeff wasn't listening. His eyes were round as he stared back at Adam. 'So why… did you kill yourself?' he asked after a few moments.

'I didn't,' Adam replied. And now indeed *was* the time to up the ante. 'You know that,' he said accusingly.

'What d'you mean? You committed suicide, Adam. In your garage, with a black hosepipe attached to your car exhaust. Carbon monoxide poisoning. None of us could understand it.'

'Couldn't you? Interesting you knew that the hosepipe was black.'

'I went to the inquest. I followed every detail. I was shocked. Traumatised, even. We all were. Poor Eva…'

'Was so upset that she dropped her support for saving Butcher's Yard and came on board with "the Clerkenwell Tower".'

'That's not true.'

'She didn't seem to be putting up much opposition in the meeting. Even poor Reuben was blindsided. Did you murder me, Jeff?'

'Don't be… rid…iculous,' he gasped.

'Were you so desperate to get your hands on the firm that you faked my suicide?'

'Of course I didn't.'

'Did Eva help you?'

'No-o-o….'

'So who did it? Because I most certainly didn't.'

Jeff was staring at him. Those replies had been a bit quick fire, hadn't they? Would someone one hundred per cent innocent be so hot on denial?

'Maybe *you* did it, Adam, and blanked it all out,' Jeff said finally. 'I've no idea what state you're in now, but don't they always say that it's the unhappy spirits that linger around…'

'I didn't blank anything out,' Adam replied, his voice rising in anger. He couldn't believe that his infuriating ex-partner was already trying to start in on the knowing blather-blather. The awful truth was that he *had* blanked it out. His own death. Why? Was it possible that Jeff was right and he had done it after all? Killed himself? And was now suffering, as both Julie and Matilda had suggested, from some supernatural form of post-traumatic shock.

No, no, no, he hadn't. Jeff was just trying to wrong-foot him. He wouldn't be fazed. In fact, he would seriously try and put the wind up the little shit. Perhaps this attempt to change the script indicated that Jeff was guilty after all.

'I didn't blank it out,' he repeated. 'Because I didn't do it.

Someone else set up that whole theatrical scenario. Hosepipe in the car. What a cliché. Are you sure it wasn't you? You certainly had the motive.'

'What are you talking about?' Jeff replied scornfully. 'You were on your way out of the firm anyway.'

'I don't think so.'

'I'd have had you out of there, don't you worry, if…'

Jeff stopped in his tracks, riled though he clearly was.

'If what?'

'If… if you hadn't–'

'Obliged you by topping myself? Something I didn't actually do. I ask you again, Jeff. What hand did you have in this, because you clearly did have a hand.'

'I did not… have any… hand… in anything to do with your sad and untimely end, Adam.'

'You set it up. Admit it. You worked with Julie. And Rod.'

'I don't know what you're talking ab-a-a-a-a-A-A-AGH!'

Jeff broke off with an animal howl of pain. Now he was struggling to breathe. 'Fuck… oh shit… what the fu…' His face was contorted into a horrid rictus as he clutched his chest with both hands. 'Call a… fu… cking… amb…' Even as he stuttered out these words, Jeff rolled off the bed and onto the floor.

There was a loud thump and then the door was thrown open.

Jeff's wife Sue stood there, in a pink floral nightie. Her indoors. Adam had last seen her over two years ago, reluctantly dolled up for a Christmas social.

Her hand reached out and she clicked on the light. Then she dived down to her husband, who was flat on the floor, not moving.

'Jeff!' she cried, kneeling beside him. 'Jeff,' she repeated, shaking him. Then she slapped him hard, three times, on the cheek. 'Jeff, Jeff, Jeff!'

She was looking round the empty room.

'What's happened?' she whimpered. She was holding her

husband's wrist, trying to find a pulse. There didn't seem to be one. She was sobbing now. What had Adam done? Murdered his business partner? Of course not. Jeff had had heart problems.

There was a noise from along the corridor. Footsteps. The door swung open. It was Jeff's daughter, metamorphosed from the perky blonde-bobbed eleven-year-old Adam had last seen up at the office on a Jeff-initiative 'Bring Your Child to Work Day' into a lanky, yawning teenager.

'Mummy,' she said, 'what's happening? What's wrong with Daddy?'

Sue was already running for the phone.

CHAPTER TWENTY-FOUR

I nnocently asleep in her studio, Eva knew nothing, yet, of her boss's terrible demise. Adam watched her as the light came up, then the early April sun started to shine on the cream Velux blind in the sloping roof. In the last nine months, since they had been an item, he had often woken to that view; to the slow, guilty realisation of where he was, who he was with, what he had got himself into.

On those mornings when he had been here, it had nonetheless been a delicious pleasure rolling over in the laundered sheets and waking Eva; a pleasure that had made all the clumsy lies he'd had to tell Julie worthwhile. 'I was up early, darling, jogging round the park.' 'I had to go into the office to use the work computer.' 'I stayed out late at a dinner, oh just a work thing, clients, bit of a bore, but you've got to do it.'

It was not a pleasure he could indulge in now. Should he have another go at speaking to her? Shaken though he was after his encounter with Jeff, he didn't feel that guilty. Would he have even been charged with manslaughter, were he still alive? No. He had just been present at an alarming medical event. He'd have phoned the ambulance himself, had he been able to: '999. Yes, I *am* a ghost, that's correct…'

Obviously it was sad that a man had died. But not that sad, because that man was Jeff, so there was one less duplicitous shit on the planet. Weirdly, Adam felt buoyed up by his success in getting through. If he could repeat the same to his beloved Eva, he could tell her what had happened. Though how shocking would she find that, even as he appeared to her for the first time?

In any case, he wanted to see how the news of their boss's sudden death played out at work. How they all took it. How Eva took it, even. Would her new-found support for the Clerkenwell Tower be dropped as quickly as it had been offered? Would he, in fact, have to go on doubting the loyalty of a woman he had once been loved-up enough about to completely trust?

So he watched her eyes open. Then close again. He watched her turn over onto her side and snuggle back down into the pillow. Then get up and visit her tiny bathroom. She showered (how Adam had hated that shower, which had mocked his infidelity with its feebleness, 'You don't *need* to be in this kind of crappy rental bathroom, you cheat') then walked around wrapped in a towel and fixed herself a light breakfast of Rachel's Organic yoghurt, sliced peach and toast, like something out of a home furnishings brochure. She read the *Guardian* headlines on her iPad. She picked out her work clothes and put them on: a favourite little black top and skirt combo this morning. She must have a meeting, Adam thought. She dabbed her favourite Miller Harris 'Peau Santal' behind her ears and clattered off down the stairs. The scent hung in his non-existent nostrils like the memory of living.

He strap hung with her on the Tube. He noted the sneaky glances of the men who fancied her in that suit, randomly, as men do, the male gaze, yadda yadda. He hovered alongside her as she paced up busy Long Acre. He queued with her in Costa, where she got her usual skinny soy latte. He followed as she turned right and then left into Sheridan Street. He floated up the central staircase of the ex-warehouse that was now Albury, Atkinson, Trelawney, to be confronted, in the first-floor foyer, with a huge, upbeat display of the Clerkenwell Tower project, complete with computer-generated watercolour-style 'drawings' of what that monstrosity might look like. With Jeff gone, was there now a chance to save it all before it was too late?

He followed Eva to her desk, watched her sip her coffee, say hi to Reuben and a couple of others, then settle seriously to her computer and her emails. Then he slid sideways into Jeff's dedicated glass cube of an office.

Sue clearly hadn't phoned yet, because Jeff's PA Asha seemed relaxed enough this morning, clearly assuming that it was going to be a late one and that Jeff would be in, at the last moment, in a crumpled linen suit, as per usual. But as the clock ticked on towards ten, and then the odious duo of Sugar and Savidge appeared, and were welcomed by office manager Lynsey and shovelled off into the conference room with Nespressos, she was visibly worrying.

What were those chancers here for now? Adam wondered. Strategy for the upcoming public 'consultation'? Bit soon after the pre-app, but you never knew with these two, they liked to keep things moving. At five to ten Asha was visibly panicking. Hovering right behind her, Adam could see that she had been trying Jeff's mobile, repeatedly, but to no avail. He drove in, so there were no concerns about him losing a signal on the Underground. Now, in desperation, after a hurried consultation with Lynsey, Asha was phoning his home number, something he always discouraged.

Adam watched as Asha's expression changed. He couldn't hear exactly what Sue was saying at the other end, but it was her all right. 'OMG,' Asha muttered, as she took in the news. Her eyes darted nervously round the office as she surveyed her heedless, and now bossless, co-workers. He watched her click off the phone, put it down in its cradle, and for a moment just stare, blankly, out. Then, after ten long seconds, she sprang into action, racing discreetly through the desks to brief Lynsey, Trevor, Eva and Reuben, before heading back to the conference room to tell the clients that Jeff was unfortunately waylaid.

'Waylaid!' Tim Savidge repeated. 'Our first public consultation is at noon. We can't go unprepared.'

Asha was doubled over in gracious apology. Trevor would be in in just a moment to take over.

'Has he been "waylaid" too? We really need to get going. Where *is* Jeff?'

In Trevor's office, he, Eva and Reuben were clearly in shock, urgently debating whether to relay the truth to the clients.

'Now is not the right moment to tell them,' Trevor was saying.

'We have to tell them sometime,' Eva replied.

'It's too sudden. We need to work out how to present this.'

'Why?' said Reuben. 'They've got to know eventually. They might be offended if they found out later we hadn't told them.'

'But if we tell them, it'll be round the houses before lunchtime,' Trevor said. 'People are going to be going mad. You remember what it was like when Adam...'

He paused and looked respectfully at Eva.

'I do remember,' she answered.

'And Jeff delayed on that for two days.'

'That was suicide,' said Reuben.

'Adam didn't have clients waiting around,' Eva said. 'Waiting to go to a public consultation. It's just not going to wash that he's not turning up. This is Jeff's big thing. Being reasonable and persuasive with the awkward squad. That's probably the main reason S & S retain him.'

Trevor looked through the glass walls towards the conference room, where Tim Savidge could now be seen pacing up and down, on his phone, gesticulating wildly.

I could just drop in here, Adam thought, and take over in a

ghostly fashion. Tell them that on second thoughts – *Woo hoo!* – Albury, Atkinson, Trelawney (Deceased Division) is recommending that they drop the glass tower and return to the altogether better idea of preserving the historic façade. Even if that did slash the Sugar & Savidge profits by ninety-five per cent and meant that Dave Purbeck might not be taking his family to Val d'Isère next year for February half-term.

'But Jeff is – was – the Clerkenwell Tower,' Trevor protested. 'What am I going to say? They might take the whole thing elsewhere.'

'Oh for heaven's sake!' Eva cried. 'Would you like me to do it?'

Trevor's curly dark mop was in his hands, his blue specs flat on the desk. 'Okay,' he said, surfacing. 'Let's do it your way. You come with me, though, please, Eva.'

It was a pathetic attempt to reclaim some authority, which Eva was visibly unimpressed by.

Adam hung around. Did he enjoy watching the commotion when the clients received the shocking news? As Tim Savidge did his best to look upset about Jeff's heart attack, his brain was visibly computing what he should do next. Trevor was a competent architect, but no replacement in the persuasion stakes for Jeff, they all knew that.

When the clients had left for the public consultation, with a scared-looking Trevor in tow, Reuben called the entire office into the conference room and formally told them what had happened. They all already knew; the news had licked from desk to desk like wildfire.

Eva made a speech. It was a terrible shock, she said, but they had to weather it. They had survived Adam's recent death (she didn't say suicide, he was glad to hear) and though Jeff was, had been, central to everything, they would be able, bottom line, to survive that too. Albury, Atkinson, Trelawney was them, all of them, working on the projects they were working on, and that creativity would continue, whatever. The structure of the firm might have to adjust a little, but that wasn't important. What was important were the imaginative solutions people were coming up with for often challenging problems.

Adam was proud of her, rising to this challenge like this. She was, whether she liked it or not, putting herself up there in the firm's unspoken hierarchy, up with Trevor who, though notionally her superior, was slipping, surely, down the credibility pole with every hour.

Adam's private yearning to speak to her was stronger than ever. He wanted to take her through what had happened to Jeff, and yes, to him too. Was her rejection of his plan for Butcher's Yard for real? Had she just been posturing with Reuben in the pub after the pre pre-app meeting? 'Life moves on. Adam's gone.' Ditto with Matilda in Tea and Sympathy?

Ridiculous though it was, after all that had happened, Adam wanted, if just for a short while, to be back *with her* again. He wanted to hear her say 'hey' in that soothing, deeply intimate way that she'd done when they had first got together; and again, sometimes, when he'd been away or not been able to see her for a while. Why had he failed to get through to her post mortem? Could that change?

He imagined that with the shock of Jeff's death the workers might all pack up and go home for the day. He was wrong about that. If anything, they seemed to be beavering away harder at their individual projects. Would Jeff, who liked to think he was the motivating kingpin of the firm, have wanted to see that? Of course the news had to be broken to clients, jitters calmed. But who was going to take charge now? It was all up in the air.

If they weren't leaving early, they weren't at least going to stay late. Adam was wrong about that too. At five thirty, as soon as the day was technically over, Eva and Reuben led a move to the pub. The Prosperous Parson rather than the New Deal. Even though Adam was frustrated that Eva was still in company, hadn't slunk home to be alone with her thoughts (and, yes, surprise, surprise, him!) he was heartened that she and Reuben and the gang had chosen *his* pub over Jeff's swankier favourite. Culturally, if not actually, they were on his side with the old-fashioned bar stools, the scuffed tables, the crisps and the pork scratchings, the familiar jugs of bitter; not the glass and chrome tables, the swanky rows of overpriced European lagers, the preposterous and expensive snacks, including of course the oversized Scotch egg that was Jeff's favourite ('a meal in itself')...

At one level he felt sad that he couldn't join them; that he could see them crunching down on the scratchings and not know that familiar, lardy, gross-but-delicious taste again, nor sample on his lips the creamy head and malty, hoppy body of a Timmy Taylor's, here on draft though not even known about over at the New Deal.

As they sat down with their drinks, the gathered gang of almost twenty-five were shocked, that was for sure. But after an initial, almost studied period of respectful calm, raucousness broke out. As the second and third pints and large glasses of wine went down, they were laughing and loud. They were remembering Jeff. In a good way? Sort of. But as with Adam at his not-so-long-ago wake, Jeff's foibles were coming out too. His love of fine food; his passion for detective fiction, in both books and TV miniseries; his taste in expensive suits, Paul Smith, Armani, Reiss, particularly of the linen variety. Did Jeff crumple them up deliberately to produce the laid-back effect he wanted? Didn't Sue have an iron? Don't be so sexist. Did Sue even exist? Oh, for fuck's sake! I've seen her. When? Once. Really? Sure it was her?

Wasn't it all a bit too soon for this kind of thing? Apparently not. Then, suddenly, in describing in more detail Jeff's work, and his approach, they had got on to his relationship with Adam. Hadn't Adam brought him into the firm? Hadn't they fallen out, creatively, with Jeff pushing for ideas that were increasingly antithetic to Adam's more regenerative approach? Wasn't it true that Adam had brought in Butcher's Yard as a conservation project, that Jeff had totally monstered him, that that had been one of the things that had driven him to suicide? No, it was the other way round, Eva said. Jeff had brought it in. And it was Stanley who had brought in Jeff.

Simone, decidedly tipsy now, thought all these deaths had started with Stanley.

'What are you saying, Simone?'

'It just seems a bit odd. Ping, ping, ping, all three of them "dead" within two years.' She mouthed the word with heavy meaning. 'The *partners*.'

Then the word 'stuffy' was being bandied about. Jeff had been the moderniser, for sure. But was Stanley stuffier than Adam?

'I don't think you could say Adam was stuffy,' Eva parried.

Thank you, Eva, my darling, you are still on my side.

'If anything, he was more forward-thinking than Jeff,' Lynsey said.

'Is preservation forward-thinking?' Pete, one of the juniors, asked.

'I think in a way it is. Anyone can build a steel and glass box. And what are you left with after a hundred years?'

'An old steel and glass box,' Asha joked.

'Ha ha.'

'Anyone who's spent time in the US appreciates what we have here in Europe,' Reuben said. 'I mean, Chicago, have you even been there?'

'I love Chicago,' said Simone.

'And you've got the sticker to prove it. D'you know what? They should send all those vandalistic local councillors and planning officers on a tour of America just so they realise what they're doing, trashing our heritage.'

'Not just America,' Lynsey said.

'But we can't stay still,' said Pete.

What did Eva think, Reuben asked, after a little more of this chatter. She had been close to both the partners, he added, mischievously.

'I was,' Eva said, 'as you know. Particularly Adam.' The group's din subsided into sudden silence, and across the pub a trio arguing loudly about the rights of eco-protesters to block major arterial routes could now be clearly heard.

It was a measure of their respect for Eva, Adam thought, that none of the gathered group mocked her statement, even though there were a few tight smiles visible among the younger contingent.

Actually Eva thought it was sad, she went on, that those two, Adam and Jeff, had developed this rivalry, after many years of working closely and productively together. It had got to a point where Jeff decided he didn't want to be thwarted, or held back, anymore, about anything, which meant he was actively trying to push Adam out: of the firm that he'd founded, that still bore his name. When in fact the two approaches could easily have been contained within the firm, horses for courses and suchlike.

'So it was lucky for Jeff,' Simone said, 'that Adam…'

'Passed on?' said Asha.

'Yes.'

'Lucky and convenient,' said Pete.

'What are you saying?' asked Eva.

'There were rumours, weren't there?'

'That?'

'Adam didn't actually kill himself.'

'So, what… Jeff was a murderer?'

'No, I wasn't saying that. I was asking, really.'

It was interesting to Adam that as this discussion continued, and got noisier again, drowning out the other pub chatter, Eva was emerging as his defender. However much she had been swayed by Jeff and his approach, while he was still alive, she seemed to have reverted to Camp Adam now that he'd gone.

CHAPTER TWENTY-FIVE

Finally she was home. Adam had been worried about her, stumbling down the street, visibly the worse for wear after the long drinking session. Luckily Reuben and Simone had gone with her some of the way. After they had got within sight of the Tube station together, and Eva had decided she couldn't, after all, face public transport, Reuben had offered to take her home in a taxi, but she had waved an extravagant finger at him, looked sideways at Simone, kissed her, and him, full on the lips, and told him she could manage alone.

But at least Reuben had flagged one down, a proper black one with a yellow light, and put her in it. Adam was worried that the cabbie would turn her away, as she had all but fallen in, then shouted, 'RIP, Jeff!' loudly while raising an imaginary glass. She had slumped to one side of the back seat, and Adam, watching from the other, wondered if she was about to make herself really popular by throwing up all over the interior. But she made it back home. Got out okay and up to her front doorstep. Nearly fell over trying to find her key in her bag.

Adam followed her up the four flights of stairs, cursing as she reached each landing, pausing, recovering herself, continuing on.

He watched as she fumbled in her bag to find her key again, then realised it was in her hand, then struggled to get it in the lock. Then she was in. She gurgled with laughter and fell back onto the purple IKEA couch, the famous Flottebo.

A minute later she was up again, over to her strip of kitchen, opening the fridge. She sighed heavily as she saw the half-empty bottle of Pinot Grigio, lightly frosted with condensation. She looked around for a wine glass, failed to see one, grabbed a convenient tumbler from the wooden rack of washed-up crocks, poured herself a couple of inches.

'Do you really need that?' Adam asked. The words were out of his non-existent mouth before he'd even made a decision about what he was going to do; try to do, indeed.

Eva span round, suddenly alert.

'I was just asking,' Adam continued. 'Do you really need that?'

'Adam?' she muttered.

God! Had he got through? So easily? He had no desire to freak her out, Jeff style. If anything, he wanted the opposite. For her to accept him at face value. Even if she were pissed.

So: 'Hey,' he said softly.

She stared blankly before her, then took a hurried swig from her glass.

'Adam?' she repeated, louder, half an octave higher.

'Yes,' he replied. 'It's me.'

'Where? Where are you?' She sounded panicked now. She put down her glass, then looked around again. 'Fuck,' she said and paced across to the kitchenette, picked up a mug that read Trophy Wife in lower-case red cursive script and filled it with water from the tap. It was a mug that Adam had bought her in Peter Jones; as a joke, but one that contained an unspoken proposal; of commitment to the idea of marriage, in due course, if not immediately. Eva stood there, drinking in long, forced gulps.

'It's all right,' he said. 'You're not drunk. Well, you are. But you're not imagining me.'

'I've never *hallushinated* before,' she slurred.

She filled up her mug again, walked over to the long mirror by the door and stared at herself as she drank more water.

'You need to stop, girl,' she told herself. She wagged a critical finger at her reflection. '*Pish* head.'

Adam was pacing himself. Let the shock sink in, he thought, then he could start to try and bring her, slowly, to an understanding of what was going on.

Eva turned back to the kitchen, took the kettle from its cradle, checked it for water, saw that it was nearly empty, lifted the lid, filled it, clicked it on. Then her lovely braceleted hands were up in the cupboards, looking for the cafetière, for the coffee she always bought from an old Greek man who had a railway arch behind Victoria station, with sacks of beans piled everywhere and a blackened roaster always on the go.

'You don't need coffee,' he said. 'I'm not a fantasy, Eva.'

She stared, disbelievingly, about thirty degrees in the wrong direction. Then she turned and slumped down on her sofa. Reached for her wine again. Knocked back what was left.

'Where then?' she asked. 'Where are you?'

'Here.'

'In this room?'

'Yes.'

'What are you? You sound exactly like Adam.'

'I am Adam.'

She laughed; a scared laugh, but still a laugh. 'How am I supposed to believe that? What are you? His ghost or something?'

'Yes. I'm his ghost. Well, I'm still Adam, but in ghostly form. Actually, it's funny. From my point of view, it doesn't feel that different. Hang on...'

It was time to materialise, he reckoned. He concentrated hard and yes, he could feel himself appearing, fingertips first, then arms, then body and head and feet. He smiled, a tad sheepishly.

Eva's eyes were wide. 'Wow!' she said. 'Matilda was right. It really is you.' She went back to her abject, if suspicious stare. 'Okay, Adam, if that's who you are, why did you decide to contact Claire and Julie before me?'

'I didn't decide – I mean, I did. You were the first person I tried to talk to. Here. I followed you home from work, the day after the funeral. You played the Beethoven *Violin Concerto* and cried. I was trying to console you, but it didn't work. Then you picked up the violin and played "Quizás, Quizás, Quizás". "This one's for you," you said. I was desperate to get through. I was shouting.'

'Were you?'

'Yes! And after the meeting about Butcher's Yard, with Dodgy Dave and Sugar and Savidge, I tried again.'

'I went to the pub with Reuben.'

'I know you did. I was there. I followed you home. You ate noodles.'

'So I did.'

'But I still couldn't get through.'

'And why was that?'

'I have no idea.'

Eva got up and went to the fridge. She took out the bottle and filled her glass to the top. She sat down again and looked back at him, at his spectral image, as if, despite all this information, she still didn't quite believe it was him. He needed to reassure her, as he'd done with his sister, with facts only he could know.

'When you were at Manchester,' he said, 'studying for a BA in architecture, you lived in a student area that had the same name, almost, as the house that I built for myself and still live in.'

'Fallowfield,' she replied, slowly.

'Correct. You lived with several other students in a house that you nicknamed The House of Death, on account of its dodgy plumbing and a ceiling that fell down twice.'

'That fucking landlord.'

'Terry.'

'Wow! You remembered that.'

'When you came in for your interview at A & A,' Adam went on, pressing his advantage, 'a little after that, it was on a sunny Tuesday and you were wearing a particularly fetching white calico dress.'

'"Particularly fetching".' Eva was smiling now. 'It's only been a few weeks and I'd forgotten how you talk.'

'Round your neck, I remember, was a string of dark red ceramic beads. You had your usual bracelets. We worked together for ages before anything happened between us.'

'I was twenty-one.'

'You were.'

'You monitored my logbook.'

'I did.'

'Took me out to sites you didn't need to.'

'But I did need to. Why else did you do so well?'

'You old goat. I always knew what you were up to.'

'But I wasn't. It never occurred to me, I swear to God. I liked you, yes, but a) I was married and b) you were far too young for me.'

'You still gave me vacation work, encouraged me to join the firm when the time came.'

'You were good.'

'Was I?'

'You know you were. Even Jeff had to admit that you were.'

She was watching him, closely; staring at him, even, as if only just starting to accept it was him. 'So what changed?' she asked.

'As you well know, there was a fight. About Butcher's Yard.'

'You were passionate in its defence.'

'As were you.'

'We went to the pub.'

'The Prosperous Parson.'

'Drink was taken.'

'Quite a lot of drink.'

'I saw you in a different light.'

'One thing led to another.'

'It certainly did. Did you come back with me to my flat?'

'Trick question, very good. I didn't that night, no. What happened between us took place in the so-called garden at the back of the pub. The next day, too embarrassed to talk to you, I sent you a tentative email and we agreed to meet for cocktails at a bar you liked in Long Acre called Redemption.'

Adam remembered the erotic nervousness cutting the air. The fear that, even though their encounter had really been no more than a drunken snog, and she had sent him a flirty email, that he had misjudged things, gone too far, got himself into some kind of #metoo nightmare. The slow realisation, as the second negroni hit his system, and she reached out for his hand, that he hadn't. That she *liked* him.

'And after that,' Eva replied, 'you did see this place for the first time.' She paused and looked at him again. 'Okay, I do believe that it is you, Adam Albury. Somehow.'

'And not a drunken *hallushination*?'

'Actually, I feel quite sober now.' She got up and went to the fridge. The bottle was empty.

'Why not?' she said, with a laugh. 'It's not a school night.' She reached below the counter and pulled out another of the same. 'Warm. Never mind.' She opened a drawer and rattled around. 'Where's a shitting corkscrew when you need one?'

Adam said nothing. It wasn't for him to comment on her drinking, especially if he wanted co-operation. The opener was right in front of him on the glass-topped coffee table.

'It's here,' he said.

'Chuck it over.'

'I can't, I'm afraid.'

'Oh right. So you can't... pick things up?'

'No. Rather disabled, us ghosts. If I'm allowed to say that.'

'I imagine you're allowed to say what you like. Since you're the ghost around here.'

She marched over impatiently and grabbed the corkscrew. Then she opened her fridge again and took out the silicon tray that made little ice penguins from the freezer section. She smashed it down on the laminate granite worktop. About ten little frozen birds danced out. She picked up four and put them in her glass. Poured in the warm white wine. Took another gulp, then turned back to face him. 'You know Jeff died?' she said. 'Last night. Suddenly. Of a heart attack or something. That's why I was a bit smashed earlier.'

It was time for Adam to tell his side of the story.

'So you killed him, basically?' she said, when he'd finished.

'He collapsed.'

'From the stress of being harassed by the ghost of his dead partner.'

'Don't be ridiculous. He had a pre-existing condition.'

'It's lucky you're dead, that's all I can say.'

Then Eva wanted to know about Adam's death. It was no surprise to her that it wasn't suicide, she said. But if it wasn't, what did that imply? Who had it in for him enough to want to actually do away with him? Julie? Had she found out about him and her? She had, he said, though how, and when, he didn't know.

'Osmosis,' Eva said. 'These things get around. Or maybe you let something slip. You weren't that careful. I know you think you were.'

'I *was* careful. Assiduous. I had the blinking burner phone. Nobody had any clue about "the secret love email".'

'"The secret lustmail" more like. Everyone at A & A knew about us, Adam. We went out to restaurants together.'

'Colleagues. Working hard.'

'You stayed over. You were always making up unlikely stories about where you were supposed to be. Julie's not that stupid. Maybe Jeff told her.'

Adam explained about Rod.

'Wow.' Eva nodded slowly, taking it in. 'Does that make you feel better? But if she wanted you out of the way anyway, knowing about us could have tipped her over.'

'Into actually going for it? Sedating me or whatever, then setting up that charade in the garage? I'm not so sure,' Adam said. 'Even with Rod on board.' Wasn't it a bit too obvious? Those two. That's what he was coming round to thinking.

'Who then?' Eva asked.

'That's the question. Would you help me find out what happened to me? And Leo too,' he added.

'Leo, yes. I heard about that. What a terrible, terrible thing. So what do you think? That that wasn't an accident after all.'

'No. It wasn't. I'm ninety-five per cent sure of that.'

Eva nodded thoughtfully, but didn't follow him up on this, or ask him why. 'What exactly is it that you want?' she said. 'Revenge?'

'No. Justice, I suppose. And closure. I just want to know: who hated me enough to want to kill me. It might sound silly, but then I'd feel free. To move on.'

'So what do you move on to? Heaven? Hell? Oblivion?'

'I have no idea.'

'But if you're in some kind of an afterlife already, doesn't that make it more likely there's more of an afterlife?'

His thoughts exactly. They were soulmates. 'Yes. That's the first thing I thought as well,' he replied. 'But the reality out here is that I'm alone.'

He had decided not to tell her about Leo. Being with him. Not particularly that he wanted extra sympathy from her. But he didn't want to complicate this moment. With her. That he had finally managed to achieve.

She was looking back at him fondly. 'What happens if you try to touch me, Adam. Can you?'

Adam held out his perfectly-detailed hologram of a hand. 'D'you want me to?'

'Yes.'

His ghostly digits hovered over her lovely dark skin; skin he had so often kissed. And loved. The texture of it. The smell of it. The colour of it.

'Go on then,' she said.

But his hands slipped through. In his dimension, his fingers could grasp each other, his palms push tight together. But not in hers.

'You really are in another world, aren't you, Adam?'

'I am.'

'It's a shame.' She looked at him, long and hard, as if seeing him, in his ghostly form, for the first time. 'I did love you,' she said softly, 'you know that.'

'I guess I did. I suppose I was never really quite sure.'

'Why?'

'You're younger than me. Lovely, intelligent…'

'Pur-lease…'

'But you are.'

'I never gave a shit about the age gap, you know that.'

'So you used to say. But it was still there. There was still part of me that wanted to be your age, so we could be… equal, I suppose. Do stuff together that couples the same age do. Have a baby even.'

'Don't be so sentimental. It's close to last knockings for me for that idea anyway. If you'd been my age, you'd probably have been off after all sorts.'

'I don't think so.'

'Whatevs. It's all over now, isn't it?'

He felt suddenly very sad, as if she were breaking up with him, which she wasn't; but then again, she was. Tears flooded his virtual eyes.

'Hey,' she murmured. 'Don't cry, sweetheart.'

'I'm not crying.' He was laughing at the absurdity of his own sorrow. 'I don't even have real eyes.'

'People might raise their eyebrows at a much older partner, but a ghost. I don't see it, really, darling, do you?'

'No.'

'So how do you imagine I can help you?' she asked. 'In your quest for justice. You want me trotting round interviewing suspects, like some feisty private detective off the telly?'

She gave him her sweetest smile.

CHAPTER TWENTY-SIX

Adam stood to one side of his shed, gazing out at his beautiful garden. Down by the natural swimming pond, the heron sculpture looked particularly fine in this pale, pre-dawn light, a tall grey outline against the deep late-April green. He and Julie had bought it from Messum's gallery, to celebrate the success of Adam's big Chinese project in Chengqing, ten years before. In Chinese culture herons symbolised strength and patience, which was hardly the mark of their marriage, but never mind, they had once watched one flapping low over the water on a sailing trip in the Camel Estuary in North Cornwall in their happier days.

Adam felt again that lurch of unreality: that he was here, and yet not here. The world was so sumptuous and colourful and extraordinary, and he was no longer part of it. How did people still in it take it so much for granted? How could they grind themselves down with petty worries about jobs and relationships and transport and money and news and social media, and all the things that kept them from just stopping still and gazing in wonder at the magical splendour of what was around them: this palest of pink dawns, the clouds turning yellow and crimson as you watched; a patch of bluebells in a green shade; a fallen confetti of blossom on the dewy grass.

A poem! But no, he didn't have a pen with him, did he? Or a notebook. Even if he had done, he couldn't have written a word. He was glad now, in this post-life powerlessness, that he had struggled on with his poetry while he was living, even if, as Julie had so memorably said, it was never going to make him money or make him famous as a poet, so what was the point? 'It's my version of mindfulness,' he'd once replied to her. The terrible irony being that it was one of his poems that had allowed his murderer to get away with his death.

Now his poetry had outlived him. It was still there, part of his legacy, such as it was; printed up, in the little handmade Christmas booklets he had distributed to his friends and favoured clients year after year. And it couldn't be that bad, could it, otherwise Roland wouldn't have been so threatened by it, would he? 'Stick to architecture, mate,' he had said to Adam once, his jagged teeth stained dark with red wine, like some literary vampire, in the bolthole of his London club, the tiny Academy in Soho. 'Those are constructions you do understand.' Patronising git, why had Adam even bothered staying friends with him?

'Hi, Dad.'

Adam span round. It was his son, materialised into hologram form, at least to his eyes, joining him by the shed, as arranged, at dawn.

'Leo, there you are! How did you get on?'

The boy was grinning. 'Lots to report, Dad. I've been all over.'

After Jeff had sped off from Fallowfields, and Adam had followed shortly afterwards, Leo had stuck around. To keep an eye on Rod and Julie. But nothing much had developed, he told his father. No obvious guilt had been displayed. And Rod was actually, Leo thought, quite a sweetie, running downstairs to get Julie's post-coital herbal tea for her.

'The creep,' said Adam. 'Of course he's going to be nice to her. For the time being at any rate.'

'Maybe he's just a nice guy.'

'Your murderer. Maybe he is.'

Anyway, Leo went on, ignoring this, after Rod and Julie had sat chatting in bed for an hour or so, they had got up and had a late lunch. A simple salad with fresh tuna, washed down with a glass of white wine.

'Which white wine was that?' Adam asked.

'What d'you mean?'

'Where was the bottle from?'

Leo didn't know. Actually, come to think about it, he did. 'Cloudy Bay, Ti Koka or something. Would that be right?'

'Te Koko! One of my best wines, the bastard. How dare he?'

'They seemed to enjoy it.'

'Of course he did. Freeloader. That's forty quid a bottle. He'll be driving my car next. And then what did they do?'

'D'you really want to know?'

'They went back upstairs and shagged some more?'

Leo made a face; he didn't need to answer.

'Did you watch?' Adam asked.

'To be honest, I don't know why I did. I think because I was alone I wasn't so embarrassed. It was weirdly fascinating. Like porn, only with people you know. But then again, completely unarousing, even though I was right there. It was like they were behind glass.'

That was exactly how Adam had felt, though he didn't particularly want to discuss that with his son. 'Sure,' he said.

'Anyway, I was doing my duty. Checking that there weren't any high-fives or more cries of "We did it!"'

'"Yeehah, we're killers!" that sort of thing. Presumably there weren't?'

'Nothing.' The rest of the day had been the same. Rod was around the house, then helping out with various odd jobs.

'What a slimeball.'

'He sorted out some jammed Velux blinds on the top floor, then there was a cracked pane of glass in one of the windows in the utility room...'

'Julie's been banging on at me for months about that. Don't tell me, he helped her in the garden as well.'

''Fraid so. They were planting marigolds.'

'Marigolds! Julie knows I can't abide them. The height of suburban kitsch.'

But there had been nothing to indicate that Rod had recently put his Mr Fixit skills to work in faking a suicide or a car accident. 'Sorry.'

Eventually Leo had got bored, nothing was happening, so he'd gone to Abby's.

'In Hendon? You got down there okay?'

'Like you showed me. Hands together. Thought about the front room. Bang. I was there.'

'And?'

Leo looked sad. His fiancée had been there alone, making supper and getting ready for bed. He had watched her, then wondered whether he should try to talk to her. And then, when she was in her nightie and had started sobbing, he decided he had to, even if it would freak her out. But he hadn't been able to get through.

'Nothing. Why, I have no idea. I tried. I was desperate to communicate.'

Adam made a sympathetic face. 'I'm afraid it's still a mystery to me, as well. Why it works sometimes and not others.'

'Anyway, I was so frustrated I decided to hop off and visit Granny. See if I could have more luck with her.'

'Did you?'

'No.' Leo laughed. But here was the news. He had found his grandmother and Jadwiga in her sitting room, discussing her will, no less. Patricia had it open in front of her and was going over it, point by point.

'Really? Who instigated that?'

'I don't know. I came in halfway through. But Granny was literally asking her what she should do with my share. Give it to Matilda, or Claire…'

'Or Jadwiga herself?'

'It didn't come to that. Not while I was there anyway. But she's definitely being an influence.'

'Although Granny does love these little power plays, doesn't she?' Adam said. 'She might just have been winding Jadwiga up, getting her advice, making sure she stays loyal, doesn't bugger off to some other old lady.'

'Why wouldn't she stay loyal?' Leo replied. 'It's a beautiful house, she's got a big room to herself, it's quiet, there's a nice view, Tempelsham's just down the road. For a carer it's a bit of a plum position.'

'So what then?'

That was it. Patricia had gone to bed. Jadwiga had given her her special sleepy drink and she'd conked out. Leo hadn't particularly wanted to spend the whole night watching her snoring with her mouth open so he'd moved on to his Aunt Claire's, arriving at the house to find her and Dan in the middle of a row. About Maya and some private school they might send her to.

'Heathcote House. Oh for goodness' sake! Don't they ever stop?'

'But then it spun off from there. It was like, "This is what you always do, Dan." And then something about him being so mean. Then suddenly they got on to the house. Granny's house. And what's going to happen to it when she dies. Now that you're dead and it's all theirs. Is that right, Dad?'

'It will be,' Adam said. 'In a few months.'

'Julie doesn't get a share?'

'Claire and I were joint tenants, so no. As I told you, "Survivor takes all". Funnily enough, that was Dan's advice.'

'Funnily enough,' Leo repeated. 'Anyway, Claire starts saying she'd like to live at Larks Hill, because she was happy there as a child, and Maya could have the kind of childhood she'd had. And then Dan was saying, "You can't go back in time, Claire. Anyway, you had a brother then..."'

'Did he say that?' Adam asked.

'Yes. "And Maya doesn't," he went on. Then Claire said, "That's not my fault," and Dan was saying, "So we're back on to that one again, are we?" and Claire was saying, "Yes, we are, and I should never, ever have let you talk me out of it," and Dan was saying, "We weren't even married at that point" and then Claire was in tears and Dan was just standing there, hands dangling by his side, saying nothing. He's such a dick.'

'What was she trying to say? That he'd forced her to have an abortion?'

'They didn't use that word, but yes, that's exactly what I thought. The next thing I know Aunt Claire is crumpled up on the couch, sobbing, and Dan's finally gone to her. And he's trying to soothe her with his big hands, and she's pushing him away, then she's saying, "What's wrong with us living in a beautiful house, and what's wrong with me trying replicate a time when I was happy?" And he replies, "Aren't you happy now?" And she says, "Why did we bother with all this, if we're not going to try and be happy?"' Leo looked at his father triumphantly. 'Those were her exact words.'

'Interesting,' Adam said. 'But pretty unspecific. Hardly incriminating in themselves.'

'But what did she mean by "Why did we bother *with all this*"?'

'They could have been referring to the tax scheme, I suppose,' Adam said.

There was silence, while the implications sunk in.

'How about you, Dad?' Leo asked. 'Did you get anywhere with Jeff?'

Adam hesitated for a moment, reluctant to tell his son what had happened. But then: why not? As he'd said to Eva, it had hardly been his fault if Jeff had had a pre-existing heart condition. Scrooge had survived a visit by his business partner. Hamlet didn't drop dead when his father appeared.

Leo surprised him by laughing. 'Result!' he said, giving his dad a high-five.

'So you don't think I'm a murderer?'

'Certainly not. Anyway, the little shit's been trying to get you out of the firm for ages, hasn't he?'

'He has. By the nastiest, most underhand methods.'

'So. Just deserts, I'd say.'

'Thank you, son. I'm glad you're here. And on my side. I was starting to feel as if it was all my fault.'

'Well, it was your fault. But nothing for you to feel guilty about. Revenge is sweet, as they say.'

Adam was about to follow up his description of Jeff's heart attack with an edited account of how the firm had taken it, his evening with all his old employees in the pub, his sad chat with Eva, back at hers – when he realised they weren't alone.

'Hello,' said Leo, eyes spinning with surprise.

The apparition he was gawping at stared back at the pair of them like a stunned goldfish (albeit a goldfish that looked somewhat like a weasel).

'Where am I?' Jeff asked.

CHAPTER TWENTY-SEVEN

'Jeff!' Adam replied. He was surprised at how calm he felt. 'Welcome. Please don't be afraid. You've had a heart attack, and now you're over on the far side. Where we spirits hang out.'

'Spirits!' Jeff spluttered. He stared hard at Adam, then his eyes took in Leo as well. 'I... I... I–'

'You've died, yes,' Adam interrupted. 'The ambulance didn't get to you in time. Sorry about that. To be honest, it was all so sudden I think you were beyond help. I might have been partly to blame, in that I visited you at home.'

Jeff swore. The memory of what had happened in his spare room was clearly coming back to him. 'You accused me of killing you. Even – setting up your suicide.'

'Did you, though?' Adam asked. 'It doesn't matter now if you say yes. I won't strangle you. I can't strangle you. With these.' He waved his spectral hands. 'I just want to know.'

'Of course I didn't, mate.' There was a silence. Jeff's ghost was shaking his head, clearly still struggling to process what was going on, what had happened to him. 'How would I have done all that?' he continued eventually. 'In your wife's garage? In any case, why would I want to kill you?'

'You wanted me out of the firm, so you'd be totally in charge, so you could put your name on the masthead and get on with pulling down the few remaining nice parts of London and making loads of money...'

'Butcher's Yard,' Jeff muttered, under his breath. 'We were supposed to be doing the public consultation... today.'

'Yesterday,' Adam corrected. 'It's Saturday now.'

'Is it?'

'You missed a day. Count yourself lucky. I was out for weeks.'

'Out where?'

'Good question.'

'But what happened at the consultation? Did those Right to Remain buggers get anywhere?' Jeff was reaching around frantically with his hands, clearly trying to find his phone.

Adam was laughing. 'Jeff,' he said. 'Reality check. You don't have a mobile anymore. You're dead. It's time to let all that earthly stuff go.'

'But Butcher's Yard – the Clerkenwell Tower – it's a flagship project. Even if... I'm not able to be there...'

'You're actually dead, Jeff...'

'It *has* to go ahead...'

'As it happens, I was at the office yesterday morning.'

'Albury & Atkinson?'

'Albury, Atkinson, Trelawney,' Adam corrected. 'Keep up, mate. The delightful duo were also there. Savidge and Sugar.'

'How could you be there? If you're–'

'Tim and Steve were obviously a bit disappointed that you weren't around for the public consultation, but they headed off anyway.'

'That's a disaster. They have no idea how to manage those things. Particularly Tim. Shit!'

'You're right. I expect they screwed it up royally.'

'Who went with them?'

'Trevor.'

'Trevor! He's crap at interface stuff.'

'Jeff, calm down. It's time to accept what's happened to you. Your life is over. Your involvement with your pet project is over. You may feel the same inside but–'

'I do feel the same inside.'

Adam laughed. 'So do I. It's weird. But you need to start letting go. Of your life on earth. Ambitions. Projects. Your family. Move on. To this life. On the other side.'

Jeff stood stock-still. It seemed as if reality was finally sinking in.

'You remember my son, Leo,' Adam added.

'Leo, shit, sorry, mate, I didn't recognise you.' As he so often was with unfamiliar people, Jeff was charm itself. 'You had a car crash. I was very sorry to hear about–'

'My loss,' Leo cut in. 'So was I. Though how or why it happened is still a bit of a mystery. The brakes on my new e-Golf seem to have failed.'

'What d'you mean, "seem"? You think it was deliberate?'

Was Jeff protesting just a little too much?

'I know it was deliberate,' Leo said.

'Okay.' Jeff looked slowly round. 'And your dad also seems to think he didn't kill himself.'

'There's no think about it, Jeff,' Adam said. 'I know I didn't kill myself.'

'What are you saying, Jeff?' Leo asked. 'You thought that Dad was really a suicide?'

'I'm afraid I did, yes.'

'Did you have any thoughts about why?'

Jeff looked over towards Adam. Now his face was creased with sympathy. 'I was shocked, to be honest. I didn't understand it. Why it had happened, really. I knew things had been difficult for him at work. But this was taking things to a whole other level.'

Adam laughed scornfully. 'You knew things had been difficult for me at work... I wonder why that was. So what *did* you think then? That I was so unhappy with what you were doing, trying to force me out of my own firm, that I'd taken the easy way out?'

'Hang on, hang on,' Jeff replied. 'I think "forcing you out of your own firm" is a bit of an exaggeration.' He was looking round to Leo for support, though why Adam's son should take his side wasn't at all clear. 'You were in your late fifties. A lot of your expertise, with drawing boards and so on, was terrific, but way out of date. You had no idea about computer modelling. Some of your attitudes, also, were, how can I put this tactfully, not exactly in tune with today's values–'

'Fuck's sake, Jeff!' Adam cried. 'My attitudes haven't changed. My architectural philosophy hasn't changed. I may not be such a whizz on computers, but let's be frank, neither are you any more. That's why we have younger colleagues. In any case, late fifties is hardly retirement age in our profession. Norman Foster is in his eighties and still cracking on. Richard Rogers was working, by all accounts, until his final illness. You know perfectly well I didn't want to give up.'

'No one was suggesting you stop completely–'

'Just not continue to work for the firm that had my name on it, is that it?'

'Guys!' Leo cut in, holding up both hands. 'Please. Let's not get sidelined here. Mr Trelawney, why did you think my dad had taken his own life?'

'Call me Jeff. We're all friends here.' Adam knew exactly what his unctuous partner was doing, playing for time as usual, while his weasel brain raced round trying to work out his best advantage. 'No,' he went on after a moment, 'I did think your father had done it. But that maybe it had more to do with his personal life than any potential changes at the firm. His marriage, as I'm sure you know, was in trouble. He was having an inappropriate affair with a much younger colleague. I suppose I thought that his problems had all rather stacked up for him.'

'Bullshit!' Adam cut in. 'There were no rules at our firm that I was aware of against seeing a colleague, even if they are a bit younger. Was that the next thing on your woke agenda? "Thou shalt not have relationships at work, even if completely consensual…"'

Jeff was shrugging and looking over at Leo. 'See what I mean? "Your woke agenda". How does fuddy-duddy claptrap like that play with our clients? Not to mention our younger staff and interns. That was just one of many instances.'

'Whereas your totally bogus, right-on mantras, visibly transparent and insincere to anyone with half a brain, weren't?' Adam spat back.

'Come on! Let's just stick to the point,' Leo cut in, glaring at his father. 'You were seriously convinced, Jeff, that problems in Adam's personal life had driven him to suicide?'

'Among other things, yes. To be honest, I thought his consistently negative way of thinking was probably indicative of a deeper malaise, some unexpressed frustration with his life and how it had turned out…'

'What utter cock!' Adam cried. 'You knew I was happy with Eva, work colleague or no. And she was happy with me. As for the rest of my life, Jesus, I'm not the one in therapy…'

'Perhaps you should have been,' Jeff snapped back. 'Was she, though?' he added.

'Was… who… what?'

'Was she that happy? Eva. Or was she just pretending?'

Adam stared at him. How offensive could he get? He imagined that Leo might be about to intervene again; but no, he seemed content to watch this one develop.

'Pretending what, Jeff?' Adam asked.

'You'd have to ask her. If she was so into you, why's she hooked up with Reuben after a mere seven weeks?'

That was a spiteful lie. And yet: 'I *did* love you,' she had said, this morning. Then: 'I never *gave* a shit about the age gap.' That, too, couched in terms of the past. But Reuben had been in the pub with her and there had been no obvious display of intimacy apart from the drunken goodbye kiss on the lips, which Simone had got too, and was in any case a bit of an Eva trademark. He had put her in a cab, for God's sake! 'I'm afraid that's simply not true,' Adam replied.

'"I'm afraid" it is,' Jeff countered. He made the quotes with his fingers in a way so annoying that Adam would have punched him if he'd been able.

'I was with them both last night and I didn't see any evidence of it,' he said, trying hard to keep his cool.

'They've still got to work together, so they're keeping it below the radar for the time being.'

'How do you know, then?'

'I keep my ears to the ground.'

'Not anymore,' Adam mocked. Then: 'Nice try, Jeff. But they didn't even hold hands.'

'Was anyone else with them?'

'Simone.'

'There you are. It's still a secret.'

'Even from Simone?'

'Even from Simone.'

'So how do you know?'

Jeff shrugged, smugly. 'You don't have to believe me, Adam. I'm just telling you how it is.'

CHAPTER TWENTY-EIGHT

L eo had taken charge at that point. Did his father really want to get to the bottom of what had happened – to him, and to Leo – or was he just going to waste his time squabbling? Wouldn't it be more interesting if Jeff was given a chance to continue with his thoughts on the case? Now that he knew Adam had been a victim of foul play, did he have *any* idea who might have been responsible?

Like, er, himself, Adam thought. But, rebuked by his son, he didn't say anything.

'If it wasn't suicide,' Jeff replied, slowly, and eminently reasonably, of course, 'I guess you'd have to ask: who stood to benefit from Adam's death?'

'Just about everybody,' Leo said with a bitter laugh.

'And what about you?' Jeff went on. 'This accident of yours. If it really was no accident, who was responsible for that? And why?'

'That would have followed on,' Adam said. 'My killer worried that Leo knew something about my death, so he had to go too.'

'*Did* you know something, Leo?' Jeff asked.

'I had my suspicions,' Leo replied. 'As you know, I didn't think Dad had killed himself.'

'Who did you share that thought with?'

'Leo only spoke about this with his immediate family,' Adam chipped in. 'And his grandmother.'

'Who is incapable of keeping a secret,' Leo added.

'So she might have told anyone in the wider family?' Jeff said.

'She probably did,' Leo said. 'Basically, she lives on the phone, and is pretty indiscreet, so anything you tell her gets widely circulated.'

'So who were you suspicious of?' Jeff asked.

'I worried – I still worry – about Granny's carer. Jadwiga. She's got in so close with Granny. She manipulates her. She's clever. She's kind of very polite and obedient, which Granny loves. She keeps out of the way when Granny has visitors. But when they're alone she's building up this intimate relationship, which Granny totally falls for. So Granny tells her stuff. About her money and everything. Even yesterday, as I told Dad earlier, they were looking over the will together.'

'So what are you saying?' Jeff asked. 'You think this carer has got your grandmother to change her will in her favour? If that's the case, why would she need to kill your father?'

'Because Dad kept a close eye on Patricia's affairs, didn't you, Dad?'

'Did you?' Jeff asked.

'I did.'

'Jadwiga knew that,' Leo said. 'She knew she'd never be able to finalise anything if Dad was around.'

'So she murders him. How would she manage that in his own garage? And why there, anyway?'

'Maybe she thought it looked likely. I mean, if you were going to kill yourself you'd hardly do it in someone else's garage, would you? What I do know is that her boyfriend is a car mechanic.'

'Her boyfriend?' said Jeff. 'Who's he?'

Leo explained about Omar. 'And Fallowfields is only eight miles out of Tempelsham, so it's not as if he had to go far. More to the point he would have known how to fiddle with the brakes on my electric car. Not everyone would know that, not even every mechanic. But that's one of the models they have at that VW place. The e-Golf and the electric ID.3 and 4. It's a growing part of their business.'

'Okay, okay,' Jeff said. 'So you seriously think it might have been these two?'

'They have the motive, the capability, the opportunity. Aren't those the things detectives look for?'

Adam chuckled to himself as Jeff nodded, seriously and sagaciously. If anyone knew what detectives looked for, it was he; at any rate in the world of crime fiction, both of the book and TV variety.

'So your electric car was in Tempelsham?' Jeff asked.

'No, London. Hendon. Where we live.'

'Hendon? Isn't that a bit of a trek for this Omar?'

Leo shrugged. 'It's only a train and Tube ride. Depends how desperate he was.'

'This was my sister's objection,' Adam said. 'It does seem a bit of a stretch.' He turned back to his son. 'If you consider the other suspects we've discussed, does anybody else seem likely?'

'Not really.' There was a longish pause while Leo considered. 'Unless,' he laughed, 'it's Walter.'

'Walter!' Adam scoffed. 'Why on earth would that dipstick–?'

'He hates you with a vengeance,' Leo riposted.

'Does he? Why?'

'Because of the way you treated Mum.'

'Ridiculous! He wasn't even around then. What does he know… about all that?'

'More than you realise. You know what he calls you?'

'No.'

'The gold-plated shit.'

'Well, jiminy-joo-jar,' said Adam. 'He actually says that in front of you, my children?'

'He simmers angrily when your name comes up. His jowls start wobbling.'

'So what? He's an idiot. Everything he's ever touched has turned to shit. If anything, I feel sorry for him.'

Jeff was leaning forward, rubbing his virtual goatee between his forefinger and thumb. 'Okay,' he said. 'I can understand how the new partner might not necessarily be enamoured of the ex-husband. But seriously – I agree – murder? What would be his motive?'

'Money,' said Leo. 'Dad's will has a big chunk in it for Serena, doesn't it, Dad?'

Adam shrugged; but there was a nod in the shrug.

'Guilt payment, is that it?' said Jeff.

'Look,' said Adam, 'I don't have to explain the reasoning behind my every last disbursement, but Julie gets Fallowfields, and most of the equity from the company and the Covent Garden property. As well you know, Jeff. Leo and Matilda get the lion's share of my investments. And yes, I did leave Serena something too.'

'For what reason?' Jeff asked.

'Put it this way, she helped me a lot with the business in the early years, and then, by the time it all came to fruition, and A & A started making serious money, she was out of the picture. I didn't see why Julie, who's hardly lifted a finger in that area, should get everything.'

'Does Serena have an income herself?'

'Not really. Other than what I give her for the children.'

'But they're grown up now.'

'I never stopped it. Anyway, Matilda's still living at home.'

'So Serena lives on that?'

'She earns something from her interior decorating.'

'Not a lot, let's face it,' said Leo. 'And what you gave her for us was never that much.'

'It was plenty, whatever she told you. I also left her my share of La Residenza,' Adam said. 'Our villa in Italy.'

Jeff was deadpan. 'That was nice of you,' he said, smirking in Leo's direction, but his irreverence was not picked up, or even noticed, Adam thought. 'Are you prepared to tell us how much Serena's share of your estate amounted to?' Jeff asked.

Adam shrugged. 'She had about a sixth. That's what I decided was fair. Though I did revise it a couple of years ago.'

'Upwards or downwards?'

'Upwards.'

'To what, if I may ask?'

'About a quarter.'

Leo whistled. 'When you and Julie started falling out?'

'Maybe that had something to do with it.'

'How much is that quarter worth, Dad?'

'As Jeff knows,' Adam said, 'we've done well with the firm, and more particularly with the real estate. In that Stan and I were lucky enough to get the freehold on a couple of warehouses in Sheridan Street, back when Covent Garden was still quite run-down. As the area has gone up and up, so has the value of the offices. Scandalous, really, but that's the way of the world.'

'So how much is Serena's share worth?' Jeff persisted. 'In total?'

Adam paused, for a moment reluctant to share. But then, he was dead, he had left every last penny of his assets and savings behind, so who really cared? 'My whole estate was worth about twenty,' he said. 'So, around five, I guess.'

'Million?' Leo whistled.

'That's a big wedge,' Jeff said. 'Especially if you've got nothing. So what about this Walter? What does he do?'

'Sponges off Mum and says he's writing a memoir,' Leo replied.

'It's the latest in a long line of things he's done.'

'Tried to do,' corrected Adam.

Leo laughed. 'That's true. He ran a restaurant for a bit,' he said. 'That went bust. Then he started an online art gallery, but that didn't come off either. Some kind of catering business, sandwiches for offices, another disaster. When Mum met him, he was claiming to be a publisher...'

'"Bridging the gap between the self-published and the traditionally published" was how he explained it to me,' Adam said with a wry smile. 'Serena had this mad idea that he might publish a collection of my poems. Typically sweet and well-meaning of her, but really, as if! *Poems By My Girlfriend's Ex*. She can't help herself sometimes, pushing people together for pointless projects.'

'So he didn't make much money by the sounds of it?'

'That was one thing he was successful at.'

'Walter is blessed with the exact opposite of the Midas touch,' Leo added. 'In that everything he fingers turns to shit. Before he moved in with Mummy he was about to be evicted from a bedsit in Walthamstow. Most of his friends had dropped him after he'd borrowed money from them and not paid it back.'

With a glint in his eye, he gave them a few more juicy details.

'How do you know all this, Leo?' Adam asked.

Leo shrugged. 'As I said before, I listen and learn.'

'Always wise to be well-informed about your enemies,' Jeff said. 'But this answers my original question: Who stood to benefit?'

'I'm sorry, it's absurd,' said Adam. 'Walter. Just posit for a mad moment that that tedious failure could have been responsible for my death; how could he possibly have done anything without Serena knowing?'

'You think your ex-wife wouldn't have supported him?' Jeff asked. 'Or turned a blind eye? To a plan that suddenly gave her what she financially deserved. Now, rather than in twenty years' time. When she'd be too old to enjoy it.'

'No,' said Adam. 'I absolutely don't think she would. Serena has a lovely nature. She wouldn't hurt a flea, would she, Leo?'

'Not a flea, no. Or a kitten. But she can be quite rude about you, Dad.'

Adam looked taken aback. He smiled in Jeff's direction. 'I wouldn't hold it against her if she were. But honestly, despite everything that happened between us, she's always been extremely reasonable. And forgiving.'

'What does Leo say to that?' Jeff asked.

'Dad's right. She is forgiving. But not about everything. She could get quite worked up about Fallowfields, for example. When we were in Italy once, she was sobbing about it. Looking round at everything at La Residenza and going on about how you'd done it together and you'd planned to do something similar at home, and had all these ideas, and then that bitch Julie had come along...'

'She really said that?'

'Sorry, Dad. That's what Mum's like. She's very gracious and gentle on the surface, but her anger runs deep.'

'Sounds like she might have been happy to bump off Julie,' Jeff said with a laugh.

'To answer your question,' Leo replied. 'I could see her, possibly, letting Walter do what he wanted with Dad...'

'Which is what?' Adam cut in scornfully. 'Murder me? Don't be ridiculous. He'd have fucked it up royally if he'd even tried.'

'But what isn't possible,' Leo continued, 'is Mum supporting him doing anything to me.'

'Though Walter doesn't like you very much either,' Adam pointed out. 'You haven't made his attempts to be a stepfather easy by all accounts.'

'For a simple reason,' Leo said. 'I never liked him. From the start. Mum kept saying, "Give him a break, darling." I did try. For a week or two. But then, quite quickly, once he'd moved in, and was established as the so-called man of the house, he tried to throw his weight around. With me, in particular. You can do this, you shouldn't do that. In the house I'd lived in all my life. Then crappy and unnecessary career advice. Why don't you sign up for this course, or try for that qualification, or go and do this shitty job for a while, it will make a man of you. "*I* once stacked shelves in Sainsbury's for three months," et cetera, et cetera. When none of it was any of his fucking business.'

'So, in fact, you loathed him,' Jeff said. 'And he loathed you, by the sounds of it. Maybe if he had murdered Adam, and he thought you were on to him, he would have found it easy to have those brake lines adjusted. Without, obviously, telling your mother. All those odd jobs he had over the years, were any of them to do with cars?'

Leo paused. 'Actually, yes. He worked in a garage, in some railway arch in Camden or somewhere. That was one of the shitty jobs he used to bang on about. As if its very shittiness was a badge of honour. Plus he has an interest in classic cars.'

'Well, there you are,' said Jeff.

'Working in a garage for a bit doesn't necessarily mean that he fiddled with your brake lines,' Adam said. 'Nor, frankly, does an interest in classic cars.'

'I suppose it's *possible* he acted on his own,' Leo went on, almost as if to himself. 'He's quite a strange guy. And I'll tell you one thing: he hates not having any money. Almost as much as he hates other people having it. Particularly anyone successfully entrepreneurial. Like you, Dad. Because he's proved himself to be the world's worst entrepreneur. He has terrible ideas, and then he doesn't have the nous or application to make them work.'

'Bit of a double whammy.' Jeff chuckled.

'I'm not sure running an architectural practice counts as being an entrepreneur,' Adam observed.

'Same difference,' said Leo. 'You've made a success of something. And financially, big time.'

'But he'd only have done anything to you, Leo, if he was scared you were going to expose him,' Jeff said.

'Did you ever threaten him?' Adam asked. 'Even inadvertently?'

Leo thought hard. 'We talked about your death quite a lot, Dad. Unlike me and Matty, he did think you could have killed yourself.'

'Bluffing, possibly,' said Jeff.

'He thought you had a depressive streak; also, quite a lot of self-loathing.'

'Did he now?' Adam said.

'He said you were always passive-aggressive with him and that was typical of someone covering up a lot of deep-seated anger.'

Adam laughed. 'I'm not sure my aggression towards him was that passive, to be fair.'

'Then he banged on about the coroner having looked into the case, and the due process of law, and all that sort of claptrap.'

'But what did you say to him?' Jeff asked. 'About Adam?'

'Just that I didn't agree.'

'That he'd killed himself?'

'Yes.'

'To which he said?'

'He said that if Matty and I didn't think that Dad's death was suicide, then we had to face the fact that the implications were shocking.'

'But you never seriously thought that he, Walter, could have done it?' Jeff said. 'Or accused him of that?'

'Only as a joke.'

'How d'you mean, "Only as a joke"?'

'I can't remember. I said something like, "Maybe *you* did it, Walter, since you hate him so much".'

'What did he say to that?'

'Something extremely pompous, as you'd expect. "That's a very serious accusation, Leo." It was in the evening, just before supper, and we were on our second gins by that point. We often have a bit of a barney when we hit the booze, particularly if it's gin. I quite enjoy winding him up. Transexuals, he gets very agitated about them, particularly when it comes to sport and ladies' loos. Statues being knocked down or chucked in the river. All that sort of anti-woke stuff.'

'Okay, okay,' Adam replied, not wanting to be distracted. 'Then what did he say?'

'We left it. He gave me the evils and that was that.'

'The evils?'

'Glare. Stare. Twitching mouth. Wobbling jowls, the full works.'

'Okay,' Adam said, after a moment. 'Let's tentatively add Walter to the suspects' list.'

'Jeff's right though,' Leo said. 'We need to think hard about *all* those who stood to benefit from your death, Dad.'

'Including Jeff,' said Adam.

Jeff laughed; rather nervously, Adam thought. 'Not anymore,' he said. 'I don't think, mate.'

'Surely we can clear this up here and now,' Leo said. 'Here you are, Jeff. Whatever advantages your widow is going to have, from what you've done or haven't done, you are not. So why not just tell us if you had anything to do with any of this? Answer please, straight up: Did you fake my father's suicide?'

'Would I really be sticking around here, speculating about possible murderers with you guys, if I was the culprit? I don't think so.'

'Where else would you go?' Adam said. He wasn't fooled by Jeff's keenness to consider other suspects. It was exactly what a guilty man would do to distract attention from himself. 'You don't yet understand how to negotiate this dimension. You don't even know how to get from A to B.'

'Look, mate,' Jeff replied, 'hand on heart, I was as shocked by your suicide as everyone else. By the sounds of it you've been keeping an eye on me since your funeral. Have I really been acting like a murderer covering up a terrible crime?'

'So why were you so freaked out when I visited you?' Adam asked. 'Why did you have a heart attack when I mentioned Rod?'

'Christ, Adam. You know I had a heart condition. I knew next to nothing about Rod. Was I freaked out, being yelled at by the ghost of my ex-partner? Yes, I was. It's been a lifelong fear of mine, ghosts, ever since I was a small boy. You knew that, because I told you, at that horrible haunted hotel in Dorset. And another time, when we were having a heart to heart one evening in the New Deal. I'm not in the frame for murder, but you should be for manslaughter.'

'Okay, enough already,' Leo said. 'I'm happy to believe you, Jeff. Dad?'

Adam stared long and hard at his ex-partner. Those dark weasel eyes, staring angrily but also pleadingly back at him, did seem sincere enough, but a) they were an illusion and b) he had been fooled in the past. Then again: what did Jeff have to gain by lying? It was all over now.

'I guess I'll have to believe you,' he said. But he still wasn't one hundred per cent sure that he did.

CHAPTER TWENTY-NINE

Seven am. Serena and Walter were still asleep in bed, though the sunlight was already shining brightly on the smart Roman blinds. There had been tatty curtains when Adam had lived there, years before, which he had got 'on permanent loan' from his mother. Funny to think how little money they had had then, how they'd had to 'scrimp and save', to use that irritating phrase of Patricia's, how Serena used come back from the supermarket thrilled with the reduced to clear items she had scooped up: meat on the turn, borderline manky salads, half-stale pies and bread rolls.

The three ghosts were lined up against the far wall, eager to observe their new suspects, whose stories and potential for guilt they had been discussing half the night.

'Shall we take a bet on who gets the tea?' Jeff joked.

'Mummy,' said Leo. 'For sure. Walter's a lazy shit.'

But when the two of them stirred a few minutes later, and the spectral trio had to watch Walter snuggling, spoon-style, into Serena's still shapely backside, it was he who agreed to go downstairs.

'D'you mind, darling?' Serena asked.

'Not at all,' Walter replied. 'I know my role. House slave.'

'Hardly.'

'Is it the tea you want this morning, ma'am. Or the freshly squeezed?'

'How about both?'

'Happy to oblige. And then I might freshly squeeze *you*.'

Even in the interests of necessary surveillance, Adam couldn't quite bear to watch this grim morning banter. 'I'll just see if Matilda's here too,' he said, sliding off down the corridor and up the twisting stairs to the attic conversion.

She was. Fast asleep, a thin beam of sunshine cutting under the dark crimson Velux roof blind to make a bright line diagonally across her recumbent body. Watching her like this, Adam felt, if possible, even more moved than if he were still alive. There was such life in her, her eyes closed tight, a smile on her face as she dreamed. Why were things so difficult for her? What did it matter if she took her time to find the 'right career' or the 'right man', or was it woman, or, no unfashionable jesting in her earshot, something in between, who would finally make her happy? She was young, healthy, energetic, beautiful, talented.

Now she was muttering. Her dream was turning bad. She was moaning fitfully.

Adam went to her. He wished he could stroke her forehead, soothe her with the touch of a hand. 'Matilda,' he said gently. 'It's okay, darling, you're just having a little nightmare.'

'Daddy!' she said, sitting up abruptly.

She looked around. Put her hands to her eyes. Rubbed them hard with the back of her palms. 'Oh my God!' she said. 'That was *s-o-o* vivid.' Then she slumped straight back into a prone position and was soon fast asleep again.

'D'you think she actually saw you?'

Adam turned. Leo had joined him.

'Shsh!' he said. Then, in a low voice: 'No. Maybe, at some

level. But I've already spoken to her. You haven't. So be careful, or she'll hear you, and then...'

'Would that be such a bad idea?'

'It might freak her out.'

'And you didn't?'

'Shssh!' Adam repeated as his daughter started again and rolled over. 'Come on, let's go. We shouldn't be talking to her just now, should we? Distracting from the main event.'

Back in the master bedroom Walter had now brought the orange juice and the tea.

'How relaxed are you feeling?' he asked as he and Serena sat up, side by side, sipping.

Now he was rubbing Serena's white belly with his liver-spotted brown hands.

'Not that relaxed, Walter.'

'It's been a while.'

God help us, Adam thought, is the old goat trying it on? With my first wife; in front of our son and my one-time business partner.

'I know, darling,' Serena replied. 'But... I'm sorry... what with everything... Leo...'

She choked up on her son's name and then started, quietly, to sob.

'I understand,' Walter said, as he held her.

'I'm sorry, Walter... it's OK... I'm fine... it's just...'

'I understand. Darling, it's awful for you... for me too...'

Adam watched in disbelief as Walter slid his hand from her waist and then purposefully downwards. 'Maybe what you need is a soothing touch of tenderness–'

'Ugh!' said Leo. 'Just leave her alone, you tosspot.'

'Please don't push it, Walter. I'm not in the right place at the moment...'

'Okay, okay. I'm sorry. I just thought... you're so gorgeous...'

'Walter, *stop* it!'

Serena looked over at the bedroom wall, almost as if she could see the ghostly team watching. Perhaps, after her visit from Leo, she was on guard.

With sex off the agenda Walter now wanted the iPad, with today's *Telegraph* online.

'Just five minutes,' said Serena, pulling herself together and sitting up. 'I did open it first.'

'Only because you insist on having it on your side of the bed,' he replied tetchily.

Serena ignored this and continued to read. Walter reached over and picked up his book. He was turning the pages rapidly, clearly struggling to find his place. Serena was chuckling.

'What's so funny?' he asked.

'Nothing.'

As Walter found his page, she read out a couple of lines of a comment piece.

'If you're going to hog the news, Serena, hog it. But please don't disturb me by reading out bits.'

'You just asked.'

'Because I wanted to read it myself. Which is a different thing. Anyway, I'm into my book now.'

'See what I mean,' Leo said. 'Arch plonker.'

'Certainly is,' Jeff agreed.

You should know, Adam thought.

'Walter,' Serena asked. 'Can I ask you a question?'

'I thought you were reading the paper.'

'I am. But, just out of interest, do you ever feel as if you're being watched?'

'Watched? By whom?'

'I don't know. Friendly spirits, perhaps.'

'Of course not. Have you gone mad, Serena?'

He took a big, noisy gulp of tea from the huge mug that read, in crimson and black, *WORK hard, DREAM big, NEVER give up.*

Then he slid his bony white legs out of bed and marched off towards the shower.

'D'you think she can sense us?' Jeff asked.

'I doubt it,' Adam replied. 'But she does know that someone could be watching her, doesn't she? So maybe she's just being careful, on the off chance.'

Downstairs, Walter and Serena had breakfast. Quite an elaborate affair involving home-cultured yoghurt that Walter had prepared, muesli that he'd mixed ('Walter's special mix'), scrambled eggs that he'd cooked, and fresh bread that he'd baked.

Matilda came down, in a dressing gown. She fixed herself a fried egg and a toasted bagel, announced that she was just going to have a shower, then she was off out for the day.

'Where are you going, darling?' her mother asked.

She was meeting her friend Olivia for coffee at the Tate, then they were going to look round some exhibition.

'What's that?' Walter asked.

'Some conceptual thing, I think. I don't know the details.'

'Can't bear conceptual,' said Walter. 'Total waste of space in my view.'

'I didn't actually ask you for "your view",' Matilda replied, heading back upstairs.

'I do wish you'd make more of an effort with her,' Serena said when she'd gone.

'You just witnessed it,' Walter replied. 'I take an interest and she jumps down my throat.'

'Was that really taking an interest?' Serena asked. 'Telling her the show she's going to with a friend is a total waste of space?'

'It's only an opinion. She's a big enough girl to answer back if she wants to.'

'Maybe it's a wee bit discouraging, darling.'

'I can't fake enthusiasm for an artistic movement I find tiresome and pointless, can I?'

'I suppose not,' said Serena, going back to her washing up.

'Now what?' asked Leo. 'Are we going to sit and watch these two bickering all day. Dick though he is, he's not exactly behaving like a man who's guilty of two recent killings, is he?'

'But how does a guilty man behave?' Jeff asked. 'Especially if his partner doesn't know what he's been up to.'

'She would, though, wouldn't she?' said Leo. 'They live together. Mummy's pretty perceptive. If he had done something, how would he keep such a terrible secret from her?'

'Murderers have been known to try and keep their crimes quiet,' Jeff observed. 'Even from their nearest and dearest.'

Serena's phone trilled. She put the saucepan she'd been scrubbing to one side on the draining board, peeled off her yellow rubber gloves, dried her hands on a kitchen towel and took the device from her pocket.

'Claire,' she said, as she swiped the screen with her forefinger.

There were bored 'aha's and 'yesses', then heartfelt 'oh my God's and 'really's.

Walter had put down the iPad and was standing by the kitchen table, attempting to eavesdrop.

'What's up?' he asked when Serena had finally clicked off.

'Adam's business partner,' Serena said slowly, 'you know, the one he calls the Weasel, has had a sudden severe heart attack and died.'

'You call me the Weasel?' Jeff said.

'You know that!' said Adam. 'Don't you?'

'No.' Poor Jeff sounded upset.

'We've all called you that forever.'

'The *Weasel*? Why?'

'Shsh!' Leo said. 'I'm trying to listen to this.'

'You're joking!' Walter was saying, shaking his head from side to side in an apparent display of sadness for a man he'd never known.

'What's up?' asked Matilda. She was down from the shower, dressed to go out, bag on her shoulder.

Serena told her.

'Wow!' she replied. 'And he was one of the ones you were suspicious of, weren't you?'

'Jeff's been trying to get rid of poor Adam for years,' Serena said. 'So I suppose I thought he was a likely candidate... for...'

'Daddy's murderer.'

'Heavens above!' Walter said. 'Have some respect.' He had picked up a tea towel, was now polishing a random wine glass he'd taken from the dark quartz surface beyond the sink, before pacing over purposefully to replace it where it belonged in the dedicated glass cupboard.

'You have to leave this idea behind, darling,' he said to Serena, casting a disapproving eye over Matty as he said it. 'I know you find it hard to accept that Adam took his own life, but he did. The inquest confirmed it. There was the note.'

'It was a poem,' Matilda said.

'It was clearly a note.'

'When did you see it?'

'At the inquest.'

'Really?'

'It was read out. If you remember. A crucial piece of evidence.'

'It was a poem. That Daddy had written. About someone else's suicide.' Matilda was regarding Walter with ill-concealed contempt. 'You never liked Daddy's poetry anyway, did you, Walter? Whatever you pretended.' She waved, pointedly, at her mother. 'Laters,' she added and left the house.

Walter had finished with the glasses and moved on to the cutlery that was propped up drying in a circular stainless-steel caddy. He took each knife, fork and spoon, studied it for smears or dirt, then gave it an individual extra dry before putting it down on the kitchen table. 'See what I mean,' he said. 'I can't win with her.' Now he had started on the crocks. 'Funny, isn't it,' he went on, 'how people so often have ambitions to do things they're absolutely rotten at when their real talent lies somewhere else? They want to paint, when actually they're brilliant writers. Or they want to write, when what they can really do is paint. Or they're desperate to broadcast, but have a terrible voice or can't pronounce their r's or are awkward in front of a camera. Your ex-husband was like that. Such a successful architect, why did he feel the need to be a poet as well?'

Leo was laughing. 'I wonder where *Walter's* real talent lies.'

'He's lying,' Adam said. His words cut across the ghostly merriment.

'He is allowed not to like your poetry, Adam,' Jeff said.

'I don't mean that. I don't give a toss what he thinks about my poetry. Or my architecture for that matter. I meant that he saw "Suicide Note" before the inquest. And before my death. He knows perfectly well that it's a poem. It was prominent in the collection I showed him because Serena was all excited about his silly old Bullfrog Press maybe publishing them.'

CHAPTER THIRTY

'This changes everything,' Claire told Serena.

'You think?'

'Jeff was my number one suspect. He's unscrupulous. I always thought he'd have done anything to get Adam out of the firm.'

'But why does the fact that he's died mean he didn't do it?' Serena asked. 'He could have killed Adam, and then Leo, and then been so stressed out by what he'd done that he had a heart attack.'

'No,' Claire replied. 'Whoever killed Adam and Leo is still out there, I'm sure of it. In any case, maybe it wasn't a heart attack. Have you thought about that? Maybe Jeff is victim number three. He was only in his late forties. It seems a bit convenient that he croaked it just a day after Leo.'

The two ladies were at a table in the window of Emperor Court, a large and airy dim sum place that Serena liked in Lisle St, Soho. There was a small white ceramic pot of jasmine tea on the table beside them, but also a bottle of Pinot Grigio, on ice, in a champagne bucket. They had both agreed, after barely a minute sitting down, that they needed it.

Fortunately the table next to them was still empty, so Adam had a place to sit and comfortably eavesdrop. He was on his own again as the other two kept an eye on key suspects elsewhere: Jeff was staying at Serena's to watch Walter, while Leo had gone off to Patricia's to keep an eye on Jadwiga. Nothing was certain, but the field, they all thought, was narrowing.

A waiter and a waitress, in identical black waistcoats and white shirts, buzzed past Adam as if he wasn't there, delivering circular bamboo steamer trays to Claire and Serena, which they piled up in neat stacks on the yellow tablecloth.

For a moment Claire broke off from her theorising to admire the spectacle, then to check out the food inside the trays. Oh, she absolutely loved these ones, she said, what were they?

'Prawn dumplings. And that one's spinach and scallop, which is yummy too.' Serena, an old hand, took the country bumpkin through the steamed pork buns, spring and bean curd rolls, fried taro paste croquettes and other delights.

'We don't have this sort of thing in Tempelsham, sadly,' Claire lamented. 'Our only Chinese is a bit bog-standard. Stir fried rice and glutinous red sauce on everything. Anyway,' she went on, once they'd helped themselves to a plateful each, 'I have a confession to make.'

'Okay,' Serena replied. There were none of the jokes Adam might have made about Claire and Dan being the murderers, just a receptive smile.

'You know how we laughed in the White Duck about Julie,' Claire began, 'being such a kook... thinking she'd seen... like... the ghost of Adam...'

'Yes.'

'Please don't think I'm completely mad, Serena. I haven't actually told anyone this, not even Dan, but the very next day, in the evening, I'd just had this huge row with Dan about Maya's education. You know how he's set on state, regardless, but her school is crap, and she gets bullied by the rougher boys and the head teacher does nothing about it? Anyway, that's by the by, this latest instalment ended with him storming off as he always does and me sobbing my eyes out downstairs. But then the next thing I knew I got this weird feeling of strength and support, like just coming out of thin air, enveloping me...'

'Go on...' Serena was nodding, smiling, encouraging.

'Yes, and then I looked up and there he was.'

'Adam?'

'Yes. I couldn't believe it. Then he started speaking. I kind of accepted that it was him straight away, and we had this surreal chat, about the row I'd just had. I asked him where he was, *what* he was, and he said he didn't know but he didn't feel any different, even though he knew he was. Then he told me that he hadn't killed himself, so we got on to the whole idea of murder, and Julie, and then I couldn't help telling him about her new boyfriend, Rod, the handyman, you know about that, yes?'

'I did hear.' Serena was failing to suppress a schadenfreude smile. 'Didn't he know?'

'He did, though he'd only recently found out. Not that he had a leg to stand on, did he? Things haven't been right between them for ages.'

'Adam was never the most faithful man,' Serena said. 'I learned to live with it. But before Julie his little flings usually blew over...'

'You're far more tolerant than I would be. If Dan ever cheated on me, I'd chop his bits off. And then chuck him out.'

'Without his bits.'

'Yes!'

They laughed; though Serena's take on their long-ago marriage wasn't strictly fair; Adam could have counted the times he'd been unfaithful to her on the fingers of one hand; to be specific, on three fingers. He had never been a serial marital shagger – like, say, Jeff.

Serena had given up on chopsticks. She had picked up a small slimy parcel of prawn dumpling, its pink centre half visible though the semi-opaque wrap, between thumb and forefinger. Now she slipped it between her lips, still full and soft, though cracked a little with age. 'I loved him, that was my problem. I suppose I thought that he was such an unusual and talented man that women were bound to throw themselves at him, and I just had to live with it and he'd always come back to me in the end. We saw how that worked out. Perhaps if I'd been firmer Julie wouldn't have got her claws into him. She was never going to be happy with just being a mistress and funnily enough, once they were together, she was much tougher about his escapades than I'd ever been...'

'It was all right for her to break you up, but nobody could touch what she had...'

'Precisely. He was seriously besotted, that was the thing. "Cunt-struck", as his friend Roland had it.'

'How very rude.' Claire was shaking her head mock-disapprovingly as she laughed. 'Roland is funny, but he's always so terribly disloyal to Adam. Jealous probably. He's been in the City all his life but never made that much money, which must be a bit of a bummer, given that's presumably why you work there. His career as a poet never quite took off either. "Poet-banker", it's not the best look these days, is it?'

'Tell me more about Adam's ghost,' Serena asked.

'Finally,' Adam muttered.

He hadn't stayed long, Claire went on. Just long enough to insist that he hadn't killed himself, and then he was gone.

'How?'

'How what?'

'How did he go?'

'It's hard to remember. It wasn't even like he faded away slowly or anything. One moment he was there, the next, not. I hope you don't think I'm completely mad, Serena, but, oh my God, I've been so longing to share this with someone.'

Serena completely understood, she said. She looked across at Claire for several long seconds. She put her palms flat on the tablecloth and took a deep breath. Then she took a prawn cracker from the little bowl in the middle of the table and chewed it slowly. Actually, she said, she more than understood, because she'd had a similar incident herself.

Claire's eyes were shining with excitement. 'Really?' she said. 'With Adam?'

She grabbed the neck of the wine bottle, lifted it, dripping, from its bucket, topped up Serena's glass and then hers, then waved it at the watching waitress, enthusiastically indicating another.

'No,' Serena said. 'Leo.' She took a hurried gulp of her wine and immediately started sobbing.

Claire leant forward and held her hand. Eventually Serena pulled out a crumpled handkerchief and wiped her eyes.

'I'm sorry,' she said.

'Don't be silly. It would be odd if you didn't cry.'

It had been Leo who had visited her, Serena said, though Adam, as far as she could understand, had been right beside him, invisible. That was why she had driven out to see Claire the day after Leo's accident. To tell her about her son's suspicions about Jadwiga.

'Why didn't Adam appear himself?' Claire asked.

'I don't know. He was there in the background, apparently, but I couldn't see him. Maybe he just couldn't face talking to me.'

'I'm sure that's not…'

'I did want to!' Adam cried. 'I do want to.' But his words were not reaching, were not, he realised, ever going to reach his first wife in a crowded restaurant like this. One thing he'd learned in his short life as a ghost was that to communicate with humans you – and they – had to be alone. 'It's just… it has to be the right time,' he muttered pointlessly into the air.

'But if Leo had these suspicions *after* his death,' Claire was saying, 'that makes it a whole lot more–'

'I should have told you,' Serena cut in, 'about his visit before. I don't know why I didn't. I felt embarrassed, I suppose. You might have thought I'd completely lost it. As the grieving mother. But it was the same as you described with Adam. Leo was right there, in the flesh, well obviously not in the flesh, but solid, pretty much.'

'Like a hologram,' Claire said.

'Exactly, that's it, perfect. Like a hologram.'

All this made Claire wonder if anyone else had had a visitation and kept quiet about it. Apart from Julie, that is. They agreed, giggling now with released tension like schoolgirls, that they would ask their nearest and dearest.

'Dan will think I'm totally mad.'

'Walter ditto. He's the ultimate rationalist.'

'What about Matilda?'

'No. She will understand. You know how much she loved her papa. Between ourselves, I think that's been part of her problem, finding a half-decent man. They never quite match up to Daddy.'

Despite himself, Adam smiled.

CHAPTER THIRTY-ONE

M atilda wasn't really going to an exhibition at the Tate. She was meeting her friend Olivia, yes, but at a very different sort of event. It was a séance, and Olivia had suggested it.

Olivia had had a long and devoted interest in the supernatural. She had shelves full of books about ghosts, both fictional and real. She had seen all the films, the documentaries about ghost hunters, the podcasts about poltergeists, Danny Robins, everything. She had even joined the Spiritualist Church, attending regular meetings at her local branch in a shop premises in North Street, Clapham. Here she had met a medium, a Pole whose name was Zofia, who lived alone in Balham. Zofia regularly communicated with the dead, though she would never have used that word, as a spirit never died, it 'passed'. On to another world. When Olivia had told her Matilda's story, of her father's supposed suicide and the subsequent visitation, Zofia hadn't turned a hair. She had, rather excitedly, agreed to organise one of her Saturday afternoon séances.

So here they all were, ten of them, in Zofia's front room, with the curtains drawn against the bright sunshine outside. They sat in the gloom around an oblong dining table, hands flat on the maroon tablecloth, fingers spread. The only other light came from a tasselled standard lamp, which was just behind Zofia, who sat at one end like the hostess of a spooky dinner party, with Matilda on one side and Olivia on the other. She was wearing a dark blue velvet dress with a low cleavage and what looked like a shopful of costume jewellery, her wrists jangling with silver bangles.

Now she was introducing Matilda, telling the group her story. Matilda had, she said, already been honoured with a visit by her father Adam. But since then, she had failed to get back in touch with him. Zofia, with her long experience of summoning spirits, was going to try again for her.

The group sat in respectful silence, ten solemn faces, not a trace of levity on any of them. From the street outside came the incongruous sound of a boy on a scooter, his mother running after him. 'Scott, come *back*! Scott, stop that *now*!' Her voice and footsteps faded away down the street.

'Adam... Albury,' Zofia called, her eyes on her notes in front of her. 'Once of... Fallowfield. Wherever you are now, come and join us. Your daughter Matilda needs you.' Slowly, she got to her feet and waved her hands over Matilda's head. 'Your daughter *ne-e-e-eds* you,' she repeated, elongating the word dramatically.

From a corner of the room, Leo was watching. Had he allowed himself to materialise, you would have seen, between those ghoulish dimples, a wry smile. When he had been alive, he would have scoffed at an event such as this. Summoning the dead – ridiculous! Such things were for gullible fools. Now that he was dead himself, his objections were different. How dare these morbid freaks be so intrusive. Was Zofia really able to communicate across the mysterious divide between living and dead – or was she a charlatan? She was making a big deal of calling for his father, but she had got his address wrong and so far completely failed to notice *him*, a bona fide ghost, sitting there watching them all.

'I feel him...' Zofia was saying now. 'I feel him coming. Come on, Adam, join us here... your daughter *ne-e-e-eds* you.' The medium's face was twisted into a grimace, but there was really no need for that, if what she was trying to do worked.

'I *fe-e-e-e-l* him coming. Come on, Adam Alb-b-b-bury...'

CHAPTER THIRTY-TWO

A t Emperor Court, Claire and Serena had settled into their second bottle of Pinot Grigio. Also, for good measure, an extra steamer tray of snowy dumplings with fish and cauliflower.

'It feels so strange,' Serena was saying, 'being here with you. My poor Leo dead in a car crash. I shouldn't be here...'

'Don't be silly. This is exactly where you should be. You need to talk.'

'I feel almost guilty, enjoying it, even just a little. This lovely restaurant...'

'Is taking your mind off things. Just for a short while. Leo would understand,' said Claire.

'He would,' Serena agreed, gazing into her wine glass.

'He would,' Adam seconded, from his adjoining table.

'Doesn't Walter ever take you out?' Claire asked after a moment.

'Chance would be a fine thing. Walter's a great chap, and very generous in many ways, but' – Serena shrugged – 'he's never had much luck with money.'

Claire sipped her wine. 'Doesn't that ever worry you?'

'Why should it? I'm not exactly broke.'

'Perhaps I shouldn't say this, but d'you ever think he might be–'

'Sponging off me?' Serena cut in, sharply.

'Please, Serena, don't take this the wrong way.'

'Sorry.' Serena took a deep breath. 'It was an accusation Leo made. He never got on with Walter. It's the whole stepfather thing. You know, those kids would much prefer it if I'd just stayed alone. Regardless of whatever happiness or companionship I might want or need. Matty doesn't get on with him that well either. It's a strain, frankly. With her in the same house. Particularly recently.'

'With the deaths?'

'Of course. And then, I shouldn't tell you this, but...' Now she was laughing.

'What?'

'Walter wants to marry me.'

'*Does* he?'

Adam leant forward. Good God! Here was a development.

'He keeps proposing.' Serena was grinning. 'In the most unlikely places.'

'And you haven't accepted?'

'I'm flattered, obviously, but I'm not sure I want to get married again. When the chips are down, it doesn't offer any more security than not being married.'

'I suppose it would if Walter had money.'

'Well, he doesn't. So it's very romantic and all that, but what, really, is the point?'

'Plus he'd presumably be tied in to a share of your house; and, I suppose, whatever you get from Adam?'

A classic, typical, barely-disguised, nosy leading question from Claire; not that Serena seemed to mind.

'This was the discussion I was having with Leo,' she replied. 'When he called him a sponger.'

'Not to his face?'

Serena laughed. 'No. Just to me. But apropos of the proposal, which Leo was completely, almost hysterically, against. You know, you'd think you can share stuff with your nearest and dearest but...' She tailed off, as if not wanting to criticise her now dead son.

'When was that?' Claire asked.

'A couple of weeks ago.'

'And you told Walter?'

'I did, eventually. I was upset. Leo's a sweet boy, but it's really none of his business what I do with my life.'

'Although it is – was – his business what you do with your money. If you married Walter that might have robbed Leo of whatever you would have left him. In due course.'

'Not if I specified in my will what I was leaving him. As I have done. Anyway, how much did he want? Adam left both him and Matty a pretty hefty chunk.'

'And you too?'

Serena smiled seraphically. 'You know, my relationship with Adam has been such an odd one. He treated me so badly when he ran off with Julie, leaving me with the kids, at the worst possible age. But then, he's always wanted to stay friends. He told me once he wished he'd never left me.'

'Did he? When was that?'

'A couple of years ago. Just before I met Walter. I must have regained my mojo big time because first of all Adam was all over me like a rash again and then suddenly there was Walter. And now, yes, there's some money too. Which he wasn't obliged to leave me at all given everything I already had in the settlement. I've even got La Residenza. Our villa in Puglia. I suppose we did build it together.'

Adam, riveted though he was by this exchange, was feeling a strange, strong, unearthly pull.

Now he heard a distant voice, growing louder. 'Adam, Adam Albury, your daughter Matilda ne-e-e-eds you...'

Matilda! What was wrong with her? No, not his beloved Matilda. He wasn't having anything happen to her. *Let me go to her now*, he willed, hands together.

And just like that he was gone, spiralling down the joint line of desire towards Balham.

CHAPTER THIRTY-THREE

J eff had stayed at Serena's to keep an eye on Walter, who had seen 'Suicide Note' before, Adam insisted, when he and Walter had discussed publishing a collection of his poetry with his tiny imprint Bullfrog Press.

'Bullshit Press, more like,' Adam had said to the other ghosts with a laugh. 'I'm not sure whether he's actually produced a single book. I only went along with the idea to be nice to Serena.'

Could it be, Adam had continued, that the very title had given Walter an idea? That a poem called 'Suicide Note' could be used as, guess what, a suicide note; and on that the rest of his murderous strategy had been built. Had he then worked with Julie and Rod on the garage set-up? Was he in league with another of the suspects? Carer Jadwiga perhaps, or Jadwiga's mechanic boyfriend, Omar? Adam didn't know, but he and the other two ghosts agreed that the whole thing was highly suspicious.

Jeff also felt he had something to prove. Despite these new speculations about Walter, Adam was clearly still not convinced that it wasn't he who had done away with him. Did that matter? Maybe not. Especially now they were both ghosts, waiting in this who-knew-where netherworld for who knew what. But he had his pride. Yes, he'd have been the first to admit that he'd wanted Adam out of the firm, that his partner was too old, too boringly unreconstructed, and frankly, too much of a liability, with all his persistent anti-woke crap. But that didn't mean he would have murdered him.

Also, Adam's death had led, pretty much directly, to his. So even though it would make zero difference to his spectral state, he did want to know who had done away with Adam, before Adam's ghost had called at his house and terrified him to death. It was, frankly, personal.

But it had, so far, been a fruitless morning. While Serena had got herself ready for her lunch date, showering and scenting herself and dressing almost as if for a man not a girlfriend, Walter had tidied up the kitchen, put everything away, wiped the surfaces assiduously, swept and mopped the dark slate floor. Was this something he usually did, Jeff wondered, or was all this busyness a reaction to a worry that he had been found out? If he really had been involved in Adam's death, had it been without Serena's knowledge? Surely his partner would know *something*, however much she pretended or protested otherwise.

When Serena had finally gone, Walter had gone upstairs to his laptop, which he'd set up on an empty table in what had been, judging by the posters and other clutter still lying around, Leo's teenaged bedroom. Leo had moved out of the family house some time ago, but his presence was still firmly there in this little side room. How long would it be before Walter had the Harry Potter and Jay-Z posters down and the walls repainted?

Jeff watched patiently as Walter worked his way through his emails.

Uber Eats
Walter, your discount is still available

easyJet
Walter, your summer plans could be hotting up

Your Funeral Plan Provider
Walter, check out your free funeral plan quotes

EuroMillionsRolloverAlert
TONIGHT, WALTER! 46,000,000 Euromillions jackpot could be yours

Or, alternatively, Jeff thought, just the five you'll be getting to share with your beloved, if beloved she really is. But no, there was nothing incriminating or suspicious here, was there?

But now Walter had closed down Outlook and was clicking into his documents. Inside a file named *Finances, private* there was a subsidiary file called, amazingly, *Journal*. Had the man never heard of Filesearch? Walter clicked it open, and up came a list of dates, reversed, for some reason, in the American fashion. As Jeff watched, agog, Walter created a new page and started typing:

Alone in my room, or rather Leo's room. Not for much longer. I think once he's buried, I can decently ask to take the posters down. At my age, Harry Potter staring at me as I write!

S has gone off for another lunch with the dreaded Claire — their second meeting in a few days. Pre-arranged, but then Claire phoned this morning to say that Adam's much-loathed business partner Jeff has dropped dead, heart attack or something, nice timing I must say. Presumably she'll come back with all the info.

Will S tell her what happened here last night? Me, on one knee, being turned down yet

```
again. I need to up the stakes. So off to
Hatton Garden it is. No woman can resist a
really huge diamond, can they? Maxed out
though I am, I have to bite the bullet. Or
rather the diamond. It's not as if I can't get
it back later, ha ha. When the poor *suicide*s
money finally comes through.
```

Jeff had seen enough.

'Hello, Walter,' he said.

Walter's head span round. Then he looked slowly and carefully around the room. He was startled, but it was clear that he could see nothing (well, there was nothing yet to see). He turned back to his laptop again.

'Hello... Walter,' Jeff repeated, after a few moments, stringing it out. There had been a reaction, which meant that Walter could hear him. In any case, his suspect (his victim?) was now on his feet, scanning every corner, looking behind Leo's old drum kit and his black leather sofa. He was veering from side to side, like an animal in a forest, checking for danger.

Jeff let him suffer for a bit. Then he went over to the laptop and pushed it shut.

'What... the... fuck?' Walter said slowly, out loud. He took the matte silver top panel and opened it again. He sat there, looking at his screen for a good twenty seconds. Then he put his hands back into a writing position on the keyboard.

```
The strangest thing just happened
```

Jeff slammed down the screen.

"King hell!' Walter cried, leaping back, staring at the machine and then at his fingers, which he'd pulled out just in time. He had quick reactions for a man of his age, Jeff gave him that.

'Hello, Walter,' Jeff repeated.

'What... the fuck... is going on?' Walter looked satisfactorily terrified now.

'My name is Jeff Trelawney. I was Adam Albury's... much-loathed... business partner. In my life on earth–'

'Your life on earth?' Walter cut in.

'Sadly over now. Funny isn't it, how everyone "sadly dies" these days. Anyway, I'm sadly dead.'

'Dead, yes! So I heard. What happened to you?'

'I had a heart attack.'

'And where... where are you now?'

'Right here.'

'Yes, but... where? I can't even see you.'

'It would be strange if you could. I'm invisible.'

'Become visible then. If you want me to believe in you. You might just be a feature of my warped imagination. A flashback of some kind. I did do some weird shit back in the day, you know.'

For all his observable fear, this man was feistier than he appeared. Jeff had respect for that. So how did he materialise? Just think about your body, Leo had said, and it will happen. Okay, so be it. Jeff imagined his very best self. He was rewarded by a slowly-dawning look of astonishment on Walter's features. Half a minute later, there he was, visible if not actually solid as flesh, dressed in one of his favourite Paul Smith linen suits, with an ironed pale blue shirt and some hip Timberlands. Who made these style decisions?

'How did you get into the house?' Walter was asking, staring at him wide-eyed.

'Easily enough. Floated through your handsome front door. Or rather Serena's handsome front door.'

Walter ignored this microaggression. 'What... what... are you? Some sort of ghost?'

'So it seems, Walter.'

'How do you even know my name?'

Jeff laughed. 'Your name isn't all I know about you. I know what you've been up to, my friend.'

'Whoever – whatever – you are, mate, fantasy or reality, you're not my friend.'

'Fair enough. Did you kill my ex-business partner, Adam Albury?'

Walter spluttered. 'What makes you think...?' He broke off.

'I don't think, Walter,' Jeff replied, summoning up the inner bad cop he had nurtured over years of reading crime fiction and sitting with Sue watching a thousand TV 'tec dramas. 'I know.'

CHAPTER THIRTY-FOUR

'Hi, Dad!' Leo said, as Adam sailed at speed into the darkened room where Zofia's séance was taking place.

'Leo? Is that you? Where are you?'

'Here. Just not materialised yet.'

'I thought you were going to spy on Granny and her carer?'

'Jadwiga. I was, but I changed my mind.' Leo laughed. 'Matilda was behaving in such an odd manner. You don't go to meet a friend to see an exhibition if you don't know the details, do you? Nor do you have to hurry to get there, unless it's one of those huge shows of very famous artists with timed slots.'

'There she is!' Adam said, relieved that he could see his daughter and she appeared to be okay. Only now did he take in the other silhouetted figures hunched around the table in the lamplit gloom.

'What's going on?' he asked.

'It's a séance,' Leo explained.

'I have summoned him,' Zofia was intoning, loudly, 'and now I fe-e-e-el his approach. Come, Adam Albury, let me he-e-e-ar you.'

'Jesus!' Adam said. 'Is that woman responsible…?'

'... for getting you here,' Leo finished. 'So it seems. Now what are you going to do?'

Adam stared at the velvet, jewelled, bangled figure of Zofia at one end, head back against the chair, carmined lips twisted into a grimace, eyes closed. 'Let me se-e-e you, Adam,' she was saying.

'Can she actually hear us?' he asked. 'Or is she faking it?'

Leo shrugged. 'Search me. She looks convincing enough, doesn't she? Though she hasn't even noticed *me* yet.'

Zofia was wriggling around like a restless python. 'Let me se-e-e you, Adam,' she repeated. 'Let me he-e-e-ar you.' She cupped her hand theatrically to her ear.

'If all she wants to do is talk to me,' Adam said. 'There's no need for all that squirming. What's her name?'

'Zofia,' Leo whispered.

'Hello, Zofia,' Adam said loudly.

'*Ojej!*' cried Zofia. She looked as if she'd been punched in the stomach. 'Who... who...?' She trailed off. A stiff smile countered her scared eyes as she looked round at the whole table watching her.

'Adam Albury,' Adam replied. 'I believe I'm the spirit you were calling.'

'Oh my God!' she muttered. 'Are you here?'

'I am.'

'He's here!' she cried. 'Adam. The spirit I was summoning.'

There was a ripple of excitement around the table. A skinny woman with long, dark, obviously dyed black hair looked petrified, hands shaking even as they grasped the rim for support. Opposite her, a shaven-headed fellow with an elaborate collage of tattoos emerging from under the arms of his black Elden Ring T-shirt had a strange, sly, slightly-crazy smile; his oft-mocked beliefs were turning out to be true after all.

'I... I... I'm so happy about that,' Zofia went on.

'Me too, Zofia,' Adam replied.

Adam wondered whether she had ever successfully

'summoned' a spirit before in her life. If she had, from this showing, it was certainly a rare event.

'Come closer, Adam.' Zofia's fingers fluttered invitingly as she held out both arms, amazingly within twenty degrees of the right direction.

Adam moved across the room. 'I'm just here,' he whispered. 'Next to you. N-e-e-xt to *yo-o-ou*!' he repeated in a spooky voice, grinning over at his son.

Zofia threw up her hands. 'Please, no need for any drama, Adam. I can sense that you are close.'

'I'm right here.'

She maintained her calm. 'Are you able to show yourself to us?'

'Check this out.' He jumped up and started spinning around in the air just above the table, arms akimbo.

'Dad!' Matilda said, her jaw dropping.

'Hello, darling. Can you see me?'

'What are you doing?'

'Showing myself, as instructed.'

'You can stop now, if you like. It's a bit embarrassing.'

'Even in death, you don't like my dancing. But I'm quite enjoying it. Though I don't seem to be visible to your friend.'

'She's not my friend.'

'Matilda, please!' said Zofia. 'Quiet now. Or your father's spirit will never appear.'

'But he has appeared. That's who I'm talking to.'

Zofia's expression adjusted rapidly. 'Are you?'

'Yes.'

'So you are the chosen one today. Can you speak to him again now? Ask him why he won't appear to me.' She sounded almost petulant. 'Especially as it was I who summoned him here.'

'Dad, did you hear that?'

'It's not that I don't want to appear to her,' Adam replied. 'I don't know why I'm not. Maybe she's approaching this in the wrong way.'

Matilda repeated this back to Zofia, who bristled visibly.

'Tell your father that I've been summoning spirits for years. I'm not going to suggest that he's stubborn, but, but...'

'But what?' asked Adam.

'He says, "But what?"' Matilda repeated.

'But – look – sometimes there are difficulties,' Zofia replied. 'Not always created by me.'

'Wouldn't it be easier to ask him what he wants to say?' Leo interrupted. He had been silently watching this exchange from the corner of the room.

Zofia's head span right round, as if she'd been slapped.

'Who's *this* now?' she asked.

'My name's Leo. I'm Adam's son.'

'Leo!' gasped Matilda.

'Adam's... son,' Zofia repeated slowly. Adam was impressed to see how quickly she recovered her poise. She looked round magisterially at her little group, as if all these surprises were intended. 'So you are here with us too. It's becoming quite the family visit.'

As she said this, Adam was amazed to see that Leo was slowly materialising.

'Now I see you, Leo,' Zofia said. 'Greetings.'

'Leo!' Matilda repeated.

'Greetings,' Leo replied, polite as ever, to Zofia. 'Hi, Matty.'

'Leo! It is you.' His sister was in tears.

'Ah, Matilda,' Zofia said. 'It's not a bad thing to be emotional when you are reunited with a loved one from the other side. Comfort her, Olivia.'

'I am,' Olivia muttered. She already had her arms around her friend. Leo was right next to her too.

'Matty,' he was saying. 'It's okay. Don't upset yourself.'

'Of course I'm upset, Leo. Seeing you like this.'

'It's okay. I'm okay. Really.'

'Are you?' Matilda's eyes were glistening.

'Yes.'

'But you're dead.'

'I know. It's fine. It's not that bad. I feel the same. And I'm with Dad.'

'So can you see your father, Leo?' Zofia asked.

'Of course.'

'That is only to be expected. Perhaps if you or Matilda speak to him, he may appear to the rest of us as well.'

'I'll do my best,' Adam said. 'I'm perfectly happy for you all to see me.'

Leo repeated this.

'Thank you, Adam,' Zofia said. 'I expect we're almost there. Manifestations don't always go entirely to plan. Sometimes there are limitations put in place by the spirit powers. What they decide is what they decide. Speak to your father, Matilda.'

'Okay,' she said. Adam sensed that his daughter was embarrassed, in front of Zofia, not to mention the ghost of her brother and this strange-looking tableful of South London odd bods. 'Hi, Dad.'

Adam felt equally constrained, though could the rest of them even hear him yet? 'Hi, Matilda. It's good to see you again. Did you want to ask me anything in particular?'

'Not really. It was just so good to see you, last time, and then Olivia, my friend here, mentioned the idea of a séance, and said Zofia might be able to summon you, so I thought... maybe... that would work...'

'And here I am,' said Adam. 'So it has worked. Is everything all right?'

'Obviously not. With Leo.'

'It's okay,' said Leo. 'It's not ideal, I'd rather be alive, but I'm fine. Really. It's quite a revelation to discover there is an afterlife...'

Matilda was smiling now, through her tears. 'Oh, Leo, you're just the same. Ridiculously upbeat, even in death. I can't tell you how reassuring that is. So then, Daddy, when I met up with Eva, that was rather cut off, because of the call from Mum about Leo. So I was wondering if everything was okay, for you, and with Eva, if you found out what you wanted...'

What a sweetie she was, still worrying about all that now. 'It's fine, darling,' he replied. 'I did manage to speak to her. We had a good talk.'

'Did you get your answer?'

'I did, yes.' Suddenly Adam was on the edge of tears, remembering how they'd left it. 'I'll try and explain another time. If I get another time.'

'But you're okay, Daddy?'

He wasn't. He badly wanted to hold her again; indeed, all of his loved ones. Matilda, Eva, Serena even. 'I'm fine,' he repeated.

'*Now* I can see you,' Zofia's shrill voice interjected. 'Oh my God! There you are. Please say something else, Adam.'

'Hello, Zofia,' he managed. 'How are you?'

'Yes! Yes!' The medium was clapping her hands. 'A real spirit. Can the rest of you see Adam now?'

Half the table nodded, half shook their heads. It wasn't clear whether any of them were telling the truth.

'Let us continue—' said Zofia.

'Zofia,' Adam interrupted.

'Yes?' The medium was well excited now.

'Would you mind leaving us alone for ten minutes. I'd just like to have a few quiet moments with my daughter.'

'But we're just getting going...'

'I appreciate that. But I really need to talk in private with Matilda. We won't go anywhere, I promise.'

'Please, Zofia?' Matilda asked.

The medium drew herself up, as if considering a weighty problem. She looked around the faces of her charges, whose eyes were fixed on her, devotedly, awaiting her verdict and guidance. 'Not a problem,' she replied. 'We can... go into the kitchen for tea and biscuits. As we normally do after our séances. Is Olivia coming?'

'If she wants to,' Adam said. He turned to his daughter's friend. 'Olivia, do you want to stay?'

Olivia looked at Matilda. Matilda looked at Adam, who nodded encouragingly. If his daughter wanted some human support from someone she knew, that was fine by him.

'If you don't mind,' Olivia said. 'And Zofia doesn't mind,' she added tactfully.

'Of course not!' Zofia replied, with a wave of the hand that was trying to be more casual than she clearly felt. 'Come on, guys,' she said to the rest of the table. 'Let's leave our friends in peace for a moment. But please don't go, will you, Adam?'

'I'll do my best.'

Zofia got to her feet, paused for a moment as if about to add something, then swept decisively out of the room, robes swishing, bangles jangling. She was, Adam noticed, visibly trembling. The others got to their feet and followed her. One fragile old lady, with hair as white as his mother's, turned and gave the four of them a long and rather hostile stare. Almost as if she didn't believe the two spectral visitors were real. Perhaps she was a sceptic, and by appearing, they had upset her belief system. Or perhaps she wasn't, and she was upset that *they* had appeared, rather than her dead husband or some other chosen spirit. Eventually, she turned round and shuffled off. The door was closed from the inside by another hand. Adam was left alone with his daughter, her friend Olivia, and his dead son.

But hang on! Where *was* Leo? He had vanished, without a word.

CHAPTER THIRTY-FIVE

'That's it, then, Jadwiga,' said Patricia with the naughtiest of twinkles in her eye, a frankly smug grin on her lips. She had the look of one, Leo thought, watching keenly from the other side of the room, who had achieved a satisfying revenge, even if only by her own lights.

Jadwiga, taking the proffered document in her trembling fingers, was nothing if not professional.

'Are you sure about this, madam?'

'Very sure.' Patricia sat back. 'I don't see why my descendants should get every last thing I own just because we happen to be blood related. Just because I wiped their bottoms when they were babies, washed out their nappies, endlessly. Endlessly, Jadwiga. You wouldn't remember, being young, but there were none of those disposable nappies in those days, cluttering up the planet, causing God knows what problems for us in the future. Well, not for us, I shan't be around, but for them, and their children, if they ever get round to having children. No, in those days we had terry nappies, horrid cloth things that you had to wash out by hand and hang on the line. That was my life for years, Jadwiga. Lines and lines of terry nappies fluttering in the biting English winter wind. And now that it's their turn to look after me, sort out *my* nappies, where are they? Swanning around. I haven't even seen my daughter Claire since my poor grandson had his accident. His sister Matilda came over for coffee, but then what did she want to know: whether I'd changed my will since her father died. He's barely cold in the ground and she's scurrying around asking about her inheritance. I do appreciate it's hard for that generation, the houses are so expensive you can't get a place of your own these days. But still, it might have been nice if she'd asked how I was, before she dives in with blunt questions about exactly who I was leaving what.'

'Yes, madam,' Jadwiga replied sympathetically. Leo was glad that he'd followed his gut instinct and come straight from the séance to Larks Hill. There was something about the sly way the carer was watching his crazy old grandmother that unnerved him. As if, somehow, she had an agenda and was just biding her time. He didn't have to look far to see what that agenda might be. The document in Jadwiga's hand was Patricia's last will and testament.

'This is the thing,' Patricia went on. 'You actually listen. To me. To what I'm saying. They don't. They zoom over here in their expensive cars, that I'll soon enough be paying for, once I'm under the daisies, and barely has a sip of my properly-brewed coffee crossed their lips than they're starting in with their blunt questions. "May I ask a blunt question?" Matilda asks. Not a word about how I am, whether I might possibly be upset that my only son and my only grandson have died. And then, would you believe it, no sooner has she found out about her inheritance, she starts ticking me off about my political views. Which I am, funnily enough, entitled to, this supposedly being a free country. Is it a crime to point out that the reason all the young people like her can't afford a house to live in is because they've all been bought up by immigrants, no offence to them, Jadwiga, but it's true. You let them in, they've got to live somewhere. It's hardly rocket science.'

'Yes, madam.'

'Actually, we should be grateful for them. If you sat down and devised a competition for the most adventurous people in the world to come and reinvigorate your country, you could hardly do better than what we have now. Those poor people in the rubber dinghies on the Channel. Risking death to get here in the freezing cold and dark. Hardly blushing violets, are they?'

'Yes, madam.'

'Unlike the idle slobs we have in this country. Softened by years and years of welfare, in my opinion. Moaning on about how poor they are when they all have TVs and mobile phones and God knows what else. Stuffing their faces full of Pot Noodles, eating out at Nandos and suchlike dreadful places.'

'Yes, madam. Now shall we drive into Tempelsham? Then we can stop off at the solicitors and go on to that nice new cake shop.'

Unthreateningly, Jadwiga held up the will. So Leo had been right; his worst suspicions were justified.

'Oh yes, the cake shop!' Patricia's eyes lit up. As Leo knew from childhood, Granny did love her cake. It had always been her treat, when she'd come to take him out from school, rushing him down the high street to the famous Copper Kettle. 'I wouldn't mind trying that new place again. Café Baba. What was it before, a wedding shop?'

'Yes, madam, it was. Though I never saw anyone in there.'

'That's because they're not getting married, Jadwiga. They're all so busy wondering whether they're he or she or LGTB&Q or whatever, they haven't got time to try and make a proper lifelong relationship, such as Philip and I had. All those dresses, sitting in the window, week after week, idle and untouched. No wonder they went bust.' Patricia waved at the will. 'There's no particular hurry with that, though.'

'We can just pop in there first, madam, it won't take a moment.'

'Once I've changed it, Jadwiga, I've changed it. You're the witness. I'm really not planning to change it back.'

'I'm not allowed to be the witness if I'm a beneficiary,' Jadwiga replied. 'It would be best to get the lawyer to do that. Then it's all done and we can go and have our cake.'

Patricia sighed. 'If that's what you want, Jadwiga.'

'Yes, please, madam. I think that would be good. And then we can have some of that nice Victoria sponge you like so much.'

CHAPTER THIRTY-SIX

'You *know*, do you?' Walter's laugh was both confident and mocking. 'So what are you going to do about it then? Haunt me into a confession?'

Jeff kept his cool. 'No need for that,' he replied.

'Anyway, even if I did have something to do with it,' Walter went on. 'What could you do? Out there. Wherever you are.'

'I'm sure I could point people in the right direction. A house search or two. A look for the evidence in the right place – the Fallowfields garage, perhaps.'

'What are you talking about? You – trying to connect with the local rozzers. I'm sure they'd be right up for listening to a ghost.'

'*The* ghost,' Jeff pointed out. 'Of the murdered man's business partner.'

'You got some ID?' Walter chuckled. 'Anyway, you clearly haven't been following the case. There's been an inquest. A clear verdict was returned: suicide. So there we are – that's that. Official.'

'And what about poor Leo?'

'Shocking accident.'

'But if they looked more closely at his car, they might realise–'

'Why would they look at his car? It's a write-off. These things happen. One and a half thousand people die on the roads every year in this country. Nobody thinks they're all murders, do they?'

'I could always call on Serena,' Jeff replied. 'Tell her what you've been up to.'

'D'you really think she'd believe you? Adam's hated ex-partner? In spectral form?'

Jeff was watching his suspect closely. Was he bluffing? 'I have a strong suspicion she knew about Adam,' he said.

'Knew what about Adam?'

'That you, Walter, killed him.'

'Why would she? That had nothing to do with her, believe me.'

'Nice of you to protect her, Walter. But I think that when she realised Adam was leaving her such a big chunk of his fortune, she started to see things rather differently. I think you both did. You've never had any money, have you, Walter? Pretty much everything you've ever touched has turned to shit, by all accounts. But here, suddenly, was your chance to save yourself and win the jackpot. You had to take it, just in case Adam changed his mind. Which he might very well have done if you'd got any closer to his first wife, married her or something like that. Or if he himself had got embroiled in a second expensive divorce, which was looking increasingly likely.

'I think you thought there was probably a time limit on this sudden sentimental generosity of his, so you needed to get on with it. I'm not sure that Serena was actively involved with your little plan, but I think she gave you her blessing. Even though Adam's final bequest to her was surprisingly large, he's never been that generous with the day-to-day stuff, has he? Serena had to make do with a bog-standard allowance, even as Adam built the house of his dreams and whisked his new lady love off around the world to all the glam places he was doing his famous regeneration projects in. Yes, he let Serena use the house they had bought together in Italy, but only because that suited him, allowed him to see his kids out there for a bit in the summer holidays before handing over to her.'

'Not bad, Jeff,' Walter said. 'Not bad at all. You're right. Serena is a much darker horse than she appears. That's one of the things I like about her, as it happens. And no, she hasn't forgiven Adam for loads of stuff, no doubt about that. Tragically, I think she thought, for a long time, that he would come back to her in the end. That Julie was just a long-term version of one of the flings she'd put up with previously, which had always petered out. But then, when he hooked up with Eva, that hope vanished. If he was going to leave Julie, it wasn't going to be to return to her. And that released, I have to say, rather a lot of pent-up anger.'

'How did you feel about that? Since you were now on the scene?'

'I didn't mind.'

'Didn't it make you feel bad that you, even as the newcomer, couldn't match up to the memory of the sainted Adam?'

'They were married for years. They have two children together. I appreciated all that.'

'But you didn't appreciate him, did you? This man who is everything you've failed to be. Successful, rich, someone who's made something of his life.'

'I didn't mind him. I didn't see him much, to be honest.'

'And what about her? This woman you'd like to be your wife?'

'She's a lovely lady, Serena,' Walter replied. 'Very warm and affectionate. I'm not going to claim that she's the love of my life, but when you get to my stage of the human parade, you take your chances.'

'I bet you do. A nice house in Tufnell Park beats a bedsit in Walthamstow that you're about to be chucked out of.'

'What the fuck do you know about that?' Now Walter looked rattled.

'A little bird told me. Actually, a rather large, rugger-playing bird. A sporty fat pigeon who likes gadgets and had recently bought an electric car. Ring any bells? You hadn't paid your rent, Penfield. You couldn't pay it. You'd alienated almost all your old friends by borrowing money from them and never paying it back. You were about to be evicted. You were known everywhere as a serial liar. None of the business ventures you'd tried your hand at had worked out. Serena's interest in you was manna from heaven.'

'You shouldn't believe all the gossip you hear about someone.'

'This isn't just gossip, believe me. Anyway, how did you even know about Eva?'

'Matilda told Serena. Matilda knew about the affair pretty much from the off. She hated Julie, always has done, so she was thrilled. But I'm sorry to say, Jeff, that yes, even though Serena was more resentful about Adam's behaviour than she appeared, none of that meant that she was onside to have him removed, did it?'

'"Removed",' Jeff scoffed. 'That's a bit euphemistic, isn't it? Sounds almost psychopathic. On which note, I also think that when Leo realised what you'd done and you had to "remove" him as well, Serena found out about that too.'

Walter was laughing again; but his confidence was visibly fading.

'What's so funny?' Jeff asked.

'I can't believe I'm having this conversation with the ghost of Adam's business partner. You've got a nerve. Trying to freak me out with this total nonsense when you're not even alive.'

'So I am freaking you out. Good. Now is it time to tell me exactly what you did with Adam? Before you set up the little suicide scene in his garage.'

CHAPTER THIRTY-SEVEN

'Where's Leo gone?' Matilda asked.

'Search me,' said Adam, scouring the darkened room with his virtual eyes. 'Unless he's just dematerialised and is hiding in a corner. Lee-oh!' he called.

'If that was the case,' Olivia said, 'surely you'd be able to see him?'

'Not necessarily. We can be invisible to each other too.'

'Lee-oh!' Matilda echoed. But there was nothing but silence. 'It's all so weird,' she went on. 'Us here and you there. Are you okay with Olivia sticking around?'

'You're calling the shots here,' Adam replied. 'Remarkably successfully, because it was you that managed to get us both here. Talking to you again. It's the first time we've been able to do that together.'

'But you wanted to come, Daddy?'

'I didn't really have a say. I was suddenly aware that you needed me, and the next thing I knew here I was, bang, right next to you.'

'Maybe that was it,' Olivia said. 'Matilda's desire. Nothing to do with Zofia.'

'Have you ever been to a séance where Zofia did summon a spirit successfully?' Matilda asked.

'This is my first time. With Zofia.'

'So why were you so keen to talk to me again?' Adam asked his daughter. 'It wasn't just to tell me about Eva, surely?'

'Ever since you told me that you didn't kill yourself, I haven't been able to stop thinking about who did.'

Adam nodded. 'Okay.'

'It's amazing, really, how many people stood to benefit from your death. I guess that's what being rich and successful means. If you can't take it with you, then whatever you leave behind gets shared around. Fought over, even. Perhaps, if you want to be safe in this world, the very best thing to be is a pauper.'

'So where did you get to, with your suspicions?' Adam asked.

'This is it,' Matilda said. 'I've worked it out. Walter.'

'Walter!' Not this one again, Adam thought. Those kids really don't like him, do they? 'He barely knows me,' he said.

'That doesn't matter. It's very simple. He's after your money. He found out that you'd left a big chunk to Mum and he realised that he could get his fat mitts on it. And solve all his problems. You know he's got debts. Really serious ones. Going back years. He's like this failed businessman, but he's also stupidly extravagant in that he likes to travel and stay in posh hotels and eat out all the time. Leo found out all about it.'

'So how did he know what I'd left Mummy?'

'She told him. He was rabbiting on about how she was so lucky that she owned her house, and she didn't realise what it was like for people like him who'd never got onto the property ladder, and how she took it all for granted, all the money she'd made sitting on her fat arse, as he put it...'

'He said that?'

'That's what I was trying to tell you. As well as being shit at everything he turns his hand to, he's not very nice.'

'Sounds like the dream man!' Olivia laughed.

'So he's banging on,' Matilda continued, 'about how one day she'd have to sell up and move to a smaller place because all her capital was in the house and there was no income and she, or rather they, needed something to live on, and she smiled and said that that probably wouldn't need to happen because one day her ship would come in. *Another* ship, he said, and you should have seen the look on his greedy face.'

'How come you were there, Matilda?'

'I just was. Lurking. With a laptop. As I do. He's basically so self-obsessed he doesn't notice other people half the time. So anyway, that's when she told him. About how much you'd left her. It was just too much. He wanted it for himself. He wasn't prepared to wait, couldn't wait probably, for however long it might be for you to die to get his hands on it. What, twenty years at least.'

'How on earth did you know what he thought?'

'I kind of listened. To some of it. And guessed the rest. It's obvious, really. Plus I chatted to Mum. She can be majorly indiscreet without realising it.'

'This is true. I guess he might also have been worried that she might get fed up with him.'

'If only. The irritating thing about Monsieur Walter is that he's very confident she won't. You know, he can be very sweet and charming – to her. He takes her breakfast in bed, freshly squeezed orange juice on a tray, that kind of stuff.'

Adam shuddered. 'Don't tell me. I've seen it.'

'He's even been quite nice to us, Leo and me, when he wants to be, because he's not stupid, and he realises that Mummy cares about what we think of him. But he made a mistake with Leo, because he tried, quite quickly, to start acting like a father, telling him what jobs he should take and so on, which coming from him was a bit effing rich…'

'D'you think he was responsible for Leo's accident too?' Adam asked.

'This is why I had to see you,' Matilda replied. 'Even though Walter really didn't like Leo at all, I never thought in a million years he could have done that. You know, arranged that crash. My first thought was that, if it was anybody, it was Julie and Rod. There's not much love lost between Julie and Leo, never has been, and Rod was actually in covert operations for a while in the marines or something–'

'So maybe he made a covert operation for himself here?' Olivia said.

'Exactly. Also, Leo didn't think it was Walter who had murdered you, Dad. He wasn't going around accusing him or anything like that, so why would Walter feel the need…'

'But Leo did know all about Walter's business failures,' Adam said, 'and his debts, which would presumably have been his motivation…'

'So anyway, then it slowly dawned on me that he did… had… done it…'

'Walter?'

'Yes.'

'Why? How?' Adam asked.

'Two things,' Matilda replied. 'The first was just after Leo's accident. And I was in the house, Harrogate Road, and I'd seen you, Daddy, the night before, not that I could tell them that, but you'd told me that you didn't kill yourself. So I was saying that. Mummy was going on about the inquest. Walter was backing her up in his pompous, annoying way. Then I said it could have been Rod, because you were found in the car in their garage, so didn't that rather point to him… and Walter was saying that was offensive to Rod, as a soldier, and I suddenly thought, one, that's quite a personal reaction, why does he give a toss about Rod–'

'You're saying he worked with Rod?'

'God no, not that. Not that at all.'

'What then?'

'Just that he was so offended on Rod's behalf, like, on the *murderer's* behalf. Weird, eh? And then, out of that, came my second realisation, which was, why was it so important to Walter that your death was suicide and Leo's death was an accident? Why couldn't he even countenance the idea of his favourite expression, foul play…?'

'And that was enough to make you think Walter was guilty of both murders?'

'No, not in itself, but just hanging around, watching him, sneaky glances, protesting too much, that sort of thing. He's been furious with Leo, anyway, because Leo called him a sponger, more than once, to his face, and made it quite clear that he didn't want him to marry Mum, told Mum, in fact, that she shouldn't, so Leo was kind of in his way, blocking his route out of all his accumulated troubles…'

'So then you decided you'd call me. Why didn't you just go to the police?'

'I wasn't sure what to do, Daddy. Your inquest is over. There isn't going to be one for Leo. Everyone thinks he's just had an accident. So I really needed to talk it over with you. See what you thought. I didn't even know if this séance thing would work. At one level, my idea seems far-fetched. At another, everything fits, doesn't it?'

'Maybe,' Adam said. 'But you have no proof. Of any of this. Bottom line, it's just your hunch…'

'I guess it is.'

'And what about Mummy? If your suspicions are correct, is she in danger?'

'What are you saying, Daddy?'

'I'm saying that if it really was Walter who saw me off, and Leo too, and it's all for the money Serena has coming to her, then maybe she's not very safe either. I don't mean immediately, because she has to get everything first, presumably. But going forward. Say he married her, and then she had a mysterious accident, the man would be home free. If he's faked two deaths convincingly, who's to say he couldn't do a third? And what about you, Matilda? If he did do all this, as you say, and he starts to think you're on to him, and could stop him...'

CHAPTER THIRTY-EIGHT

'That was *very* nice, Jadwiga,' Patricia said as the pair of them arrived back together at Larks Rise. 'Just what the doctor ordered.'

Leo was with them, on the back seat, not that they had any idea about that, he was still as invisible as air.

'Such delicious cakes, madam. Better even than we have in Poland.'

'You see,' Patricia went on, obliviously, as Jadwiga hopped out of the driving seat and ran round to hold her stick for her and help her out of the other side of the car, 'it's interesting, isn't it, how things work. People bang on about how Amazon is destroying the high street, and how we shouldn't get stuff from them, or indeed receive any online deliveries at all. My daughter Claire is always trying to make me feel guilty about that, even though I am ninety-two, and I lived through the war, and rationing, for goodness' sake, in any case how am I supposed to go round the supermarket, even with your kind help, Jadwiga? My point is, life moves on, presumably the very few people who are still going in for conventional weddings are buying their dresses online, and so now we have a lovely cake shop.'

'Yes, madam.'

'It's progress. I mean, I can remember the days when *everything* was delivered. In little vans, the grocer, the butcher, they came up all the time, to the tradesman's entrance. You wouldn't know about that; it was a special door for people with trades. It sounds terribly snobbish nowadays, but actually it had its uses. You wouldn't have the butcher getting in the way of your lunchtime guests, embarrassing them and himself. You'd never have had him marching in through the front door, like Ocado seems to think is okay. But despite that, we're back to all those deliveries, the wheel has turned full circle.'

'Yes, madam.'

'I suppose the worrying thing is that the only shops that'll be left in Tempelsham and everywhere else will be shops that you *need* to visit, like hairdressers and coffee shops and estate agents and I suppose shoe shops, because it's nice to try on shoes, and actually it's good to try on clothes, isn't it? I've bought quite a few things on the internet that look very good on the laptop but then you get them delivered and the fabric's awful or they're too big or baggy–'

'So where are we going, madam?' Jadwiga asked, accommodating as ever. 'Upstairs for a rest, or along to the sitting room to listen to music with Alexa?'

At least she has a sense of humour, Leo thought. He was watching her like a nervous hawk. The last will and testament had been signed and witnessed and left safely with the solicitor, and now he was panicking that Jadwiga was going to try and finish off his grandmother right away. She wouldn't be so stupid, his more rational self told him. Or impatient. If she were planning something, she would surely wait a few days. Or weeks, to be sensible.

'Upstairs for a rest, I think,' Patricia replied.

'Very good. Shall I bring you one of your sleepy drinks?'

'That would be lovely, Jadwiga. I hardly slept at all last night; I don't know why. I get off all right and then I wake up at two o'clock and I simply cannot get back again. It's all whirring round in my head, the news, the terrible things going on in the world...'

Leo followed Jadwiga downstairs to the kitchen, keen to see what she put in one of her famous sleepy drinks. Perhaps, after all, it was nothing more alarming than Horlicks.

But now Jadwiga was going to a cupboard, reaching up for a small square plastic box, in which were two bottles of pills, some cylindrical red ones in a glass bottle and some small round pale blue ones in a little plastic tub. Jadwiga unscrewed the bottle and tipped out four red pills onto a side plate, one of the pieces of Patricia's lovely blue and white Wedgwood Portmeirion dinner service. Then she took eight of the blue ones from the tub and started crunching them down to a fine powder. This was some sleepy drink, Leo thought. But then again, if his darkest fears were about to be realised, she wouldn't be so stupid as to leave evidence, would she?

If she really was about to murder her unwitting charge, did that mean that she was the likely killer of him and his father too, possibly with Omar's help? Looking at her now, a hunched, set-faced figure, going determinedly about her business, it was hard to believe. Perhaps Patricia's 'sleepy drink' really did require all these pills? His grandmother had been taking tranquillisers for years, ever since Philip had died; perhaps this was what she needed these days to get her off...

As he watched Jadwiga pour on the hot milk before adding, yes, two spoonfuls of Ovaltine and one of sugar, Leo had no idea what to do. Race off and try to find the other two – who were where? Still at the séance? Back at his mother's? The three ghosts had agreed to rendezvous for a catch-up at the Fallowfields shed at eight o'clock this evening. At this rate, that might be way too late.

CHAPTER THIRTY-NINE

Walter was out in the garden. It was a warm afternoon and now he was sitting with a *Financial Times* under the big parasol that his sadly dead benefactor Adam had bought, years ago, before he had left home and the woman he, Walter, was now happy enough to call his partner.

It was good to feel the calming sun all around him. Had he actually gone stark raving mad? he wondered. Adam's ghoulish business partner had seemed real enough, but perhaps 'Jeff' had been a figment of his nervous imagination? Perhaps all those illegal substances he'd indulged in, years before, had returned to haunt him? A hallucinatory flashback? He'd had a few, back in the day. Was this what happened, if you did something as outrageously heinous as killing someone? Even if, in both instances, it hadn't felt that bad at the time. Had, in fact, been surprisingly easy. Turning up at Fallowfields with Serena to 'talk about Leo's wedding', then returning to the idea that he and Adam had discussed before, that Bullfrog Press might publish a collection of his poetry. As if!

He and Adam had sat together round that funky pink polyethylene round table, designed for him, as he liked to tell you, by one of his famous chums, Patrick-some-effing-celeb-or-other, with the fat file of doggerel, which had included 'Suicide Note', the poem that had given Walter the brilliant and irresistible idea for his murderous scenario.

Then he had slipped the powerful, impeccably researched Zimovane sedative into Adam's second coffee, before waving cheerfully goodbye and heading off with Serena for lunch at that nondescript gastro-pub in Partlesfield, The Duck and Sparrow, where there was no risk of anyone recognising them. Returning an hour and a half later to find Adam in just the right state to be dragged round to the garage. It had taken both of them, the body was so much heavier than he'd imagined, even though Adam was still alive at that point, if comatose. At that moment, Walter had rather regretted having the sticky toffee pudding as well as the lamb shank and the duck pâté starter. But Serena, who had managed no more than the soup of the day and half a roll, had been fine. Lady Macbeth wasn't a match for Adam's quietly vengeful ex-partner, as she'd encouraged Walter on.

Serena had taken care of Julie, too. Brilliantly, by arranging for her to meet up for lunch with Claire in Tempelsham, so that Claire could tell her 'something important', i.e. the news about Eva. Originally, Serena had told Claire she'd be there too, but then she'd dropped out, making her totally free from suspicion, while dumping Claire firmly in it. If things hadn't gone so smoothly at the inquest, Serena might well have had questions to answer about why she'd set up the lunch in the first place. Claire, of course, had been more than happy to pass on Serena's hot gossip. 'See how the little bitch likes that,' Serena had said.

As for the tricky technical stuff, as it happened the post-mortem team had been blindsided by the carbon monoxide. Of which there had been plenty. Into the lungs and out again. So that they had hardly taken into account the significance of the Zimovane sedative, nor the Propofol that had finished Adam off. That had been the only unsavoury aspect of the whole thing, getting that gas down his throat while he was still, just, alive. But it was Walter who had thought all that through. That Adam couldn't actually 'be dead' until he'd inhaled a goodly amount of carbon monoxide, to achieve the appropriate symptoms, the lividity and all that, to fool the investigators. But that, by the same token, Walter and Serena couldn't hang around until Adam did actually die of carbon monoxide poisoning, because that would have kept them there, at the scene, for dangerous hours.

People called Walter an idiot. 'A serial failure,' had been one of Adam's nastier jibes, gleefully repeated to him by his smug entitled rugger bugger son Leo. But in this little instance, guess what, he had been serially successful. With poor Leo's sad demise too. Which had been equally tricky to set up, but had worked equally well. Four sets of brake lines punctured with the tiniest pin, the warning light disabled. About that neat, technically assured operation Serena had had no idea. A daytime trip to Hendon, which Walter knew well, from the last but one of his grim living places. He really hadn't wanted to do it, but needs must. Quite apart from how annoyingly inquisitive Leo was about his past and, more to the point, obstructive about his intended marriage, Walter had realised he knew the truth about Adam's 'suicide'.

Dear, dear, poor Adam. Such a success in one world and yet he had this little Achilles heel. Well, more than one. He had a soft spot for the ladies, though that was hardly original. But then, more tellingly, he had wanted, desperately, to be taken seriously as a poet as well. Consider the excitement in his eyes when they had discussed the edition of his poems that Bullfrog Press might produce. Consider how weirdly jealous he was of his old friend Roland Herrington, who had been published, frequently, in magazines, and had three well-received collections to boot.

Adam had designed all those amazing buildings. There were parts of central London he could stroll through and think, *that's all mine*. There was a whole chunk of Pimlico that was effectively his baby. There was that Chinese city, Ching-dong-something-or-other, where he'd taken the old centre and completely regenerated it, so that it was now a famous place to hang out, a kind of Covent Garden of the Far East. Why did he need to be Simon Armitage too?

What must it have been like to have reached this age, Walter's age for Pete's sake, almost sixty, not that old when you got to it, and have all that behind you? A proper career of which you had made such a thorough success. That meant that when you died you got a half-page obituary in *The Times*, not to mention a spot on that Sunday night Radio Four programme that Serena had made him listen to. Not the dreadful fuck-up that had been Walter's life, with all those ideas that had got so close to working and then hadn't quite.

He had thought of mail-order clothes retailing back in 1989, two years before bloody Dicky Dryden had got going with a Sloaney designer friend and a few Jiffy bags in his flat in Notting Hill. And look at Dicky now. Multimillionaire with a global brand. Middle-class mums and dads and their pretty little offspring across the globe entirely dressed in Dryden outfits (with their strangely large-bottomed trousers).

Sandwiches for office workers. That had been another of Walter's beautiful – and entirely original – ideas, dreamed up, he remembered, after a magnificent sinsemilla spliff in The Bulldog, Amsterdam's oldest and finest 'coffeeshop'. He and Lulu McNair had spent two long years trying to make that work, and perhaps their mistake had been actually delivering the sandwiches, by hand, in plastic trays, to the offices, because then along came Pret, and look where that was now. In every blinking high street in the country.

Nor could we forget the inspired idea of the Intimate Dating Café, where there had been phones on numbered tables so you could call the girl or bloke you fancied across the room, *while you were eating*. Walter had had plans for a chain, with screens, so a woman in Leeds could hook up with a man in Liverpool. And then along came the internet.

A success with any one of these things would have made Walter rich. Money begat money, didn't it, and with one business under his belt, it wouldn't have been hard to launch another. He could have had an empire, a penthouse flat in Mayfair, a charming country house for the weekends and summer, a pool, a collection of classic cars, like that rock manager he'd met once who had 150, stored in a huge warehouse on his estate outside Monmouth.

Instead, he had spiralled down, taking stupid risks that had ruined him. He lost his flat over a secured loan for the Intimate Dating Café. Then he made the mistake of involving his friends. He had always been persuasive; and now he was again, getting them to invest in sure-fire projects that turned out not to be so sure-fire. With the result that, in the end, they had ganged up on him and called him all the names you could imagine. Even Dicky had showed him the door eventually. 'Sorry, Walter, old boy, but in the end, you have to stand on your own two feet,' he had pompously intoned at the door of the Wolseley, after a meal that had probably cost more than Walter was asking for in the first place.

The humiliation. He'd ended up in a bedsit in Walthamstow of all places. In a dreadful house full of immigrants and thieves. It had been a stroke of pure golden luck that at an art show in central London he had met Serena. Bless her. She hadn't noticed how down at heel he was; had thought that his threadbare shirts and battered brogues were just scruffy boho chic. When in fact his weekly fare-dodging trips down the Victoria Line to Green Park were to give himself a free glass of hooch or two and on a decent night a few canapés too.

Sometimes those social snacks were as good as a meal. Mini shepherd's pies, mini burgers, soups even. Some of the better galleries in Dover and Cork Streets even did bijou little puddings to follow. So who needed to root around in bins at the back of restaurants, or get the thrown-out sandwiches from Sainsbury's Local, although Walter had often enough, whisper it, been reduced to doing that too.

He still had the voice, that was the thing. The old upper-middle class educated English voice. Even in these days of alleged equality for all, of wokedom and check your privilege and all the rest, that voice still cut through. Taxi drivers still called him 'guv', even if he was wearing filthy jeans. More to the point, scrubbed up, he could gain the respect of a gullible bird like Serena. She would actually listen to him, warm white wine in hand, as he bullshitted on about the figurative and the abstract and the conceptual and synergies and opaque and transparent discourses, you name it, he could talk about it...

But now, with this latest venture, murder, he had suddenly and finally got himself to a place where he was looking forward to being free of the insecurity that had dogged him all his life. When Adam's money came through, which it would, very soon, he and Serena would be able to pay off the last chunk of her mortgage and own the Tufnell Park house outright. For the first time in his life he would be in a bricks and mortar property that was totally his. His, his, his.

Well, Serena's obviously, but also his, once she accepted his marriage proposal, which she surely would before too long, especially if he bought that big diamond. Leo was out of the way and Matilda would come round, and if Serena were still with him, surely she was happy with him, otherwise why hadn't she kicked him out? The rest of the lump sum could be invested, in the financial markets, which is what Walter was getting up to speed with right now. He would buy equities and bonds and maybe commercial property too. One thing his various business failures had taught him over the years was what worked and what didn't. So he would, he reckoned, have a shrewd nose for the up-and-coming companies that nobody else had yet spotted…

And here *was* darling Serena, back from her lunch with Claire, coming out through the sliding door from the kitchen. He put down his paper and smiled up at her.

'Hello, my love. How was it? Are you stuffed with yummy Chinese treats?'

'Pretty much.'

'How was Claire?'

'She seemed fine.'

'Is that all? No gossip to report? How about the dreadful Jeff?'

'He's got a nerve,' Jeff muttered to himself. After his earlier confrontation, which had ended with repeated denials rather than anything approaching a confession, Jeff had vanished from Walter's sight. But he had not left the house, eager to see what Walter might get up to next, now that he was spooked and on edge. Then Adam had joined him, hot foot from some séance where he'd seen his daughter Matilda. 'He knows perfectly well what happened to me,' he said to his partner now.

The two ghosts were on tenterhooks as Serena gave him the news about Jeff's heart attack and Walter reacted with badly-acted surprise.

'Dan behaving himself?' he asked eventually.

'They're still arguing about Maya's schooling.'

'That's the latest, is it?'

'So it seems. Claire thinks she should go private. Dan has his principles.'

'"These are my principles and if you don't like them, well, I have others."'

'What's that?'

'Groucho Marx, never mind. Bottom line, Dan's just chippy. He doesn't want his daughter to be posher than he is.'

Serena was laughing. 'I really don't think that's the case,

Walter. I actually quite respect the way he sticks to his core values.'

'Even if the poor girl is bullied and unhappy with a shit education as a result? You can't change the way the world works, can you? But you can look out for your own. Well, you know what I think, don't you?'

'I certainly do, my darling. Now how about a soothing cup of tea. Why on earth are you reading the *Financial Times*?'

'I find it interesting. Actually, this weekend edition has very good arts coverage. And it's not so politically biased as the other papers. They have good people on all sides of the equation. The travel section is excellent too. This place looks like the perfect honeymoon destination.'

'Walter! Stop it! I've told you I'm not interested.'

'Maybe I shouldn't stick around then.'

'Oh come on, don't sulk, you silly man. It's nothing personal, I just... I've got that particular T-shirt, you know that. Anyway, marriage can change things. We have a great time as we are. Why spoil it? It doesn't have to be a honeymoon. We could go on a nice holiday. Where is it?'

Walter passed the paper over.

'Rarotonga!' said Serena, reading the headline, and looking at a photograph of steep jungle-covered peaks rising from golden sandy beaches. 'Looks amazing. Where is it?'

'The South Seas. I've always wanted to see the South Seas. It's in the Cook Islands, which used to be British, and are basically a satellite of New Zealand, as far as I can see, so no language problems. Coral reefs, lagoons, beaches, exciting trails through empty mountains, delicious seafood, what's not to like?'

'A week's half-board at the Crown Beach Hotel and Spa and flights with Air New Zealand from £3,975,' Serena read. 'Per person. That's way more than we can afford.'

'Is it?' said Walter.

'What an idiot!' Jeff said. 'He just can't help himself, can he?

Serena hasn't even got your money yet, and already the fuckwit is trying to spend it.'

'Is she in danger?' Adam asked. 'Exciting trails through empty mountains doesn't sound great to me. Especially in a remote spot like that.'

'He's not going to do anything right now, is he?' Jeff said.

'Let's bloody well hope not. What would we do if he did?'

'Listen up,' said Jeff, nodding at Walter. 'This could be what we've been waiting for.'

'Why did we do what we did, darling,' Walter was saying, 'if not to have a good life together. Why have the money if we're not going to–'

'Shsh!' Serena had her fingers to her lips. 'You never know who–'

'Oh come on! Are you seriously expecting me to believe a ghost might be watching?'

Serena shrugged. 'I told you what happened before.'

'It was probably an hallucination, darling. When people are under stress, their minds can play tricks on them. Funnily enough, I wasn't going to tell you this, but just this morning…'

CHAPTER FORTY

'Ah, here you are, Jadwiga...'

Patricia was in her big double bed now, propped up on a pillow, her phone in front of her, a pile of books and notes on the near bedside table, her Alexa Echo 3rd generation speaker on the farther one.

Outside, beyond the pretty, classic William Morris curtains, there was a fine view down the long garden, the mighty boughs of the ancient cedar in the foreground. Leo had always loved that tree, with its swing, and then later, the rope ladder up to the end of the zip wire that ran down over the lawn to the woods at the far end. Such fun they'd had on it, over the years. He and his friends. It was a shame to think that when his grandmother passed on, and the house was inevitably sold, this beautiful dark evergreen would fall victim to some tree surgeon's noisy saw, as the lovely old garden was replaced by the kind of horrid cheap housing his father had hated so much, like so many of the once-pristine fields round here.

Jadwiga put Patricia's favourite little Portmeirion 'Botanic Garden' mug down on the nearside table. It was filled to within half an inch of its rim with Jadwiga's famous 'sleepy drink'.

'...thank you, that's very kind,' Patricia said.

Leo was on edge. Should he try and stop this now, before his poor deluded frail old grandmother took a sip? Of a drink that, if it wasn't in itself going to kill her, was surely going to put her in a position where she could be done away with: sedated, then suffocated with a pillow – and who would possibly guess that that's what had happened, with an old woman of over ninety? He wasn't even sure if he could, with both of them there together. Perhaps if Jadwiga left he would have a chance.

Where was his father? Not still at that séance, surely. And Jeff, who had been watching Walter at his mum's house in Harrogate Road. Was he still there, or perhaps they'd both gone back to base at Fallowfields? Oh for a ghost-friendly mobile phone! He wanted them here, now, to advise and help.

'What's that boyfriend of yours called again?' Patricia was asking Jadwiga now.

'Omar, madam,' she replied, with a smile that was trying hard not to be tense and impatient. *Get on and drink your sleepy drink, you stupid old hag, then I can smother you.* Leo could see the thoughts written on her face.

'Did you say he was from Turkey?'

'Yes, madam.'

'I must say he's very handsome.'

'Thank you, madam.'

'I hope it's not too personal, but do you see a serious future there, Jadwiga?'

'I hope so, madam.'

'So do I, so do I, although you are from very different cultures, that's always something to watch as far as marriage is concerned...'

Patricia picked up her mug, very slowly, and smiled indulgently over at her carer, who smiled back, a touch nervously, it had to be said. Patricia made as if to sip. Then she put the mug down again.

'Is this the normal drink you mix me, Jadwiga?' she asked.

'Yes, madam. Just the same.'

'Are you sure? It looks, somehow, darker, more colourful.'

'It is! Don't touch it, Grandma!' Leo shouted. But to no avail. There were two of them there and he wasn't getting through.

'No, madam.' Jadwiga went over and pretended to study it. 'I don't think so.'

'It's wonderfully effective, I must say. What exactly do you put in it?'

'It's basically milk and honey, with a sprinkle of nutmeg...'

Leo was right above it now, ready to strike before it was too late. He concentrated as hard as he could, then thrust his hand down towards the mug in a wild sweep.

Nothing.

Why? When his poor deluded old grandmother was about to be murdered, surely now was the time that he should be allowed some agency?

Desperate, focused, fingers out, he tried again.

Nothing.

The mug sat there mocking him.

'Is that all?' Patricia asked, as she picked it up. 'Milk, honey and nutmeg?'

'More or less, yes,' her carer replied.

'Bollocks!' shouted Leo. 'Grandma, put it down!'

But Patricia was cackling, that familiar endearing child-like laugh of hers. 'You expect me to believe that?' she said. 'You must have thought I was born yesterday, Jadwiga. And a load of sedative, surely, isn't that it?'

Despite herself, Jadwiga was laughing, too, a nervous, high-pitched giggle. 'No, madam. Maybe a little. Just to help you get off.'

'I have to say, my dear, it works every time.' Patricia yawned, expansively. She lifted the mug to her lips and then, just as she was about to drink, put it down again. 'Funnily enough, on second thoughts, I don't think I need it this afternoon. That little trip to the lawyer's has *completely* tired me out. Either that or that lovely carrot cake. What a very nice place that is, Café Baba, don't you think?'

'It is, madam, very nice. Now drink up, before it goes cold.'

'Such a great addition to Tempelsham,' Patricia replied. 'I expect, when I'm gone, you and Omar will enjoy visiting it together.'

A puzzled question mark had appeared on Jadwiga's forehead. 'What d'you mean, madam? We don't expect... you... we hope, rather... that you are not gone... just yet...'

'"Just yet",' Patricia repeated. 'Are you sure about that? Then why are you knocking me out like this? Now that you've got my will signed. And in your favour. Safely witnessed by the lawyer.'

'Madam, please, I don't–'

'I must say, I do applaud your speed of action. You don't exactly hang around, do you? But then I suppose you're off again next week.' She smiled, then: 'Why don't *you* try drinking this?' she asked, her tone hardening as she tapped the edge of her mug sharply with a gnarled forefinger.

'Madam, no, I have things to do this afternoon.'

'Like smother me with a pillow, and then call your so-called boyfriend to tell him the job is at last done. He's not your boyfriend, anyway, is he? He's your husband. You're married partners in crime.'

'What do you mean, madam?' The carer was trying to keep composed, but she looked rattled now.

'Okay, Jadwiga. Drink the drink. Go on. Prove to me that you don't have any bad intentions towards me.'

'Madam, please, you are being silly. It would make me sleepy. And then I wouldn't be able to wake you later, make your tea...'

'But I'm not going to wake later, am I? This is it. A few more irreverent thoughts from the barmy old bird and then off she goes into her final sleep, isn't that it? *Requiescat in pace*. And good bloody riddance, too, I don't doubt.'

'I have no idea what you mean. Why are you saying this?'

'Because I'm not stupid. Do you actually think I'm a *kretyn*, Jadwiga? To use the rather unwoke word you still use in Poland.'

'Of course I don't, madam.'

'You've been canvassing me quietly for months to change my will. Every time I've suggested that it might be nice for you to be rewarded for all your hard work, you've told me not to bother, but then you've always made it very easy for me to find the will, get it out, consider the changes, haven't you?'

The carer was looking thoroughly discombobulated now, her usually composed look replaced by wide and fearful eyes. Leo watched agog. All his concerns about his grandmother had been unnecessary. The mad old bat had been on the case all along.

'And now at last I've done it,' Patricia continued. 'I've even surprised you with the substantial share I've given you. You can hardly believe your luck. You almost couldn't hold the document you were shaking so much as you dropped it off at the solicitor's and phoned your husband. Don't think I don't notice these things. Leaving me there staring at the teapot for a good ten minutes. Unlike some of the old dears you've worked with in the past, I still have my marbles, enough of them to see through you anyway.'

'Madam, please, this is most unfair and not true, at all. I've just been doing exactly what you told me. It was you that wanted that document placed safely at the lawyer's office.'

'Was it, Jadwiga? I don't think so. Anyway, don't worry, because that's not the only document that she's got there, nice Ms Kumar of Kumar, Rogers and McPherson. When you were watching me sign it this afternoon, so eagerly, you failed to notice the date I was putting on it. The thirtieth of the third month, not the fourth. Ms Kumar already has another, later version. Which I'm afraid, very sadly, gives you nothing. Nothing at all, Jadwiga. Not a single British penny. Sorry about that.'

Jadwiga was speechless, her face a picture of conflicting emotions. This moment, Leo thought, that Patricia was so visibly enjoying, was probably the most dangerous of all. If Jadwiga had planned to sedate her and then smother her, there was nothing stopping her just getting on with it right away. The smothering, that is. Except if Patricia was telling her the truth there was no benefit in it for her. And presumably some risk. Because if she had told Ms Kumar about the carer's alleged intentions, who else had she told?

'You've done this before, haven't you?' Patricia said.

'Madam, I'm sorry, this is crazy…' The carer was shaking her head in studied disbelief.

'D'you want to know how I know?' Patricia went on. 'Well, obviously, I've had you checked out, but why were my suspicions aroused in the first place? I guess when Jane from the agency told me that you were very good with the very old, that you had indeed cared beautifully, as she put it, for a number of old ladies who had sadly passed on. That you didn't mind calling your old ladies and gents "madam" and "sir", as some of the better-off ones liked to be called. Even "your Ladyship" in one case. That you were perfectly comfortable in big old houses, even if they were a bit remote. Jane didn't find any of that suspicious, but I did. Even before you'd arrived, I had my eye on you, Jadwiga.

'And then, when Adam died, you were so interested in all that, the inquest, the suicide verdict, whether he had left any money, whom he might have left it to. Naturally, some curiosity was to be expected, but not the level you demonstrated. It was almost as if you wanted to find out who his killer was so you could team up with them.

'Actually, for a very short while I thought it might be you. You and your greedy husband, who had seen an opportunity with Adam to branch out to an altogether younger type of victim. But of course that wasn't the case, because how would you get him to leave his money to you? It was just a horrid coincidence, that here you were with me as your next target, and all the while poor Adam had fallen foul of someone else.

'Who was it, Jadwiga?'

Silence from the carer. Had Patricia, Leo wondered, remote in her eyrie, worked this one out too?

'Was it that appalling business partner,' Patricia went on, her thumbs pushing nervously back and forth against her palms as she spoke, 'who I knew was a wrong 'un from the first moment I set eyes on him. Adam was always such a sweet man, very trusting, even as a little boy, always wanting to see the good in people. A big mistake, obviously, in life, but particularly when it came to what's his name...'

'Jeff.'

'Ha ha, you see, you *did* follow it all closely. I knew you did. But I didn't,' she went on, 'on careful reflection, think it *was* Jeff, no, even though he's been trying to get Adam off the board for years. Of his own company. How ruthless is that? But the very fact that Jeff was bothering to do that, and going to quite dramatic lengths to get his own way, told me all I needed to know.

'So who else could have set this up, this so-called suicide? That second wife of his had found herself a new love interest, hadn't she?'

'How did you know that?' Jadwiga's face was a picture.

'Body language. You can always tell. It hadn't been good for a long time between her and Adam. The fuckathon was over.'

'The *fuck-ath-on?*' Jadwiga repeated slowly, as Leo gurgled with appalled, but unheard, laughter.

'That's what he used to call it,' Patricia went on. 'When he first got together with pretty little Julie. Don't think I didn't pick up on that. Anyway, all that sexy stuff was long gone, and then suddenly, there she was, being very touchy feely with him again.

In an obviously fake way. So I realised then that she must have someone else. But though she would have fought tooth and nail in the courts to hang on to that beautiful house he had built for her, she wasn't going to actually do him in. And if she was, not in her own garage, for goodness' sake, where she would be the prime suspect.

'So who was it? Someone, for sure, because my Adam would never take his own life. I know there are plenty of mothers who delude themselves about their offspring, most, let's face it, but never forget, we know them best. We were the ones who brought them into the world, saw their first smiles, watched their first steps, listened to their childish worries.

'I can still see the look on Adam's face now when he first started walking. He was showing off, as he always was, but ah, that grin of delight when he made it across the room in one go! With both of us watching, Philip and I. It was only matched by the look he had when we gave him his first set of coloured pencils and he started drawing. Hours and hours, he spent, sketching people, and houses, and people in houses, often very elaborate ones. He was always concerned, right from the off, about how comfortable people would be. Would they have a nice bath? Would they have a nice garden? Could they have a swimming pool? I hoped then that he might end up as an architect.

'Then he went through a sweet phase of building fairy houses at the bottom of the garden. By the stream down there. Those fairies, honestly, they had some great places to live and play. There was a whole complex of diving boards and steppingstones for them to enjoy. Honestly, it made you want to be a fairy yourself.

'I knew his upsides, and his downsides. He was a randy little sod, not very faithful to his doting girlfriends, or to his poor first wife. But one thing that shone through, always, was his love of life. His interest *in* life. Yes, he had his bleak moments. I can remember several, when he was a teenager, and in his twenties, before he finally settled with Serena. He used to come back here and shut himself in his room. For days sometimes. You couldn't move him. But there was never ever any suggestion that he would run away. Which is what suicide is, isn't it? In my humble opinion anyway. Running away from life, the ongoing difficulty of it, the awful anxiety of it, but not caring about who or what you leave behind. Very selfish. Brave, obviously, but selfish too. He would never have done that. Sorry. So I knew someone had killed him. The only question was who, and why?

'And then at the inquest, I suddenly realised who had done it. It was just the look on the face of a woman I knew well. Though she hadn't done it all by herself, had she? She'd got her tame feller to do most of her dirty work for her. And in return, what, money and security for life. He's rather a ridiculous character, I'd say, wouldn't you, Jadwiga? One of those people who mess up almost everything they touch. But never mind, she thought old Blunderfingers could manage this little job.'

'Who are you talking about, madam? I'm sorry. I don't understand.'

'The mother of my grandchildren. Serena. Smile and smile and be a villain, that's her. Always far too reasonable and nice to be real. Adam, I'm afraid, did not behave well towards her. She seemed so forgiving, always, but he didn't realise the anger she'd stored up over the years. When she'd enabled his success but wasn't allowed to take the credit for it, or enjoy it, as any woman should. People laugh at me when I say that behind every successful man, there's always a strong woman. These days, of course, it may be the other way round, or possibly, who knows, the successful man has *become* the strong woman.' Patricia cackled again, as she often did when she thought she was being clever. 'But believe me,' she concluded, 'if it isn't, and you deny that strong woman her just rewards, God help you!

'Her accomplice, Walter, was a man at the end of his tether.

She saved him from the arches, as far as I could make out. The arches, Jadwiga. Do you know what they are?'

'No, madam.'

'A place in London where you wouldn't care to live. Philip had a dear friend, a *Times* leader writer no less, who ended up there, freezing to death in a grubby sleeping bag. But that's another story.'

'I don't believe it, madam. Walter, maybe. But not Serena. She wouldn't have killed her own son.'

'Exactly,' Leo muttered to himself. He was struggling to accept that his own mother could have been involved, in any way at all, with Walter's suicide scenario for his father; but the idea that she'd have had anything to do with his accident was inconceivable.

'She didn't,' Patricia said. 'Walter did. He had to. Because he thought Leo knew about what they'd done. He was convinced of it. He was wrong about that, as about so much else in his inadequate life, but that didn't help poor Leo.'

'It certainly fucking didn't,' Leo muttered. His grandmother was right. Though he'd found it hard to believe that his father had killed himself, he hadn't been convinced that the suicide set-up represented murder. Even if it had, he had never pointed the finger at either Walter or his mother. If someone had done it, he'd thought, it was most likely, surely, to be Julie and Rod. Who else would have risked getting caught in the Fallowfields garage?

'It probably didn't help that Leo was dead set against Walter marrying his mother too,' Patricia went on. 'But you're right. Serena didn't know, doesn't still. She thinks it was an accident. Which will be her fate too if she doesn't watch out. Walter will take her on holiday, to the Amalfi coast or the Grand Canyon or somewhere, and push her off a cliff. Or on a cruise, even better, where he can shove her over the railings on the top deck, his crime in the hands of an absentee policeman from Panama.'

Patricia flashed her carer a winning smile, then turned to her other, more reliable assistant. 'Alexa,' she commanded. 'You can tell the police to move in now if you like. Here. And there.'

No sooner had she said that, than there was the whoop of a siren outside. Jadwiga went to the window and her face fell. The house, Leo could see, was surrounded.

'Here, madam. You mean–?'

'The nice police people will read your rights to you, I'm sure. But they've already tracked your accounts, they know exactly what happened with those last three clients of yours. Lady Pilkington, was it? Mrs Choughamford-Taylor of Choughamford Hall. It was always a giveaway, to me, dear Jadwiga, that you pronounced it 'Chumford', as is of course correct. Only someone who had spoken at length to English people, and to English people of a certain class, the class with money tucked away discreetly, would have known that. And yes, finally, your shining star, Dame Dierdre du Cann. Ah, dear dear Dierdre du Cann. How I loved her movies back in the sixties. *The Right Case.* Wasn't that one of hers? With Michael Caine? It must have been a real privilege to live with such a fascinating legend. Before she sadly and abruptly carked it.'

Jadwiga was blank faced. 'And there...?' she asked. 'What do you mean by "and there"?'

'Omar, obviously. Your handsome Turkish hubby is being pulled in. At the Volkswagen showroom in Tempelsham. And down in London, Tufnell Park, where Adam bought them their first house, with our money, Philip's and mine, would you believe, Serena and Walter. The police were just biding their time with those two. Or that's what they told me when they came to call the other afternoon. The SIO, that's the Senior Investigating Officer on the case, was very complimentary about my observations. Told me I'd give Miss Marple a run for her money. I can't say that was *quite* the comparison I'd have chosen, but never mind.'

CHAPTER FORTY-ONE

A dam had been as gobsmacked as Jeff when Leo had filled them both in, back in his office at Fallowfields at their evening rendezvous, about what had gone down at Patricia's. Though he wasn't surprised that his beady mother had managed to rumble Jadwiga and catch her out, even as she posed as yet another helpless old lady for the carer and her husband to prey on.

He was amazed that she had managed to rumble Walter and Serena's involvement too, though she'd never been a fan of Adam's first wife, for reasons that he hadn't ever quite fully understood. Even now, when he was forced to accept that Serena had been prepared to do away with him, he was struggling to understand why. Yes, obviously, there was the money, which would have set her and Walter up comfortably for the rest of their lives. But then again, you'd have thought Serena would have had some respect for the unnecessarily generous settlement that Adam had voluntarily given her. Yes, he had left her, for no good reason other than his own wanderlust and waywardness; but there had never been any 'hell hath no fury' about their ongoing relationship, especially when it became clear that running off with Julie had been a huge mistake.

Adam's pride had meant that he had never admitted as much to her, though he had come close to it a couple of years ago, before Walter had appeared on the scene, and when Eva was still just a colleague. There had been a couple of sneaky dinners with Serena, and they had laughed together about the fact he hadn't told his second wife he was out on the lam with his first. He had never suggested they get back together, though he had, for a few months, been tempted. He had been under the erroneous belief that he and his first wife were friends, that that was all good for the children, that sins had been forgiven and resentments buried. Clearly not.

He could only blame Walter for taking it as far as they had done. Walter, that twisted failure, whose string of repeated cock-ups had made him bitter and resentful rather than sensibly accepting of his own dire limitations. Adam's success had not been handed to him on a plate. He had worked for it, job by job, client by client, using all kinds of ingenuity to win projects and get them over the line, against the relentless forces of negativity that had included jobsworthy and grudge-bearing planning officers, devious rivals, unimaginative and unreliable clients, you name it. He had sacrificed plenty of good times and days in the sun to stay late in the office and get things finished. Serena had always seemed to support him, when he prioritised deadlines over time with his children, but perhaps she hadn't, perhaps the hidden hatred had started there.

Walter had always had a problem with Adam, not that Adam had cared tuppence about that. He had assumed, blithely, that was because Walter knew, deep down, Serena still loved him. He had always been polite to the wazzock, even as he'd struggled to hide his contempt. Of course he wished his ex-wife well, he wanted her to be happy, his guilt dictated that, but to be happy with that dickhead! It was her choice, he supposed. Perhaps, retrospectively, it had been a mistake slagging him off repeatedly, and he had always thought amusingly, to his children. He had known that his meaner comments might get back. But he hadn't cared. What power did tragic and useless Walter have over him? None.

That had been his error. It turned out he'd had all too much power – if only he was prepared to cross the line into the resort of the failed, the weak, the desperate, the disillusioned, the cynical, the useless and the mad: criminality. Adam would never have countenanced Walter as a murderer, even if he had properly understood how terminal his circumstances were. The idea that Serena would have happily helped him was inconceivable. But there you are. What had happened had happened. And it only went to show, as Jeff had observed, that it was always the quiet ones you had to watch out for. The quiet ones and the nice ones. Fizzing away furiously under their warm and apparently forgiving smiles.

As for Leo's accident, Adam could only explain that in terms of panic. Leo had made it obvious from the start that he didn't like Walter, that he thought his mother was selling herself short. Leo was dead set against her continuing with the relationship, certainly against her marrying him. So Walter's plan to save himself and be financially secure was in jeopardy. And then, it seemed, Leo had realised about his involvement in the so-called suicide. There was no way Walter was going to discuss what to do about that little problem with Serena. She would hardly support murdering her own son. But it had to be done. And what better, for a young man who was known for his love of fast cars, than a tweak of the brakes, and an accident.

Now it was over. The human perpetrators were all facing human justice. Adam and Jeff had been at Harrogate Road to witness the efficient police swoop and round-up, the shock on the faces of Serena and her partner in crime as they realised they had been found out; then the sheer and unforgiving horror on his first wife's face when Walter's second charge was read out.

But Adam was relieved to find that now he knew exactly what had happened to him, his hatred and anger towards them had entirely gone. As it had towards his unfaithful spouse Julie and the human condom, Rod. Good luck to them! And to his sister and her husband also. She had made her choice. She could have made another, easily enough, but there you go, if what she really wanted as a life companion was a CGI cartoon with personality deficiencies, so be it. It wasn't for him to be entangled in their destinies; any more than it was now with darling Eva. He had floated one last time past her studio, seen her tucked up in the big white 'Songesand' double bed with a happy-looking Reuben, and had wished her well. She had her life ahead of her and he hoped it would be a good one, filled with all the tangible rewards the real world has to offer those who strive hard enough to find them.

After their excited mutual debriefing, and the satisfaction of knowing who was responsible for putting them where they were now, the three ghosts had been left with nothing to say, stunned into silence. What now? was on each of their minds. Would they stay in this spectral state for eternity; for a year; for a day? They didn't know or understand, any more than they knew or understood exactly how and why they could visit their human counterparts sometimes and not others.

Jeff had been surprisingly focused in helping solve the mystery of Adam's death, but now that was resolved, Adam could see, from the lurking fury on his face, that he still had unfinished business with the man who had frightened him to death. The last thing he wanted or needed was his ex-partner muscling in with undeserved recriminations, even though for the moment Leo's presence was enough to keep them apart. If time was going to be short, he wondered, how could he get away and spend a little quality time alone with his son, have a chance to tell him how proud he'd been of him, how much he loved him, and how sorry he was that their destinies had got mixed up in the tragic way they had.

But even as they sat, or rather floated there together in that empty Fallowfields office, none of these logically human developments came to pass. Instead, it seemed to Adam as if, even as the watching faces of his companions faded into the background, he was suddenly drowned in brilliant light.

Far away he could hear music, slow and ineffably soothing, like a twangle of harps accompanying the hugest choir. There were violins in there too, Eva's beloved violins. Was it 'Quizás, Quizás, Quizás' they were playing? Oh my God, yes it was. Segueing mysteriously into another of his favourite pieces of music, Chopin's Etude Op 10, no 3, sometimes known as *Tristesse*. Tears filled his virtual eyes, but they were, God help him, tears of happiness. He felt as he always used to feel, walking up a sandy path with his children at the end of a day on the beach, nothing more to worry about, his task over. He could have done with another twenty or thirty years, he could have done with another life, but if that was not to be, so be it. It was time to let go of this beautiful world.

Images flashed through his mind, if mind it still was. Himself as a child, with the set of coloured pens his parents had given him for his tenth birthday... reading out his poem at the school poetry competition, 'The Air, A Dream', the thundering applause and the furious look on Roland's crimson tomato of a face... at Bristol with Serena, drinking cider with their good friends Belinda and Eric on a summer's evening in the cobbled yard outside the Llandoger Trow... up in London in that crazy first term at the AA, Stan over 'a Four Seasons with extra tuna', his default pizza, in Kettner's in Soho... Serena on honeymoon in Lipari, that dazzling terrace at the Roche d'Azur, negronis at lunchtime, her lovely nakedness back in the shuttered siesta bedroom... Matty as a toddler, with that winning smile, that jet-black curly hair... Leo's magician phase, how old had he been, thirteen? the shiny grey suit they had bought him, the spinning red bow tie... Julie at that lunch at the L'Arbre Bleu in Chelsea, cute in her cream suit, her bobbed blonde head back, laughing, slipping him her card... a boat ride with her up the Camel Estuary, a tall heron guarding the grey stone beach, the sun going in, that sinking feeling that he'd made a huge mistake... Eva with her logbook, her attentive face out on some site meeting when she was still a student...

They flooded in, these memories, faster and faster, like some PowerPoint presentation gone mad. Then, abruptly, in a moment, they were gone, whirling away forever like autumn leaves in the wind. His past was vanishing, as if it had never been. As if, in truth, he had never been. The music had ended on a perfect cadence, but Adam found he no longer cared. He tilted up his hologrammatic jaw and melted effortlessly into the brilliant nothingness beyond.

Now this is the ultimate living space, he thought, as he faded away.

THE END

ALSO BY MARK MCCRUM

Fiction

THE FRANCIS MEADOWES MYSTERIES

The Festival Murders

Cruising to Murder

Murder Your Darlings

Non-fiction

Happy Sad Land

No Worries

The Craic

Castaway

Robbie Williams: Somebody Someday

Going Dutch In Beijing

Walking With The Wounded

ACKNOWLEDGEMENTS

I am grateful to Paul Davis for his insights into the life and work of a successful architect; to Sarah Hare, for more thoughts on that subject; to Julie Costley of Gwyn James Solicitors for chapter and verse on the complex details of inheritance tax; and to Ashley Klinkert of Tintern Garage for explaining how car brake lines work.

Thanks as always to the kind friends who read and commented on early drafts: Katrin Macgibbon, Ben Craib, Duncan Minshull, Linda Hughes, Jackie Nelson, Richard Cobourne, Margaret Iggulden, Toni Harvey; to my agents Jamie Maclean, Lisa Moylett and Zoe Apostolides for their enthusiasm for the idea and their dramatic edits; and to Abbie Rutherford for being a gentle but beady editor. Finally, of course, to my wife Jo, for looking after me and being always, as a reader, impressively impartial.

A NOTE FROM THE PUBLISHER

Thank you for reading this book. If you enjoyed it please do consider leaving a review on Amazon to help others find it too.

We hate typos. All of our books have been rigorously edited and proofread, but sometimes mistakes do slip through. If you have spotted a typo, please do let us know and we can get it amended within hours.

info@bloodhoundbooks.com

R

Printed in Great Britain
by Amazon

34717362R00184